Soulbound: Des
Amanda Al

Copyright © 2024 Amanda Albery
All rights reserved Second Edition
First originally published by Page Publishing, Inc. 2015
No portion of this book may be reproduced in any form without written permission from the author except as permitted by U.S. copyright law.

This is a work of fiction. Names, characters, places and incidents either are the product of the author's imagination or are used fictitiously. Any resemblance to any persons, living or dead, events or locals is entirely coincidental.

Table of Contents

Olivia 1 1
Dreams 2 3
First Glimpse 3 5
Evil In the Woods 4 15
The Scent 5 23
The Date 6 31
Alone 7 41
A Fairy Tale Begins 9 67
Betrayal 10 87
Assaulted 11 99
Emeline 12 109
Disappeared 13 125
Frightening Truth 14. 155
Revelation 15 167
World Of Kings 16 183
Abducted 17 219
Althea 18 231
Through The Veil 19 247
The Binding 20 257
Soul's Torment 21 263
Conviction 22 275
Awkward Beginnings 23 281
Absolution 24 291
Dangerous Kinship 25 301
The Sealing 26 309
Bittersweet Good-Byes 27 317
Invasion Of Es'Mar 28 333
A Visit to Kardaun 29 347
Transitions 30 365
The Yule Ball 31 387
Decimation Of Innocence 32 415

Locked Away 33	441
The Seduction 34	453
End Of A Winter Dream 35	461
About The Author	469

Dedication

A wise man once told me, "Life is like a ladder; when you're ready, take the next step up." This is my next step. I love you, Daddy.

Preface

The sound of battle whirled around me. I tried to cover my ears to squelch the sound of metal scraping metal and of the screams— the sickening screams of the dying! The flames of the fire blazed up a bloody red with every heart thrown into the tormenting heat. It seemed to flicker outward like long greedy fingers reaching to fill a gluttonous appetite.

Acknowledgements

To my mother, for helping me type my handwritten work and deciphering the hen's scratch that came with sudden epiphanies and late-night sleepy ramblings on paper. Rest peacefully, Ma.

To my boys, for being a constant inspiration.

To my granny (Delcie), for her support and allowing me the use of her name.

To Aunt Nita, for character inspiration and all the times she babysat to give me that quiet time. To my best friends, Autumn (Fall) and Tiffany (Sissy), who both believe in me and support me through everything.

And to Daniel, for reading my book all the way through and telling me how much he liked it.

Olivia 1

As far back as I can remember I've been a part of this tiny corner of the world, tucked away in the mountains of East Tennessee. Here, everything glides along at a slower pace. Neighbors still lend a willing hand, and your word still means something.

I've been hidden away, sheltered and tightly nestled in these aged mountains. Life here still holds tight the sanctity of family, bound by tradition and undying faith. These are a people held together by strong beliefs and ancient stories steeped in superstition.

I've never been one to join in with large groups. As much as I outwardly appeared deeply rooted in this life my parents had chosen for me, I never felt like I truly belonged. My friend Jenna was eager to jump headfirst into the big world surrounding this little safe harbor. She was excited to ride the storm that seemed to whirl unending in the world outside.

I had no desire to leave. *Where would I go? Why would I want to?* I thought. I would feel just as strange and out of place no matter where I went. I'm not sure why I felt that way. It was just something deep within me. I never felt like I was anything special...nothing more than just plain Olivia Ryan.

Tailors Mountain is a quaint little town. I'm sure within the borders of the entire county, a head count would reveal maybe a smidgen over twenty-five hundred people. Town consisted of the usual gas stations, pharmacy, a couple of grocery stores, etc. But I'm quite sure we topped the list for small private-owned businesses. I chose to work in just such a place: Rooter's BBQ and Grill on Laurel Street. It was a little off the beaten path, but the food was good; along with the fact that it was always open till midnight, it had earned Rooter's local fame.

It was the summer of my nineteenth year. I was still battling idea that destiny was about to make its first move. Indecision. I didn't have a clue as to what I wanted to do with my life or where I wanted to carve out my little niche in the world. I had no idea that destiny was about to make its first move.

Dreams 2

I finished filling a few pitchers of tea for my relief and carried a tray of dirty dishes back to the kitchen then walked back by the office door to punch my timecard and go home.

I pulled off my pink apron and nametag as I walked through the dimly lit parking lot to the teal-colored Cavalier parked in the back of the employee parking spaces at the side of the building.

I threw the apron onto the passenger seat and put the key in the ignition. I've been trying to save up enough to get an apartment of my own. My parents are so deserving of this time alone now that they have completed their work in bringing me into adulthood. They have shown great patience in their wait for solitude, and if they had any reservations or worries over my procrastination about moving out, they didn't show it.

I turned off onto Ryan Lane and pulled into the driveway. Having your street named after you was a little odd for most places, but pretty much the norm for here. They always seemed to use the last name of the residents of the last house on a dead-end road. It was ten o'clock, and the moon was almost full. I could see the house as if there were a huge lamp looming over the top. My parents were never ones to attempt living beyond their means. Our house is a small, comfortable dwelling with pale-yellow siding and maroon false shutters lining the sides of each window. There is a covered front porch that runs about half the length of the house. It only has two bedrooms each with a private bath and a small bath in the hall. The living room and dining room are one open space. The kitchen area is small with two entrances, one from the dining area and one from the hall. There is a small table with four chairs in a little nook at the far end of the kitchen. No, it's nothing elaborate, but it's comfortable and it's home.

I trudged into the house on aching feet, focused on my room at the end of the hall. My parents had already turned in for the night, and I tried to move quietly so I wouldn't disturb them. I turned on the lamp by my bed, pulled an oversized tee shirt from the dresser, and went in to turn on the shower. As I stood in front of the mirror, toothbrush in hand, studying my plain, pale reflection, I tried desperately to see myself as others seemed to; but the vision totally escaped me. There were certainly prettier girls around. I just wasn't interested in dating; even in high school, I never went through the raging-hormone stage. In the entire four years, I went out with one boy twice, and since I failed to see the satisfaction in it, I just dropped the whole thing.

What's wrong with you? I said to my reflection. *It's no wonder you don't have a real life of your own. You could have found a nice guy and been happy in a relationship...but no...you have to be weird and apparently void of hormones!* I gave myself a disgusted look, took a long breath, and turned out the light. I crawled into bed, thankful I had tomorrow off.

First Glimpse 3

I woke from a restless, dream-filled sleep—dreams that left me trembling and weak. My mind kept replaying the nightmare over and over as I lay there. There are usually people in my dreams, but not this time. It was different and confusing. I remember standing in the woods at dusk, staring into the sky. There was an object moving very fast. It was falling! As hard as I tried, I couldn't make out what it was. It disappeared below the trees, and I heard a sound like thunder to my left. I couldn't seem to move my legs, and I remember feeling utterly terrified! When I finally started toward the sound, I saw a huge fire with black smoke rising for miles. There was an odor coming from the flames—a horrible, sickening scent. Just before I could see the cause of the torrent, I woke up. It's not the first time I had this dream; it seemed to be haunting my sleep more often this past week.

As I sat up and pushed the hair back from my face, I noticed the tears still damp on my cheeks. I forced myself out of bed to get dressed. I put on a pair of faded jeans and a tee shirt and took some old sneakers from the closet and a pair of socks from the drawer.

I tried to think about my plans for the day, hoping to dissolve the remnants of my nightmare as I glanced at my window. Oh no... it wasn't supposed to rain!

I walked over and stood by the window, watching the drops roll to the bottom of the pane. I could see now, down to the tree line at the edge of the woods. The gray light of daybreak, along with the foggy ground cover, gave everything an eerie look, only adding to my foreboding feeling.

As I peered out at the disparaging gray, my mind rehashed the past fifteen months since my high school graduation. I thought of the disappointed look on my parents' faces when I announced I was not going to college right away. Instead, I took a job at Rooter's BBQ.

I remembered poor Reverend Butler and his wife, Grace, at the funeral of their daughter, Savannah. Just two short weeks after graduation, she was found out by Saylor's pond, bruised and scratched almost to the point of mutilation.

There were bear tracks leading away from where they found her body. I suppose that was enough to squelch any real investigation. They ruled her death accidental. Savannah was a timid girl with big brown doe eyes and long blond hair. Why she was in a secluded area, alone at night, still remains a mystery. What a shame, I thought, that she spent her last year of life devoted to an arrogant jerk like Jimmy Stanton. Jimmy was a tall, lanky redhead with freckles dotting his cheeks and nose. He was clumsy and awkward with arms that seemed too long for his body. The Honorable Judge Stanton's son was nothing more than a spoiled little brat. I couldn't, for the life of me, understand what Savannah saw in him.

Oh, he tried to make a show as the bereaved sweetheart at Savannah's funeral, but he wasn't very convincing. It certainly didn't take him long to get back to "business as usual." Personally, I didn't think Jimmy was capable of compassion or empathy toward any human being.

I recalled the recurring dream I had of Savannah lying still in the moonlight with her eyes wide-open in fear. I shook my head and wiped a tear from the corner of my eye. Death seemed to plague this town and my dreams.

I had dreamed about Tommy Haines just six months ago. In my dream, he was white as a sheet, leaning against a rock wall. They found his body down by the old mill. The police couldn't determine his cause of death, and it's still unsolved. He was a gentle sort, with short brown hair and a stocky build. He was the only boy

I had dated in high school. I liked him, and it saddened me to hear of his untimely passing.

There were other incidents, like the hiker found on Cutler's Ridge about twenty miles from here. The poor girl was ripped to pieces! The game warden said there was a pride of mountain lions in that area. Her death, too, was ruled accidental. I totally rejected the mystery and accidental-death theories, but I kept those feelings to myself. I never understood the dreams or why I had them, only that they were back...just as frequent...and just as ominous.

Something caught my eye in the tree line that pulled me from my despairing reunion of memories.

"Someone's out there!" I whispered aloud. I steadied my gaze into the fog, hoping to focus better. There it was again! I was certain it was a man moving between the trees!

I was about to call my dad to come see when it stepped out into the clearing! I couldn't believe my eyes! I blinked and focused again. It couldn't be, but there it was! A panther! I caught my breath as I stared at the magnificent beast. He was enormous and black as the night! "How beautiful," I breathed.

I stood there motionless, fearing the slightest movement would scare it away. I watched as it paced back and forth. Then...suddenly it stopped and looked straight at the house. The cat's stare was so deliberate I felt almost as if he were looking straight at me.

I glanced to see if my camera was still on the bookshelf by my window, but it wasn't. I turned back to look, and the beautiful creature was gone! I sat down on the corner of my bed; my heart was pounding. I took in a deep breath.

I couldn't believe how exhilarated I felt! I was about to bolt from my room, screaming out the scene that had just taken place, when I came to my senses. Was it real? Did I really see a panther outside my window, or was it just a sleep-dazed hallucination? I better approach this subject calmly. I'll bring it up to Dad in a nonchalant way. Right, Olivia, I told myself. Like bringing up panthers in the backyard is just normal conversation! They're going to think you've finally lost it! I inhaled deeply and let my breath out slow, pulled my hair back in a ponytail, and started down the hall.

I stood quietly in the entrance to our cozy little kitchen, watching my parents interact. They made a relationship look easy... uncomplicated.

To look at them, one wouldn't even place them together as a couple, Mom with her thick locks of auburn hair and green eyes. Her petite five-foot-four size looked almost childlike standing next to my dad. His six-foot-one frame towered over her. I could see how time had changed them. The years were beginning to show around Mom's eyes, and her hair had lost some of its luster. She wore it short now; I guess she figured it more befitting an older woman.

Dad sported black hair and brown eyes. He had a darker complexion. His skin had a swarthy appearance, caused no doubt by the long hours spent outdoors on a construction site. Time had changed him from a tall, slender man to one of a portlier stature. His hair was graying at the temples.

As I studied them, I smiled. I was proud to be the daughter of James and Anna Ryan. I could remember sitting in front of the mirror as a little girl, picking out our similarities. I too had emerald-green eyes like Anna's, only thicker dark lashes, along with her same pale skin. I carried midnight-black hair to my shoulders the same color as James's, and I was close to Anna's height at five foot two. As I stood there, I wished with all my heart I had been born to them.

"Olivia!" Mom placed her hand on her heart. "We didn't hear you come in!"

"Sorry, I didn't mean to startle you." I grinned.

"What are you doing up so early?" Dad's expression was priceless.

"I thought I'd take a ride up to the lake today...wanna come?" Unlike most young people, I enjoyed spending time with my parents.

"I can't, Mom has a honey-do list this long!" He raised his hand to gesture above his head and laughed. Mom smiled and warped him on the shoulder with her dishtowel.

"Thanks for asking though. Maybe next weekend."

"Okay, we'll plan on it then." I smiled as I poured a glass of orange juice and took a sip. Now is as good a time as any, I thought.

"Dad..."

"Yeah, hon," he answered.

"I thought I saw someone in the woods this morning." "Are you sure?"

"I dunno...I saw something. Do we...umm..." I hesitated.

"Do we have any panthers in this area?"

"Panthers?" Dad chuckled. "Why?"

"Well..." I busied myself at the cupboard so I wouldn't have to make eye contact. "I thought I saw one out my window this morning...a black one." I added. Dad snickered a little. Just like I figured. He thinks I'm nuts!

"Well, honey..." he continued, trying to resist his urge to outright laugh. "We have mountain lions and bobcats, but...panthers are strictly a jungle cat."

"Oh..." My eyes were still not meeting his gaze. "Well, I'm sure I saw something out there this morning!" My voice must have sounded a little defensive. Dad took on a more serious tone, even though his eyes still twinkled with amusement.

"Olivia, think about it; even if there were such a thing here, you couldn't have seen one if you saw a man out there too, right?"

"Yeah...that makes sense." I was beginning to regret even bringing it up.

"I figure it's one of two things." The amused twinkle was still there. "It was either old man Blevins out running his hounds this morning or the dim light and fog playing tricks on a young woman's overactive imagination!" he said, and then he laughed. I felt the need to defend my sanity.

"Dad, I did not imagine seeing something!"

"Well then, my bet's on old man Blevins," he said.

Mom stayed silent as she finished his breakfast. It was plain to see she too was amused by our conversation.

"So, are you going alone?" Mom asked as she placed Dad's food on the table.

"I'm sorry...alone?" I wasn't following her question.

"To the lake. Are you going alone?"

"Yeah, Mom...just me," I answered.

"You know, Liv. I'm not comfortable with you being in the woods by yourself. James, maybe you could put your chores off till tomorrow and—"

"Now, Anna," Dad interrupted. "Olivia is all grown up and perfectly capable of taking care of herself." He winked at me.

"Mom, I've been up there hundreds of times, everything'll be fine." I insisted.

She looked up at my dad, hoping he would back down and side with her. When it didn't happen, she sighed.

"Well, all right, but be careful!" she said, her finger pointing at me.

"I will...promise," I said, smiling.

"Have fun, girl." Dad smiled broadly and kissed Mom on the cheek.

SOULBOUND: DESTINY'S MOVE

"I've got work to do. I'll see ya later, okay?" He grabbed another piece of toast and kissed the top of my head as he passed by.

"See ya, Dad." It was only a few minutes until we heard a loud clattering on the back porch.

Mom poured a cup of coffee and sat down at the table with me.

"Honey...are you sure you wouldn't rather go somewhere with a couple of your friends?"

"Mom..." She knew my look all too well.

"Can't blame me for trying." She smiled and took a sip from her cup.

I put some sandwiches and chips in a small cooler and grabbed a couple of sodas from the fridge.

"I'll see you later," I said as I kissed her on the cheek and left her sitting alone, staring after me.

I had my fishing gear on the front porch. I needed some time alone to think, and that required a fishing pole. Dad had trained me to this custom when I was little, and I learned to enjoy it very much.

I couldn't understand Mom's concern. Nothing had happened since Tommy Haines, and as far as the police were concerned, they both, Savannah and Tommy, were freak accidents.

I walked out into the sticky, damp air, breathing in the fragrance of wildflowers along with the aroma of Mom's roses, strategically placed on a trellis beside the covered porch. Our house was set slightly on a hill in the middle of five acres. Purposely placed, I was sure, for the view. Today the scenery seemed exceptional.

The rain had stopped. The shades of green on the hills and in the valleys were a veritable rainbow. It was late August, and the hottest month of summer was finally coming to an end. I stood there on the porch, admiring the view. The fog was starting to lift.

"Smoke on the Mountains" we called it, because the fog rose in soft spirals from the tops of the trees, giving the illusion that every hilltop was smoldering. It was absolutely beautiful. Once I had my fishing gear and lunch secured in the trunk, I headed for the lake and my day of solitude.

SOULBOUND: DESTINY'S MOVE

Nikolas stood up, pressing both hands flat on the granite top of the kitchen counter. His eyes were wide in disbelief.

"You what! She saw—Tristan! What were you thinking?"

"Hold on, Nick. She didn't see me...like this! I was phased!" Tristan tried to explain.

"Oh, and that's supposed to make it okay?" Nick walked around the counter to stand in front of Tristan.

"Come on, Nickie, calm down. I just wanted to get a closer look. Don't tell me you wouldn't like to get just a few feet closer!" Tristan's knowing gaze pierced through Nikolas.

"Of course I would, Tris, but we have to be careful. As hard as this is, we have to maintain control." Nick raked his fingers through his soft blond hair as he spoke.

"Look, Tris, if I gave in to my desire to get closer, you know what would happen. I may be able to get you off the hook if you had to face the council over it, but you know it wouldn't exactly be the same if I had to face them. It would be a little awkward, don't you think? Since I'm head of the damn thing!" Nick looked frustrated, knowing he could not act on his desire as Tristan had.

"You standing before the council would be interesting to watch—at the least!" Tristan laughed.

"Haha! They wouldn't be very happy. I can tell you that!" Nick walked back over and sat on the bar stool at the end of the counter.

"Tristan don't get reckless. What part of the law don't you understand? Not until she's twenty!"

He felt Tristan needed reminding, even though he knew if he had the chance, he would do the same.

"Don't worry, Nick. I'll stay back from now on. You know, we really need to bring that up at the next council meeting and see if we can't make some kind of amendment to the law, at least allowing someone in our position regarding her, to at least be allowed to meet," Tristan said.

"I'll try to keep that in mind, Tris." Nick laughed.

Evil In the Woods 4

I parked the car down by the boat ramp. There weren't many boats on the lake today, so it seemed like I would definitely get my peace and quiet.

I followed the trail through the woods leading to my favorite fishing spot. It gave me not only seclusion but shade as well. I rarely sat in the sun, at least not without a ton of sunscreen. After arranging everything on the ground, I realized I had forgotten to bring my fold-up chair. I scanned the area, looking for a suitable seat, and spotted a log lying against a tree near the shoreline. Perfect! I thought. I readied my hook, cast out, and settled back on the log.

I had originally planned to come out here to contemplate a decision between school and my regular job, but I couldn't see any reason to expend the energy when I knew I would remain at the restaurant.

My thoughts wandered back to the events of this morning. Regardless of Dad's explanation, I was quite sure I did not see old man Blevins and his hounds. I knew what I saw, and I knew I couldn't wait to see it again or at least hoped I would. That cat was the most magnificent creature I had ever seen!

My stomach growled. The fish may not be hungry, but I was. I reached into the cooler and retrieved a bologna sandwich and a canned soda. I leaned back on the tree and let myself continue daydreaming about the beautiful black cat. What would it be like to get closer? I imagined. To actually touch it!

My eyes suddenly flew open. I realized I had fallen asleep. Crap! It's almost sunset. I'll hear it now! I rushed to gather my things and get back to my car while there was still enough light to see the trail. Halfway into the woods, I heard something in the brush behind me. I looked over my shoulder to see who or what it was and barely caught a glimpse of something black out of the corner of my eye. Was that a bear? I shook my head. It's just your imagination, Liv, keep moving. I could hear brush breaking with every step I made. Something was following me! Just keep walking, don't look back! My heart was pounding. God, please don't let it attack! I prayed.

I stumbled as I tried to hurry my steps. My heart was racing, and everything around me seemed like a blur. All I could think of was ending up like Savannah or the hiker—mutilated or ripped to pieces! My foot caught on a tree root. I fell to the ground, my armful of belongings scattering all around me. Get up! Get up and run! my mind instructed me, but I couldn't move. I breathed in deeply, trying to regain my strength.

As I inhaled my next breath, calm came over me. There was a different scent to the air, a wonderful, delicious scent. I let the aroma envelop me. It was like nothing I've ever experienced. I was suddenly oblivious to whatever had been following me. *Had I already been attacked?* I thought.

Everything around me began to look hazy, out of sync. I kept breathing deeper and deeper. If I was about to die, I wanted my last feeling to be the sheer pleasure the intoxicating aroma had brought. I heard footsteps coming toward me and then...nothing.

"Olivia, can you hear me?"

As my eyes opened, everything appeared foggy.

"Where am I?" I mumbled. I tried to focus on my surroundings.

"Olivia, are you all right? Can you talk?" I turned my head toward the voice and blinked to focus.

"M-Mike?" I stammered. The voice belonged to Mike Zita. I hadn't seen him since graduation.

"Yeah, it's me. Are you okay? Do you need me to call the rescue squad?" He looked worried as he spoke.

"No...I mean, no, Mike, I'm fine."

"You don't look fine. Maybe I should call 911." He pulled out his cell phone.

"No!" I shrieked. He stopped, looking confused at my vehement protest.

"Is there some reason you don't want to be treated?" His smile was mischievous, and his blue eyes were full of intrigue.

"We aren't up to no good tonight, are we?" he asked as his smile widened. Mike was always one drawn to trouble. He is a good-looking guy, definitely resembling a California surfer—sun-bleached blond, tan, and muscular. Yeah, Mike was well aware of his appeal to women.

"Is she going to be okay, Mike?" a feminine voice sounded from behind him.

"Yeah, babe, I think so." Mike popped the top on a soda "Here, Liv, sip on this till you catch your bearings."

"Thanks." I took a sip of the drink and finally noticed I was sitting in the front of my car with the seat tilted back. I struggled to set myself in an upright position. Mike reached down and pulled the seat up.

"So what happened?" he asked.

I collected the events that led up to now. I glanced up at him, scrambling to arrange everything in my head. I sat silent, playing with the tab on the soda can as I thought of an explanation. *I can't tell him that I got spooked and fell. That would only make me the topic of everyone's jokes. I could hear Mike now. "Poor Olivia Ryan is so afraid of the dark she knocked herself out running from ghosts!" Ugh! I could never show my face in town again.*

"Olivia...what happened?" he repeated.

"It's kind of embarrassing." I smiled at him.

"Well, tell me anyway." He smiled back.

"I had gone fishing this afternoon. I got a little too comfortable and fell asleep." I was really beginning to feel the heat in my cheeks as his eyes held a steady gaze on me and his mouth was fixed into a smirk.

"Well, when I woke up, I realized how late it was and tried to hurry to get home—*before* my mom sent out a search party. I was carrying too much stuff to really watch where I was going...and you know me...Queen Klutz...I tripped on a tree root, and the next thing I remember is...you."

"So no one or nothing else caused you to be lying unconscious in the woods?"

"No, Mike, no mystery, no evil in the bushes...just a dumb accident." I looked down at the soda can in my lap. I didn't like to lie, and I wasn't good at it. "So what are you doing up here tonight?" I asked.

"Oh, umm...me and Kenzie were meeting Terry and his girlfriend. We're having a little weekend camping trip, roast some hot dogs by the campfire, do a little cat fishing, you know."

"Oh, sounds like fun." I looked around Mike and saw McKenzie Robbins standing behind him with a most vibrant crimson coloring her cheeks. I smiled and waved. "Hey, Kenzie."

"Hey," was all she managed to say. It didn't surprise me to see the two of them together. Ken and Barbie, what could be more natural? I smiled.

"Hey, if you're not up to driving, I could take you home. Kenz can follow in my car." His offer took me by surprise. He wasn't the same person I remembered. The Mike I knew didn't go out of his way to help people. Maybe this relationship with McKenzie was good for him.

"Thanks for the offer, but I'll be fine to drive...really."

"Well, if you're sure. You do have a pretty-good-sized pump knot on the side of your head."

He had obviously attempted to assess my damage while I was unconscious. I reached up and winced as my hand passed over the goose egg. "It's fine, just a little sore. I'll put some ice on it when I get home."

"Okay then, we're going to head up to the campsite." Mike leaned back from the door and eased it shut.

"Thanks for helping me out," I said as I fastened my seatbelt.

"No problem." Mike smiled. "Glad we could help. Take it easy going home, okay? I don't wanna find you in a ditch tomorrow."

"You won't...promise." I laughed. "See you guys later." I turned the ignition and started easing back.

When I walked into the house, Mom was frantic.

"Olivia! You're all right! Where have you been!"

"Relax, Mom, I'm fine. I leaned against a tree and fell asleep."

I could hear the roar of my dad's laugh coming from the living room.

"The sign of a true fisherman!" he called out. Mom was in no mood for Dad's joking. "Hush, James, this isn't funny!"

"Relax, Mama, she's fine! Don't make a big deal of it." Mom's reprimand didn't seem to affect him at all.

"Well, just don't scare me like that again. Understand?"

"I'm sorry, Mom; I'll be more watchful next time...promise."

"All right, see that you are. Your dinner's in the oven." Mom's voice softened. I knew she wasn't angry; she can't help overreacting when it comes to me. Being overprotective just comes natural to her.

"Thanks." I felt terrible for worrying them. I decided the details of my evening were better left alone. *If she knew what really happened tonight, I'm sure that would send her over the edge.* After only a few bites of the saved meal, I rinsed my plate and headed for bed. My stomach was in knots, and my head hurt. I put some ice in a dish towel and called out to them as I started down the hall,

"Night." I heard them echo "night" as I closed my bedroom door.

I slipped on my night shirt and got some Tylenol from my medicine cabinet. My head was throbbing now. I eased into bed and lay there with the towel full of ice plastered to the side of my head. If it weren't for the pain I was feeling, I would swear this whole day had been a dream. I kept seeing the flashes of black in the woods and that scent! That absolutely divine aroma! I shivered and drifted off.

"I TOLD YOU, TRISTAN, you're getting reckless! You were following her too close!" Nick's fist came down on the thick hardwood table beside his chair, causing it to crumple in a pile on the floor.

"We can't allow Lucas or his minions to get near her. We just have to be more careful to keep our distance in the open like that, but still stay close enough to keep her safe." Nick looked more than worried; he looked desperate.

"I understand, Nick, but it's not going to be easy." Tristan was pacing uneasily as he spoke.

"We have to be more careful, Tristan. If we don't keep our distance, we won't have to worry about Lucas. She'll kill herself trying to get away from us!" Tristan could see the fear in Nick's eyes—the same fear he too felt.

"Whatever happened to quiet? You sounded like an elephant in a china shop out there!" Nick exclaimed.

"That's bull in a china shop," Tristan corrected as he struggled to hold back the snicker fighting to escape.

"Whatever!" Nick waved his hand in frustration.

SOULBOUND: DESTINY'S MOVE

"Nick, I know you're on edge, so am I! It's August. Everything out there is dry. A damn feather would break that brush!"

"I can't lose her, Tris." Nick's voice had calmed.

"You mean we can't lose her." Tristan stopped his pacing and looked at Nick with the same fear and desperation that his friend had just exhibited.

"I'm sorry, Tristan, sometimes I lose sight of the fact that it is as much you're right as mine. We have to stay aware though, that her choice has to be her will."

"I know. Are you as terrified of that choice as I am?" Tristan asked nervously.

"Yes, my friend...I am," Nick answered.

"Who's watching her now?" Tristan started fearing she was left unguarded.

Nick stood and walked a few steps, resting his arm on the mantel of the huge stone fireplace.

"Don't worry, Galen and Safrina are there. They'll summon us if there's trouble," Nick said.

"She's amazing, isn't she?" Tristan broke the silence with his question.

"She most certainly is."

Suddenly Nick's eyes widened as Tristan straightened in his chair. His electric-blue eyes narrowed, and a low growl erupted from his throat.

The Scent 5

"Liv, are you planning to sleep all day?" The sound of Mom's voice raised me from my finally restful sleep. I had a terrible night.

"What time is it?" I called through the closed door.

"Almost ten."

I must've been exhausted, I thought as I rose, shaking my head.

"I'm going to take a shower. I'll be out in a few minutes," I called again through the door. I heard Mom's footsteps retreat down the hall. I sat up on the edge of the bed, my head still hanging on to a dull ache and my pillow was soaked from the towel of melted ice. I proceeded to strip my bed, leaving the discarded sheets in a heap on the floor, took two more Tylenol, and stepped into the shower.

My right shoulder seemed stiff and sore. I turned to examine it in the mirror. I didn't realize I hit the ground that hard. There was a huge bruise appearing in the deepest purple shade around my shoulder blade. So much for a cute halter top today. I squinched my face and sucked air through my clenched teeth as I ran my hand over the dark spot. I knew I couldn't explain this to my parents, and I didn't want to try.

I dressed in a pair of denim shorts, some flip-flops, and a V-neck tee. I was thankful the knot on my head had receded and was now the size of a pea, but still tender. I held my breath and squinted in pain as I pulled my hair into my usual ponytail.

"Good morning, sleeping beauty!"

"Morning, Dad, aren't we cheerful this morning." I yawned.

"Oooo...sounds like someone had a bad night," he teased.

I reached in the cupboard for a bowl, poured some cereal, dropped in a few of the fresh blackberries Mom had placed on the table, and poured the milk.

"Yeah, I didn't sleep well. There was the loudest commotion! I've never heard so much growling and hissing. It sounded like a war zone outside my window."

"Next time I see Jeb, I'll talk to him about hunting so close to the house, okay?" Dad said.

"Oh, Dad...don't. Mr. Blevins is a nice old man, and the only thing he really enjoys is running those dogs at night. He'll stop as soon as the weather starts to get colder." I didn't want to start any trouble with Mr. Blevins, and I was sure he really didn't have any control on where the dogs ran when hunting.

"Okay, if you're sure. I don't mind speaking to him about it."

"I'm sure. Besides, that's the first time I've ever heard him get that close."

"All right. So...how would you like to go to the movies this afternoon?" Dad loved catching me off guard. He said I always got that "deer in the headlights" look. His chuckle told me he got it again.

"I'd love to go!" Tailors Mountain didn't have a theater, so going to a movie was rare. The best cinema was an hour away in Virginia.

There were more people than I expected for a Friday afternoon. We had to wait in a long line for the tickets. The air was miserably hot and sticky, but I was willing to suffer the uncomfortable wait. I was just glad to get to see a movie *before* the DVD went on sale.

Vampire movies were my favorite, and I had been excited to see this particular movie. Dad enjoyed a scary movie as much as me. Mom, well, vampire movies were not exactly her pick, but she was content to feed our dark side now and then.

SOULBOUND: DESTINY'S MOVE

How odd, I thought as I stood there melting in the heat. *Even though we don't share one single strand of DNA, how much James and I have in common.* James and Anna adopted me when I was two. I had been made a ward of the state, with no known relatives, except of course my birth parents, who were killed in a car accident.

James and Anna saved me from being shuffled from one foster home to another. They were both only children, so I never had the luxury of a favorite aunt or uncle in my life. Anna's parents passed before the adoption. I only knew them through pictures. I did experience grandparents with James's mom and dad.

I loved Grandpa Larry and Grandma Jean, but that experience too was short. Grandpa had a heart attack when I was seven, and Grandma passed with cancer when I barely turned twelve. The three of us was all that was left of the Ryan family.

I noticed Mom had found an envelope in her purse and was fanning impatiently.

"Finally, I thought I was going to have a heat stroke!" Mom hated extreme heat as much as the winter's cold. I smiled to myself. I guess I have something in common with her too.

After loading up on junk food, we managed to find seats near the center. From the moment the lights went down I, felt strange...like someone was watching me. I couldn't seem to focus my full attention on the screen before me. I did enjoy a few moments watching Mom cover her eyes or look down at the floor, and I got a kick out of her constant fidgeting. A giggle escaped when my poor dad winced in pain as she dug her nails into his leg! He must've thought the movie was having the same effect on me, since he paid me no attention.

I couldn't shake the feeling someone's eyes were directly on me. I scanned the darkness but didn't see anyone paying any unusual attention.

As I leaned back again to relax, I felt the air move around my neck. It was warm...burning warm, like someone's breath! I wanted to turn around to see where this was coming from, but I couldn't bring myself to move. All at once my body began to tingle, like small jolts of electricity pulsing through my veins. My pulse quickened as my heart rate sped up. *What's happening to me?* I started to tremble, then I heard what I was sure to be a low, steady growl, almost a purr!

Instantly the mysterious feeling was gone. I jerked my head around to look behind me, but there was nothing there. I sat back and took in a long breath. *I have got to lay off the scary movies*, I thought. *My imagination is definitely starting to run away with me.*

We left the dark, cool theater into the blinding sunlight and scorching heat of the parking lot. I'm glad no one asked me about the movie. I couldn't remember one scene.

"Those vampires are such beautiful creatures. I don't understand why they can't be good." Mom's assessment of the undead only gave Dad permission to open fire on her antics inside. I admired the way they loved each other—comfortable, easy, uncomplicated.

The great thing about matinees, they give you plenty of times to do other things, like go shopping. Dad feared a department store as much as Mom feared a horror flick. I guess he figured if she could endure the undead for him, he could survive an afternoon clutching a cold metallic cart.

I couldn't believe Mom's energy! I picked up a few essentials I was lacking at the house and a new sweater from the fall clothing now starting to appear on the racks. It was getting dark when we left the store.

Dad just had to satisfy his craving for shrimp. *Ughhh, wouldn't you know it—another line!* I tried to convince them how good a burger and fries would be. Not even going to happen!

SOULBOUND: DESTINY'S MOVE

I trudged to the end of the line. At least the night air was more tolerable. I inched forward as another couple came up behind me. I glanced back and wished I hadn't. The girl was polite, and she smiled, so I smiled back and gave a quick hi to her. She was a chubby, rosy-cheeked young woman with red hair and blue eyes. Her escort, however, was another story. He was tall and extremely thin, with long scraggly hair that appeared as if it had never been washed. He hadn't even tried to "clean up" before he brought the cherub-faced girl to dinner. He apparently worked in some sort of garage; his clothes were all grease stained. The smell of it was still clinging to him, along with a stench that was obviously natural. His mouth turned up into a broad smile to show a row of yellow teeth.

"Hey, darlin', here alone?"

"No," I answered quickly and pointed to my dad. That ought to squelch any more attempts at conversation. I just wanted to turn around and ignore them. He made a step toward me anyway, and the quiet girl reined him back. The way he looked at me made every nerve in my body twitch. It was very unsettling.

A slight breeze moved the stale air, and there it was again! I wrapped my arms around my waist and breathed in the aroma. I shivered with pure delight. What was it? It wasn't perfume or cologne. It was intoxicating, and somehow, I felt like it belonged to me.

I looked around. Why doesn't anyone seem to notice? It is so overpowering! I started to feel faint, and then it was gone! I stood there trembling, trying with all my might to remain standing. I was intent on keeping my balance, not letting anyone see my weakened state. I especially didn't want Mr. Smooth behind me putting his greasy hands anywhere on my person.

Dinner seemed to take forever. I was glad to finally be out of the overcrowded restaurant. I opened the door of the silver Lincoln MKZ and seated myself in the back. I was glad Dad had finally bought a good vehicle for Mom. This was the only real luxury I had ever known them to allow themselves. I leaned my head back against the cool leather seat. Thank heavens this day is over! I made it to my room with slow, forced steps on my aching feet and collapsed onto the bed.

NIKOLAS WAS STARING out the window into the night. "I can't understand how they got that close!"

"I don't know, Nick. They found her sooner than I expected." Tristan moved from the chair to stand by the fireplace.

"I know. It's those traitors like Harold and Lydia! At least we won't have to worry about Harold anymore. Thanks to Galen and Safrina," Nick said. His eyes never left the stillness before him.

"Yeah, but Lydia got away, the little weasel!" Tristan paced, his breath heavy and labored.

"He knows who she is now," Nick stated.

"We have to find a way to get closer to her! It's too hard to watch her this way!" Tristan insisted as his back-and-forth pace quickened.

"We can't, Tristan. Not until she comes of age, just six more months." Nick sighed.

"This time is crucial, Nick. This is when it always happens!" Tristan's fist slammed into the wall beside him, causing a piece of the stone fireplace to crumple in a heap of powder at his feet.

"This is the closest we've ever been; it's not like before when we had never actually seen her." Tristan's voice trembled. Everything about him— his expression, his voice, his movement—all gave away the dire hopelessness building in his chest. "The attempts to get to her will be more frequent now."

"I know, and many will die." Nick turned back toward the window, his expression far away and sad.

SOULBOUND: DESTINY'S MOVE

"I don't want to sit here and stew about it. Let's go see if there's anything in the kitchen to eat and try not to dwell."

"You're right, let's go find something. You heat up the leftovers, and I'll pour us something to drink," Nick said, trying to sound less concerned, but he knew the next six months was going to be hell.

Tristan heated some leftovers while Nick poured himself a drink from the metal pitcher in the fridge and handed Tristan a tall glass of cold milk.

"So, where did you go this afternoon?" Nick only asked for the sake of conversation. He knew all too well where Tristan had been.

"I followed her to the movies," Tristan answered as he swallowed half of the huge piece of pot roast in one bite. "I got close enough to her today to literally taste her scent! I have to tell you, it was sweeter than I could've imagined!"

Nick's teeth clenched tight, and his knife dug into the meat on his plate with more force than he anticipated.

"What's wrong?" Tristan smirked.

"Nothing." Nick knew his friend meant no harm in sharing this information. Still the thought that Tristan could get closer than he could hope to for the next six months didn't set well with him.

"So...anything happen?"

"Oh yeah." Tristan downed his glass of milk before he finished speaking. "I almost blew it!"

Nick felt a little uneasy at that remark and looked at Tristan with one eyebrow raised. "What do you mean you almost blew it? How?"

"Well, being that close, breathing in her scent, tasting her, I became so enraptured that uncontrollable little growl started up in my throat!"

"You mean...you started purring! Nick leaned back and burst into a fit of laughter.

"Shut up, Nick. I don't purr!"

"Oh yes, you do!" He tried to regain his composure, but he couldn't shut out the mental image of Tristan leaned over on the chair, purring like a kitten waiting for a belly rub.

"I do not purr, and that's about enough from you!" Tristan's face flushed with his irritation.

"I'm sorry, Tris. I know you can't help it; purring comes naturally."

"I told you. It's a growl! I don't even like that word. It sounds so...so...feminine!"

"Trust me, feminine is not a word that would ever come to mind when describing you, my friend!"

The Date 6

I had the afternoon shift at work. I hated working days. I was much more comfortable closing. I walked into the kitchen to get something to drink before leaving for the restaurant. Mom had already prepared a quick lunch for me.

"Mom, you didn't have to do that." I smiled.

"I know, but you can't tell me that you don't get a little tired of eating the same old thing every day." She continued plating the salad as she talked.

"I do get a little tired of it; after all, no matter how big the menu is, it's still the same options," I answered as I grabbed a baby carrot and took a bite. "I don't think I'll need to worry about eating there today. It's Saturday, and the place is going to be slammed. I probably won't even get a chance to take a break." I groaned. I sat down and enjoyed my meal. "Well, I guess I better get going. Thanks for lunch, Mom," I said as I stood and picked up the ugly pink apron from the chair beside me.

"You're welcome, hon...be careful." Mom always said that; it didn't matter if you were going across the country or to the mailbox.

My day turned out exactly as I expected. I managed five minutes to go to the bathroom all afternoon. Danny was in rare form today. He had such a good disposition sometimes everyone at work, me especially, forgot he was the boss. At least the joking and camaraderie between us made the day go by easier.

I was glad when my shift was finally over. I walked back into the short hall to clock out. Danny was standing by the office door.

"Headin' home?" I could hear that tone in his voice again.

"Yeah, I'm exhausted." I tried to avoid eye contact. Danny had asked me out a couple of times before, and I could tell he was about to do it again. I didn't want to hurt his feelings, so I always tried to have at least a decent excuse for not being available. He was persistent though; I'll give him that.

It's not that he was a jerk or bad looking. He was medium height with short reddish hair and hazel eyes. It was obvious he worked out. I'm sure any girl would be thrilled to capture his attention. I just didn't feel any chemistry between us, and dating your boss I was sure not to be a good idea.

"I was wondering," Danny started as he shifted his stance and placed his hands in his pockets.

Here it comes. My mind was racing to stay ahead of the inevitable question.

"I was wondering...if you'd like to go somewhere and grab a bite to eat before you head home." He looked down at his feet as he spoke. It was almost like a teenager approaching his first crush. His behavior was actually kind of sweet.

"You want to go somewhere else to eat?" I asked, not quite seeing the logic since he owned a restaurant.

"I thought it would be more private. Besides, I don't like everyone knowing my business, you know." He smiled sweetly at me.

"It's really nice of you to ask, but I promised Jenna I'd visit with her tonight. I kinda need to get home and change...sorry." For some reason, this time I really was sorry. I didn't exactly lie about Jenna. I wasn't actually going to see her, just call.

"Another time then." His expression was again disappointed. I felt bad about turning him down again. Maybe I should just go grab a quick bite or a cup of coffee with him sometime. I'll consider it next time he asks...if there is a next time.

I walked out the front door, shaking my head. It was eight thirty. The sun was starting to drop behind the mountain. Darla McCoy was just getting out of her car. She must've been able to tell by the look on my face.

"Did it again, didn't he?"

I jumped when she spoke. "Hey, Darla. Yeah...I wish now we had changed shifts. I could've avoided the uncomfortable confrontation."

"Well, at least you'll get a couple of weeks' reprieve before he tries again." She laughed. Darla was a sweetheart. She was about four years older than me and twenty years wiser. Her straight cropped strawberry-blond hair seemed to accentuate her chubby cheeks, giving her face the appearance of being larger than it actually was. She was a short, heavy-set woman with a lively attitude. Darla married Chad McCoy right out of high school and immediately started a family. She had three kids, twin girls and a boy, all under the age of six.

"You know, Olivia, all joking aside, a date with Danny isn't the worst thing you could do. You know what they say about 'all work and no play.' Everyone needs a social life. You could use a little recreation, instead of always filling in for someone else to take a night off." She was leaning against my car, working on the wrapper of a candy bar, smiling in a mischievous way.

"Darla, don't you even think what I think you're thinking!" I exclaimed. "I don't do blind dates, okay?"

"Even if he's gorgeous?" Her smile held fast.

"Not even if he's Adonis! Besides, your idea of gorgeous and mine may not be the same." I elbowed her in the arm good-naturedly, not wanting her to feel bad about the offer.

"Well, gotta go, time to clock in." She smiled, letting me know that no offense was taken as she started out across the parking lot.

"Call me!" I yelled after her.

"Okay," she said, her arm waving as she walked.

I stood there thinking about what Darla said. She's right. Maybe it wouldn't hurt to socialize a little. It wasn't like an evening out was a commitment. I looked around and noticed Danny's car still sitting in the lot. I turned around and headed back inside. He was sitting in the office, going over some paperwork.

"I thought you quit for the night." I startled him, and he jumped, nearly knocking the folder and its contents to the floor.

"Hey, Olivia, and I thought you went home." He smiled.

"Well, my plans for this evening got cancelled, and I thought I might take you up on that offer for dinner...that is if you haven't already made other plans." Now I understand my dad's amusement when he caught me off guard. So that's what a deer in the headlights looked like. I suppressed a giggle and managed a smile.

"No," his voice squeaked. "Uhmmm...I mean no, as a matter fact, I haven't," he said with a beaming smile.

"Great, I'll wait for you outside, okay?"

"I won't be a minute," he said as he was piling up the papers in a disheveled heap into the folder.

Walking back out the door, I smiled to myself, pleased with my decision. I pulled my cell phone from my back pocket and dialed home. I decided not to send Mom into a panic twice in the same week.

"Mom...yeah...everything's fine. I just wanted you to know I'd be late tonight. Danny asked me out to dinner. I didn't want you to worry." I had no idea how concerned everyone had been about my lack of male companionship. Mom sounded ecstatic about the news.

"That's wonderful, hon. Do you have your key?" she asked, a little too exuberant.

SOULBOUND: DESTINY'S MOVE

"Yeah, so you don't have to leave the door open, and please don't wait up, okay?" I really hoped she wouldn't; I don't think I would feel comfortable being questioned about my evening.

"Okay then. I won't." Mom's voice had a knowing tone to it.

"Thanks, talk to ya later." As I hung up, Danny walked out.

"Everything all right?" he asked, glancing at the phone.

"Oh yeah, just a courtesy call."

"Ready to go then?" he asked, motioning toward his car. "Do you like Mexican food?"

I nodded my approval. Danny at least wasn't going to leave any awkward silence tonight, thank goodness.

Dan opened the car door for Olivia and started around to the driver's side. The black Mercedes Roadster with dark tinted windows, parked in the back of the front lot, came to life.

Nick sat frozen in his seat. "What is she doing?"

Tristan stared with an expression of shock as he relayed his conclusion to Nikolas.

"It looks like she has a date, and from the way she's laughing, about to enjoy it!" Nick was so stunned he could barely speak; his voice trembled with each word.

"This is something I hadn't anticipated." His eyes widened. "We can't allow this!"

"And what do you propose we do about it, hmmmm?" Tristan asked, still looking straight ahead at the white VW Jetta backing out of the parking space. "We've been so absorbed in our own cause that we failed to take into account that she's young, very beautiful, and bound to be desired by other men!" Tristan's hands were shaking, and his heart began to pound wildly in his chest.

NICK PULLED OUT OF the parking lot behind them, eyes wide and, if it were possible, paler than usual. They parked again in the rear of the small shopping center lot and watched Dan and Olivia enter the restaurant.

"This place is too small for either of us to go inside without being noticed. Damn!" Nick punched the center panel of the dash, and the air conditioner vents and the stereo panel shattered onto the floorboard.

"Nick, look in that Chrysler convertible." Tristan pointed. They were both out of the car and at the side of the two men instantly.

"Good evening, Darius...Lawson. You two don't strike me as the spicy-cuisine type." Nick sneered.

Darius's thin lips turned up in a broad, arrogant smile. Everything about Darius was long and thin, from his wiry bone-like fingers and straight pointed nose to his thin graying hair. Tristan stood beside the passenger door, looking down at the fat round-faced man. Lawson's cheeks were flushed like his blood pressure had suddenly shot up.

"Nikolas, it's been a long time!" Darius said, still smiling as he opened the car door and stood beside Nick.

"Not long enough. Shall we find a suitable place for a more private reunion?" As he spoke, he placed his hand on the back of Darius's neck, gripping him with such force it caused the wiry man to stumble.

"Certainly, old friend—lead the way." As quickly it seemed as Darius spoke, they were on the mountain behind the building. Nick threw him to the ground. In the same instant, Tristan found he was face-to-face with a huge brown bear. His smirk became a wide smile as he looked up at the bear now standing upright on its hind legs.

"This is going to be interesting!" Tristan's eyes narrowed, and his lips curled back, revealing huge sharp fangs jutting down from an equally sharp row of teeth. The panther released a bloodcurdling scream.

Darius made one leap, landing on Nikolas as the two rolled several feet down the hill. The black cat made a leap for his opponent's throat, landing the bear soundly on the ground.

Nick rolled to a standing position, only to meet Darius's foot as it connected with his chest, throwing him through the air several yards into a tree.

"You're pathetic, Nikolas, to think you can protect her! Lucas will win—as always!" Darius hissed.

Nick righted himself easily, showing no sign of pain or distress from the impact he had just experienced. "Don't count on it, Darius, she's stronger this time!"

"Ha! You're delusional. She's a mere mortal, a little animal to keep around for amusement! Is that what you and Tristan are up to, finding a family pet?" Darius snarled.

Those would be the last words he would utter. Nikolas hissed loudly and, in the breath of a second, was on Darius. The only sounds were that of flesh tearing and a sickening gurgle.

Nick stood there like stone, staring down, his eyes cold and black. In his hand laid the jugular from his adversary's throat, as the blood gushed down onto Darius's chest. A loud roar caused Nick's head to jerk, looking up to where his friend was engaged in his own battle. He then heard another bloodcurdling cat scream, the sound of bones breaking, and an agonizing moan.

In a few moments, the cat emerged to stand beside him, holding Lawson's heart in his mouth. He waited as Nikolas separated Darius from his. They placed the two hearts in a small hole dug by the huge panther paw and covered them with dry leaves.

Nikolas took out a lighter and set fire to the small mound. As the flames took hold and the hearts turned to ash, so did the two still bodies. They stood silent, heads bowed, sorrow in their eyes.

"We need to get back." Nick's voice was now calm, his breath even. At the edge of the woods he stopped. "Wait here, Tristan." It seemed like only an eye's blink when he returned carrying a gallon of water, a bowl, and some clothes. He placed the bowl and clothing on the ground and filled the container with water.

As the panther lapped the water to rinse his mouth, Nick washed the remains of the fight from his hands. He picked up the bowl and turned to walk as Tristan spoke.

"I know how you feel, Nick. I too am saddened by the lives that ended tonight."

"It's only the beginning." Nick sighed and walked away.

They were again seated in the car, and Nick shook his head. "I can't understand why Lucas insists on this bloodshed. There is so few of us left!"

"Lucas has only one agenda—to destroy you."

His jaw clenched tight at Tristan's words. "I know...I just wonder if this insane war will ever end!"

"Not as long as Lucas lives!" Tristan turned to stare out the window. His mind seemed worlds away.

Olivia and Danny emerged from the restaurant, walking close together, still talking and laughing.

"It's not enough we have to deal with Lucas. Now we have him!" Nick gestured toward the couple ambling slowly before them.

"What can we do?" Tristan shrugged.

"It would be easy. All I have to do is follow him home and—"

"Nick! You can't do that! Besides, it would only implicate her! We just have to find a diversion to keep them from being together."

SOULBOUND: DESTINY'S MOVE

Tristan was surprised at his friend's suggestion and was worried by the look on Nick's face that he just might follow through with it.

"Fine, Tris, but look. He's got his arm around her waist!" Nikolas watched them as his eyes burned into Dan.

"In the future, please try and refrain from pointing out every detail, or I just might agree with your plan!" Tristan sniffed.

"All right, you work on the diversion." Nick's eyes narrowed. "But so help me if he kisses her."

"Just try and stay calm. We'll get the situation under control." His eyes were just as fixed on the couple as Nick's.

"Take the Chrysler, Tristan. The keys are still in the ignition. I'll get Safrina to dispose of it tomorrow."

"See you at the house, right? Don't do anything stupid," Tristan warned.

Nick followed Dan and Olivia back to Rooter's BBQ and watched as Dan waited for Olivia to unlock her car door. *Don't kiss him...please don't kiss him* were the only words going through his mind.

Alone 7

"I really enjoyed dinner tonight," Dan said as he started fidgeting again.

"I did too, I'm glad you asked me." My smile was genuine. I did enjoy myself.

"Maybe we could go out again sometime? I mean, on a real date." Dan's cheeks were flushed, and he kept his eyes lowered. I would never have taken him to be timid that way.

"I'd like that." I looked at Dan and smiled softly, suddenly feeling a little awkward myself.

"Maybe the next time we're off together," Dan suggested. Since he made out the work schedule, I was sure that would be soon.

"All right then, I'll check my schedule Monday after work."

No sooner had I agreed than he made a step toward me. I opened the car door quickly so that it would be between us. I wasn't ready for the goodnight kiss thing, not just yet.

On the way home, I started second-guessing my acceptance of a second date with Dan. I was hoping there might be some chemistry between us, but tonight didn't reveal it. *Is it fair to him to go out again... when I'm almost positive that this is not going to develop into anything more than the friendship we already seem to have? I want to give it at least a decent chance, maybe—oh for cryin' out loud, Olivia, just give it up!* My thoughts were only making me frustrated, and I was glad I was home. Mom had left the light on for me. I guess I was just doomed to grow old, the cranky spinster, and a victim of my own hormonal impotence.

I started across the yard to the front porch, when I heard something in the woods. I stopped and instinctively searched the tree line. I felt the hair on the back of my neck bristle as I rubbed the goose bumps on my arm. It felt again like I was being watched. I hurried into the house and locked the door behind me.

I turned out the lamp burning on the end table and made my way down the dark hallway to my room, feeling uneasy as I dressed for bed. I just couldn't shake the feeling something or someone was out there. *You're just being paranoid.* I shrugged off the strange feeling and got into bed, hoping for a peaceful night's sleep.

I wish I could make out what was falling from the sky. It seems so small…so far away! My heart was pounding louder and louder! The thunderous boom to the left of me started my body convulsing in terror. I started running faster. I could barely breathe! What's burning? The flames were so high! My breath quickened, and the odor caused me to gag! *Wake up!* I told myself. *Wake up!* I dropped to my knees and looked up at the bright blazing inferno.

I blinked at the sunlight glaring through my bedroom window and sat straight up, gasping for air, my stomach quivering. *Is this nightmare ever going to end?* I thought. I got out of bed and ran to the shower. I couldn't shake the fear this morning. The dream was becoming more vivid. I just stood there, letting the stream run over me until there was no more hot water. The blast of cold jolted me back to reality. *Relax…it's only a dream,* I told myself as I dressed with trembling hands.

I walked into the kitchen to find my parents laughing and making plans. Dad seemed extra cheerful as he greeted me this morning. I reached in the cupboard for a pack of Pop-Tarts and dropped them in the toaster. "You two seem pretty happy, what's up?" I asked.

Mom poured a glass of orange juice and placed it on the table in front of me. She was positively glowing. "We have some exciting news!" she bubbled.

"Oh…" My eyebrow rose as I took a sip from my glass.

Mom placed the Pop-Tarts on a saucer and handed them to me.

"Uh-huh, tell her, James."

"Our anniversary is coming up, you know..." Dad began, but Mom impatiently took over the conversation again.

"This year is our milestone anniversary of twenty years—"

"I know," I interrupted. "And..." I waited.

"And...Dad has surprised me with a trip to Las Vegas, isn't that great!" Mom gushed. She was so excited I thought she might pee her pants any second!

I smiled at how she resembled a child finding out she's going to Disney World for the first time. She was absolutely precious. Mom never got out much. Travel just wasn't in the family budget, so I could understand her exuberant reaction to the news.

"It's a long drive. When are you going?" I asked, finishing my last bite of pastry.

"We'll be flying out tomorrow!" Mom's eyes twinkled. It was her first time on a plane. I stopped chewing and stared at the two of them. I forced myself to swallow and washed it down quickly with some juice.

"So soon, can you be ready that quick?" I should be happy for them, but for some reason, the only thing I could feel was a knot in the pit of my stomach.

"Oh, sure, Mom can have us packed and ready to go in two hours." Dad leaned back as he looked at her with absolute confidence.

"What time does your plane leave?" I asked.

"Ten o'clock in the morning, but we have to be there an hour early. We'll leave here about seven thirty," Dad explained. He had everything all figured out.

"Great, so...I guess you guys have a lot to do today." I tried to sound excited for them, but my ability to deceive held true, and Mom for certain could tell I didn't share in their joy.

"Are you all right, hon?" Mom asked, hoping I would confess my disapproval.

"Yeah, I'm fine. I'm going to go call Jenna. She came in for the weekend, and I at least want to talk to her before she leaves again." I tried to smile, but I'm sure it looked as phony to them as it felt to me.

"Okay, Liv." Mom looked warily at Dad as she sipped her coffee.

I decided not to prolong my stay at the table.

I sat on the edge of my bed and dialed Jenna's number.

"Jenna...it's me...how's everything?" I was glad I caught her before she went back to school. I hated the fact that we never got the chance to get together for lunch or something while she was home.

"Olivia, hey! I was beginning to think you forgot about me."

"No, I couldn't forget you! Things are just a little crazy around here, that's all."

Jenna was my closest friend from high school. I can't remember how our friendship started or why we ever became friends. We were exact opposites. Jenna was tall and slender. I always thought she would be a model. She certainly had the height at around five foot nine or ten. She was very outspoken and outgoing. Jenna was the type of person that lived for change.

Her hair was currently blond with red highlights. She had changed colors so many times I didn't even remember what her natural color was. Once, she got contacts to change the color of her beautiful blue eyes. "I like the idea of changing my eyes with my mood," she would always say. Personally, I thought it was creepy.

"So...have ya missed me?" she asked.

"Of course I miss you! What kind of question is that? Now that you're away at school, I don't have anyone to turn to for the dirty deeds of the county." I teased.

"Olivia Ryan! I am not a gossip; every word is straight up!" She laughed.

"Yeah, yeah." I tried to be teasingly sarcastic, but the playful mood just wasn't there.

"Hey, girl, is something wrong?" Jenna always had a way of seeing through me even if we weren't face-to-face.

"Nah, I'm fine." I tried to sound convincing but failed.

"Come on, Liv; spit it out before it eats you up!"

Aside from being a terrible liar, confiding was also not one of my strong suits. "I'm just a little jittery about my parents' trip this week," I told her, trying not to play it up as a big deal.

"Your parents are taking a trip, that's great! Where are they going?" I could almost see her eyes dancing at the prospect of spreading the news.

"They're going to Vegas for their twentieth anniversary."

"How great is that, so why are you so down? You're going to have the place all to yourself!" she pointed out.

"And what will I do all to myself?" I didn't mean for the words to sound so bitter.

"You don't want them to go without you, do you?" Her question made me feel defiant. I wanted her to know my attitude about their trip had nothing to do with my independence.

"That's not it, Jen. I'll be fine here by myself."

"Awe, Liv, you're feeling abandoned, bless your heart."

I knew Jenna was trying to understand me, but sympathy was the last thing I needed...or wanted. "Jen, I'm not feeling abandoned, for crying out loud. I just...just..." I was so frustrated I couldn't think of a word to describe how I felt!

"For goodness' sakes, Olivia, get a grip!" she scolded. "Your parents are great! They've spent so much time and sacrificed so much to give you a great childhood!" she continued. "Surely you can't begrudge them an anniversary celebration! You're a grown woman, for the love of Pete!"

"I know what I am, Jenna!" I was annoyed at her assessment of my maturity.

"Look, Olivia, you've never spent any time away from your parents. It's only natural that you would feel anxious about the separation. I felt the same way when I left home for school," she pointed out.

I realized Jenna was absolutely right! My parents deserved this vacation, especially Mom. Suddenly I felt childish and very selfish. It occurred to me that Jenna was waiting for a response.

"Jen, you're right. I'm glad I talked to you about it. I feel a lot better now. My words were a lie. I knew they deserved to go, but I couldn't shake the apprehension."

"Well, what are friends for? I'm just glad I could set you straight before you had a meltdown and caused a scene!" She was joking again. I turned the conversation to her and got the low-down on the college scene before we said our good-byes until her next visit.

As I walked into the living room, Mom was placing suitcases by the front door. I didn't realize I had been on the phone with Jenna that long. The sight of the luggage made my stomach wrench.

Mom walked over and sat down on the couch, turning toward me. "Come here, Olivia." She patted the cushion beside her.

"What is it, Mom, is something wrong?" *Of course something was wrong, everything inside me was screaming it.*

"Well, there's nothing wrong with me. I want to know what's bothering you." Her eyes were locked on me, and she used that easy mothering voice, the one that makes you feel guilty about withholding information.

"It's really nothing. I guess I'm just nervous. I'm not used to being away from you and Dad."

"Oh, I see." Her eyes danced with a hint of motherly amusement.

"Olivia, dear, we're going to miss you too. After all, we're not used to being away from you either." She smiled a warm, loving smile. "Maybe this trip will help us both; give you the courage to step out on your own and your dad and me the courage to let you. Think of it as a practice run." She chuckled.

"Yeah, I guess you're right." Of course she was right—as always. It was just a little separation anxiety.

"I'm going to fix supper, come and help." She grabbed my hand and pulled me from my seat. I helped prepare my favorite meal: pot roast and chocolate pie.

We enjoyed a leisurely dinner, laughing, joking, and reminiscing about my stunts and schemes growing up. After cleaning up, Dad stretched his arms. My stomach fluttered at the sign the evening was about to come to an end.

"It's getting late; we better get some rest, Mama. We've got a big day tomorrow." Dad stretched again, emphasizing the urgency to turn in with a huge yawn.

"I suppose we should get some rest." She looked at me as though she didn't want the evening to end. I definitely felt the same.

"Night, Liv," they chimed as both kissed my cheek. Mom hugged me tightly.

"Turn out the lights, dear." "I will. I'm just going to watch a little TV." "Not too loud," Dad remarked.

"Okay, I'll see you both in the morning." I switched through the channels and found one of my favorite old vampire movies. I leaned over on one of the throw pillows on the couch to enjoy it. My eyelids began to feel heavy, but I wanted to see the ending.

The clouds suddenly turned gray; everything had the appearance of dusk. I looked up into the sky again to see the object falling.

Immediately I heard the thunderous sound to my left. I looked to witness the torrential fire and again experienced the black smoke and the stench. I began running toward the blaze, but instead of reaching it, I found myself looking up to watch the object fall again. This time, just before it was out of sight, I heard a scream and my name!

I shot straight up, my chest heaving. My hair was wet with sweat. I couldn't focus. I couldn't catch my breath. Every muscle in my body was trembling. I wrapped both arms around my waist and began to rock slowly bank and forth, trying to ease the pain in my chest and stomach. It was some time before I regained my senses.

I had fallen asleep, and the nightmare had taken over again. The television was still playing some silly comedy, filling the room with unessential noise. I grabbed the remote and clicked it off.

I walked into the kitchen to get a drink. My hand was still shaking as I took the glass from the cupboard and grabbed the Tylenol bottle from the back counter. As I poured two into my hand and popped them in my mouth, I noticed the time on the microwave clock. It's six a.m. Mom and Dad will be up soon.

I rushed into my room and threw on some fresh clothes (I didn't want them to know I hadn't gone to bed), hurried back into the kitchen, and started preparing breakfast. I had put on a pot of coffee and started the bacon when Mom entered the room, dressed in a pale-blue knit top and white capris, smiling and excited.

"Olivia, how nice, you didn't have to cook for us this morning!" The smile on her face told me she was pleased I had.

"I know. Peanuts and crackers are not a sustainable food in my book." I hoped my attempt at enthusiasm was convincing. I was still trying to stop the trembling in my legs.

SOULBOUND: DESTINY'S MOVE

Dad came in with his nose raised high in the air, taking in big whiffs of the bacon and coffee. "Mmmmm...that smells good. I'm starved," he announced as he rubbed his rounding middle. "It's really nice of you to make us a farewell breakfast." He smiled, gesturing to the pans on the stove. The farewell comment was almost the straw that broke the camel's back.

Time passed too quickly. I stood on the front porch as Dad loaded their luggage in the trunk of the car. I wanted to drive them, but he insisted on leaving the car at the airport. "I don't want you driving that crooked road at night. Besides, we'll be returning late," he said.

I felt numb. Why couldn't I just break down and beg them to stay home? I couldn't do that. I knew how much they were looking forward to this vacation.

"We better get going if we plan to catch that plane." He placed his arm on my teary-eyed mother's shoulder.

"I want to give you your anniversary gift now. It's nothing elaborate." I wished that I could have afforded something more, but most of my meager salary went on insurance, gas, and a constant demand for car parts. I was pleased with my parents' gift at graduation, but it was an older model, and after the first six months, things started breaking down. It managed to keep a pretty steady need for repairs since. I figure, at the rate it's going, in about a year I should have a whole new vehicle with the exception of the distributor.

"Oh, honey. Thank you." Mom wiped a tear from her eye and opened the small package as Dad watched. Mom pulled out the tiny crystal cube with the laser-imprinted picture of the three of us.

"Oh, it's beautiful!" she exclaimed, holding it up in the light as the tears started to flow freely.

Dad took the crystal and smiled approvingly. "Technology, it amazes me what they can do these days. Thank you, Liv."

I clung desperately to each of them as I said good-bye, not wanting to let go. It was all but impossible to stop the tears. I stood there on the porch and watched as the silver Lincoln disappeared down the road. I leaned over the porch rail and vomited.

My parents called when their plane landed. Mom was excited, and I was glad her trip was off to a good start. I felt more relaxed then. *You have been paranoid for nothing,* I told myself. *They're fine.*

Work had been pretty quiet today, and just as I suspected, my next day off with Danny was tomorrow. He had some plans to take up the entire afternoon. I was glad; it would save me from rambling around the empty house.

The week went by faster than I expected. Danny had made an attempt twice more since Tuesday, but something always seemed to get in the way, so I filled up the cancelled dates working for Darla or Michelle. My parents called often. I enjoyed hearing about their adventure.

Saturday had finally arrived, and Mom and Dad would be home sometime after midnight. I busied myself with housework to pass the time. I didn't want Mom to come home to a trashed house. My idea of neat and hers were totally different.

Mom called at eight thirty p.m. It was only five thirty there. "We just wanted to call before we boarded to say good night and tell you we love you." Dad took the phone from Mom. "We love you, honey. We'll see you in the morning."

"Okay, Dad, have a nice flight, and I love you both, more than you know."

"We love you too." Mom spoke for the both of them. "We'll talk to you later, okay?"

"Okay," I whispered into the phone, and it went silent.

I went back over to the movies on the shelf, picked one, and sat back to relax. Around nine thirty, a wave of nausea came over me.

SOULBOUND: DESTINY'S MOVE

I got a glass of ginger ale from the kitchen, passing the sick feeling for having eaten my own cooking for the past week.

I hadn't made it back to the living room when my legs buckled under me, my chest ached, and I dropped to the floor, panic racing through my entire body. The glass slipped from my fingers and rolled onto the carpet beside me. The flashes of my dream were tearing through my mind in repeated succession.

I just sat there in my stupor, unable to fathom what was wrong with me. I heard a knock at the front door, and I glanced at the clock on the wall. It was a quarter past ten. I forced myself from the floor; my hands were shaking so violently I could barely unlock the door.

I opened it to find Sheriff Whitman and...Grace Butler? Why would Grace be with the sheriff? The expression on his face made my heart skip a beat. Please...God...let him be here to warn me about a prowler or something! I silently prayed.

My heart began to race as I looked into the somber face of the sheriff, obviously trying to control his emotions. He pulled his hat from atop his balding head, and I didn't like the look in his eyes.

My body began to shake violently as he reached out to grasp my shoulders.

"Olivia...I have some news." He spoke very soft, his words apprehensive. "There's no easy way to say this."

"Then don't say it!" I gasped through uneven breaths. "Wait till morning and tell my parents!" The tears were burning my eyes and one escaped down my cheek.

"Liv..." he paused, searching a way to proceed. "There was an accident...the plane went down in the woods just out of Grand Junction Colorado around seven thirty p.m. That's...um...nine thirty our time." His eyes were filled with pity and remorse.

I couldn't hear this! "My parents..." I breathed, my voice barely audible.

"I'm so sorry..." he paused again "There were no survivors."

"No!" I screamed. "Oh, God...no! My dream..." Everything went black.

SOULBOUND: DESTINY'S MOVE

Five Months Later

AMANDA ALBERY

First Meeting 8

THE PAST FEW MONTHS had went by in a blur after my parents' tragic death. I threw myself into work. I don't know how I would have survived had it not been for the selflessness of Grace Butler. She spent almost every waking moment with me in the weeks following the accident. She was my rock at the memorial service and such a help settling my parents' affairs.

I always assumed they sacrificed a lot of things like travel, weekend trips, new furniture, and the like because the income just didn't stretch far enough to allow for these things. I couldn't have been more wrong! They had chosen to prepare for the unforeseeable and had managed to pay off a twenty-five year mortgage in eighteen, leaving the only name on the deed, Olivia J. Ryan.

They had provided me with sizeable life insurances from each of them, along with a large savings. Everything they did and everything they did without was for the sole purpose of taking care of me. Thanks to their love, devotion, and hard work, I, should I choose, would never have to work again. As thankful as I am, I would rather it be like it was—sharing life with them.

My budding relationship with Danny slowly burned out. I lost interest for several months after the news. We never seemed to be able to get a real date anyway; something always seemed to interfere. I figure it just wasn't meant to be.

I stood at the kitchen window sipping a hot cup of tea. The snowflakes started to fall as I stared out at nothing. It was February 26, my twentieth birthday. I certainly didn't feel like celebrating. Everything about this sucks! I hurled the teacup into the wall and sank to the kitchen floor, sobbing.

The phone rang. I debated on whether or not to answer but decided another voice, any voice, would be better than this dreadful silence and my agonizing memories. I glanced at the caller ID.

"Hey, Dan..." My voice was a giveaway that I'd been crying.

"Olivia...is everything okay?" I could tell he was genuinely concerned.

"Yeah, everything's fine. What's up?"

"I hate to call and ask again. I was hoping you might come in and work for just a couple of hours. I'm really shorthanded."

I was relieved. I needed to get out of here even it was only a couple of hours.

"Sure, Dan, I'd be glad to. Oh, do you have an extra apron? Mine's in the wash."

"Don't worry about that. Right now I wouldn't care if you waited tables in your pajamas," he teased. I knew he could sense that I was feeling down and was trying to lighten my mood.

"All right then, I'll grab my coat and be there in about fifteen minutes."

"Great, see ya then," Dan said.

I grabbed my coat, keys, and purse, flipped on the porch light, just in case, and headed to town.

I walked in through the front door of the restaurant. Although there were several customers scattered about the room, the only staff I could see was Dan and Michelle.

"Man, you weren't kidding. Where is everyone?"

"It's the weather. You know how it is. Every time it snows, the callouts start." Dan smiled.

"Yeah," I sighed. "Let me clock in and I'll get started. What tables do you want me to work tonight?"

"Before you do, will you go on back to the break room and get that stack of folders on the back table for me and take them into the office. I have to check on some things in the kitchen." Dan glanced up and smiled as he started toward the kitchen doors.

"Sure, be back in a flash." I smiled back, turned, and started down the hall. I opened the break-room door to the loud roar of "Surprise!" Everyone I worked with was standing in the room decorated with crepe paper streamers and balloons. In the center of the table sat a beautiful cake.

"Oh my stars! You guys didn't have to do this! I don't know what to say." The fact that they had taken the time to arrange this for me touched me deeply. As I wiped a tear from my eye, Darla came up to me with outstretched arms.

"Happy birthday, Liv. We just couldn't stand the thought of you sitting at home eating junk food...when we weren't there to share it!"

"You guys are great! Thank you so much!" I heard a noise behind me and turned around to find Danny smiling, eyes twinkling.

"Can I get a hug from the birthday girl?" he said, holding out his arms.

"Of course you can!" I reached to give him a hug and got much more than I expected. Dan's lips came down on mine, strong and forceful, holding me tightly. After I had pried myself free of the vice grip, he had on me, I just stared at him in disbelief, ignoring the sounds of applause and whistles.

My cheeks were colored scarlet, not from embarrassment, but anger! I couldn't believe he would take advantage like that! He looked down at me, eyes still shining, apparently feeling very smug about his brazen display.

"Happy birthday." He was so caught up in his little coo that he didn't even notice my reaction.

"We need to talk—later," I said as I turned back to my friends and threw myself into the little party with as much enthusiasm as I could muster. My surprise party was short and sweet since most of the guests had to get back to work.

After everyone had cleared the room with the exception of Dan, I wheeled around on him, my anger building by the second.

"How dare you pull a stunt like that—in front of everyone here to beat it all!"

"Olivia, calm down, it was just a harmless kiss!" Dan's posture became defensive.

"Harmless! Now everyone I work with thinks we're a couple!" I couldn't believe he didn't see the implication of his actions.

"So, I'd like to be." He stood there, waiting for my response.

"Like to be what?"

"A couple." He sounded so confident in his announcement.

"What? Do you honestly believe that kissing me was all it would take to turn everything around?"

"Well...I just assumed..." He had the audacity to look shocked at my reaction.

"Assumed...you had no right to assume anything!" I yelled.

He looked embarrassed now and hurt. I realized he had put his feelings on the table in front of everyone. Even though he went about it entirely wrong, it must have taken every ounce of courage he could muster to attempt this declaration tonight.

I suddenly felt bad about my surge of anger, and I softened my tone. "Danny, I realize what you did was meant with good intention, and maybe I'm just overreacting." A smile started to show in the corner of his mouth.

"I'm sorry, Liv. You should have had a choice, and I didn't give you one."

"I'm sorry, but I just..." I was so at a loss for words. "I just don't see us together...romantically. I'm sorry; I don't share your feelings. Please try and understand. I do like you as a person...and a friend... but nothing more."

He walked over and placed his hand under my chin, pulling my face up gently to look at him.

"All right, Olivia, we'll be friends, if that's what you want. You know how I feel, and you can't blame me for trying or stop me from hoping." He bent down, kissed my forehead, and started for the door.

"Danny?"

"Yeah?" He stopped and turned back toward me.

"Do you still want me to work?" He shook his head and smiled. "Register and cleanup," I said meekly.

"Yeah, I know you hate it." He tried to laugh, and I just smiled.

NIKOLAS PACED BACK and forth in front of the fireplace. "She's finally twenty!" His voice was nervous and his eyes full of excitement.

"I know, Nick. The pull to be close to her is almost more than I can bear!"

"Now that we can approach her, I don't know how!" He kept pacing, all the while wringing his hands.

"Well, I don't think it would be wise if both of us went barging up to her at once. This is her night off anyway. How would we approach her tonight?" Tristan felt a sinking feeling as he realized this. "It's not like we can just walk up to her front door. We don't exactly have a legitimate excuse to go to her house." Tristan had begun to pace alongside Nick.

"Maybe one of us could pretend to be a salesman or something," Nick suggested. "Oh yeah, I can see it now. You ring the doorbell, and when she answers, you smile and say, 'Avon calling.'" "I don't think that'll wash." Tristan laughed.

"Well, we have to think of something!" Nick was starting to get impatient. His cell rang. "Galen, is there a problem? I see. Thanks....No, Tristan and I will keep watch." Nick hung up the phone, smiling. "Good news, Tris. Galen told me that Olivia had been called in to work tonight. Now we just have to decide which one of us gets the first meeting." He started unconsciously pacing again. "Got any ideas, Tristan?" He stopped again, waiting to hear any suggestion Tristan may have.

"The only fair thing I can think of is for us to flip a coin."

"It sounds a little corny, but it's better than anything I can think of at the moment." He reached into his pocket and pulled out a quarter.

"Okay, Tristan. Heads, I meet her first. Tails, well, you know."

"Sounds fair to me—wait a minute, I want to look at the coin."

"Oh, that's mature, Tris. What do you think? I've got a pocket full of two-headed coins?" He looked at Tristan as though he'd lost his mind.

"With you, my friend, I can never be sure." Tristan's face lit up in a broad smile.

"Would you like to toss?" Nick held the coin out to Tristan.

"You go ahead." He stepped back, folding his arms across his chest.

Nick tossed the coin, caught it, and placed it on the back of his hand, keeping it covered.

"No hard feelings, whoever meets her first...right?" He gave a suspicious look at Tristan, unsure if he would be a graceful loser.

"Right, so let's see, the suspense is killing me!" He stepped closer to see the coin Nick still had covered on his hand.

Nikolas gently raised his hand, and Tristan smiled.

"Looks like you've just developed a huge craving for pulled pork, Nick." He started walking out of the room. His irritation at having to wait was evident. "Where are you going?" Nick called after him.

"For a walk, pick me up one of those roast beef sandwiches... rare." He raised his hand to wave off any more conversation as he continued walking.

AMANDA ALBERY

I REACHED INTO MY PURSE and retrieved my nametag. I had just recently started carrying the shoulder bag. I hadn't seen the advantages that my friends kept telling me about. I hated it. It so far had proven to be more hindrance than help.

The close proximity to Dan after the break room fiasco made me uncomfortable, not to mention the stares and whispers of my coworkers. I was glad for the rush that filled a good portion of the tables. I was busy enough that I barely had time to look up.

I had started restocking the cabinets underneath the front counter and was kneeling down with my head half inside the first compartment when I sensed someone at the register. "I'll be with you in just one minute," I called without looking up.

"That's okay, I'm in no hurry."

When I heard that perfect angelic voice respond, I immediately stopped what I was doing. *If silk had a voice, that would be it!* I thought. I stood up slowly, and there before me was the most beautiful man I'd ever seen!

He stood about six foot two, broad shoulders and perfectly built. His muscular chest tapered off to a narrow waist. From the top of his forehead to his jaw line, the angles of his face were symmetrically perfect! He had soft blond hair layered down to the edge of his jaw, with tiny wisps of it across his forehead and...beautiful full lips that formed a perfect Cupid's bow. His skin was smooth and pale, almost luminous...and those eyes! Dark thick lashes formed around perfect shaped lids. The color wasn't the vibrant blue you would expect, but black as midnight—gorgeous and mesmerizing! I stood there just staring at the angel before me. I blinked and tried to compose myself.

"Can I help you, sir?" My words made an unusual crackling noise.

SOULBOUND: DESTINY'S MOVE

"Please. My name is Nikolas. You can call me Nick," he said, handing me his bill. The European accent only made him all the more alluring.

I had averted my eyes to ring up his purchase; my mouth was dry and my stomach in knots. As I looked back up, I felt the heat burning in my cheeks. *Get a grip! He's just a man, a beautiful god of a man, but still a man,* I told myself. I caught my breath and attempted a casual smile. It wasn't until he smiled back did I feel my legs turn to water! Then he spoke with that silken voice again.

"It was nice meeting you, Olivia," he said. The sound of my name rolling off his tongue seemed to have melted my brain! I should have been content to keep quiet.

"You know my name?" I hadn't noticed Kandi standing next to me until she reached over and flicked my nametag, making me wish I could melt into the floor! I attempted an annoyed glance, but she didn't notice since her eyes were fixed on Nick as well. I straightened myself and tried to appear more confident.

"Thank you, Nick, enjoy your evening."

"I'm sure I will. It's certainly off to a great start."

I quickly turned crimson again at his obvious flirting. I watched as he started toward the door. He moved so effortlessly and confidently. It seemed as though he never touched the ground. I turned to Kandi, still awestruck.

"Was he real?"

"Honey, if he wasn't, I wanna be in your dreams every night!" Kandi was still staring at the front door as she spoke.

I noticed Dan had been watching as Nikolas exited the building. He stood there leaned against the wall at the entrance to the hall, arms crossed over his chest, eyebrows knit, and a pout forming in the corners of his mouth. I placed my hand over my mouth and snickered. He resembled a grumped-up bulldog at that moment.

It was only seven thirty, and I dreaded going home. I was parked out front instead of the employee lot. I began fumbling through my purse for my car keys. I never had this problem before. I would have just reached in my front pocket. Pocketbooks are an atrocious pain in the—before I could finish my thought, I dropped it, scattering its contents all around me.

I bent down, placing my gifts gingerly on the snow-covered pavement, mumbling words my mom would have referred to as "unbecoming a young lady." A pale hand reached out to hand me the keys. I looked up into the pitch-black eyes and smiling face of Nikolas.

"I assume there was a party in your honor?" He gestured toward the gifts as he spoke.

"Yes, a surprise party actually...for my twentieth birthday. *He didn't need to know my age!*

"Well, happy birthday." His voice was soft.

"Thank you...and thank you for your help." I pushed a lock of flyaway hair behind my ear and unlocked the car door.

"Olivia." His beautiful, gentle voice broke the awkward silence, and my heart skipped a beat.

"Yes, Nick."

"I know this may seem sudden...being we just met," he began. "I was wondering, since it's still early...if you would do me the honor of joining me for dinner?"

"Didn't you just..." I pointed to the restaurant.

"Oh, that's just some roast beef for tomorrow."

I just stood there looking at him. This just wasn't happening.

"Would you? Have dinner with me tonight?" he asked again. "I promise you, I'll behave like a gentleman." His captivating smile was very convincing.

"I'd like that very much." Any other time I'm positive there would be a red flag waving about now. For some unknown reason, I didn't feel the least bit apprehensive about accepting his invitation.

"Great. Do you like seafood? I would like to try the new restaurant that just opened." He handed my gifts out to me, and I placed them in the passenger seat of my car and locked the door back.

"You mean the one on Waverly Street?" I asked.

"Yes, that's the one. The Triton, I believe."

"Seafood is my favorite. I've wanted to try it myself." I smiled.

Nick walked slowly as he escorted me to a silver Hummer with dark tinted windows. It sparkled flawlessly under the post lamp. He opened the door and waited until I was comfortably seated before closing it. I noticed Kandi and Darla standing by the front door, looking out at us. I gave them a quick wave as Nick climbed into the driver's seat. I was almost afraid to look over at him. I've never been so nervous. My heart was pounding so hard I was sure it could be heard a mile away.

Thank goodness for a small town, it didn't take long to reach Waverly Street. We walked into the restaurant, and I noticed immediately the eyes of every woman (and a few men) turn to Nick. He seemed oblivious to the attention. After being seated, the waiter gave us our menus.

"What can I get you to drink?" the young man asked.

"I'll have a cup of hot tea please," I answered, smiling politely.

"I'll have the same," Nick said, opening his menu.

We began discussing dinner options as if we'd done it a million times.

"What looks good to you?" Nick asked casually.

"I don't know, they do have a good selection," I remarked as I scanned the entrées. "The braised salmon and wild rice sounds good."

"Yes, it does. I believe that settles it." He smiled and closed his menu. The waiter brought our tea along with a small pot still steeping. I closed my menu and waited. Nick ordered for both of us. Then things got quiet.

I felt a little awkward about starting a conversation; I hoped he wasn't one of those silent types that would leave me to carry the vocal part of dinner.

"So...why don't you tell me something about Olivia?" he said, pulling up the sleeves of the navy-blue crew neck he was wearing. He seemed very comfortable and relaxed. He leaned up on the table, folding his arms in front of him, waiting.

"There's really not much to tell. Let me see...I'm Olivia Ryan, I'm a waitress, I like movies, music, long peaceful walks, fishing, camping, outdoorsy things, cozy fires, herbal tea and...good company. That's about it. Now it's your turn, tell me something about Nick." I smiled.

"All right. I'm Nikolas Riggs, I'm an attorney. I have a branch office of my firm about thirty miles from here. My main office is in New York City. I too like music, movies, long peaceful walks, coffee and tea, cozy fires and...good company." He winked, and I caught my breath.

"So you're not into the outdoor scene?" Judging from his pallid complexion, I guessed I was on the money there, but then again, I didn't exactly look rustic myself.

"Well, I'm just not much of a day person, work takes up most of that."

I found eating to be a little more difficult, with all the butterflies taking up the space in my stomach. It only got worse whenever I would meet his gaze straight on. Looking into those beautiful black eyes seemed to pull me into an almost trancelike state. He managed to keep the conversation flowing, and I discovered how easy he was to talk to.

SOULBOUND: DESTINY'S MOVE

By the time he returned me to my car, I felt as if I'd known him forever. He ambled along beside me as we made our way back to my parking space. It was only ten o'clock, and Rooter's parking lot was pretty full.

"Olivia, may I see you again?" The question nearly stopped my heart!

"Nick, I would like that very much."

"I have to work tomorrow, and I'm not sure what time I'll be through. Can I call you?" he asked as he held my car door open.

I pulled a piece of paper from the back of an envelope, wrote down my number, and handed it to him. "I'll be looking forward to it." I tried so hard to remain calm, hoping not to appear too enthusiastic.

He took the paper carefully from my hand. His eyes glistened, and he flashed that leg-weakening smile at me. My heart immediately began its uneven rhythm.

"I'll see you soon," His silken voice cooed. He stepped back as I started the engine.

"Good night, Nick."

"Good night, Olivia."

In the silence of my car, I replayed every second of this wonderful evening. I hope this isn't some cruel dream, and even if it is, I don't want to wake up.

I pulled into the driveway, glad that I had left the porch light on. This night seemed extremely black, even with snow covering the ground. I walked into the quiet, dark house and switched the light on.

There in the floor lay the broken pieces of the teacup and the sticky mess from the spilled liquid. I sighed and began cleaning up the reminder of my earlier meltdown.

I didn't think it would happen again in my life. I was happy. I felt lighter, as if a weight had been lifted from me. I turned on some music and started singing and dancing around. Nikolas was the reason for my exceptional mood. He was absolutely wonderful! I turned around and caught my reflection in the mirror hanging on the dining room wall. I stopped and looked at the glowing face shining back at me. "Olivia, I was wrong. You do have hormones after all," I said out loud.

Dancing around to the rhythm of the music pulled a memory from four years ago. My parents walked in on me after they returned from shopping to find me doing this very same thing. The memory didn't make me sad; instead it brought a smile to my lips. My dad didn't give me time to be embarrassed. He just scooped Mom into his arms and started dancing around the room with her. They were so happy. I always admired their love for each other. I dreamed of a relationship like that back then. Now at twenty, I would settle for nothing less.

My birthday had turned out much better than I expected. This evening seemed perfect! After this day, I felt different. It was weird, almost like something inside me had shut down. I knew, though, that it was my subconscious desire to remain in this wonderful dream forever.

A Fairy Tale Begins 9

I placed the kettle back on the stove. What's that noise? I turned off the music and listened. A loud growl came from what sounded like my front yard! Suddenly something let out a growling yowl! I quickly locked the doors and checked all the windows. My heart began palpitating as the fear started to quicken my breaths. The sounds outside seemed to grow louder, and the screeching and hissing were terrifying! What was that? What's out there? I kept thinking. It sounded like something from a horror movie!

I sat on the end of the couch, my knees pressed hard against my pounding chest, jumping with each renewed sound. I reached for the telephone with trembling hands, just as it rang. The unexpected phone call startled me even more, causing me to feel weak and disoriented. I grabbed up the receiver and answered it before the caller ID could pick up the number.

"Hello!" I answered anxiously, my voice trembling.

"Olivia, is everything all right?"

I instantly knew the voice. "Nikolas?"

"Yes, what's going on!" he asked, sounding alarmed.

"Umm...some animals are fighting outside. They seem a little close to the house, is all." I tried to sound calm, but I couldn't control the shaking in my voice. Just then there was a loud bang out by the front porch. I screamed into the phone!

"Olivia!" Nick's voice was starting to take on the tone of panic.

"Okay..." I panted "Something just hit the side of my house!"

"What's your address?"

I gave Nick my address without hesitating. "Please hurry. It sounds like there's something on my porch! Oh god! Nick, it's hitting my front door!" I began to cry.

"Olivia, stay on the phone with me. I'm not far away!" As he spoke, I heard the sound of his engine accelerating. It seemed like only seconds when the lights of his vehicle turned in the lane. The minute the light flashed onto the road, everything went silent. I just sat there, trembling and listening.

"Olivia, I'm here. Can you open the door?"

"Yes, hold on." I hung up the phone and raced to unlock the door. Nikolas stood on the front porch, seemingly calm and composed, which is more than I could say for me.

"I picked up your trash can. There definitely was something out here. I'm afraid it made a pretty good mess of your porch. I think the headlights scared it away. You stay here. I'm going to check out the wood line and make sure everything is okay." He smiled and held up a flashlight.

"Be careful please!" I whispered. He nodded and quickly disappeared into the darkness.

<hr />

NICK ENTERED THE WOODS and turned off the unnecessary flashlight. He stepped out into a small clearing, glaring at the three figures before him.

"What the hell is going on out here!" He focused his stare on two of the three poised for attack. "Ahh...Kael...Lari, don't you two have better things to do than go around scaring innocent young women in the middle of the night?" He glanced quickly back and forth, assessing the situation. "Hasn't anyone ever taught you that it's rude to fight two on one?" Nick looked at his comrade in full panther form.

Tristan's hot breath's wafting up like smoke into the cold night air, a feral grin shown from the huge black cat as he glared at the wolf before him. Nick's smile was loathsome and contemptuous.

"So the tables are turned. The cat chasing the dog, how amusing!" He turned his attention fully on Lari, confident his friend had everything under control.

"Lari, this is your lucky night. You see, I'm feeling exceptionally gracious," Nick spoke, showing no sign of emotion in his face.

"*My* lucky night," she hissed." I don't need luck, Nikolas, but you will!"

He fended off her attack easily, knocking her to the ground. He placed his foot on her throat, holding her down, and hissed through his teeth, his fangs sharp and menacing. "Like I said, Lari. It's your lucky night. You see, I'm going to let you live!" A pitiful yelp interrupted his words. He turned his head to see the still form of the wolf as Tristan proceeded to rip the heart from its chest. "Tristan, however, does not share my lenient attitude! Take a message back to Lucas." Nick seethed as he looked into the wide eyes staring up at him. "Tell him she's come of age! He'll have to find another way to get to us now, because it will be impossible to get to her!" His breath was quick and his eyes cold. "Now go. Before my patience and good grace come to an end!"

As soon as she was released, Lari disappeared into the night. Nikolas looked at his friend. "Clean up this mess, Olivia is scared to death!"

Tristan's voice suddenly rang out into the night. "Do you think Lucas will take heed?" he asked.

Nick turned to find him bent down lighting a small fire. Lying in place of the wolf was the body of a young platinum-haired man. The fire caught, and he disappeared into a pile of ash.

"No, but at least now he knows we'll be with her. He'll understand his attempts will assuredly result in the death of more of his people," Nick said as he again turned to leave.

Tristan's hand touched his shoulder. "Nikolas, what's she like?" His voice was low but still rang clearly in the night air.

He smiled and looked at Tristan with a softened expression. "I can hardly find words to describe her. She's more exquisite than either of us could have imagined." His eyes expressed a deep understanding of the longing Tristan felt.

"You'll get to meet her soon, my friend."

"I hope...very soon," Tristan said.

Nick nodded, feeling empathy for the torture his friend was suffering, and decided to change the subject. "Tris, try to keep things like this away from her home. Negotiate a little!"

Tristan smiled broadly. "You know I've never been good at formality, that's your area of expertise."

Nikolas laughed. "True, but just the same, at least try. She doesn't know anything yet, and right now she's most important." With that, he turned and walked back toward the house.

※

I JUMPED WHEN NICK came through the front door.

"Everything is fine. I caught a glimpse of a bobcat crouched over a raccoon. My guess is your front porch got in the middle of the chase." He walked into the kitchen as he was talking. I had my back to him when he entered the room, and I didn't realize he was standing behind me.

"Thank you for coming to my res..." I turned to find him standing an arm's length away. This totally upset my newfound confidence. "Cue," I finished as I averted my eyes in embarrassment. "You must think I'm such a coward," I said more to the floor than to Nick.

"No, living out here alone, your reaction to everything seems quite normal to me."

His understanding managed to relieve some of my disgrace. I quickly turned back to the stove. "I was about to have a cup of herbal tea. Would you like some?"

"Yes, thank you."

I could hear him shuffling around behind me. I put all my effort into finding the courage to turn around and face him. I knew I wouldn't be able to control the rise in blood pressure I was sure to experience at the mere sight of him. I wonder if he had a clue how extreme his effect on me was. *You made it through dinner face-to-face, so what's your problem?* I scolded myself.

Nikolas took in his surroundings, memorizing every detail that made up the life of Olivia Ryan.

I took in a deep breath and turned toward him. He was stunning! Nick smiled sweetly and started toward the kitchen table.

"Please, have a seat in the living room, and I'll bring it out when it's ready." At least I sounded a little more confident and far less distressed than when he entered the room.

"As you wish, but I have to tell you; I'm starting to feel lonely already." His eyes were shining and staring intently at me.

I smiled, bit my lower lip, and turned back to the tea. *I swear, for someone who rarely blushed in her life, you're sure making up for it now!*

I placed the cup and saucer on the end table next to the chair and took a seat on the couch beside him. He then started a conversation that lasted past one in the morning. Nikolas wanted to know about every picture on the walls, my family, and my friends. It was as if he were committing every detail of my life to memory.

When he stood up, I took in a quick breath; I didn't want to be alone tonight. He made no effort to leave; instead, he walked over to the shelf that held the collection of movies.

"You have a wonderful collection of old movies, even some of the black-and-whites," he said as he continued to browse leisurely through them.

"Yeah, Mom loved them. She was a big fan of Bogie and Bacall. I have to admit, I enjoy them too, even if I have seen them a million times." I had walked over to where he was standing. I immediately found I had made a mistake. The extremely close proximity of our bodies made me weak in the knees. My heart rate accelerated. Nick looked down at me and smiled. I swear he acted like he could hear it!

"Do you mind? This is one of my favorites." He held up an old black-and-white I didn't see the name on the cover.

"Of course, be my guest." I tried to behave casually as I looked up at him, but I was beginning to feel dizzy, and it was getting harder to breathe. I walked back to the couch and sat down, hoping my wavering steps didn't give me away.

Nick placed the movie in the DVD player and turned on the TV. He came over and sat beside me on the couch. *Oh, I'll never be able to watch this, not with him so close!*

It was odd; as long as we had been indoors, it felt like the cool air from outside was still drifting off his clothing. *Maybe my body temperature was warmer than normal. That did make perfect sense; after all, I was sitting next to this beautiful Adonis!*

The sunlight bouncing off the snow-covered ground blinded me as my eyes opened. I was lying on the couch covered with one of Mom's Afghans. Nikolas was gone.

I would have to apologize for falling asleep when I see him again. *I hope I see him again.* I had known him one night and already I felt lost at his absence.

I had the afternoon shift. Darla and Kandi were waiting to pounce when I walked through the door.

"Did I see you get into a Hummer with that gorgeous man last night?" Darla stood wide-eyed.

"Yes, you did," I said and flashed a quick smile.

"Oh, Hon-ee, if that had been me in that vehicle, he'd have to take me straight to the ER!" Kandi was fanning her hand in front of her face, smiling.

"Kandi." I rolled my eyes at her and giggled.

"Why?" Darla asked, looking lost at Kandi.

"To get some oxygen, that man takes my breath away!" Kandi's comment brought about a round of laughter.

Kandi Martin had moved here from Birmingham Alabama about six months ago. She was a very private woman. All I knew about her was that she was around my age, and she didn't have kids. She was a beautiful woman, with a smile that was so radiant. She had perfectly shaped brown eyes and a petite figure. Her skin was a smooth cocoa brown. Today she was positively glowing as she drilled me for information about my date with Nick.

"Where'd y'all go last night?"

"Kandi, I don't think that's any of your business!" I grinned.

"Girl, I know that, now tell me anyway!" She giggled. Her face was beaming with curiosity.

"You know what they say, curiosity killed the cat." I smirked.

"Yeah, and satisfaction brought him back. Now quit avoiding the subject!" she said, leaning over to prop on the bubblegum machine.

"Oh, for heaven's sake, you guys didn't grill me like this when I went out with Dan!"

"Face it, Liv. Dan's nice and all, but this guy is way different!"

Darla's eyes were dancing. "What's he like?" "Yeah, Olivia, dish!" Kandi shifted impatiently.

"Oh, all right. He came up to help me pick up some things I dropped in the parking lot. He asked if I'd join him for dinner."

"Just like that?" Darla stared in disbelief.

"Yeah, just like that." I smiled and playfully nudged her shoulder with my hand. "We went to the Triton. We talked, he brought me back to my car, asked if he could see me again, took my number, and left."

"That can't be all there was to it! You look way too happy." Darla crossed her arms and scowled at me.

"Well, he was supposed to call me tonight. Instead, he called me last night to see if I got home all right with the slick roads and all."

"At least we know he's a gentleman. That's rare these days." Darla sighed. I assumed that meant Chad didn't have a gentlemanly bone in his body.

Kandi stood up straight. "You're holding out on us, Liv!"

"No, I'm not!"

"I believe you are. I don't blame you though. I'd wanna keep every detail of that honey to myself too." She winked.

"Are you going to see him again?" Darla's question caused both me and Kandi to turn toward her with gaping mouths.

"Duh, Darla, of course she's gonna see him again. Wouldn't you?"

"Dumb question, huh?" Poor Darla, her face was lit up like a candle.

"I hope he calls tonight. I need to apologize to him anyway," I commented.

Darla's mouth flew open. "Apologize...what did you do?"

"I sort of fell asleep," I answered as I squinted my eyes. Kandi looked completely mortified!

"You what!"

"Fell asleep," I repeated sheepishly.

"You nodded off in the car with a gorgeous man like that sitting beside you?" Her eyes were as big as dollars now.

"Of course not. I fell asleep on the couch." I rolled my eyes as I spoke.

"On whose couch?" Darla jumped back into the conversation, in full protective mode.

"Relax, Darla. My couch!" Instantly I realized what I had told. Olivia, you should have kept your mouth shut while you were ahead, I scolded myself as I looked into the faces of my two stunned friends.

"You just said he called you. You mean he was at your house... alone with you?"

I could feel Darla's reprimand coming. Kandi stopped her next question in its tracks.

"I knew there was more to it than you were telling, you little devil!" Kandi's eyes gleamed with excitement and mischief.

"It wasn't like that, Kandi! Get your mind out of the gutter! Nick was a perfect gentleman." I didn't want them to walk away now with the wrong impression of him or me.

"Mmmmm...I bet he was perfect."

"Kandi, nothing happened!" I protested emphatically. I knew she was just teasing, but I felt insulted just the same.

Kandi held her hands up, palms out toward me. "All right, honey, if you say so. You just spent an entire night with the most beautiful—no, gorgeous...hell! He's so good looking there isn't even a word to describe him, and you just sat there looking at each other! Okay, I'll buy it. I just have one thing to say about it...ARE YOU CRAZY?!"

I laughed at the teasing expression on her face.

"I guess I am." They both burst out laughing too.

Dan walked up, amazingly still looking like a bulldog, with a bark to match. I wondered how much of our conversation he had heard.

"I hate to break up your little party, ladies, but this is a workplace, not a social club, so clock in and get busy!" he huffed and stomped off.

"Man, who peed in his Cheerios?" Darla glared at him as he walked away.

"Well, Darla, after that lip-lock in the break room last night and Mr. Wonderful showing up, I'd say…Olivia did!" Kandi smiled and winked as she punched her timecard.

I let out a heavy sigh. "Great, that's all I need!"

The rest of the day drudged by. I spent most of my time avoiding any contribution to Danny's grumpy mood and attempting to ignore his dagger-throwing stares. I hoped—no, we all hoped—he would get over this jealous tirade and get back to being the Dan we were used to. He wasn't just taking his anger out on me. He was making it rough on everyone.

The next few days didn't prove to be any better at work, but my nightlife had certainly improved. Nick and I had gone out twice this week, and he came by my house every night. It always seemed to end the same way. I would fall asleep and wake to find him gone. I hadn't slept in my bed since the night we met.

I was glad I had to work every day this week. Staying busy during the day helped me maintain my anxiousness to be with Nick again. Dark had become my favorite time of day.

It was Friday, only five days into March. I wished spring would hurry up. I desperately needed some warm sunshine and short sleeves. I came home from another miserable day at work. *Boy, could Dan hold a grudge!* I stepped up on the porch and noticed a huge box and a bouquet of roses.

I unlocked the door, gathered up the gifts, and headed for my room. I sat them on the foot of the bed, gathered the roses, and filled a vase. After gently placing the flowers in the water, I walked into the dining room and placed them in the center of the table. I turned on the weather channel, holding just a glimmer of hope that tomorrow would be as nice as it seemed to be outside today.

SOULBOUND: DESTINY'S MOVE

Yesss! It's supposed to be seventy degrees tomorrow. *Hallelujah, I'm breaking out the fishing pole!* I hurried to the utility room in the back of the house to gather up my gear. I made sure to put everything on the front porch so as not to waste one single minute of my reprieve from winter. Oh, the box. I got so excited about the warm weather I completely spaced out the gift on my porch.

I needed to get ready before Nick arrived, so I took a quick shower before I actually looked at the package wrapped neatly and tied with an emerald-green bow. I stood at the edge of the bed wrapped in a towel, eyeing the box, and feeling a little nervous, in a good way, about opening it. I reached down and pulled the note from under the ribbon. It simply said "This is for tonight" in a beautiful, almost calligraphic script.

My eyes widened as I lifted the lid to reveal a gorgeous evening gown! I reached for the dress and noticed a small velvet box in the upper corner. My hands trembled as I gingerly lifted the lid. I stopped breathing. Inside were a delicate diamond pendant and earrings!

I gently pulled the emerald-green satin gown from its container and spread it across the bed. He had a perfect eye for these things. I couldn't have done better, if I'd chosen it myself. The gown was simple but elegant, no fancy sparkles. It had a modest neckline with long sheer flowing sleeves. The back of the gown had a low V-cut. Soft sheer material lay from the shoulders in panels, edging the open back and a flattering A-line bodice cut full at the bottom.

As I stood admiring the garment, panic set in. *Where could he be taking me that I would need this!* I thought. *I don't have any shoes!* I raced to my closet to find the only thing that came close to a heel was a pair of silver pumps. *Please let the dress be long enough to cover my feet!* I prayed under my breath.

I began dressing, first pulling my hair up into a tight bun, with the exception of a few strategically placed wisps around my face.

I downplayed the makeup since I rarely wore it at all and put in the diamond pierced earrings. They hung in a teardrop just barely below my lobe, and I placed the pendant around my neck. It lay delicately just under the hollow of my throat. Finally, I slipped the dress on and breathed a sigh of relief. It fell to the floor, covering the atrocious shoes.

I was finally ready. Standing in front of the mirror, examining my appearance, I couldn't see even in this beautiful gown what could possibly be special enough to attract someone like Nick. *Well, I guess this is as good as it's going to get. I just hope Nick isn't disappointed.*

My nerves were on edge as I went to answer the knock on the door. I wish I had been more prepared! When I saw Nick standing there in the black tux, sporting a deacon's collar rather than a tie, I nearly fainted! He was absolutely breathtaking!

The tux fit so perfectly (tailored, no doubt), and the black material, in contrast to his soft blond hair and deep black eyes, was almost more than my heart could stand! The black full-length cape draped across his shoulders gave him the appearance of royalty. I just stood there in awe of him.

Nick stood without speaking as his eyes scanned me from head to toe.

"Olivia, you look exquisite!"

I lowered my eyes, and a faint blush crossed my cheeks. "I'm glad you approve." I smiled timidly.

"Approve, *that*, love, is an understatement. I have never seen anything so truly beautiful!" he exclaimed.

The pet name that unconsciously fell from his lips made me feel faint. I composed myself as much as possible and slowly lifted my eyes. I could have sworn Nikolas caught his breath at that moment.

"Thank you, and you are quite stunning yourself." I smiled, trying not to be too self-conscious of my every movement.

SOULBOUND: DESTINY'S MOVE

"Ahh...you are very gracious." He smiled as he held out his arm. "If you're ready."

I reached for him and realized I had no coat.

"I'm sorry, Nick. Please excuse me for just a minute. I need to get a coat." I started to turn, and Nick spoke.

"Forgive me, love, but I was so stunned by you I nearly forgot about this." He reached beside him to the chair on the porch and produced a full-length white cape etched in fur.

"Oh, Nick...it's beautiful! As everything you sent." I reached up and touched the pendant.

He smiled and held up the cape to drape over my shoulders, then held out his arm again, and I took it.

Every nerve in my body shivered; it was the first physical contact since we met. The feel of his arm even through the jacket sleeves was firm and strong. My pulse quickened at the errant thought of the rest of him. My eyes widened in surprise yet again. Nick had exchanged the Hummer after the snow melted for his everyday car. I was expecting the sleek Mercedes to be our transportation, but instead parked in the drive was a limousine!

"Oh, Nick." I looked up at him. "This is so extravagant. I feel like a princess!"

"Oh no, love, you are definitely more like a queen to me," he whispered. I smiled at his gracious compliment. He helped me into the limo and seated himself beside me.

"Where are you taking me tonight?" My nerves were starting to jump again.

"It's a surprise. I'll tell you on the way."

We pulled up at the airport next to a leer jet.

"Ohhhh..." I gasped. "Are we getting on that plane?" My heart started racing, fear suddenly gripping me with such fury I couldn't move!

"Olivia, you've never flown before?" he anxiously asked.

"No…my parents…my mom had never been on a plane until their trip…" my voice trailed off.

"Olivia. Darling, I'm so sorry, I didn't realize." Nick looked as though he'd been shot.

"No, really, it's not your fault. I never said anything about it! Please don't feel bad."

"Olivia, I would never…" His eyes lowered as he spoke.

"I know. Just give me a minute to gather myself." I couldn't let this happen! He had gone to such lengths. *Olivia, get a hold of yourself. You cannot live in fear because of one accident. People fly all the time. Grow up!* I chastised myself vehemently for my behavior.

"We can go somewhere else, or I can take you home if you'd like."

"No, Nick, what I would like is for you to escort me onto the plane and take me to wherever I was meant to be in this beautiful gown."

He looked into my eyes with such tenderness I thought I would melt away any second.

"Are you sure?" He sounded apprehensive.

"Yes, I am quite sure." I smiled as confident as my nerves would allow.

He came around and opened the door, offering his gloved hand. "All right then, shall we?"

Inside, the jet was completely different than I expected. There were four tan leather seats with belts, a huge matching leather sofa with tables at each end, and two swivel chairs set on each side of a round table. It looked more like a house than an aircraft. Nick seated me in one of the belted chairs.

"This is only temporary until we're in the air, then you'll be able to move around as you please." He smiled and patted my hand, trying to ease my tension.

When the plane began to taxi down the runway, my fingers tightened on the armrest. As I felt the aircraft lift off from the ground, I held my breath and squinted my eyes closed.

"You can relax now, love, we're in the air," his silken voice whispered in my ear. I released my grip, let out my breath, and opened one eye. Nick chuckled, and I opened the other one. His smile was radiant, and his eyes danced with amusement.

"Olivia, you are priceless! Come, look out the window." He unlatched the seatbelts as he spoke.

"Oh, I don't think that's such a good idea."

"Are you afraid of heights?" His eyebrow rose inquisitively.

"No," I said flatly.

"Then come and look, it's beautiful. He reached for my hand, so I walked over and sat on the sofa by the window. It was beautiful and exhilarating!

"Oh, Nikolas, the lights look like tiny diamonds scattered on a black cloth!"

Nick leaned over, brushing a wisp of hair with the back of his hand, barely touching my cheek. My heart immediately began to spasm, and I felt my body begin to warm.

"I promise you, Olivia, no harm will ever come to you as long as you're with me," he whispered. His black eyes were looking at me with such conviction I truly believed him.

"So, you promised to tell me where we're going."

"Oh yes, I did. To New York."

"New York City?"

"Yes."

"Okay, where in New York City?" Nick smiled, enjoying the tease.

"Nick, tell me," I pleaded. "I can't take the suspense another minute!"

"All right, we are having dinner at my favorite restaurant and a night at the opera." He patiently waited for my response. I was totally speechless. He wasn't sure what to make of my silence.

"We can skip the opera if you wish."

"Oh no, I'd love to go!" My voice came out breathless. "This is fabulous!" Nick could see the excitement in my expression and quickly fell at ease.

"I almost forgot. I have one more, little thing that you may need tonight." He quickly stood up and strode toward the back of the plane. A woman walked in carrying a tray.

"Just put it on the table, there." He pointed to the two swivel chairs.

"Thank you, Abby," he addressed her by her first name. My heart gave a quick thud at the sound of his familiarity with another woman.

"Good evening, Ms. Ryan." She smiled cordially. "I brought tea and a light snack," she continued, still holding the polite smile. "Enjoy your evening," she said and started back toward the rear of the plane.

She was a tall brunette that carried herself more like a model than a stewardess. She had the same pale complexion as Nick and the same perfect features. She was very statuesque. Abby gave a low nod that resembled more of a bow than a courteous gesture. Nikolas acknowledged her with a curt nod and quickly returned to the table where I sat nibbling on a cracker.

"I would have sent this with the dress, but they weren't ready." He handed me another box. I opened the lid to find a pair of satin heels. The emerald-green color was an exact match to my dress.

"I had them specially dyed to match." Nick was obviously an expert at planning formal engagements. He seemed to know my exact taste and size it was just uncanny.

"You certainly thought of everything." I smiled. He bent down to reach for my foot, and I hesitated. *Oh, what's the use, he's going to see them sooner or later!* I held out my foot, and I saw the corner of his mouth twitch at the sight of the silver shoes. When he slipped the green satin shoe on my foot, I looked at him and suddenly realized what Cinderella must have felt like trying on the glass slipper.

The entire evening was like something from a dream. Dinner was very romantic. The restaurant was so elegant, with candles, beautiful crystal, and white linens. We dined by the fire; it was all so perfect.

We were escorted to balcony seats at the opera. I had no idea how well-known Nikolas was. He was greeted with smiles and handshakes everywhere we went. Some seemed almost reverent when he appeared, bowing their heads much like Abby did on the plane.

When the limo pulled into my drive, I couldn't believe it was four a.m. and I was still wide awake. We walked slowly to the front door. Nick unlocked it for me and handed me the key.

"Nick, this was the most wonderful night. Thank you, for everything."

"It was totally my pleasure."

I was close enough to feel his breath as his eyes gazed down at me, and I could hear his uneven breaths. I looked up into Nick's eyes, longing for that first kiss, but it didn't happen. He gently raised my hand and kissed it tenderly, and the blood began to pulse through my veins. His lips were soft and cool against the warmth of my hand.

"I feel like Cinderella," I admitted to him.

"Not even close, love. I told you. You are my queen." His fingers traced my face from my cheek down to the hollow of my throat. I shivered with delight at his touch, even though his hands were still covered by gloves.

"Good night, love. I'll see you tomorrow." His voice was a soft whisper.

"Good night," was all I managed to say before he turned and walked away.

NICK ENTERED THE KITCHEN to find Tristan pacing.

"Is something wrong? Was there a problem?" Nick tensed as he spoke.

"No, everything is fine, Nick." He continued pacing.

"Then what's the matter with you?"

"It's been eight days, Nick, eight since she came of age! I'm about to explode! I can't hold out much longer!" Tristan's chest heaved, and his eyes were almost glazed.

Nikolas smiled as he looked at Tristan.

"Well, my friend, you won't have to. She's going fishing at the lake tomorrow. I saw her fishing pole on the front porch."

Tristan let out a long breath and smiled. His electric-blue eyes were dancing with excitement.

"Thank goodness for sunshine!" he quipped.

"That is your opinion." Nick laughed. He was genuinely pleased that Tristan would finally meet her.

"I know what you meant about tasting her scent now." He began as Tristan turned in shock.

"You didn't!" His eyes began to narrow.

"No! No, Tris, I wouldn't, not without her consent!" Nick defended.

"Then what do you mean?"

"I kissed her hand. Just as you can taste her scent when you're close, I can taste her blood. You're right, it is incredible!"

SOULBOUND: DESTINY'S MOVE

"How did you manage to take her hand without her noticing those popsicles you call fingers?"

Nick threw the white gloves on the counter with a smug look.

"Well, that was just brilliant!" Tristan threw his head back and laughed.

"Enjoy your day, but remember, you can't kiss her on the lips. You know what will happen," he reminded Tristan.

"Relax, Nick, I have it under control."

"You say that now, but trust me, once you meet her, you'll see just how hard that control is going to be." Nick sighed. "Just keep in mind...her will, not ours."

"I will. Rest well, Nick."

Betrayal 10

I woke at eight a.m. Even though I didn't get in the bed until five o'clock this morning, I felt rested. *I must still be charged from my fantasy date last night,* I thought.

I decided on a bowl of cereal for breakfast. I couldn't wait to get to the lake. My thoughts kept wondering back to Nikolas. *How did I get so lucky?* The memory of his gentle touch as he kissed my hand caused me to tremble. *I just don't understand how someone could do that with no effort.* I smiled. *Imagine what he could do if he was trying!* I swallowed hard, and my pulse quickened just at the errant thought!

I opened the refrigerator to get some orange juice. *Man, I really need to go to the grocery store!* It was obvious from the bare shelves that lunch today would be a bologna sandwich and the single can of soda left in the door. I took out the last two slices of lunch meat and attempted to spread some mustard on a piece of bread. The squirt bottle was almost empty, and all I managed was a drop and that disgusting sound that signaled you should have known better in the first place. I tossed the empty bottle in the trash, along with the watery mess on the slice of bread. Plain bologna would have to do. I've been too wrapped up in Nick to even think about eating. I knew that my obsessive behavior wasn't healthy, and now I was certain. I'll remedy the grocery problem tomorrow. Today I had better be on my game, because I'd have to eat what I caught.

The morning air was still cool, so I slipped on a light jacket. The sun was shining bright, and I could feel the air starting to warm as I gathered my gear to head out to the lake.

I felt a little skittish as I walked down the trail, still remembering my last trip here. I opened my canvas chair and got ready to cast out my line. I sat back and relaxed as the warming rays of sunshine beamed down on me. This side of the bank would get the heat of the sun until about one o'clock; by then I figured it would be warm enough to withstand the cool shade that would follow.

It was so peaceful listening to the sounds of spring birds beginning to sing in the trees. All at once my bobber disappeared. I began reeling in my catch, quite pleased with the larger-than-normal bluegill dangling from my hook. *A couple more of these and I'll have dinner.* I put another cricket on the line and cast out again.

My eye caught a movement in the trees just ahead of me on the far bank. I just sat there, frozen and wide-eyed. There, standing just a short distance across the water, was the enormous black cat! I was afraid to breathe. He was so beautiful! I must have moved too quickly; the cat raised his head from drinking and disappeared into the trees. My heart was pounding in my ears. I opened the can of soda and took a long drink. I felt positively wired! How could I be so lucky? To see that magnificent creature twice! I kept staring intently across the water, wondering—no, hoping—it would come back.

I was startled when I heard a smooth deep voice behind me.

"I'm sorry. I didn't realize there was someone here," he said.

I turned to see a gorgeous man with the most shocking electric blue eyes. He must've been at least six foot five and beautifully built. He had the broadest shoulders I'd ever seen! His thick black hair was pulled back in a ponytail, and his smooth almond skin seemed to glow in the sunlight. He greeted me with a broad smile that revealed straight vibrant-white teeth. I was so taken with his appearance I forgot how to speak.

"I'm sorry to have intruded." He continued to smile as he turned to walk away.

"That's okay, you're not intruding," I spoke quickly. For some reason, I didn't want him to go. "Have a seat, there's plenty of room." I don't know what came over me. I just knew I had to invite him to stay. He placed his fishing gear on the ground and opened a canvas chair that was an identical match to mine.

"Had any bites?" he asked, seating himself in the chair that seemed too frail to accommodate his mountainous size. I was staring—no, gawking—so intently I almost didn't register his words.

"Huh...oh, not much...I caught one since I've been here," I responded, a little shaky.

"Hopefully it'll pick up. I'm Tristan Rilz. It's a pleasure to meet you." He held out his hand as he spoke.

"Oh, I'm sorry. Olivia. Olivia Ryan." I reached out to shake his hand. As soon as he made contact, I felt like thousands of tiny sparks ran through me, and my heart sped up.

"Olivia, that's a very pretty name." He released my hand, and immediately I began to collect myself.

He cast out his line and leaned back. "So, do you come out here a lot?" His beautiful eyes locked on me. It made it hard to think, hard to form words. I averted my eyes to check my fishing pole.

"As often as I can," I said.

"I can see why, it's gorgeous up here and very peaceful."

"It's a good place to think," I said, gazing off into the water.

"I hope you don't take this the wrong way, but...I rarely ever see women take the incentive to go fishing—alone." His smile widened.

"Oh, yeah...well, my dad got me into the habit," I said with a small giggle.

"Well, if you're going to have a habit, this is about as good as it gets." He flashed a quick wink, and my heart caught in my throat. Oh, this day was going to be much better than I thought!

Tristan put me at ease right away. I found that we had a lot in common. He enjoyed the outdoor things as much as I did. We caught several fish, a couple of bass and few more bluegill.

"Olivia, I have to ask. I see that you're a good fisherman, but do you clean them too?" Tristan was hoping she was not that adept at the sport.

I laughed, but he did have a good question.

"Actually, my dad used to do that, but I figure, how hard can it be, right?"

"It's a little more time-consuming than you might think, especially scaling them."

"You have to scale them?" I blushed at my ignorance.

He let out a small chuckle. "Yes, how were you planning to eat them?"

"Cooked." I grinned.

His eyes twinkled at my sarcasm. "We have a pretty-good-sized catch here. If you'd like, I'll help you, and maybe you'll be able to take care of it on your own next time."

Funny, I felt no more apprehension at accepting his offer than I did the night I met Nick. Nick. I hadn't thought of him in the last few hours. I suddenly didn't know what to say to Tristan.

"Could you?" His voice brought me back to the conversation.

"Could I what?" My mind was disoriented.

"Could you use the help?" he repeated.

Why not? I told myself. *After all, it's cleaning fish, that's pretty harmless.* "Um...yeah, I suppose I could."

"All right then, I'll follow you home and we'll get to work." Tristan stopped as he caught the sudden tense look on my face.

"Olivia, you don't have to worry. I'm as safe as a kitten... promise." He winked again, and my legs went numb.

He put his belongings and the fish into the back of a vibrant metallic-blue Jeep Wrangler and smiled.

I started my car and pulled out, the Jeep following behind me.

What are you doing, Olivia? Have you lost your ever-lovin' mind? You have a beautiful angel like Nick, who not only makes you feel like the most special woman on earth, plus he's drop dead gorgeous, and... I sighed, so is Tristan. I tried hard, too hard, to justify taking this beautiful man home with me. I tried to make myself believe there was no harm being done. *I could have friends. Tristan is just a new friend.*

He pulled into the driveway behind me and grabbed the stringer of fish from the back. I opened the door, and Tristan followed me to the kitchen.

He put the fish in the sink and proceeded to run some water to cover them. He then turned around, propping his hands against the sink.

"What's in the cooler?"

"It was going to be my lunch." I hung my jacket on the back of the chair as I answered.

Tristan lifted the lid and brought out the sandwich.

"Ugh. Don't you know this stuff is bad for you?" He held the sandwich bag up between two fingers, eyes squinted, and nose wrinkled.

I laughed. "Yeah, so I've heard. Are we cleaning fish or what?" I smiled.

"Don't you think we should wait until they quit flopping?" He smirked.

"Flopping?" I didn't get it.

"Some of them are still moving, unless you plan to decapitate them alive." He looked at me as thought he was suppressing a full-blown laugh.

"No! Of course not!" I defended. My sad lack of knowledge in this area was very evident now.

"Now as to this..." He waved the sandwich bag in the air and dropped it back into the cooler. "I think you need a good dose of wholesome food."

"Oh, what do you have in mind?" My inquiry brought a huge, breathtaking smile to his face.

"Pizza," he stated.

"Now that's just what I need."

"Great! What kind do you like?" He stepped around the table and waited.

"Meat, lots of meat." I wanted him to know I was not a vegetarian. I'm not sure why, just a feeling that would so not be his type. *Why do you care? You're seeing someone!* I scolded myself.

"Oooo...a woman after my own heart," he teased. I smiled. I don't think it was his heart in question today.

"Tell you what, you wait here and I'll go out and be back before it has a chance to cool."

"Okay, I've got a few things to do anyway." I lied.

Tristan turned and walked out the door. I sank into the chair at the kitchen table, placing my face in my hands. It was only five and a half hours till Nikolas would be here. I wonder if Tristan will have left by then.

Oh, what am I thinking! What am I doing? I'm crazy about Nick, but I couldn't stop myself. There was something about Tristan that I just couldn't resist. Maybe he won't ask to see me again. If he does— deep down I know I won't have the strength to refuse.

Tristan returned as promised with a piping hot Philly Cheese Pizza. We enjoyed our quick meal and began the task of prepping the fish.

As much as I enjoyed this entire day, my eye kept glancing at the clock. My nerves were beginning to edge. Tristan helped clean up. It was five thirty when we finally finished.

He turned from the sink, drying his hands on the towel.

"Now that we're finished and as much as I hate to, I have to go...gotta work tonight." His voice had that tone in it. The same tone I was familiar with fending off dates with Dan.

Here it comes. He's about to ask, and heaven forbid, I'm about to accept! I was right.

"Olivia, I'm going hiking tomorrow. I was hoping, if you weren't busy...maybe you'd like to come along?" Tristan stood waiting for my reply; his eyes, his beautiful electric-blue eyes, gave away his fear of my rejection.

"Oh, Tristan...um..." I debated. I was really trying not to accept, but I just couldn't help myself, and the words were unstoppable. "I'd love to." The unsavory deed was done, and now the tight knot in my new relationship with Nick had begun to slip.

"Great! I'll pick you up around nine."

I looked up, almost craning my neck to look at him and smile. Why did the look on his face remind me of a wild beast that had just conquered its prey? I shrugged that image away quickly as I walked him to the front door.

"I'll see you tomorrow then," I said.

"I'll be looking forward to it." His eyes had softened as he brushed the hair back from my face. This trivial touch sent the heated jolts again through my body. I was trembling with sheer excitement as I closed the door behind him.

Olivia Ryan! I mumbled to myself as I started back through the house. *You are without a doubt the most loathsome, disgusting excuse for a human being that ever lived! How could you? How in the name of everything good and right could you do this to someone like Nick!*

I walked to the cupboard for a glass and noticed it was six thirty. Nick will be here in an hour! I forgot about a drink and ran to get a shower.

I blow dried my hair and dressed quickly. I pulled out the thin emerald-green V-neck sweater I bought the last time I went shopping with my parents. I don't know why I hadn't worn it before now. I took a pair of stone-washed jeans from another hanger and some black clogs from the shoe rack. Nick and I were going out to the movies tonight, and I wanted to look nice but still be comfortable.

I was ready when Nick arrived and had started putting some dishes left out this afternoon in the dishwasher when he knocked at the front door.

"Come in!" I called. Nick walked to the kitchen entrance, sporting a white tee shirt, black leather jacket, faded jeans, and sneakers. He looked gorgeous, but then, when didn't he? The man could walk in dressed like Fred Flintstone and still melt you in your shoes!

"Hi, Nick. I'll be ready in a minute." Damn, I thought. I've got to control my tone of voice. I sounded guilty. But then I was—guilty as sin.

"No hurry, love, did you get a cat?" he asked.

"No, what made you think that?"

"Well, I—"

I interrupted as I realized the fishy smell in the kitchen. It did sort of resemble cat food. "Oh that. I went fishing today. I had a pretty good catch to ready for the freezer." I turned back to the dishwasher, not wanting to give him the slightest hint that my day consisted of anything more than my solitary fishing trip.

"Oh." He smiled. "I'm glad to hear the trip wasn't for nothing." His eyes twinkled like he knew something he wasn't telling, and it amused him greatly.

My heart started beating rapidly again. Calm down! I thought. *He doesn't know—he couldn't know anything more than you're willing to tell, so relax!*

SOULBOUND: DESTINY'S MOVE

MY WEEKEND SHOULD HAVE been exhausting, seeing Tristan during the day and Nikolas every night. Somehow, the more I saw them, the more energized I seem to be!

Dan knew I would rather work nights, but he had me opening every day this week. From the look of my hours, I didn't see the point in even bringing me in. I was scheduled for only ten hours in five days. Since I didn't like the morning shift, maybe that was a blessing. Then it dawned on me, fewer hours, working early. That meant more time with Tristan. No night work meant more time with Nick. I smiled at the irony. Danny was trying to punish me, and instead he's giving me more time to spend with Nick! He doesn't know about Tristan.

"Ha, he just made my life easier!" My smile remained as I copied my schedule onto a piece of paper.

"Who made your life easier?" Darla had walked up to hear me talking to myself. I flicked the piece of paper and held it up in the air.

"Danny, that's who." The smile was still plastered on my face.

"How?" Darla asked.

"He cut my hours."

"And you're not upset about that? If it were me, I'd be raising the roof!" She stood there, looking confused at my reaction.

"Don't you get it, Darla? Think about it. He just made all my nights free this week!"

"Oh. Ohhh, I get it now!" She grinned. I wondered if she really did. Darla was so smart when it came to advice about life, but bless her heart, she wasn't quick-witted.

"Still seeing Nick?" Kandi had walked up behind me as I finished bussing a table.

"Yep, he comes over every night."

"Oooo, I'm surprised you're still able to stand, honey."

"Kandi, I told you our relationship isn't like that! Don't you have something better to do? Did you come here to eat or harangue me?" I snipped.

"I came in for lunch. I'll just seat myself." She threw me a sideways grin. I finished the table and went to ring up some of the patrons waiting to pay their bill. I bent down to pick up a dropped quarter and stood up to find Tristan standing there, all smiles.

"Hey, Tristan." My heart skipped a beat when I saw him. He was such a captivating man.

"Hi, sugar, do you have to work all day?" He looked disappointed that I had to work at all. It gave me butterflies when he called me that.

"No, actually, I'm off at ten." I was trying not to look directly into his eyes. The effect they had on me was way too dramatic for here.

"So that means you're free this afternoon?" he asked.

"Yes, it does." I grinned.

"Good, how about I meet you at your house, say…eleven o'clock?"

"Eleven's good. Did you have something in mind?" I could see a hint of mischief in Tristan's expression.

"How do you feel about horses?" His perfect smile broadened.

"Horses! What are you talking about?" I didn't know anything about horses, and the look he gave me made me nervous.

"I'll tell you when I get to your house." He leaned over the counter and whispered in my ear, "I'll take care of you, don't worry." He picked up his order and winked.

I was frozen. My legs were numb, and my heart was beating like I'd just run a marathon.

"What was that all about, Liv?" Kandi's voice startled me.

"It was nothing." I started fidgeting. She didn't miss a thing.

"Olivia, where are these gorgeous men coming from? And where did you meet that beautiful treat?" Kandi looked at me with her wide brown eyes.

"Umm...I met Tristan at the lake Saturday."

"Girl, does Nick know about—"

"Of course not, Kandi, do you think I'm stupid?!" I scolded through my teeth, trying to keep the volume down.

"Honey, from what I just saw, the word fool comes to mind, but definitely not stupid!" she said as she watched Tristan get into a crimson Mustang Convertible. "Well, I gotta go," she said, grabbing her purse off the counter.

"Where are you going?" I asked.

"To the sport shop. I've got to get a fishing pole!" She winked.

I started laughing out loud. "Kandi, honey, you just won't do!" I teased.

She smiled a wicked little smile and strutted back to her seat.

Assaulted 11

I guess the old saying is true. Time does fly when you're having fun.

It's already mid-June. The time glowed four a.m. on the microwave. I had spent another glorious day and night with Tristan and Nick. In spite my lack of sleep, I felt energized. They were both so amazing! I decided to try and rest before I went to work in a few hours.

I woke at seven o'clock again. I was tense and nervous. I dreamed for the first time since my parents' accident. There was a shaky, queasy feeling in my stomach. I could remember seeing bats flying around in my dream. It was dark, and I sensed someone there, but I couldn't see who, and then I remember being on the ground. Everything else played out in shadows.

As I replayed the dream, a stabbing pain hit me in the stomach; suddenly I felt sick. I wasn't dreaming about someone else—it was me!

I continued this dream almost every night for the next week. I remained preoccupied with my nightmare. It was starting to get in the way of my time with Tristan and Nick.

"Olivia, what's wrong?" Tristan looked at me with concern.

"It's really nothing." I tried to just push my despair aside. It wouldn't be fair to ruin my day with him again.

"It's not healthy to keep things bottled up, you know."

"I'm not bottled up." I sat down, pulling a throw pillow onto my lap.

"I think you are. Olivia, I know we've only been seeing each other a few months, but I hope that you know by now you can trust me." Tristan was determined to get everything out in the open.

"I do need to talk, I guess...even though I doubt it will do any good." I fiddled with the tassels on the pillow. "I'm just not good at confiding," I admitted.

"Why don't you try? It may do more good than you think." He looked as though my depressed state caused him physical pain. Come to think of it, Nikolas seemed to have the same reaction.

"I really don't know where to begin," I said. I was still looking down at the pillow in my lap.

"I don't care, baby, where you start." Tristan had sat down beside me. His look was gentle and loving. He reached up and stroked my hair. Oh, the heat that burned in my veins when he touched me. I couldn't concentrate on the words! I trembled and sighed. Tristan must have noticed. He pulled back his hand and whispered, "Tell me, baby." I loved it when he called me that.

After I calmed myself, I began telling him about my dreams. I told him about Savannah, Tommy, my parents, and finally my latest dream.

Tristan had listened intently, never speaking, never disturbing one single detail. He stood up and lightly paced as he listened. He stopped in front of me as I completed my story. I looked up at him with tear-filled eyes. It appeared as if he winced in pain when he looked down.

Tristan knelt on the floor in front of me. It's the first time I had seen him at eye level. He was truly beyond words!

"So, you see, Tristan, all my dreams have come true...and this one I can feel is going to happen too! I just don't know when." A tear fell onto my cheek. "I'm going to die!"

Tristan's eyes narrowed, and his breath became more rapid. "Olivia, sweetheart," he began gently, trying desperately to control the fear my dreams had instilled in him. "You don't know that. You didn't dream you died!"

"No, Tristan, but I know someone was trying to kill me, and I feel it deep down. They're going to succeed!" He was pacing again. I could see he was trying to stay calm, to make sense of everything.

"How long have you had these dreams?" he asked.

"Since I was about seventeen, at least that's when I remember them starting," I answered.

"Have they always been about death?"

"No, not always, sometimes good things happened." I wiped a tear from my cheek. "Once I dreamed that my friend Jenna would be crowned homecoming queen in high school, and she hadn't even been nominated yet."

"Did it come to pass?"

"Yes, I remember how exited she was when they announced it."

"Did you tell her about your dream?" He continued his line of questions.

He knelt back down in front of me, placing a hand, palm down, on the cushion to rest on each side of me, taking in every word. He never laughed or scoffed at my fear.

"You are the first person I have ever told, Tristan. Now I'm worried you'll think I'm crazy."

"No, no, baby, I don't think that." He pushed my hair back behind my ear. You could never do or say anything that would change my feelings about you." I could tell he meant it deep in his heart, but I knew different. I could destroy everything he felt and everything Nikolas felt.

I was more afraid of hurting them than I was at the thought of dying. Tristan handed me a tissue as the tears fell like rain now. He reached to stroke my hair again, still kneeling in front of me. His eyes looked at me with longing and helplessness. I could feel his desire to hold me in his arms and comfort me. Why didn't he? I wanted him to.

"Olivia..." He brushed a tear from my cheek as he spoke. "Believe me when I tell you, nothing will happen to you as long as you're with me." I knew he meant every word just as Nick meant it, both I feared couldn't stop the inevitable.

I confided my dreams and my fears to Nick again when he came over. I felt that he deserved to know as much as Tristan. His reaction to my story almost mirrored Tristan's, except Nick's eyes gave away hatred pure and deep for my unknown assailant.

The next week went quickly. Tristan and Nick seemed to be putting extra effort in keeping my mind occupied with something other than my perilous nightmare.

It was the end of June, and the full weight of the summer heat was starting to show. Nick had to put in more hours at work, but Tristan had more free time. It's funny how things work out sometimes.

I had to close at work so I wouldn't get to see Nick until after midnight. I used to love this shift, but now, I passionately hated it!

Business was slow, so Dan told me to work on the stockroom. I was placing some canned goods on the shelf, when I heard someone behind me. I turned thinking it was Dan; instead I was face-to-face with Jimmy Stanton!

"Can I help you with something, Jimmy?" My voice came out uneven. I was uncomfortable and wary.

"Maybe." He smiled an evil, menacing smile. "Or maybe...I can help you." His eyes scanned me from head to toe. His expression made me feel dirty and afraid. He stepped toward me, and I could smell the alcohol on his breath as he grabbed me around the waist and pulled.

I caught my breath and tried with all my might to push him back.

"Get away from me!" I yelled. "Let go!" He held tight. I screamed out, "Get away!"

SOULBOUND: DESTINY'S MOVE

Dan came running into the stockroom. He reached out, grabbed Jimmy by the back of his neck, and jerked him loose from me.

I just stood there as Dan wrenched Jimmy's arm behind him and practically drag him to the back entrance. He threw him out and threatened to call the police if he tried to come back into the restaurant. Dan ran back to where I stood still frozen in the same spot. "Liv, are you all right? Did he hurt you?"

"No, I'm okay...just a little shaken. He's drunk." I was still peering at the entrance to the stockroom as if I expected Jimmy to come barging in again any second.

"I know. If he remembers, he'll probably regret it in the morning," Dan said.

"Yeah, he probably will." I agreed for Dan's sake. I knew Jimmy, and his remorse was doubtful.

Dan put his arm around my shoulder to attempt comforting me. "Why don't you get something to drink and take a little break?"

"Okay...yeah...I'll do that." I was still dazed by the incident. Lee Daniels, one of the cooks, came over and took my arm to aid my steps to the break room as my friends and coworkers looked on in shock.

I emerged about thirty minutes later, appearing calmer and more composed, at least outwardly. Inside my nerves were jumping, and my stomach was still tied up in knots.

I finished my shift. I even managed to joke around a little with Darla; Kandi had already gone for the night.

"Olivia, would you like me to walk you out tonight?" Dan asked.

"No, I'm fine. The lot is pretty well lit. Besides, Jimmy's long gone by now. He's probably passed out somewhere." I gave him a fake but confident smile.

"Yeah, I'd say you're right, but if you're the least bit uncomfortable—"

I interrupted him. "I'm fine, don't worry. Thanks for offering just the same." I patted his shoulder and slipped on my jacket.

It seemed darker than usual. I noticed when I rounded the corner that a couple of post lamps near the back where I was parked were out. It felt creepy. I wish now I had accepted Dan's offer. *I could turn around and go back inside. Dan would understand,* I reasoned with myself. *No, there's no need to. You've been out here at night hundreds of times. There is no sense in being paranoid.*

I started on to my car, reaching in my pocket for my keys to unlock the door, when a hand came around from behind me, covering my mouth! I was being dragged behind the building! I was petrified! My heart was pounding wildly, and I started to struggle, but the grip became more powerful.

"Be still, precious, and you won't get hurt," came the slurred voice of my assailant.

Jimmy, what was he doing! I was suddenly slammed back into the brick wall, knocking the breath out of me. His hand was still covering my mouth. He seemed to be reveling in the fear my eyes gave away.

He leaned against me and pulled out what appeared to be a small gardening tool. It had three prongs, very sharp prongs! He placed it on my neck just under my chin.

"Be quiet, sweetheart." He breathed in a gruff, raspy voice as he pressed the prongs against my skin. "I'm going to move my hand. I swear if you try to scream, I'll rip your throat out before the first sound escapes, understand?" he threatened. I nodded to let him know he was perfectly clear.

"Jimmy, what are you doing?" I whispered, still struggling to breathe.

"What I've wanted to do for a long, long time!" He leaned into my face, the sickening smell of alcohol and bad breath almost smothering me. My eyes were darting all around, searching desperately for an escape.

"You uppity bitches are all the same," he sneered. "You try to act like you're not interested or too good. You think I'm not good enough, don't you, Olivia?" He slammed me hard against the wall again. I could feel the sting of broken skin from the rough bricks against my back.

"No, Jimmy. I don't think anything like that!" I had to focus, concentrate on his words. I had to try and remain calm if I was going to get out of this alive!

"Oh yes, you do! Well, I'm good, precious, and I'm going to show you just how good!" He was starting to breathe heavier now. I could see the lust in his eyes.

"Oh, dear God! This can't be happening! I blinked back the tears. I can't let this happen! He reached up at that moment, gripping the collar of my tee shirt. He jerked hard, ripping one side to my waist.

"Oh god...Jimmy, please don't do this!" I cried.

"That's what Savannah said. All she had to do was be still!" he rambled.

I was trying with all my might not to allow my fear to overtake me and cloud my judgment. The prongs of the sharp instrument pierced my skin. I could feel the warmth of the blood dripping down my neck. Jimmy leaned into me, running his filthy hands along my body.

"It shouldn't be too hard for you, Olivia; after all, I've seen your two pansy-assed boyfriends. I bet they won't even notice their little whore let someone else take a dip in their pond!" he whispered, still groping me rough and dirty.

"You vile bastard. You'll pay for this!" I spat the words like venom.

He threw his head back and laughed; he staggered and loosened his grip. I tried to run, but he was faster than I expected. He grabbed the back of my hair. I jerked loose and turned to defend myself, but instead his fist connected with my jaw, sending me sprawling onto the pavement. I felt flesh scrape and tear against the asphalt as my head hit the side of the metal Dumpster.

I just lay there, unable to move, staring at the light on the lamppost at the end of the rear parking lot. I watched as the bats flew around, chasing the elusive moths. My dream...Everything started spinning. I felt the sticky wetness in my hair as blood gushed from the gash in my head. I heard a loud hissing sound and a horrifying growl. As my head began to spin faster, everything became blurry. I saw nothing but shadows as I lost consciousness.

"WE WOULD HAVE BEEN here if it weren't for that damn roadblock!" Tristan said as he examined the injury to Olivia's head. "She needs x-rays immediately!"

"I'll call 911." Nick pulled out his phone and dialed. "I've been so fixed on keeping her safe from the danger in our world. I never gave any thought to humans being a threat!" Nikolas was in total shock at what had just transpired.

"Nick, you can't take all the blame for this! It was just as much my fault. I didn't see any danger from mere mortals either!" Tristan stood up from his rushed examination, being careful to leave her body in the exact position he found it.

"Is she going to be all right?" Nick's eyes searched Tristan's face, desperately seeking confirmation of his hopes.

"It's hard to tell here." Tristan's face gave no hope to Nick.

"Tristan, take the body up on the mountain. Make sure you leave his scent for the dogs to track. I'll meet you in a few minutes." Tristan nodded and started to turn.

"Oh, Tris."

"Yeah, Nick."

"Save something for me." Nick spoke in a low cold monotone. Tristan nodded. He knew that Nikolas loathed drinking directly from mortals, but this time he was sure that his friend would take great satisfaction in draining this human. He picked up the limp, lifeless body of Jimmy Stanton and disappeared up the mountain.

Nick's eyes never left Olivia's still body. He knelt down and dipped his finger in the blood puddled on the ground by her head. He slowly raised his hand and touched the red liquid to his tongue.

As soon as he tasted the sweet droplet, he raised his eyes to the sky, fangs bared, and let out a bloodcurdling screech!

Emeline 12

I regained consciousness, unaware of my surroundings. It took a few minutes to realize I was in the emergency room. My head hurt.

"Ms. Ryan? I'm Officer Snyder," a low, raspy voice spoke.

I turned my head to find a short heavy-set policeman with an extremely receding hairline standing by my bed.

"How are you feeling?" he asked in his most sympathetic tone.

"Like I've been hit by a truck," I replied.

"I'm sorry I have to put you through this right now, but I need to ask you some questions." He reached into his pocket for a notepad as he spoke.

"It's okay, I'm just glad I'm here to answer them." I tried to smile, but my face hurt, especially the right side.

The officer began asking his questions. I told him about Jimmy, what he did and what he said. I informed him that he had admitted to killing Savannah Butler. When I had finally finished, he patted me on the hand. "We'll find him, Ms. Ryan. Don't you worry." The officer's attempt to comfort me was appreciated, but not helpful. As he turned to leave the room, a nurse walked over, put something in my IV, and I was out again.

I woke the next morning in a hospital room. At least now the only thing hooked to me was the IV. If I had my way, that would be gone as soon as the doctor came in.

I raised my bed to a sitting position. Oddly, I didn't seem to hurt as bad as I remembered. I felt my head. It didn't hurt any worse than the night Mike Zita found me. Then again the huge bandage may have cushioned the pain.

I heard a voice just outside my room. It was low and muffled. I could see blue scrubs through the small opening in the partially closed door.

"Thank heavens the doctor's here," I mumbled under my breath. I leaned my head back into the pillow and closed my eyes.

"Well, it looks like your x-rays are okay and there's no sign of internal bleeding." That voice! My eyes flew open.

"Tristan!" I exclaimed.

"Good morning, sugar!" His smile was positively radiant!

"What are...you're a doctor!" I was totally stunned.

"Yes, baby, I'm a doctor." He pulled a stool beside the bed and sat down.

"Why didn't you tell me?" My eyes still wide in shock.

"You never asked." He grinned.

Tristan brushed my hair back from my face. His expression became somber. "Olivia, I'm so sorry this happened. I feel like I failed my promise to keep you safe." His expression was anguished, and his eyes, those beautiful, mesmerizing eyes, sent a pain through my heart to see the torture emanating from them.

"Oh, Tristan, don't! This wasn't your fault. Sweetheart, you didn't fail me. If you remember, I wasn't with you last night. This was one of those unforeseeable things." I tried to comfort him. I wanted so desperately to ease his pain. "This was caused by a drunken psychopath."

"Still, I should have..." His voice trailed off.

I reached out to touch his hand. As soon as I made contact, I felt the burning inside me. He had the most dramatic effect on me. I believe if I were dead, just his touch could bring me back.

"Last night...when I saw you lying there...bleeding, I can't begin to describe the rage inside of me. If I had known about him before..." The pure hatred for Jimmy Stanton seethed from him. "I took over your treatment, the only thing I could think of then was saving you, I couldn't bear life if you weren't part of it!" He looked at me as if his words were coming straight from his soul.

"Oh, honey, as you can see, I'm fine, thanks to you. Please, Tristan, let's not dwell on last night. I want to put this behind me as quickly as I can."

"I'll do whatever it takes to make that happen." He smiled.

"Have you had breakfast?"

"No, not yet, and I am starting to feel a little hungry."

"I'll be back in a few minutes then, with something more edible than what they're about to bring you." He stroked my hair gently and rose from his seat.

"Umm...Tristan?" I called as he turned to leave.

"Yes," he answered.

"I'm feeling much better, so do you think we could take this thing out? It's really uncomfortable." I tried to put on the sad eyes. He laughed and shook his head.

"I believe you can do without it now." He reached over and began removing the IV from my arm.

"Thanks," I spoke softly.

"I'll be back in a few minutes." He winked.

Tristan had barely been gone five minutes, before there was a knock on my door.

"Come in," I called. It was Kandi, Darla, and Danny, each bearing a bouquet of flowers.

"How are you feelin', honey?" Kandi looked as though somehow this was all her fault.

"I'm doing okay. I'm pretty sure they won't keep me in here long." I made an effort to sound upbeat. Darla and Danny were standing against the wall, staring at me.

"I'm so glad to see you guys!" I reached for Darla to take my hand.

"Olivia, I didn't know!" Her eyes were fixed on me.

"Didn't know what, Darla? What are you all staring at?" They were all three gawking at me like they were trying to decipher the origins of a piece of roadkill! Dan finally spoke. "Darla is trying to say, we didn't know how bad you were injured until we came in. Olivia, I am so sorry! I should have insisted on walking you out!" Dan's face was full of remorse. I didn't want him feeling guilty.

"Dan. It's all right, it wasn't your fault! No one could have known Jimmy's true intent. Please, don't blame yourself." My words were meant to be comforting, but from the look in his eyes, nothing I could say would make a difference.

"Now, tell me what everybody is staring at."

"You haven't seen yourself?" Kandi asked in surprise.

"No...why?" I was beginning to feel alarmed.

"Darla, do you have a mirror in your purse?" Kandi asked.

"Yeah, hold on a sec." Darla thrust her hand inside the shoulder bag and pulled out a small compact. Kandi opened it wide and handed it to me.

I looked in the mirror; my eyes widened in horror! My right eye was swollen and reddish blue. A huge purple bruise radiated from my jaw to cheekbone. I had a series of scratches on my forehead, and my lip was cut! Down further I could still see the faint prong marks from Jimmy's weapon on my neck. It took every ounce of my strength to contain my emotions. I felt sick inside. I made a feeble attempt at a fake smile as I closed the compact and handed it back to Darla. I tried to clear my throat before I spoke. "It really isn't as bad as it looks." Dan just dropped his head. He really was taking this hard.

"Come on, you guys, lighten up! I'm going to be just fine! They will find him you know!" Dan looked up as I spoke, his eyes moving back and forth between Kandi and Darla.

"You haven't heard?" Kandi's voice was uncertain. Since no one had told me, she was afraid it would be too much.

"Heard what?" My heart sped up. "Please don't tell me he got away!" I felt panicked.

"No, he didn't get away. They found him this morning," Dan answered. I leaned back against my pillow.

"I'm glad he's in jail. He killed Savannah Butler, he admitted it. He intended to kill me too." My eyes filled again as I trembled just thinking about him.

"Maybe you should wait until you're feeling better to talk about this." Darla reached down and picked up my hand, patting it tenderly.

"I want to know. Did he try to deny what he did? Did he put up a fight? What happened?" I searched each of their faces as I spoke.

"No. Jimmy's dead," Dan said flatly. Before I could get the details from my three friends, Tristan entered the room.

"Good morning," Tristan spoke in his most all-business tone. "I hate to interrupt, but Olivia needs to get some rest, and it's time for her medicine." Tristan smiled politely at them.

"I'm sorry. I'm being rude. Kandi, Darla, Dan, this is Dr. Tristan Rilz. Tristan, these are my friends." Tristan smiled brightly as he reached to shake their hands. Darla turned crimson, and Kandi bashfully lowered her eyes. I noticed both women tremble slightly as soon as he touched them. Dan, however, was not so cordial. He refused to shake Tristan's hand. His look was far from pleasant. Kandi sat down on the edge of my bed and leaned over to whisper in my ear, "I didn't know you still liked to play that game." Her voice was barely audible.

"What game" I silently mouthed as she sat back. She leaned back down and whispered, "Doctor!" I giggled and nudged her in the shoulder. Tristan glanced at the two of us, smiled, and winked. I knew it was impossible, but he acted like he heard every word! I couldn't help blushing. Kandi stood up and looked at me with those mischievous dancing eyes. "We'll talk later." She grinned.

"Okay, see ya." I smiled.

"It was certainly a pleasure, ladies." His voice was so smooth and sweet. I swear he could have melted an iceberg; he was so charming. Poor Darla, I thought for a minute she was going to faint dead away! He chose to ignore Dan. His steady glare didn't seem to intimidate Tristan in the least.

They said good-bye and promised to see me in a couple of days. When the door closed behind them, I drew in a long breath and exhaled slowly.

"Your friends are very nice," Tristan commented.

"Yeah, they're great!" I replied. "So, are we the hot gossip around here now?" I teased. I did wonder what people were saying about Dr. Rilz spending so much time in my room.

"Well, you seem to have broken a few hearts, Ms. Ryan." Tristan's smile was teasing.

"What do you mean, I've broken some hearts?"

"It seems…I've recently learned…several of the younger nurses and a few of the older ones have a crush on me." Tristan looked sheepishly at the floor as he spoke.

"Ohh, and you're surprised!" I quipped.

"Well…" He shrugged his shoulders as he unwrapped my breakfast. "Until you came here, it hadn't occurred to them that I had a social life, or that I was seeing someone!" He chuckled. "So as of now, you are definitely the topic. I'm afraid, honey, and I hate to say this, so don't get mad. You are the most hated woman in the building!"

I smiled a huge, proud smile. "That's fantastic!" I exclaimed. My joy in this knowledge caused Tristan to look up in utter shock!

"You're happy all these women hate you?" Tristan's expression was priceless.

"Of course I'm ecstatic about it!" My face was beaming. He just sat there, eyebrows knit and clueless.

"Tristan, sweetheart, they hate me because I have you and they don't! You have no idea what a huge compliment that is!"

"Women are definitely curious creatures." He smiled.

"I suppose we are, and that, I'm pretty sure, is the reason you men love us!" I laughed.

"You're probably right." His eyes glistened as he reached across me to adjust my blanket. He was close enough for me to feel his breath on my lips. My heart raced unevenly. Oh, how I ached at that moment! He shared my feelings. I could see it when he looked at me. I wanted him to kiss me more than I wanted to breathe! He pulled back, and I released a nervous sigh. We sat in awkward silence for a moment. I spoke first.

"Aren't you neglecting your other patients?" I smiled timidly.

"No, as a matter fact, I'm off duty, so it looks like you're stuck with me." His eyes shifted as he looked at me, no doubt, as I was, still feeling the effect of what just happened.

"So," he started. "Did you enjoy your visitors?" I knew he was attempting to change the heated atmosphere between us.

I looked down solemnly at my hands as Dan's words came back to me, and the beautiful moment was gone.

"Dan said Jimmy was dead." My words came out in a low monotone. "What happened?" Tristan was not prepared for such a drastic subject change.

"Umm...well..." he stammered, trying to regroup his thoughts. "According to the police, he ran off into the woods after..." He never finished the sentence. "From the condition of the body and the tracks, they figured he got between a bear and her cubs."

"How ironic. He died exactly like he tried to make Savannah's death appear." My vocal chords seemed to tighten as I spoke. My eyes filled so quickly I couldn't contain the tears that began to drop one by one onto my cheek.

Tristan sat silent. He looked confused, unable to grasp this emotion toward someone so horrible and cruel. My tears were not from grief though. I was relieved! Maybe I should feel bad about Jimmy's death. After all, he was still a person, no matter how insane. No, I was glad, glad he couldn't hurt me again and satisfied knowing Savannah's death had been vindicated. Tristan just sat there, patiently waiting for me to speak. I took a tissue and dabbed away the tears.

"I'm sorry. I'm a horrible person." I felt guilty that I found solace in someone's death.

"You don't have to apologize, and you're not a horrible person just because death makes you sad!" Tristan had misunderstood.

"I'm not sad. I'm relieved, that's why I'm so horrible. I'm glad he's dead!" I turned my face from him in shame.

Tristan seemed to relax after my confession. He behaved as though any sadness or pain I felt over Jimmy's death was caused by his own hand. He took my emotions much too personal.

"Baby, it's perfectly normal to feel the way you do, especially after what he did to you...what he tried to do! No one can blame you for the way you feel!" His expression was intense, hoping I would be able to see and understand that my feelings were justified. I relaxed and smiled at him. He knew I understood.

Tristan immediately changed the subject. "It seems your friend Dan doesn't like me." He laughed. "Ex-boyfriend I'm guessing." He raised a curious eyebrow.

"Not exactly." I smiled. I remembered Dan's bulldog look the first time he saw Nick; the thought of Nick made my heart ache. I missed him so desperately. *Does he know what happened? I wondered.* Tristan's voice pulled me from my thoughts.

"What do you mean not exactly?"

"I went out with him a couple of times. He kinda took things more seriously than me. I told him I didn't feel the same, but he doesn't seem to be willing to let it go," I explained.

"Well, sugar, I can certainly understand his pain. If you ended our relationship right now, I would never get over it!" There was something in his voice and the way he looked at me. I believe he truly meant every word.

I knew without a doubt I would die if he wasn't in my life! Tristan's reference to us as a couple thrilled me to my very depths. I guess we were wrapped in a beautiful platonic relationship. It consisted of all the feelings, the tender looks, the want, and the need, yet completely void of physical contact, with the exception of a light touch to my hair or hand.

As for me, aside from Tristan's hand, I had never really touched him. Come to think of it, I had never touched Nikolas either, with the exception of his arm—once. My relationship with Tristan was exactly the same as with Nick! Still, somehow it felt right. If this was all to spite my longing, it would have to be enough. Just to be near them made me feel content and complete.

"Tristan." I must have been quiet longer than I realized. My voice startled him. "There never was a relationship with Dan. I don't see why he can't get over it. After all, I'm nothing special. I looked away. I knew this was true, and I didn't understand why Tristan would be hurt if I left. He could do so much better, I thought.

"You are special, Olivia. You may not be able to see it but trust me—you most definitely are!" The emotion in his voice and the longing in his eyes stirred me to my very soul.

Tristan abruptly came to his feet, breaking the trance I was falling into.

"Where are you going?" I was afraid I had said or done something to make him leave. I couldn't stop the fear from showing on my face. Tristan reached down and ran his fingers down through my hair and smiled warmly.

"You need to rest." His voice had regained its normal tone. "I'll be back with your dinner later. Any special requests?" He grinned.

"A burger and fries sounds good. After all, you did insist on a more wholesome diet!" I giggled.

"I did. One wholesome serving of meat and potatoes coming up!" He bent down and kissed the top of my head lightly. I quivered and caught my breath. I could die happy this very moment! I leaned back and sighed. I had just experienced a little taste of heaven!

An elderly nurse came in with a small cup containing an assortment of pills.

"What's that?" I inquired.

"Dr. Rilz ordered these. He said they would help you to relax and rest." She poured some water from the pitcher and handed the cup to me.

"All right." I downed the medicine and relaxed onto the pillow. "Would you like your bed lowered?" the kindly woman offered.

"Yes please." I smiled. She reminded me a little of Grandma Jean.

"Now if you need anything, just push the call light. I'm Emeline, and I'll be your nurse for the rest of the day." She smiled, patting my hand as she spoke.

"Thank you, Emeline. You are certainly nicer to me than most of the other nurses here." I was looking out the window as I spoke.

"Never you mind about those other women. That Dr. Rilz is quite a catch, and they're just jealous!" Her aged eyes danced as she looked at me. "If I were, oh, say, about forty years younger, I'd probably hate you too." She smiled and winked. Her light-blue eyes glistened. I could tell behind the aged skin and white hair, forty years ago she would have been one to reckon with.

"Now that I've been here and saw for myself what all the fuss was about, I can see why Dr. Rilz can't stay away." Emeline smiled, causing her eyes to almost completely disappear. I couldn't help giggling as I watched her expression.

"Ms. Emeline, you are being kind." I flushed a pale rosy color.

"Don't you go mistakin' this white hair and cute dimples for sweet, honey." She wrinkled her nose. "I call it like I see it." She spoke over her shoulder as she walked out of the room. I was still smiling as the door closed behind her. What a treasure she must be to someone, I was thinking as I yawned.

I slept most of the afternoon, waking only long enough to eat the meal Tristan had brought. He ordered another round of sedatives for ten o'clock and told me he would return in the morning.

Just past sundown, I was finally awake, staring out the window in the silent room. A dim light glowed just above my bed. It was never a good thing for me to be alone; the memories came flooding through my mind. I could see the smiles and hear the voices of my parents as clear as if they were standing in this room with me... if only they were. I missed them so very much. I had to get my thoughts on something else. I thought of Nikolas. I hadn't seen him since the night before Jimmy...

I needed to see him. I felt lost without Nick, and I ached deep inside. I visualized every perfect feature of him. The longing to be near him made it hard to breathe. If only I could get in touch with him, just hear his voice.

I heard a light knock on my door.

"Yes. Come in," I called. My heart skipped a beat, and the butterflies in my stomach went crazy!

"Nick! I'm so glad you're here!" His beautiful heart-stopping smile could be seen across the dim-lit room.

"How are you feeling, love?" His silken voice made me weak.

"Much better now, I was just thinking about you." I wanted to leap from my bed and fling my arms around him, but the unspoken no-contact rule overrode my impulse. He handed me a gorgeous bouquet of spring flowers and pulled a chair up to the side of my bed.

"I brought something I'm sure you miss." He smiled.

"Unless you are referring to yourself, I can't think of a thing!" I couldn't take my eyes off him. The light from behind the chair made the appearance of a golden halo around him. He looked like an angel sitting there, and I was totally enraptured by his appearance.

I heard the sound of paper rattling and glanced down to see him unwrap a thermos and cup. When he opened the lid, I smelled the aroma of hot tea and lemon. Aside from my usual herbal tea, I had grown accustomed to drinking this with Nick every evening.

"Oh, that smells sooo good, but I don't know if I'm allowed. The caffeine may not be good for—"

Nick stopped me. "Shhh...don't worry, I cleared it with your doctor." He smiled, seeming very amused at my sudden wide-eyed expression.

"You met Dr. Rilz?" The guilt gave a hard thump in my chest.

"Yes, he seems like a very nice person...very professional."

"You think so?" I was starting to feel nervous, knowing they met even for the briefest moment. Stop it, Olivia! I scolded myself. Concentrate on Nick only!

"I feel much better knowing Dr. Rilz is in charge of your care, he has an extraordinary reputation," Nick said.

"I'm not surprised, he's very good," I muttered. My eyes were set on the night sky rather than Nick, where they should have been. I turned back to direct the conversation away from Tristan. Nick was staring at me; it was almost like he was trying to will away all my injuries. I was glad the lighting was dim. I wanted so badly to hide my face from him. I hoped he couldn't see just how gruesome I really looked.

"Olivia, I blame myself for what happened, for not meeting you at the restaurant when you got through at work. I am so very sorry. My promise to keep you safe has been broken." Nick looked at me with such strong remorse. His pain was so intense it felt like a knife in my heart. He sat there looking down at his hands. I could see his jaw clenching at the thought of my attack.

"No, Nick, you couldn't have known this would happen."

"I did know! You told me about your dream! I should have been more watchful!"

"Oh, my dream...but you couldn't have known it was Jimmy!" I tried to assure him that he had no blame in this.

"You knew your assailant!" Nick's head jerked up in surprise.

"Yeah...I went to school with him. I didn't like him then either." Visualizing Jimmy in my mind pulled up anger that I didn't realize I was capable of.

"I hate myself for allowing this to happen!" Nick's voice was thick with self-contempt. "I wish I had known who." He stopped there.

The look on his face told me, if I could have put a face on the shadow in my dream, Jimmy Stanton would have never lived to attack me. This made me realize there was more to Nikolas Riggs than I imagined. This beautiful romantic angel had a dark side, and it was black and...lethal! My hands started to shake as I took a sip of the hot tea.

"It's over now, Nick. Jimmy's dead," I said.

The corners of his mouth turned up into an almost sinister grin. He seemed to take great pleasure in that fact, as if he had the satisfaction of snuffing out Jimmy's life himself. I was frightened of the man I saw at that moment. I knew in my heart that this was not the person Nikolas was, yet I was positive this was a side of him I didn't want to pursue.

"How did you know I was here?" I asked.

"I went to the restaurant when I didn't find you at home. Your boss, Dan is it?" I just nodded in response. "He told me what happened. I came straight here. Olivia, I've never felt fear like I did the moment I saw you lying in that room." He looked at me with those beautiful black eyes, his expression gentle and loving. My Nick was back from the darkness I had just witnessed.

"I couldn't live if something happened to you!" he whispered, his voice desperate. There were no words to express the joy I felt at his proclamation. He did feel the same as I did for him!

"Shhh..." I whispered. "I'm fine, love."

The bright light from the hallway flooded the dimly lit room as a nurse walked in carrying another cup full of pills. I noticed how beautiful she was. Her skin was like silk, smooth and flawless. She wore her long blond hair pulled back. Even through the unflattering attire of nurse's scrubs, you could see her perfect silhouette. It confounded me as to why Tristan would choose me over someone like her.

"Do I have to take these?" I asked as she poured a glass of water from the pitcher.

"Yes, ma'am, doctor's orders." She smiled politely. Mercedes was one of the many nurses Tristan had informed didn't like me very much. I'm sure she would have been rude had Nikolas not been sitting there. I swallowed the pills like a good girl, and Mercedes turned to leave the room, giving a low nod to Nick as she passed. He in return nodded slightly in acknowledgment.

"Nick, I don't want to go to sleep!" I whined. "I want to spend every second with you!"

"Olivia, don't worry, you need to rest. I'll stay in case you wake. Please, love, sleep."

I leaned back, tense, determined to fight the medication. Suddenly I caught a waft of that beautiful unknown scent in the air. I breathed in and became oblivious to everything around me. I was so lost in the glorious feeling I let out a soft moan and drifted into sleep.

"Too bad we can't bottle that stuff up." Tristan laughed as he walked into the room.

"YOU'VE TAKEN GOOD CARE of her, Tris. She's been through quite an ordeal." Nick had placed his hand on Olivia's as she slept, unaware of his touch.

"It's painful to see her this way." Tristan's voice was low and whispered.

Nick just nodded. "I wish I could take this from her." Nick's voice held a helpless desperation.

"This is so hard...not being able to touch her, to get close to her. How long will this have to go on?" Tristan asked.

"I'm not sure...till she's showing some sign of choosing, I guess. Tris, it would be so easy for either or both of us to take her and she wouldn't even realize what had happened. We both know how wrong that would be, because it wouldn't have been her choice. You and I would be no better than the lowlife that put her in here!" Nick looked at Tristan, both silently communicating the still-present loathing for the dead man.

"I know, my friend, but she is so strong and so breathtakingly beautiful it's hard not to think of it." Tristan's eyes were back on Olivia, gazing at her with such desire, such painful need.

Nick knew that Tristan's feelings for her were every bit as deep and strong as his. He was now positive that Olivia's pull on both their souls was equally powerful.

"I hope she makes her choice before the council convenes again. If she hasn't, you know what will happen. We will not have a say in the decision." Nick's eyes lowered as he spoke. No more words passed between them concerning the matter.

"She is so amazing, isn't she?" Tristan spoke adoringly.

"Yes, she certainly is!" Nick removed his hand from Olivia's as she made a restless move.

I must be dreaming. I hear Nick and Tristan's voice! My guilt is now haunting my sleep. I'm a horrible creature! I felt my eyelids flutter and, for a brief moment, thought I saw them together in my room. I could still hear Tristan speaking, but I couldn't see him.

"Have you eaten?" he asked Nick.

"No," Nick answered, shaking his head.

"Thirsty?" Tristan leaned against the wall.

"I could use a drink." Nick looked up as Tristan tossed a packet of blood to him.

"Thanks." He didn't need to say anything more as he bit the container and began to drink.

"I have rounds to make, Nick. I'll see you later."

Nick nodded and tossed the empty container into the trash as Tristan left the room.

Disappeared 13

Life has many turns and twists to keep you off the beaten path. Luckily, destiny has a way of turning the corners to keep you on course. My fear that Tristan was suspicious of Nick was put to rest. Once I was released from the hospital, Tristan never brought him up again.

I had to be the luckiest woman alive! I was positive I was the most frustrated woman on the planet! I had managed somehow to spend every minute, every waking hour of the past eight months with two men that were so beautiful they shouldn't even be real! Yet here I stand today with my virtue still intact! What in the name of all that's right am I doing wrong?

The summer passed so fast it seemed like a blur. Tristan kept my days filled with adventure, excitement, and fire! Nikolas flooded my nights with romance and fantasy! The more time I spend with them, the harder it seemed distinguishing them as separate entities. In my heart they were melding together as if they were one man—one perfect man! My mind knew differently. This fantastic fantasy would soon come to an end. I could feel it.

I had just spent my first day since we met without seeing Tristan. He had to leave for a four-day seminar in Boston. I barely made it through the day and was sure the next three would be worse. It was the middle of October. Tristan would be home the evening of the sixteenth, and I would see him Sunday morning. I stood at the front window, admiring the beautiful bright fall colors. There was a light breeze blowing, and I watched a few of the withered leaves separate from the limbs and float to the ground. Somehow it seemed sad, and it tugged heavily at me.

My parents had been gone a year; I thought of them often. As vibrant as everything still seemed, fall to me was a time of separation and ending. I was feeling very melancholic. Tristan's absence only made it worse. I felt like one of the dry, withered leaves falling before me. I was glad the light of day was coming to an end. That was the good thing about this time of year, shorter days. I continued to watch out my window, remembering and longing to bring my memories to the here and now. I wiped a tear from my eye and dropped the window blinds.

As the last of the sunlight disappeared behind the mountain, the butterflies in my stomach started. Nick would be here soon, and I needed to get ready. The days were still warm, but the nights had begun to cool down, so I decided to wear a slightly heavier sweater. I didn't know what he had planned, so I dressed casual.

It was getting harder to maintain my self-control when I was with either of them. I trembled inside almost constantly, and my hands would shake much more than they should. I could tell this platonic relationship was affecting them too. Nick's voice seemed to tremble when he spoke, and Tristan's breathing was quicker and more erratic when he was close to me. It seemed like the more difficult it was to control their emotions, the farther away from me they became. I had a long list of whys: Why didn't either of them hold me? Why hadn't they tried to kiss me? Why wouldn't they touch me? Why couldn't I make the first move, and most of all, why couldn't I choose one of them? I was certain if this continued, although I may not lose my virtue, I would definitely lose my sanity!

Just as I started down the hall, Nick walked through the front door. Both Nick and Tristan spent so much time here we had dispensed with the formalities of knocking long ago. I stopped as I caught my breath at the sight of him. He was wearing a charcoal-gray sweater and black fitted stonewashed jeans. I studied every inch of him. The firm muscles of his shoulders and chest pushed against the sweater, accenting his tight abs and perfectly shaped hips. I swear he gets more beautiful every day!

Nick had stood there looking back at me the same as I had just been looking at him; his eyes were filled with such longing. I could feel his desire from across the room. How much more of this excruciating torture could I endure?

He cleared his throat. "Uhmmm, well, love, are you ready to go?" His voice trembled.

"Yes...umm..." I suddenly felt awkward and at a loss for words. "Okay." I started for the door, trying to keep my eyes steadily in front of me.

The air was crisp as we walked. I listened to the sounds of the night around me. I could hear an owl in the distance calling out of sync with the constant hum of the crickets. The night was so peaceful. Nick and I made little conversation; he seemed to be deep in thought. The dry leaves crackled softly beneath our feet as we walked through the trees. We came out into a small clearing at the edge of the creek.

Nick spread a blanket on the ground, placed the basket he carried beside it, and motioned for me to sit down. He had always taken me to such romantic places, but tonight was different; it was more perfect than anywhere we had been. It felt as if we were the only two on the planet.

I sat down on the blanket, and Nick took his place beside me. He leaned back on one arm, the other resting on his bent knee. It was a beautiful night, clear and brightly lit under a full moon. For a long time, we sat quietly, listening to the sound of the water rolling along over the rocks.

Nick leaned forward and reached into the basket, brought out two stemmed glasses and a bottle of Bordeaux. I broke the silence between us.

"Oh, Nick, you certainly think of everything." My voice came out soft.

"This night is almost as perfect as you and is deserving of a good wine." He smiled as he poured the drinks. He handed me a glass along with a single red rose. I bit my lower lip tenderly and lowered my eyes. I could have sworn once again I heard him catch his breath.

I lifted the rose and breathed in its sweet bouquet. He leaned back as before, resting his arm on his knee as he held the glass, again looking up at the stars. I took a sip of the wine and examined the flower. The rose was still closed in a tight bud; each petal was perfect, without any visible flaw. The thorns had been removed, and the stem felt smooth against my skin. He had taken such great care in the choice of this one thing, I thought.

I turned slowly toward him. He was still leaned back, gazing at the night sky. He was a gorgeous man, but now that word was not befitting. His soft blond hair glistened in the moonlight, his face was softer, and it showed every angle of his perfection. No, gorgeous was not the word; he was, without a doubt, beautiful beyond words.

I relaxed into his slow, steady breaths as he sat at ease and sipped his wine. A tiny taste of the drink glistened on the upper corner of his full lips. His tongue slightly moved across them to catch the drop, and I stopped breathing! How I ached from my very depths to know the feeling of those lips on mine. Yes, moonlight was definitely his element!

I forced my eyes away, sat my glass on the ground, and lay back on the blanket, content to gaze at the heavens with him.

"The sky is beautiful tonight." My words were soft and low.

"Yes, but there is one star...more radiant...more beautiful than any you can see. And only I am privileged to see it tonight. It's mine." As he spoke, his eyes were still locked on the sky.

I rolled over and rose up to rest on one arm. "Share it with me, Nick, show me where it is," I whispered softly. He had lifted the rose from my hand and ran the soft petals along my cheek, tracing down to the hollow of my throat as he looked tenderly into my eyes. He gently placed the petals under my chin.

"It's right here," he whispered low. My pulse quickened, and I became flushed. "Olivia, you are more stunning than anything on this earth or in the heavens. There is nowhere on this planet, or this universe, that I would rather be than right here, right now, with you," he cooed softly. I suddenly realized how very close he was. I stared into his eyes. I could almost see his thoughts, feel his emotions. They were more tender, more revealing than any time we had been together.

I felt as if I had been hypnotized. I couldn't look away. I didn't want to. That scent was in the air, more powerful than it had ever been. It seemed to fill my senses so fully, so exquisitely; I became weak, intoxicated, and euphoric! I continued looking deeply into Nick's eyes. My mind became foggy, and I felt like I was beginning to float, to be pulled into the dark pools staring back at me. I could feel the breath from Nick's lips almost close enough to touch. I began to fall deeper...deeper...Just as our lips were about to meet and our souls were about to touch, Nick turned away and abruptly sat up.

I felt like I had been dropped from the top of a cliff! My entire body ached, and I felt broken.

"I'm so sorry, Olivia! I can't do this, it's not right!" His breathing was still heavy and erratic.

"Do what? I'm sorry, did I do something wrong. What did I do wrong to ruin this wonderful moment? I thought. "Please, forgive me, Nick. Nick!" He turned toward me, his eyes full of sorrow and regret.

I blinked back the tears.

"I...I don't understand," I stammered.

"You have no need to apologize, love, this is my fault! If it were only my choice...if you only...I would make you a part of me this very instant! I've never wanted anything more totally in my entire existence! If it were just up to me, I'd make you mine this night, this very second, and you would be mine and I would be yours—forever!" His expression was beyond desperation. He stood up so fast I didn't even see him move! I rose to my feet, still trembling.

"We have to go. Now!" His voice was anxious, and he seemed angry. He had gathered the basket blanket and its contents. Before I realized it, we were heading back through the trees toward the vehicle. The night air had chilled more, and it caused my face to sting as it rushed against my wet cheeks. The tears were now streaming uncontrollably. It seemed like only minutes when the engine of the black Mercedes purred to life.

I couldn't speak. I just sat there silent, dazed, and numb.

"You can never know my remorse for the pain I've just caused you."

Nick's voice came through to pull me for a brief moment from my torment. I slowly turned to look at him.

"To see your tears, to know I caused them, it burns through my veins like hot coals!"

I don't know how fast he was driving. No sooner had he stopped speaking, we were in my driveway. I still could not find my voice. I had not uttered a word; it was as if I had been totally dumbstruck! Nothing would form in my mind.

"Olivia, I swear to you, there will never be another tear fall from your eyes, caused by me! There are no words to express my sorrow, you must forgive me!" His pleading got through to me.

"Nothing happened, Nick. There's nothing to forgive!" The words squeaked out of my throat in broken pieces. He stood there on the porch, looking like a man tortured. His eyes were so full of pain. He reached to touch my face. I wanted him to! I wanted him to take me in his arms. To let me feel that I hadn't lost him! He dropped his hand, holding it clenched to his side.

"I need to go...I..." He never finished speaking; he just turned and walked away.

I locked the front door behind me and flung myself onto the couch, sobbing violently. I had never felt the pain of loss as deeply as I did at this moment. I didn't care if he never wanted me in that way! I just needed to be near him, beside him. The tears came again. The ache was stronger, and I felt empty.

The bright October sun was blinding to my red, swollen eyes. I needed to pull myself together before I went in to work for the few hours Dan had me scheduled. I don't know how many times I replayed last night in my head. Every time ended in a wave of tears.

I had cried more in one night than I'm sure I had in my entire life!

I turned on the shower and tossed my work clothes on the bed. *Please, God, don't let him be gone for good!* I prayed as I stepped into the steaming cascade. The thought alone of Nick never returning caused a shaking in my chest. My breath felt short again, and I held back my overpowering urge to cry. I missed Tristan terribly, but I was glad he couldn't see me this way. I know I could never explain without losing him too! *I couldn't live! Oh, God, how was I going to get through this miserable day?* I thought as my chest heaved and I fought for self-control.

I barely made it to work on time, and Dan was in his usual ill mood. Everyone was going about business as usual, but I didn't feel like usual.

"Trouble in paradise?" I was startled at the voice; my thoughts were far away on Tristan and Nikolas. I turned around to look straight into the gleaming brown eyes of Michelle. *She would be the first to notice something wrong!*

"No," I answered curtly. I had no intention of sharing one second of my business with her. She had never been happy to see my life going well. Michelle hated knowing she for once in her golden life couldn't capture the attention of someone she wanted!

"Michelle, would you work at the register please?" Kandi asked. She had been watching me all morning.

"Sure," Michelle answered as she snickered under her breath. She was getting way too much pleasure from my misery! If there were only one person in this entire world that could truly test my tolerance of others, Michelle was that person!

"Olivia, it's time for your break." Kandi was standing beside me, and I hadn't even noticed her. She had been promoted to assistant manager. We were all happy for her, and she helped alleviate some of the wrath of Daniel.

"Kandi, I don't get a break today. I'm off in an hour," I reminded her.

"Just do what I said, honey, and go to the break room," she ordered.

"Okay," was all I said and started toward the back of the restaurant. I walked into the empty room and sat at the table against the back wall. I put my head down on my folded arms, fighting the quaking inside me that was certain to start the tears flowing.

"Uhmmm..." I heard and slowly looked up to find Kandi standing there, looking worried.

"Umm...hey, Kandi...did you need me back out front?" I started to get up as I spoke.

"No, honey, just sit back down. I sent you back here 'cause I wanted to talk to you. I noticed you aren't your usual happy self today, and I saw your expression when Michelle started with you." Her eyes were not showing her normal playfulness.

"I'm sorry, my mind has been on other things. I'll try to pay more attention," I promised.

"I'm not talking about your work, girl. I'm worried about you. What's going on?"

"It's nothing, really," I assured her.

"Hogwash! You might convince those guys out there." She nodded her head toward the front. "This is me you're talking to, and what you're selling, sister, I'm not buying!" She wasn't going to let me be; that was certain.

"It's Nick!" I admitted and released a long breath.

"I was afraid this was going to happen," she said.

"Afraid what was going to happen?" I asked.

"Nick broke up with you, didn't he? I told you, Liv, if they ever found out about each other—"

"He didn't break up with me!" I interrupted. "At least I don't think he did!" *I wasn't sure what was happening right now, so how could I begin to explain it to Kandi?* I thought. "They don't know about each other. I still have that under control, okay!" My defenses were starting to kick in. I was beginning to feel annoyed by her assumption.

"Then what do you mean by 'I don't think he did'?" She raised her hands to make the little quotation marks in the air.

"Kandi, I'm sure you don't want to hear about all this."

"Oh yes, I do! I've been living my dreams through you for the past eight months, and if they're coming to an end, I wanna know!" She raved.

I knew she was concerned, but I had no idea she was that caught up in my life. That fact left me feeling a tad bit uneasy.

"Oh, all right, sit down, but if I get into trouble, I'm blaming you, okay?" I tried to smile.

"You won't. I told Darla to clock you out, and I'm on my lunch hour." She grinned as she sat down across from me. "Now start talkin', honey."

"Well, how do I begin? Last night Nick took me out. It was so romantic...so perfect! At least I thought it was. Nick was beautiful, and I felt like...like..." I was reliving every sound, every vision of him, every word.

"Hey, Olivia." Kandi snapped her fingers. "It musta been some date!"

"It was...and I thought everything was going great! Then...all at once he took me home!" I teared up as the pain of his leaving hit me again.

"Just like that...out of the blue...no explanation." Her eyes were focused, waiting for further explanation.

"Yeah, he just took me home! He seemed angry, not at me, but at himself! He just walked off my front porch without a word! I don't know what to think! I can't, for the life of me, figure out what I did wrong!" My words were catching as I tried to keep from bursting out in tears again.

Kandi had leaned back, looking at me with wide eyes and a gaping mouth.

"So, what do you think?" I waited for her to assess my situation.

"You two haven't..." she started.

"No! Oh no, Nick is far too much a gentleman!" I don't know why I felt the need to defend my honor, or his for that matter; after all, we were both adults!

"Then I can assume things got a little tense last night?" she asked.

"Yeah, you can assume." I blushed.

"Uh huh...well then, Nick's problem is obvious," she knowingly stated.

"Well, I'm glad it's obvious to you! Why don't you give me a clue?"

"He got scared, Liv."

"Scared? What are you talking about, Kandi?"

"It's simple, Liv. Things started looking too serious last night. He realized just how close you two were becoming, and it scared him!" She gave a smug look, confident in her analogy of the situation. "Sometimes, honey, men aren't always sure of themselves, or what they want. Just give him a few days and he'll be back." She seemed quite sure of her conclusion.

"I hope you're right."

"So, what about the doctor? He's still around, I'm guessing." She looked at me with her eyebrow raised. The mention of Tristan threw me and the sadness of his absence shown on my face.

"Oh no, don't tell me there's trouble there too!" Kandi leaned back onto the table, surprised.

"No. Tristan had to go to Boston for some seminar or something.

He'll be back on Saturday night," I explained. "Oh, and you miss him, huh?" "Terribly!" I answered.

"Olivia, you know you can't keep this up much longer. You're gonna have to make a choice sooner or later," she scolded.

"How am I supposed to do that?" The mere thought of choosing gave me an anxiety attack!

"Isn't there something that makes one of them stand out in your mind more than the other?" she asked.

"No, that's the problem. They're so alike in many ways and so perfectly different in others!"

"How so?" Kandi looked intrigued.

"What do you mean?"

"How are they perfectly different? The alike is pretty obvious, they're gorgeous!"

"Kandi!"

"What! I have seen them, you know!" Her eyes were wide and shining. I could tell, if either of them gave her the slightest hint of interest, our friendship would not stand in the way.

"Still, I'm not sure I like the way you said it!" I felt a little defensive.

"You don't need to get all huffy, girl. You have to know that every woman that lays eyes on them would love to be in your shoes even for a minute! Those two men can't see anyone or anything but you!" she exclaimed. I was embarrassed.

"Now how are they different?" she repeated.

"Well, Nick is so gentle and romantic. He makes me feel like Cinderella. Everything with him is romance, fantasy, and well... euphoric!" I sighed. "Tristan, he makes my blood boil! With him, everything is electric, exciting, and passionate!" The strong desire I felt for the both of them was evident on my face and in my voice.

"Whew, girl!" Kandi was fanning her hand in front of her face. "After that visual, I'd get a cold glass of water, but it might give me a stroke!" she commented, still fanning her hand wildly in front of her.

"Kandi, I'm serious!" I was beginning to get frustrated with her antics.

"Yeah, honey, and you think I'm not!" She grinned.

"Anyway, you asked my dilemma and now you know." I sat back and folded my arms to sulk.

"I wouldn't call it a dilemma, darlin', more like a blessing, a beautiful blessing. I should be so lucky!" She laughed. "You're in love with both of 'em, aren't you?" My eyes widened at her words.

"In love...that's a pretty strong word! Attached to both of them, yes, but I don't know about love! Neither Tristan nor Nikolas has really made any remarks about commitment, so I don't think they feel that way either!" I couldn't be in love—not yet and certainly not with two men! I thought.

"Hmph...if you say so...you're still gonna have to figure out who you are more 'attached' to. You know it in your heart, Liv. You can't go on stringing them both along forever!" she continued to lecture. "You need to do some serious soul-searching!" The concern on her face was real.

"Well, if Nick doesn't come back, I won't have to, will I?" I couldn't stop the tear that glistened in the corner of my eye. Kandi picked up my hand and gave it a gentle squeeze.

"He'll be back, honey, mark my words," she spoke softly.

"Thanks, Kandi, you're a good friend." I wiped away the droplet from my eye and smiled.

"I hate to leave, but my break is over, and Dan will be furious if I'm not back on time," she said.

"I'm sorry about that. It's my fault he's acting like that, you know. He really needs to grow up, get over it, and move on." I hated the way Dan treated everyone since I started seeing Nick. It only got worse when Tristan came into the picture.

"Yeah, but he's not gonna let it go. Somehow his mind has tricked him into believing he's still got a chance." She turned up the corners of her mouth in a wicked little smile. "I don't know what you've got, but I damn sure wish you'd share!" She laughed out loud. We were heading out the door as she spoke.

"Hmph." I laughed and lowered my eyes.

"Go home, Liv, relax, okay? Things have a way of working themselves out, don't worry." She meant her words to be encouraging, but until I could see Nick again, I just didn't believe it. Nothing but being near him again would make me feel better.

I picked up a few groceries and started home. I hadn't been in the house long when the phone rang. It was Tristan!

"Hey, sweetheart, how's the seminar?" I tried to sound casual even though my heart was racing.

"Boring," he answered. "Are you all right?"

"Yeah, of course, except for missing you."

"Are you sure, baby? Your voice sounds a little off."

"Just a rough day at work, nothing you need to be concerned about," I lied. As long as Tristan couldn't see my face, I'm sure I convinced him.

"I miss you too. This is going to be the longest four days in my entire existence!" I could tell by the tone of his voice he was hurting as much as I was by the separation.

"Are you working tomorrow?" he asked.

"Yes, but only a few hours in the morning. I wish I could be busy all day so the time would pass more quickly," I told him.

"I know, sugar, it's passing slowly for me too. I can't talk long today, but I want you to know I'm thinking of you every minute. Remember, only two more days." *Only two more days he says, I feared I wouldn't last two more hours!*

"I have to go. I'll call you tomorrow." He sounded as sad as I felt at the thought of hanging up.

"Okay. Tomorrow then. Bye." Now, I was left to a huge black silence.

Nightfall came, and I waited— Nick didn't show. I spent another night crying until I fell asleep sometime around four a.m.

I drudged through another day. Darla and Kandi tried their level best to lift my spirits, but their efforts were futile.

Friday night I waited again, still no Nikolas. *Maybe Kandi was wrong this time. Maybe he isn't coming back.* I started to shake as soon as the thought crossed my mind. *Where is he? Does he know what he's doing to me? I can't imagine never seeing his beautiful face or hearing his silken voice. He can't be gone forever, he can't!* I dropped to my knees, crying desperate tears.

SOULBOUND: DESTINY'S MOVE

Saturday morning, I felt a little better as I got dressed for work, only because Tristan would be back in town this evening. He told me he was planning a hiking trip Sunday morning and asked me to be ready early. I couldn't wait.

My mind kept drifting away all morning, and I just didn't want to go to work. Why I even kept that job was a mystery to me. I had only planned it to be temporary. *Two years is not temporary,* I told myself. I really didn't need to work now, so why did I continue to put myself through the aggravation of getting reprimanded by Dan and disrespected by the customers? Maybe I just felt obligated, who knows.

Work went pretty fast, and I was glad. Kandi and Darla felt better being around me when they saw just a hint of my better mood. They knew Tristan was back and was sure now I'd be all right. I tried very hard to make them believe it, but inside I wasn't. I knew I would never be truly happy again as long as Nick remained out of my life. Where did he go? Why hadn't he at least called? The desperate feeling started to fill my chest again. Breathe, you can't fall apart here! You cannot let everyone here see this happen! I fought desperately for self-control.

I walked down the short hall to clock out, glad this day was over. Dan called me into the office.

"Hey, Dan, what's up?" It wasn't like him to call me in for a private talk. He preferred to spend his days sulking and avoiding me.

"Olivia, we have a problem." So, this wasn't just a friendly talk; he was all business.

"We do?" I couldn't imagine anything that had went wrong today.

"Yes, it seems there has been a discrepancy with your register."

"Excuse me? Discrepancy? I'm afraid I don't understand."

"You've been coming up short. I tried to overlook the first couple of times. I hate to say this, but after today, if it happens again, I'll have to let you go." There was something in the way was he was looking at me that made me shift uncomfortably. There was more to this little conversation, I feared, than he was saying.

"I know I've been a little off lately, but it couldn't be that bad! Aren't you overreacting?" I couldn't believe that after two years he'd just toss me out over nothing.

"Look, Olivia, I don't want to fire you. The past three days your combined loss has been almost one hundred dollars. Why don't you have dinner with me tonight, and we can talk about it?" he suggested in a quiet, gentle voice.

"There's no need to go out, Dan, I'm sure we can resolve the problem here."

"I would rather our discussion be more private," he insisted.

"I just don't think that would be appropriate, Dan, as you know I'm seeing someone," I reminded him.

"I know, two someone's." He gave a strong emphasis on *two*. Discussing this with Dan made me uncomfortable.

"You know, I have a theory on that," he said, attempting a smile.

"Oh, so just what is your theory?" I didn't like where this conversation was going.

"You see, I believe you're still dating them both because you're not over us yet." He seemed so sure of himself.

"Us...Dan, we never had a relationship to get over!" I was stunned that he actually believed what he was saying.

"I don't know why you insist on denying that we were meant to be together, Olivia. I suppose it's just going to have to take something drastic to force you to open your eyes and quit playing this game." He looked at me with such conviction. *He has convinced himself that I belong to him!*

"What do you mean drastic? I don't see what this has to do with my register."

"Unless I have a very good reason to overlook the problem, I can't see myself allowing it to continue," he stated.

Did he honestly believe this job was that important to me, that I couldn't work anywhere but here? It was very obvious to me now that Dan had finally snapped! "I can't believe this!" My voice raised in astonishment.

"Believe what? Money is disappearing!" He spoke louder to ensure any eavesdroppers wouldn't catch on to his true intent.

"Ohh, so that's how the game is played, huh? Since I won't agree to drop Nick and Tristan for you, you're going to accuse me of stealing! Dan, do you honestly think that ruining my good name is going to endear me to you?" I was becoming more infuriated by the second. "You're insane!"

"I'm not accusing you of anything, Ms. Ryan!" I could hear the nervousness in his voice.

"Oh, Ms. Ryan is it now! Well, let's get something straight right now! Number one, I have never stolen anything in my life and I'm damn sure not gonna start now! Number two, I do not now, nor will I ever need a job badly enough to be blackmailed into keeping it!" I yelled.

Dan took a step forward as if to assert his authority. "Now, Olivia, you don't want to go there!"

I glared at him. "If you think for one second, I'm the least bit intimidated, you had better think again! You have been a pompous—" I caught my breath in. My voice had gained momentum, and everyone within earshot was leaning in by now. "You know what you can do with your job! I'll be in next week to pick up my check. On second thought, mail it! Good day, Mr. Baker!" I walked out of the office, leaving Dan standing with his mouth open as I slammed the door behind me with enough force to have shaken it from the hinges. I was so furious I barely glanced at the wide eyes and stunned expressions as I passed through the dining area to the front door.

I had calmed down by the time I reached the house. *I'm glad Dan tried his little power play today,* I thought. I started to feel relieved. At least now I wouldn't have to explain my business to everyone around me. No more audience to judge my every move. I was tired of being the topic of people's backroom gossip. I wouldn't be hearing bits of low conversations with words like *tramp* drifting out. *Not that I really cared what anyone thought.* It's just annoying to think they have nothing better to do in their mundane little lives than to trash someone's reputation. I felt like a huge burden had been lifted, and for the first time in my life, I felt free!

Kandi called as soon as she got home. I explained what happened and promised to call if I needed anything. I heated a TV dinner in the microwave, knowing I needed to eat something, but I just didn't have an appetite. My stomach stayed twisted so tight I couldn't hold anything down. *Nick, where are you? Please—please call!* I needed to see him, but I didn't know how to get in touch with him. I had gone three days without a word. If only he realized what a huge hole he's left in my soul. Sleep was almost nonexistent; a couple of hours were all I seemed to manage. On top of my anxiety, the dreams were back. I knew it had something to do with me, but nothing seemed familiar. I could see a small room; it was dimly lit and very cold and damp. There were scraps of what appeared to be food scattered on the floor and this smell, a moldy stench, almost like I was trapped in a basement or something. I remember a woman very tall and thin. She was pale, sort of like Nick, and she had huge amber eyes and short spiked brown hair. I wasn't familiar with the way she was dressed. It seemed like she was wearing some sort of armor, only not metal. And she had a sword hanging on her side. I was frightened by her presence and debated with myself as to whether or not to tell Tristan. *You've just been watching too many movies, that's all,* I told myself. Still, this dream worried me more than even my dreams about Jimmy or my parents.

I was up early, excited to see Tristan. I hurriedly pulled out a pair of dark jeans, my blue knit sweater, and hiking boots. I took a quick shower and dressed. I went to the hall closet, grabbed my backpack, and proceeded to fill it with emergency essentials: firstaid kit, blanket, dry socks, etc. Then I made a steaming hot thermos of cocoa and slipped it into the side pouch. I went over to the coat closet in the living room, got a jacket, and placed it in the top of the pack. *Now,* I said to myself as I looked around, *I think I have everything.* After reexamining my gear, I was satisfied that I hadn't left anything vitally important.

I poured myself a cup of coffee and walked to the window. The sun was coming up. It was going to be a gorgeous day. Something moved in the trees. I sat my coffee cup down on the counter and leaned against the sink to watch. It was the panther! He stopped and just stood there, still as a statue!

He was breathtaking! He seemed to deliberately look straight at me! No one is going to believe this! Then it hit me. Get the camera, dummy! I could get a picture and show it to the wildlife agent. I started to turn; the camera was just behind me, clipped to the backpack. Before I made the full circle, Tristan walked in the door. I glanced back out the window, and the beautiful cat was gone.

"Tristan!" I squealed. He looked totally fabulous. His hair was down this morning, and he was dressed in a red pullover and faded jeans. His mesmerizing electric-blue eyes were staring intently at me, like it was the first time he had ever seen me. His gorgeous smile lit up the entire room, and I shivered from head to toe as I looked at him.

"Hey, sugar, are you ready?" His voice was so deep and smooth.

"I think so. I'm so glad you're back. I've missed you so much." My eyes lowered, and a blush burned in my cheeks. Tristan had walked over to stand in front of me. He placed one finger under my chin and lifted my face as he looked into my eyes. As soon as he touched me, I felt my blood start to heat; the electric jolts started to pulse through my every nerve, and my lips started to tremble. *Why didn't he kiss me? Could he tell the fire he ignited just with the slightest touch?*

"You have no idea how painful it's been to be away from you. I promise never to let them talk me into going to one of those things again!" He stepped back into that *safe zone* again, only to leave me trembling in my shoes.

"We better get going." His breath was beginning to quicken as we stood there.

"Yeah, I guess we should go." I locked the door while Tristan tossed my pack into the back of the jeep.

"Where are we hiking today?" I asked as we started down the main road.

"I thought we'd head over to North Carolina, hike some of the back trails on Grandfather Mountain." His stare was so intense I could feel it burning right through me. It made my heart pound, and I started to fidget.

"That's great!" My throat seemed to have closed up. My words came out broken. I cleared my throat and attempted again to speak.

"The fall colors are at peak now, it'll be gorgeous!" I rambled. He seemed a little preoccupied, and I felt like I needed to carry the conversation.

"So, did you see anything strange this morning?" I asked. Tristan slowly turned back toward me.

"No, like what?" His blue eyes were shining, almost as if my question was amusing.

"I was looking out my kitchen window this morning and a huge, beautiful cat walked out of the trees! Are you sure you didn't see it?" It had to have been standing there when he drove up! I thought.

"What kind of cat? Like a huge house cat, a mountain lion, bobcat?"

"No...more like a panther...a black one," I answered. Tristan grinned as if I were telling some crazy joke.

"I didn't see anything, let alone a panther, which by the way are not indigenous to this area. If we lived in the Amazon, maybe." He chuckled. "Are you sure the light wasn't playing tricks on your eyes?" he mused.

I was right—no one is going to believe me. "Maybe." I decided not to attempt convincing him I was sane. We rode in silence for what seemed like an hour.

"Tristan..." I started. "Umm, I've been debating about telling you something." His head turned quickly toward me with a panicked expression, like he was expecting me to say something he didn't want to hear.

"What is it, baby? Is something wrong?" His voice sounded nervous.

"No. Oh, honey, I'm sorry. I didn't mean for it to sound that way!" Sometimes I just didn't think of how I worded things. The jeep bounced suddenly as we turned off onto a back road that obviously saw little traffic.

"I've been having weird dreams again," I told him. Tristan had pulled into a turnout at the foot of a small trail overgrown with brush. He turned off the engine and adjusted himself in the seat to face me.

"What have you been dreaming?" He seemed to be genuinely interested in what I was about to say, so I guess it was safe to assume he didn't think I was too crazy. I proceeded to tell him about the dark, damp room, the scraps on the floor, and the woman. His eyes seemed to widen as I described her to him.

"I'm sure it's just a lack of sleep and too many movies," I concluded.

"You're probably right, sugar. I can't see that there is anything in the dream to associate with your normal day-to-day life," he assured me.

"That's what I thought too. I just don't understand why it bothers me so much." I sat with my head down and my eyes fixed on the floorboard.

"Maybe you're just stressed about my being gone and your problems at work," he said.

"Oh yeah, about work, I forgot to tell you I quit yesterday." I must have sounded pleased with my announcement. Tristan smiled as if he were just as pleased to hear the news as I was to give it.

"You're probably right. The dreams are most likely the stress." I seemed to feel better about it now, and I was sure Tristan was right— he always is.

"Well, are you ready for the treacherous terrain?" he teased.

"I am. So, let's get to it!" I smiled, feeling more relaxed. I walked to the back of the jeep and lifted my gear out.

"Olivia, I need to walk up the hill and make a quick call. My pager is on vibrate, and I want to make sure there's no big emergency before we start up the trail." He looked apologetic about the delay.

"Sure, honey, I'll just take the opportunity to rest while I can," I teased.

He smiled and started walking toward the embankment. "I won't be long, promise!" he called back over his shoulder.

SOULBOUND: DESTINY'S MOVE

TRISTAN WAITED UNTIL he was well out of Olivia's sight before he picked up his speed to reach the clearing at the top of the hill. He hit the speed dial on his cell phone.

"Tristan, aren't you out with Olivia?" Nick's voice sounded surprised.

"Yes, Nick, she's waiting down at the jeep. I needed to call you, it's important. She's having dreams again!" Tristan informed him.

"What are they about?" Tristan filled him in, being careful not to leave out even the slightest detail.

"Nick, you know who she's describing!" Tristan's voice was beginning to sound panicked.

"Althea!" Nick answered.

"They're planning to kidnap her! We have to keep it from happening somehow!" Tristan exclaimed.

"I'm doubling the guard around her house as we speak. Safrina will be able to pick up their scent should they try anything tonight. I'm planning to see her later. I've missed her terribly," Nick admitted to Tristan.

"What do you mean you've missed her?" Tristan was surprised that Nick had not been with her recently.

"I left Wednesday night, and I was called to an informal hearing of the council. They, by the way, were happy to excuse your absence due to your duties in Boston. You know I couldn't call her from there! I also had a little run-in with a couple of Lucas's little puppets," Nick explained.

"You mean she hasn't seen either one of us in three days! No wonder she's stressed and dealing with a huge bout of anxiety." "Tristan, you have no idea how anxious she is right now, so please take good care of her today." Nick sounded distressed as he spoke.

"I always do, my friend," Tristan spoke kindly to Nick, sensing something was weighing heavily on his mind other than the immediate problem.

"We'll talk more later. I can't keep her waiting much longer." Without another word, he turned off the phone and walked out at the jeep in the breath of a second.

"EVERYTHING ALL RIGHT, or is the treacherous climb cancelled?" I asked as Tristan walked up beside me.

"Yeah, everything's fine; we have the rest of the day to ourselves, undisturbed, promise." Tristan smiled as he pulled his backpack out of the jeep.

We started up the overgrown trail. Tristan was much better at this than I was. He moved along the landscape with such confidence and stealth. Although I wasn't quite as sure-footed, I managed to keep up easily enough.

The hike was quiet. Tristan still seemed a little distant. The silence gave my mind time to play with me. *Maybe he's found someone else, someone at the seminar. He's surely not taking me up on top of a mountain to tell me it's over!* I knew that didn't make sense, yet he has been preoccupied all morning; he does seem different since his return. *She must be beautiful. I'm about to lose him!* A pain shot through my chest at the image in my mind. I stopped and sat down on a log. I was clutching my chest with both hands, trying to breathe. *I can't lose him, I can't!*

In an instant, Tristan was beside me. "Are you hurt? Olivia!" His voice sounded frightened. "I'm so sorry. I forgot you're not used to a climb this steep. Why didn't you tell me you needed to rest?" When I didn't respond immediately, his expression became panicked. "Olivia, can you speak?" He was starting now to sound frantic.

"I'm okay, just give me a minute," I answered. He let his breath out as if he had been holding it the entire time.

SOULBOUND: DESTINY'S MOVE

"Just don't scare me like that! I thought you were having a heart attack!"

I looked at him, bewildered. "Why would you be worried? You're a doctor for crying out loud! You can handle anything." I smiled, trying to put him at ease.

"No, not anything. I couldn't handle something happening to you and definitely could not handle being the cause! With the exception of last June, I've never been more scared, no, that's not the word"—he breathed—" totally petrified in my entire life as I was just now!" He meant it; I could see sheer fear etched in his face.

"Please, don't ever do that to me again!" he begged.

"Tristan, I'm so sorry. I'm fine, see, just a little winded, that's all." I felt guilty for my childish behavior. I had let my overactive imagination get the better of me again and, as a result, nearly gave poor Tristan a physical breakdown. "Let's continue the hike. I'm sure we can find a better view than the one from this log!" I tried to be playful.

"Are you sure? We can stay here."

I looked down at his face as he remained seated. His expression let me know how very concerned he was for my well-being. Knowing this gave me a warm, comfortable feeling.

"Trust me, I'll be fine," I insisted. Tristan stood up and waited as I readjusted my pack and started out behind him. We hadn't been on the trail that long, maybe forty-five minutes, when we came onto a huge rock jutting out over the side of the mountain. You could see the hills for miles! "Tristan...look...it's beautiful!" I gasped." Do we have to go any farther? I think this is perfect!" Tristan walked over beside me and admired the beautiful view.

"You're right, this is perfect." He dropped his backpack, and so did I. I rummaged around and pulled out the blanket. Tristan spread it out on the grass beside the huge stone. It didn't seem to alter the view.

I unclipped the camera from the strap and sat down cross-legged on the blanket. As I prepared for my first shot, I felt Tristan lean in beside me. I immediately felt the electricity through every nerve in my body.

As I put the camera down, I felt his arm brush across my back as he reached up to release my hair from the ponytail. As my hair fell to my shoulders, he ran his hand down to the tips.

"I like it down against the blue." He breathed into my ear. My pulse quickened, and my breathing became shallow and erratic. Tristan had never been this close to me. He had always remained just outside that personal space. Now, he was crossing into it! He moved around, gently easing me back until my head was lying on the blanket.

He was sitting with his arm across me, looking down. His long black hair hung down, shielding our beautiful private moment from the outside world.

"You are positively radiant," he whispered. I have never been privileged to anything so stunning as you, Olivia Ryan." His voice was deep, almost a low growl. His eyes were intense. He placed his hand to my face and traced my lips with the edge of his thumb. My entire body trembled! His tender touch ignited a fire within me that I thought surely would turn me to ashes. *If he doesn't kiss me, I'm going to spontaneously combust!* I thought.

I reached to touch his face, expecting him to pull back, but he allowed it. I traced every curve of it. Tristan let out a soft moan and trembled at my touch. I was surprised he would have the same reaction as I did a moment ago. He leaned closer; I could feel his warm breath on my lips. I looked into his eyes, those mesmerizing electric-blue eyes! Suddenly, I saw the fire burning deep inside. The flames were bright, and the heat was as intense as the fire burning within me.

I wanted to get closer. I wanted the flame inside him to wrap itself around me! I kept getting closer. I could feel it, but I still wasn't part of it. I was almost touching it.

Tristan rolled over! *Oh god. This isn't happening—not again!* My mind was whirling.

"I'm sorry, Olivia, that shouldn't have happened!" Tristan's head was down as he sat with his back to me. He was still breathing heavily. I hadn't found the strength to move.

"Tristan—what's wrong? Did I..."

"No!" Tristan stopped me. "You did everything perfect...you are perfect! I have never ached so badly for anything more than I ache for you!"

"Then why?" My voice was low and weak. He turned back toward me, his face anguished as he looked at me lying there, my cheeks damp with the tears that had silently started flowing. He reached down and gently wiped the tears from my face. His expression was soft as he spoke.

"Because it's not right. I can't...When its right, we'll be together," he whispered. "I've got to hold on!"

"Hold on for what? I don't understand." I searched his face, trying hard to make sense of what was happening.

"I will have you. We will be a part of each other. I know it!" His voice was almost a breath. "Please, baby, don't be angry with me. I lost control, and for what I've done, for what I was...about to do, I am deeply sorry!" He looked hurt...like...like a wounded kitten.

"Tristan, sweetheart, I'm not angry, please don't disappear!" He looked down at me as if my words were a dagger that I had just thrust in his heart.

"Disappear! I couldn't. I need you near me. If only...if it could just be..." Tristan never finished a sentence.

This was happening! The same words as Nick spoke before he disappeared. I'm sorry, I can't, if only. What kind of curse am I under that I would lose them both? I just wanted to die. I couldn't bear this torture, this loss! "Tristan, please..." Suddenly everything became hazy and then black.

I woke on my own bed, a blanket spread over me, and my feet were bare.

"What happened?" Everything was still hazy.

Tristan appeared at my bedside. "Olivia, I'm glad you're awake." He knelt by my side, gently stroking my hair as he spoke. "I'm so sorry for what I've done...for what I was about to do." Tristan's voice was soft and intent on fervently seeking forgiveness for something.

"Tristan, you have nothing to be sorry for. I'm sorry I fainted. You must think I'm crazy!" I was so embarrassed.

"No...no, baby, you have more strength than I expected."

"What do you mean, than you expected?" *Just what was he expecting?* I wondered.

"Not now. We'll talk another time, just rest now. I have to go, but I'll be back in a couple of days." I started to protest, but Tristan placed a finger on my lips, only to ignite the burning again.

"I promise, day after tomorrow. I just need some time to think." His words were meant to reassure me; instead, I became weak and afraid. He stood and looked down at me.

"Simply amazing!" were the only words he uttered before disappearing through the doorway. I just didn't have the strength to sit up. I was so exhausted I drifted off. My dreams were all jumbled up. I tossed and turned in my sleep, moaning. Falling...the black cat...

Nick's eyes...burning...scraps of food...floating...the woman... flames...darkness...Tristan's blue eyes.

I was startled awake by my own voice calling out to someone. I sat up on the edge of the bed and pushed my hair back. I couldn't take many more days like this! I noticed the time; it was almost four o'clock in the evening. I had slept for four hours!

Frightening Truth 14.

I walked into the kitchen to get something to drink and sat down at the kitchen table. I couldn't stop thinking about my last night with Nick and what had transpired today. I saw the hurt in both their eyes, both men uttering almost the exact same words before they left. I wish I could understand. Where did they go? Why did they go? I needed to hear Nick's voice. I needed to be near him! I missed Tristan! I felt so totally abandoned and alone.

I walked to the sink to pour the rest of my juice down the drain, when the phone rang. It was so quiet around me and so unexpected I dropped the glass, shattering it into a million pieces.

I grabbed the phone before it could ring again to further my nervous state. "Hello." My heart was still pounding.

"Olivia," then it stopped as I heard the silken voice on the other end.

"Olivia, are you there?"

I tried to fill my lungs with enough air to speak. "Nikolas!" I gasped.

"Yes, love. I want to apologize for not calling you sooner. I had some urgent business out of town, and it was a remote area. I haven't been able to think of anything but the look on your face when I left the other night. I have agonized over leaving things the way I did. I wish I could find the words to express how sorry I am." His apology was so heartfelt and sincere. I still didn't understand why he was torturing himself like this.

"Nick, I'm just so glad to hear your voice," I answered breathlessly. "I thought I'd never hear it again!" My heart was in my throat. I've never been so relieved, so...filled with pure joy in my life!

"Olivia, I have caused you so much pain!" His voice sounded hurt and full of remorse.

"Nikolas, please. I've never been angry with you."

"I need to explain everything to you. I called in hopes that you would come to dinner tonight at my house." He sounded nervous.

"I would love to have dinner tonight. I'm not coming to hear an explanation; I just want to see you." My heart was pounding so hard I could hear every beat. I hadn't lost him. "Then I'll pick you up at six thirty."

"I'll be ready." I knew I sounded a little too enthusiastic, but I couldn't help it.

"I'll see you in a little while then. Olivia?" "Yes, Nick," I answered.

"I do love green." His voice was soft as he spoke. I smiled to myself. I knew exactly what he wanted.

"I'll try to remember that," I said and hung up. I looked at the clock. I had less than an hour to get ready!

After my shower, I blow dried my hair and pulled it back in a tight bun on the back of my head. It took a little more effort since my hair had grown several inches since last spring. I dressed in my emerald-green V-neck sweater and a pair of black knit slacks. My soft leather slip-ons were purely for my comfort. I hoped Nick's attention would not be on my feet! I reached into the jewelry box and pulled out the delicate gold chain that held the diamond pendant he had given me and the small diamond stud earrings that were a gift from my parents.

I examined my overall look in the mirror. It seems my nervous lack of appetite, combined with Tristan's vigorous outings, like hiking, rock climbing, and dancing, has definitely paid off. I was in the best physical condition of my life! I was quite satisfied with my appearance. I only hoped Nick would be.

SOULBOUND: DESTINY'S MOVE

All my efforts seemed moot when Nick walked through the door in all his perfection. He was dressed totally in black, black button-up shirt and black slacks to his black dress shoes. My lord, he was stunning! Just the sight of him made my knees weak. Nick took in a long breath as he seemed to scan me from head to toe. Ugh, I knew I should have changed the shoes!

"Olivia, you are absolutely breathtaking!"

I lowered my eyes, my cheeks turning a nice rose color. No matter how many times Nick or Tristan gave me compliments, it always seemed to embarrass me. That perfect smile crossed his lips, and my heart sped up.

He looked down at me and winked. "Shall we go?" He waved his hand forward, still smiling.

He held the car door for me as always, and soon we were headed east out of town. We turned off the main road and drove for about ten minutes then made a left turn onto another paved road. We went around a couple of curves and turned again onto a well-graveled road that seemed to wind around forever. All the while we were on a steady incline up the mountain.

"Where is your house? On top of the mountain?" I was totally lost, and I thought I knew all the back roads there were in this county.

"Well, kind of." Nick smiled.

"It's certainly secluded," I remarked.

"I like my privacy," Nick answered as we came to a stop at what appeared to be the middle of nowhere. "Why are we stopping?"

"We're here, love." Nick grinned.

"Where's the house?" I thought he was joking.

"It's right there." Nick pointed to my right. If it were not for the faint glow of a lamp through what appeared to be a huge, tinted window, I would never have seen it!

I stepped out of the car and looked up as Nick turned on the outside lights. All I could see was what appeared to be logs framing a row of huge, tinted windows and a front door. From there up and back, nothing but mountain and trees.

Nick walked around and opened the front door. My eyes were wide in astonishment. He took my jacket and hung it on a coat rack just inside. I followed him down about five steps into a large foyer covered with the most beautiful brown-and-tan marble tile. There was a huge set of double doors to my right and a gorgeous arched staircase with an intricately designed wrought iron railing. To the left was a short hall that led to another room.

"I thought we could have dinner in the kitchen area tonight. It's much more comfortable than the dining room." I jumped when Nick spoke. I was so enthralled with my surroundings.

"Oh, I'm sure that would be perfect." I kept staring at the huge staircase. Nick noticed my preoccupation with it.

"Is something wrong, love?" Nick asked.

"No, I didn't see a roof, so...how can there be an upstairs?" I asked in total wonder.

Nikolas chuckled. "Well, my house is built into the mountain, not on it," he answered.

"Oh..." my face turned crimson. "I've never seen a subterranean home before. It's nothing like I imagined. This is beautiful!" I breathed.

"Thank you, I'm glad you like it. Maybe after dinner you'd like to see the rest of it?" he asked.

"Yes, I would. This is fascinating!" I knew I was behaving like a wide-eyed child, but I was totally fascinated with this outwardly invisible house.

"Dinner is ready. Shall we?" Nick motioned for me to follow him. His eyes were sparkling as if my amazement brought him the same joy as watching a child at Christmas. I blushed again and followed him down the hall.

The kitchen was on the left side of the hallway just past the stairs. It was half the size of my house! The floors were a sand-colored ceramic tile and the countertops black granite. There were tons of cupboards, all-natural wood and every appliance stainless. It was so light for a room with no windows.

Nick pulled out a chair at the beautifully set table. When I was seated, he lit the candles in the center and dimmed the bright lights. He poured a glass of white wine and began serving the meal. He had prepared a light salad and then served a perfectly cooked trout almandine over a fluffy bed of rice pilaf. He then poured fresh brewed coffee and served the most delicious black-forest cake I had ever tasted.

"I enjoyed the lovely dinner, Nick. I had no idea you were a chef." I smiled. Nikolas was breathtaking as I studied him across the table.

I recalled our last night together and the way the moonlight had enhanced what was already perfect (*if that were possible*). I remembered the look of his soft blond hair shaping a perfectly framed face, accented with those beautiful full lips. I loved his deep black eyes, the kind of eyes you could fall into and never stop. *I had almost done that very thing.* I couldn't help allowing my assessment of this gorgeous man to wander along the silhouette of his upper torso; I must be dreaming. I couldn't imagine a vision of perfection like Nikolas Riggs ever being truly interested in me. I was so mesmerized it caught me off guard when he spoke.

"Thank you, but I'm far from chef quality, it's just a hobby." He smiled.

"Um...well, thank you just the same," I responded with a light pink to my cheeks.

"If you're finished, I did promise you a tour of the rest of the house." He reminded me as he stood. My heart skipped a beat when he took hold of my chair and motioned toward the hall. We made a left and again descended another three steps. We entered a room on the left, and I noticed a doorway that obviously was a second entrance up to the kitchen area. I realized then what Nick meant by the kitchen being more comfortable for two people. The dining room was enormous. The huge dark-wood table held twelve chairs. The room was very elegant, meant solely for entertaining important guests. Nick smiled as if he could read my thoughts.

"It is a bit ostentatious, but it does serve a purpose, I assure you." He grinned. "Let's move on." He motioned me back into the hall. He then led me through a short corridor that came out into another smaller foyer that mirrored the entrance hall at the front door. We entered Nikolas's study. It was lined with bookshelves; our community library would be envious of this collection. There was a corner fireplace on the back side of the room, and just to the left, centered near the back wall, was a beautiful mahogany desk with a high black leather chair. Nick's computer was set up on one end. All the furnishings were leather, and the hardwood floor was partially covered with a rust-and-gold Persian rug.

"I prefer to do a lot of my work at home." Nick broke the silence. I was so amazed by the house I hadn't realized I had not uttered a word since we left the kitchen.

"You certainly have a nice office," I muttered, not quite knowing how to respond.

"Well, I figure, just because it's work doesn't mean it can't be comfortable." Nick was ambling over to turn off his computer as I gazed at the collection of books on one of the shelves.

"Have you read all these?" I asked as I gave a swooping gesture toward all the bookshelves.

"Every single one, some several times," he answered.

The rest of the house was just as remarkable. He took me into a media/game room that was set up with comfortable chairs and ottomans for watching movies on a huge projection screen and a beautiful billiard table. There were chairs positioned against the wall for the comfort of the players, and a well-stocked bar and another fireplace in the corner. A set of double doors led into a huge indoor pool. We exited the game room and walked over to another corridor that led to yet another smaller staircase.

"I think you will enjoy this most of all," Nick said as he led me to the top of the stairs. We came out onto an open sunroom that led to an outside garden. Nick turned on the outside lights to show a fabulous array of floral beds brightly colored with fall flowers. There were so many hues of red, yellow, green, and burgundy. The winding stone paths of the garden seemed to have no end. Wooden and wrought iron benches dotted the walkways.

"Oh, Nikolas! This looks like it was designed from a fairy tale. It's gorgeous! You're right, I would probably spend most of my time right here." My eyes were lit up like candles. Nick seemed pleased by my approval. It was almost as if he had this designed with me in mind. I smiled up at him as he stood silently beside me.

"Now show me the upstairs." I was most curious about the size of rooms that could be built inside on a second floor without being visible to the outside world.

We climbed the staircase from the back foyer. The upstairs hall was open straight to the front stairway. There were only three rooms on the second floor. One of the rooms was just to our right at the end of the hall. It was a very large room, masculine in its furnishing. The huge king-sized headboard looked as if it came right out of a sixteenth-century castle. The colors were done in rusts and tan with accents of black in the bedding. The bath was large and luxurious.

"I assume this is your room?" I timidly asked.

Nick shifted awkwardly as he answered. "Um...yes, it is." He averted his eyes.

How strange, I thought. *Someone as strong and confident as Nick would be uncomfortable showing a woman his bedroom.* I was sure I wasn't the first female to enter these doors.

He took me then to the far end of the hall just past the staircase into another masculine-designed room. This was just as large, only decorated with more modern furnishings. The bed and chests were oak, and the colors were earthier, greens and tans.

The last room was amazing. It was decorated with a feminine hand. There was a fireplace against the back wall, just facing the center of the room, and a huge chaise lounge with a reading lamp in the corner. The other side of the room opened up to a walk-in closet and a luxurious full bath with a whirlpool tub and a cascading shower. The king-sized canopy bed in the center of the room was covered with a white eyelet comforter and surrounded with intricate white lace curtains. It looked like the bed where the prince would have found Sleeping Beauty! I wondered what woman had occupied this room. Nikolas must have loved her very much to create such a room for her personal sanctuary. I didn't want to dwell on that thought.

We went back downstairs to the double doors I saw when I entered the house.

"This is the sitting room. I have a nice fire going in the fireplace, and I thought we could relax in here to talk," Nick said as he opened the doors to reveal a large room with an enormous stone fireplace in the center. The walls on each side were lined with more books. The far-right wall had the row of tinted windows I saw out front. The remaining walls were decorated with beautiful paintings and antique wall hangings. Delicate tables of dark wood were strewn about the room, topped with crystal vases and hurricane lamps. Three huge, overstuffed chairs were arranged in a semicircle around the fireplace. This was definitely the kind of room someone could relax in.

Nikolas gestured to one of the chairs by the fire. I took my seat, and he sat directly opposite. The chairs were arranged in closer proximity than they appeared.

"Nick, thank you for showing me this extraordinary home. It is without a doubt the most beautiful place I've ever seen!" I raved.

"I am so glad you liked it. So, this is somewhere you could be comfortable even though it has very few windows?" He smiled.

"Yes, most definitely!" I stated.

Nikolas shifted uneasily in his chair. I could tell there was something pressing seriously on his mind.

"Nick, you told me on the phone there was something you wanted to talk to me about. I mean something to explain." I wanted him to be comfortable in knowing I was still expecting this talk.

"Yes. That's why I wanted you to come here tonight. I knew we would have the privacy and plenty of time to talk." He fidgeted as he spoke. "There is something about me you need to know... to understand, I mean...before you choose your path." Nick continued to fidget as he obviously searched for a way to continue. This was the first time I had ever seen him nervous or unsure of himself.

"I don't understand what you mean by...choose my path. Life just comes at you, and you have to move with it, you know?" I said, trying to impress my disbelief in fate, karma, and all that junk.

"Oh," he mumbled. "This is going to be more difficult than I thought," he almost whispered. As he spoke, he stared into the fire. After a long pause, he began again.

"Olivia, some things come at you out of the blue or seemingly so. You may not always accept it, but you learn to live with it," he started to explain.

"Exactly, like I said, you just learn to move with it!" I felt a great comfort in our mutual understanding.

"No, that's not exactly what I mean. I'm obviously not very good at this. Let me try to explain this in a different way. Take the loss of your parents for instance." Nick looked at me compassionately. I felt the sting of the memory but tried not to let it show. Still he could tell how painful the memory was; he hung his head down and sighed then looked back to me and continued.

"You had told me about your dreams, and even though you may not have realized it, you were not totally surprised by the news," he said. The memory of the dreams flooded my mind. The guilt I felt for not revealing them to my parents caused me to shiver, and the salty sting of tears began to form in the corner of my eyes.

"Please forgive me. I truly do not wish to cause you pain." Nick's eyes told that he wished he had not used this particular scenario for his explanation for whatever he was trying so desperately to tell me.

"I know," I whispered as I tried to choke back the sob pushing to escape. He reached out to touch my cheek but pulled back. I wish I could understand why he would not touch me. Maybe before this night was over, I would find out. I hoped.

"Olivia, you are stronger than you give yourself credit." His soft silken voice brought me back to the conversation and the stinging pain it had caused. "Even though we don't understand why, it is the journey one's soul must take. The more informed we are, the better our judgment. You follow?" His gentle eyes were assessing my expression for a hint of understanding. Since he apparently found none, he continued. "We are never in complete control, but with enough knowledge, we are more capable of living with surprises, so to speak." He continued searching my face, but I just sat there, staring blankly.

"Nick, I don't have a clue what you're getting at; why don't you just say what's on your mind?"

"I'm trying to...it's just hard." He turned his eyes back to the fire.

"Why?" I asked.

"I'm not sure how you're going to react." He ran his hand nervously through his hair.

Oh no...he's going to tell me he doesn't want to see me anymore! I should have known it was too good to last. My stomach tightened, and my heart began to palpitate. "You're scaring me." I told him as the fear was now gripping every fiber of my being! I couldn't live if he wasn't part of my life. I didn't want to! I hadn't realized this before. *How could I be so selfish...and cruel? I have the same feelings for Tristan! Kandi was right. I am in love with both of them!* My mind was spinning. I love them both—equally! I didn't want to be without them...ever! Olivia, I scolded myself, what mess have you made now? How do I tell him about Tristan without hurting him, and how do I tell Tristan about Nikolas? Does Nikolas know? Is that why he made the remark "Before I choose my path"? *Oh, this is bad,* I thought, *really bad!* Before I could chastise myself anymore, Nick interrupted my thoughts.

"Olivia, are you all right? You look upset."

"Yes, I'm fine." My voice came out low and shaky. "The memory of my parents is hard for me." It wasn't a lie, but that pain seemed far less to me right now than the pain of losing him...or Tristan. I suddenly felt sick.

"Nikolas, would you excuse me for a moment?"

"Certainly, are you sure you're alright?"

"Yes, if you would please remind me where the bathroom is?" I needed to collect myself, prepare for the inevitable words that would rip the life from me. He had walked back to the staircase and was about to point me in the right direction when the front door came crashing in!

I fell back, catching my heel on the bottom step, slamming my ribs into the stairs. My heart felt like it was in my throat, and I was clutching the rail so fiercely I was sure I'd left an intention of my fingers in the iron.

"Nick, what the hell do you think you're doing? We agreed, and you've gone back on your word!" The intruder growled. "You were not supposed to bring her here!"

"Back off!" Nick hissed. Slowly I opened my eyes to see the intruder.

"Tristan? H-how...you followed me?"

"No!" he snapped, causing me to jump.

"Then how..."

"He knows!" Tristan answered, nodding toward Nikolas. "You've got some explaining to do!" He rasped as he turned his gaze back to Nick. "And you only have a few seconds!" Tristan glared as he spoke.

Revelation 15

Nick never seemed to lose his calm, but his voice told otherwise. He never moved, never flinched, even when Tristan made a step toward him.

"I do not now, nor will I ever owe you an explanation for my actions. Do you understand me?" It was obvious Nick was trying to control his anger. Tristan stood there, and it sounded almost as if he released a low growl.

"I wouldn't do that!" Nikolas warned. "Don't even think about it. She's not prepared!" Tristan immediately took in a long breath, and the calm returned to Nick's voice.

"Out of respect for Olivia and the situation, I will explain why she's here." Nick calmly looked at Tristan as he spoke.

I looked at the two standing there, Nikolas pale, angelic, and statuesque. Tristan was taller, broader shouldered than Nick with dark almond skin and jet-black hair. Just as Nick had perfect features, so too did Tristan. Both men were so beautiful, so exquisite. It occurred to me that my evil ways had caught up to me. What a deceitful, vile person I was. I always knew this would come to no good. *That's what you get for burning the candle at both ends. It's bound to meet in the middle.* Suddenly a look of pure shock crossed my face. I stood up.

"Hold on. You knew I was seeing Nikolas, and, Nick, you knew I was seeing Tristan? Oh my god, you know each other!" I slumped back down onto the stairs. The tables had turned; I was no longer the player, but the one being played. I became infuriated. The heat started to burn on my face as my anger rose. "You have been lying to me, all this time?" My breath quickened.

"In the hospital, you pretended you only met briefly. Why would you do that? Why would the two of you deceive me like that?" The hurt at their deception started to override the anger, and the tears started to spill down my face.

"Under the circumstances, we wanted to relieve you of some of the stress you were under. We knew you worried about us finding out about each other, and we wanted you to get well," Nick tried to explain.

"Did you both think this was a joke or some kind of game?" My anger was starting to rise again. "Did you enjoy yourselves; did you enjoy watching me squirm? I bet you got a good laugh, huh!"

"Calm down, Olivia. This has never been a game...or a joke. This is not what you think!" Tristan spoke with his palms out, urging me to be still.

"Well then, *please* tell me!" I glared at them as I spoke through clenched teeth. Nikolas stepped toward me, and I flinched back, suddenly feeling frightened.

This is what Nick meant about "choosing my path." They were going to make me choose! What was I going to do? I couldn't...I didn't know how! All at once I couldn't breathe. The tears began to fall in despair. I was no longer angry. How could I condemn them for the very same thing I thought I was doing? Nick and Tristan were talking, but I was too numb to pay any attention.

"Tristan, I wanted to tell her about us before she chooses her path. I want her decision to be her own will," Nick explained.

"I see." Tristan nodded. "Don't you think I should have been invited for this, Nick?"

"Surely, Tristan, you can see how...um...awkward that would have been," he said as he gestured to me. A smile broke across Tristan's face, a beautiful, perfect smile.

"Yes, I do see, and she does need to be informed before she makes a choice." Tristan's eyes glanced toward Olivia.

"Good, we're in agreement!" Nick relaxed. "Let's calm dear Olivia and return to the sitting room," Nick suggested as he reached to shake Tristan's hand. Tristan helped me to my feet. As Nikolas patted Tristan on the back, he looked over his shoulder and laughed.

"You owe me a front door."

Tristan chuckled. "This is going to be a long night."

"Yes, I know." Nikolas sighed. He left Tristan to help me relax into the chair by the fire and returned with a cup of hot chamomile tea.

"Sip this, love, and try to calm yourself," Nick said. I took the cup from him and sipped the hot liquid.

"What about your door? It's going to get cold in here tonight." I don't know why I was so concerned; he didn't seem to be.

"Don't worry. I have a maintenance man living on the grounds. I called him when I went to make the tea. He's going to come up and fix it." Nick smiled.

"Now, you were about to explain." I looked directly at them both when I spoke.

"Well, for starters. Tristan and I have known each other for a very long time. We were aware of each other's...uhhh...how do I put it politely...social engagements concerning you." Nick smiled an impish smile as he spoke.

"As I stated before, Olivia, it's not a game, and we want to explain," Tristan added.

"Okay, this had better be a very good explanation," I warned. "I assure you, love. It is!" Nikolas was still smiling impishly.

"I mean extremely good, or I'm walking, got it!" I tried to sound stern.

"Oh, trust us, the explanation is...life altering!" Tristan smirked.

"All right then, start explaining." I leaned back in the chair and took another sip from my cup.

"Olivia, we need you to think very carefully right now," Nikolas urged.

"Think about what?" I asked, not following his request.

"About the odd things that seemed to happen since dating us and even before we met." Tristan smiled as he spoke.

"For instance?" I needed some kind of nudge to put my thoughts in motion.

"Let me see. Do you remember waiting in the line at the restaurant with your parents last summer?" Nick asked.

"Yes," I acknowledged. "Everything seemed pretty normal. Except..."

"Except what?" Nick leaned forward in his chair, waiting for my response.

"While we waited in line, I remember this strange scent in the air. But it wasn't the first time I experienced it."

"Did it seem odd to you that no one else seemed to notice it?" Nick pointed out.

"Well, yes, but how did you know that?" I was beginning to feel uncomfortable. I hadn't met Nick then. Now there was a red flag! Tristan laughed out loud, and both Nikolas and I looked calmly around at him.

"Go on, Nick." Tristan was still chuckling. "This is about to get real interesting."

I looked back toward Nikolas. What does he mean? My curiosity was beginning to override my growing fear that something wasn't right about Nick's knowledge of these events before we met.

"Oh no...you've been stalking me!" I gasped.

"No, Olivia. I do not need to stalk. I was just watching over you...to keep you out of danger. It wasn't time yet," Nick reasoned.

"Danger? I don't recall being in danger!" I snipped.

"We'll explain that later," Nick protested, not wanting the conversation to get sidetracked.

"Fine, so what was the scent, and why didn't anyone around me notice it?"

Nikolas cleared his throat and sat forward again. "It was me," he stated matter-of-factly.

"You? Impossible, I don't smell it now and you're sitting right here!"

"I have the ability to release it at any time," Nick said this as if I was supposed to believe it without question.

"Right, I don't know what kind of idiot you think I am, but I do know people can't release pheromones in the air at will!"

Nick's eyes widened. "You know what that scent is?" He seemed stunned.

My face started to burn. "I'm right then?" I asked, feeling more embarrassed.

"Olivia." Nick smiled gorgeously. "You are priceless, love, and much more astute than you give yourself credit." "We'll see," Tristan mused as he walked over beside my chair. "Now do you remember the movie earlier that day?" Tristan coaxed.

"Of course, it was the last outing with..." My voice trailed off as I thought of my last day out with my parents.

Tristan reached over and stroked my hair. "I'm sorry that memory brings you pain, baby."

"No, it's all right actually I treasure that memory."

"I'm glad." Tristan's voice was soft and comforting. "Now what do you remember?" He asked, bending down by my chair.

I thought intently, trying to recall every detail. "Yes, I remember getting a tingly electric feeling, sort of like"—I blushed—" how I feel when you're close." My eyes lowered from

Tristan's. "I also thought I heard an animal loose in the theatre. I know it's absurd, but I could've sworn I heard a growl."

Tristan's eyes danced. "That was unintentional." He laughed.

"Are you telling me you go to movies and make growling noises in the dark?"

"Um...not exactly, I just got a little caught up in everything." Tristan looked a little embarrassed. Nikolas caught our attention with a loud chuckle.

"I would so love to have been there." He continued his snickering.

"I'd rather be remembered for a growl than a stench!" Tristan rebutted.

"Not a growl, Tris, a purr!" Nick teased.

"By the way," Tristan turned his attention back to me. "Why do you watch those mindless movies anyway?"

"They're not mindless. They're entertaining," I defended. "Besides, vampires, werewolves, and the like fascinate me."

"Well, sugar." Tristan leaned back in his chair. "Sit back and prepare to be thoroughly fascinated!" His grin was wide and mischievous.

"What are you two trying to tell me? I don't see how making fun of my interest in mythical or supernatural beings has anything to do with the explanation concerning you both!" My irritation was definitely showing. "So, are you about to tell me some vampire story, or is it some other scary supernatural tale? Surely you didn't plan all this for an elaborate Halloween trick?"

Nikolas turned to Tristan with a look of total dismay.

"After that statement, how am I going to convince her of a single word that comes out of my mouth?" Nikolas threw his arms in the air.

"Nick, trust me, she'll believe us when we're finished." Tristan seemed quite entertained by my Halloween comment.

"I'd appreciate it if you both could try to remember I'm in the room! You could address your questions or concerns to me." I was really beginning to get aggravated.

"Of course, love, my apologies."

"And why don't you just say sorry, Nick, like everyone else. Tonight you have seemed so, so...formal! Not that you don't talk like that at other times, but not so much as now."

"I don't think he'll ever fully get the hang of talking like normal people. It wasn't in his upbringing. Trust me, I've tried to bring his mannerisms and speech into this century. I think he's done quite well up until tonight." Tristan laughed.

"This century? You talk like he's a hundred years old or something," I commented, trying to make light of my criticism.

"Or something," Nick added, smiling.

"Okay, you two, don't you think you've beaten around the bush long enough?" I asked.

Nick looked at Tristan as if I had just spoken some kind of mystery language.

"She's asking why we haven't gotten to the point yet," Tristan translated.

"Oh, well. We're trying to." Nick's voice sounded a little frustrated. "Promise you'll keep an open mind? Please reserve your opinions and learned prejudices until we're through." Nick's words were almost pleading.

"I promise, my mind is an open book. My opinions and prejudices, as you say, are now erased. I'm a fresh, clean page." I crossed my legs under me and took a sip of my tea. I was feeling quite smug at my ability to hold my own between the two of them. "Fine, then I will continue." Nick leaned forward. "As we had begun before this conversation got out of hand, you remember several strange happenings?"

"Yes, like the weird noises and the abrupt halt on my attack by

Jimmy Stanton."

"Uh-huh," Tristan acknowledged. "Go on," he prompted.

"Let's see, the cat I saw in the woods. There are no panthers in this area. Bobcats and mountain lions, but no panthers." I studied their faces as I gave my account of strange happenings. They sat quietly, neither one moving to interrupt my recollections. "It always seemed when I was feeling stressed or frightened, I would smell that wonderful aroma in the air and calm down almost immediately." My memories were starting to form a pattern. "I remember seeing the panther at the lake the last time I went fishing alone. No sooner did it disappear, Tristan showed up. I saw it again from my kitchen window, and before I could make a full turn, Tristan walked through the door. Wait a minute, are you saying all these weird things are connected to the two of you?"

I was trying to put the pieces of this puzzle together, but it still didn't make sense.

"The weird dream I had in the hospital?"

"What dream in the hospital?" Nikolas had sat to the edge of his seat as he glanced at Tristan.

"You never told us about any dreams after your attack!" As Tristan spoke, he stood up and walked to the edge of the fireplace.

"Well, I figured it was just all the pain killers you loaded me up on." I grinned sarcastically at Tristan.

"What was the dream?" Nick sounded a little impatient. It was apparent he did not take my dreams lightly.

"I dreamed you were both in my room, talking to each other. Tristan asked if you were thirsty. You said you could use a drink and then—" My sentence stopped cold. "It wasn't a dream, was it? Please tell me I'm in the middle of a nightmare!" My revelation almost caused me to bolt from the room. I got cold, shivering cold. Both Nick and Tristan were standing silent as if they were giving me time to process my epiphany. I dropped my cup to the floor, frozen in the chair. The chills were flowing over my skin in waves, my heart was beating so wildly I was certain it would burst any second, and it felt like the air had been cut off from my lungs.

"Olivia, please try to remain calm. You're in no danger!" Nikolas tried to reassure me.

"Olivia, tell us what you're thinking. Please!" Tristan was begging, and his eyes looked fearful. I looked without blinking, working desperately to keep my wits about me. I tried to speak, but nothing came out. Think, Olivia! I urged myself. I knew I had to regain my self-control. Nikolas just said I was in no danger. I looked back and forth between them. I jumped as Tristan repeated his question in the same fearful tone. This time I managed to utter only three words: "This is real!" my voice barely a whisper.

"We're not mind readers, love, what is real?" Nick tried to keep his voice soft and low. Just as in Tristan's, I could see the fear in Nick's eyes.

If they were telling me what I think they are, why should they be frightened? I pulled in a deep breath and found the courage to speak.

"Are you telling me...you're a...a..." My finger was pointing at Nikolas.

"I'm a what, love, what?" he coaxed.

"Vampire!" I whispered.

Nick took a long breath and released it slowly. "Yes, Olivia, that's exactly what I am." His voice and actions were still gentle, nonthreatening.

I turned to Tristan. "And you...are you some kind of werewolf?" I looked back at Nick. "But aren't you supposed to be enemies?"

"No. I am most certainly not a werewolf! Werewolves are dogs!" He gave an indignant sniff. "I am what you call a shapeshifter," he said with pride.

They had decided that for whatever reason, terror or ignorance, I wasn't going to try and escape. They seemed to relax enough to return to their seats.

"W-w-what's going to happen to me?" I asked, trying to control the trembling in my hands.

"Olivia, please try to calm down and relax. If you were in any danger from us, do you think you would be sitting here now? You would have been out of the picture a long time ago." Nick tried to reason.

"I'm not so sure. Maybe this whole thing has been a game for the two of you, you know, let's see how long we can play with our meal. The first to bite loses!" I couldn't imagine where I found the sarcasm let alone the courage to employ it.

Nick and Tristan looked at each other as if they were mortified by my insinuation.

"Olivia, we do not play games like that. I can see, though, why you might feel that way. Please trust that we are not planning you any harm," Nick insisted.

"This is ludicrous. I must be having another dream!" I exclaimed.

"No, baby, you're not dreaming," Tristan said. He was now sitting on the arm of my chair.

I hadn't even noticed Nick had left the room until he sat another cup of tea on the table beside me. I picked up the cup and took a drink. I studied Nick for the longest moment before I spoke.

"Nick, you are not playing a trick on me, right?" I watched his expression carefully for some sign as a giveaway to an elaborate joke. This was just too unbelievable.

"No tricks, love, promise." He smiled.

"But...you don't have...fangs!" I pointed out that I had noticed. Nick shook his head and smiled that gorgeous, perfect smile.

"I do when I need them," he explained. My look of disbelief left him at a loss.

"Show her, Nick," Tristan urged. "After all, seeing is believing." "I'm afraid she may faint or something." Nick looked worried.

"Nick, don't worry!" Tristan pointed to himself. "Doctor, remember!"

"No, Nick, I won't faint. I'm here and resigned to whatever my fate is. If this is real, show me. I'm stronger than you think." I wanted him to know—no, both of them to know—they were not going to kill a frightened little mortal. I would defy them if I could.

"All right, Olivia." Nick still seemed apprehensive. I saw him move his tongue across his teeth. As he did, I watched in amazement as the fangs lowered. I caught my breath as I stared, frightened, helpless, and...awed! I was mesmerized by the display. I jumped, pulling my feet up into the chair, as something touched my arm. My head whirled to see what it was.

There he stood, the magnificent black cat with the electric-blue eyes! It was the same beautiful black panther I had dreamed of getting close to since the first time I saw him out of my bedroom window.

"Tristan..." My voice was an anxious whisper. I reached my hand toward him as the panther lowered his head for me to make contact. His fur was soft and warm.

"What happens now?" I hesitantly asked, expecting the news of my impending doom any second. I realized my hand was still on the black cat's, I mean Tristan's, head. I quickly pulled it back and continued my steady gaze at Nikolas.

"Now, love, Tristan and I are prepared to answer your questions and explain why you're here." Nick's fangs were now retracted, and he looked far less menacing. He was again tender, beautiful, and comforting.

"So, sugar, are you thoroughly fascinated yet?"

"Very!" I was startled as I looked at Tristan now in his human form.

"H-how did you do that?" I stammered.

"Do what?"

"Change back without my noticing, and you're fully dressed. I figured you wouldn't have…" My cheeks were scarlet.

"Olivia dear, I've been doing this for a very, very long time! I've perfected my technique." His smile was wide and radiant. "Besides, I'm really fast!" He then laughed out loud. Nick dropped his head to hide a smile.

"What about when you're out? Do you carry clothing with you?" I was very curious as to how he managed in the woods.

"The short explanation, our people have developed a material that will withstand the change, and it's worn under my clothing. As for tonight, it's not that far to my room," he informed me.

"Before the garments, you wouldn't believe some of the clothing I've caught him wearing!" Nick was trying desperately to suppress an urge to laugh.

"I remember once back in the '70s I caught him running through the backyards of a residential area in Boston wearing a dark blue halter dress." Nick could barely contain himself now. "You were stunning." He chuckled. "Blue is definitely your color!" The vision of this massive man in a dress with the long black hair. Tristan lowered his head, and his face turned scarlet. My efforts to control myself were useless as I began to laugh uncontrollably. By now, Nick had held back as long as he could and joined me. It was the first time I had ever heard him really laugh out loud. It was the most beautiful sound!

"I had to go through that residential area. I couldn't remain in my animal form, and, well, you just needed to be there!" Tristan defended.

"All right, Tristan. I get the picture," I said as I regained my composure. I had concluded they didn't plan to kill me, at least not tonight. I started to feel more at ease in the room and found a higher level of confidence. It was odd, I thought, that I grasped this so quickly. It was as if the words "I'm a vampire" or "I'm a shifter" were as common as saying "I'm a doctor" or "I'm a lawyer."

"You told me you were ready to answer my questions now." I changed the subject.

"Yes, love. What would you like to know?" Nick leaned up in his chair, preparing to answer.

"First of all, I would like to know why I didn't meet Tristan the same night I met you."

"We were both very anxious to meet you, but we didn't think it was appropriate for both of us to show up together," Nick told me.

"We had to decide who would meet you first," Tristan continued.

"How did you make this decision?" I asked.

Both men turned and looked at each other. I could tell my question made them uncomfortable. My eyes shifted between them as it dawned on me. I giggled.

"What, did you do draw straws?" I asked. "No," Tristan said.

"Then what?" I asked again, still smiling.

"We flipped a coin," Tristan mumbled under his breath as he steadily stared at the floor.

"Excuse me, you what?" I coaxed him to speak up.

"We flipped a coin!" he piped up. I looked at them for a second then burst into another loud raucous of laughter. Both men sat silently in their humiliation until I got it out of my system.

"You mean the two of you, highly intelligent, grown men, a doctor and a lawyer, couldn't come up with a more reasonable and mature solution than flipping a coin?" I was using all my restraint to hold back another outburst.

"As Tristan said a while ago, it's another one of those situations that you just had to be there to understand." Nick kept his eyes averted as he spoke.

"All right." I smiled. "So, Nick won the toss, and everything from there is history."

"Yes..." they piped together.

"Next question *please*," Nick pleaded and then smiled timidly.

"I would like to know what's wrong with me." My statement seemed to leave them both wide-eyed and stunned.

"Wrong with you!" they exclaimed in unison.

"Yes, wrong with me! For instance, why, Tristan, as many times as I've seen you morphed or warped...or whatever it is—"

"We call it phasing."

"Okay, phased then, when I'm all alone and not once have you attacked me or threatened to attack me!" I pointed out.

"I could never harm you!" He was completely shocked that I would even suggest such a thing.

"I know you wouldn't in your human form, but as a panther, isn't everything more...instinct?"

"In some ways, yes, but try to understand, Olivia. Even when I'm phased, I'm still Tristan. I know you, I know my own mind, and I know your scent."

"That makes sense, so you still *think* human?"

"Not completely. If you were to come across me, say, when I'm engaged in a fight, you may not be as safe, but I would be able to stop before I hurt you."

"That's a comforting thought!"

Tristan looked sheepish at my errant comment, as he shifted in his seat. Nick chuckled.

"Don't cross him at the dinner table either!" Tristan shot a dirty look his way.

"Nikolas, that's not funny!" I couldn't help the giggle that escaped. It was obvious they were trying to squelch my fear. I could see now a deep friendship between them.

"I wouldn't be so quick to laugh, Nick. You're next!" I scolded.

Tristan sniffed and leaned back in his chair, stretching his legs in front of him. He locked his fingers together, crossed his feet, and smiled. "I can't wait!"

"So..." I continued. "It's apparent you change during the day, but does it have to be like certain phases of the moon or something?" I inquired.

"Please don't compare me to dogs. Olivia, I'm a shifter, not a werewolf. I can phase at will." Tristan's pride was evident in his tone.

"Sorry. My mistake." I felt bad about not choosing my words more carefully. "I will repeat my question. What's wrong with me then? Do I smell bad to you or something?" My eyes remained a steady gaze, waiting.

"No! Oh, sugar, no. Your scent is, well...exceptionally desirable." Tristan's eyes burned as he looked at me, and I felt the electricity spark my veins.

"I haven't harmed you for the same reason he hasn't." Tristan threw his arm out, gesturing toward Nick. I looked over at Nikolas just in time to see him readjusting himself, trying to avoid being drawn into this with Tristan. Too bad, he was about to be.

"As for you..." I turned to Nikolas. He immediately corrected his posture. He reminded me of a schoolboy that had just been unexpectedly called on by the teacher. I suppressed another giggle.

"I'll ask you the same question, what-is-wrong with me?"

"There is nothing wrong with you, love. You're perfect!"

I rolled my eyes and peered at him. "Then why, in all the times we have been alone, have you not tried to bite me!" I knew something had to be wrong if I could thwart two very dangerous predators for eight months! "Is my blood tainted, or sour maybe?"

"No!" I could see in his face he was desperately searching for a way to explain. "Just as Tristan can smell your human scent, I too have your scent, only the scent of your blood, and trust me, love. It is exquisite!"

As he spoke, I thought I saw a hint of...fang! Should that make me feel better about the tasty factor? I wondered. I cleared my throat, hoping what I just saw was my imagination.

"Then why? Why haven't you attacked me?" I was insistent. Nikolas and Tristan both seemed to straighten in their chairs at that moment. As they did, I felt a strong tingling sensation, and it raised goose bumps on my arms. They turned toward each other, a strange look on each of their faces. Had my repeated question caused them to reconsider their decision not to kill me?

"Olivia, do you mind giving us a moment?" Nick asked politely. His request seemed harmless.

World Of Kings 16

"Certainly." I leaned back to await their return. I watched them cross the room for their private chat. My eyes never faltered in my stare. They were so marvelous. I couldn't understand what they could want with me, plain little me. They were truly a dream. Neither of them was supposed to exist, yet they did exist, and they had identities! They had notched out a place for themselves in the universe. They both had a purpose in the scheme of things. I, on the other hand, did not. I hadn't established my own identity. I was nothing special, nothing more in this universe, this existence, than a speck of dust floating in the air—invisible...insignificant.

How arrogant you are! I thought. *To believe for one second that you have the right to question them, let alone expect an answer! What interest could they have? I'm just Olivia, plain and simple.* I continued to sit there, watching them talk quietly across the room.

"Nick, Lucas has taken a mate! This is going to pose a problem." Tristan was worried.

"I know, Tris, but there is nothing we can do about it now. At least we know why we were able to save Olivia." Nick looked at Tristan's knowing expression.

"He just wanted to keep us occupied so we wouldn't seek out his soul mate. He has decided to produce an heir to his throne. Nick, I have a very bad feeling about this!"

"Now that he's bound, Olivia will be in even more danger! We cannot afford to let our guard down for a second," Nick said. "We need to tell her as much as we can tonight."

"Let's hope it won't be more than she can handle this soon," Tristan responded.

"She's strong and very astute. I'm sure she'll handle everything quite well." Nick smiled and started back toward Olivia.

They returned, both sure of what they wanted to say, but very unsure of how to begin.

"In order for us to explain why we haven't attacked you; we feel that we need to explain ourselves better." Nick sat, arms resting on his knees as he nervously rubbed his palms together.

"All right, Nick, you have my undivided attention." I sat up straight and crossed my feet in the chair.

"Let's see. For starters, erase from your mind everything you've been told about vampires, shifters, werewolves, witches, immortals, and elves. All those stories are myth, with the exception of a few small truths humans accidentally got right." Nick's eyes studied me as he spoke.

"Oh, so you're saying that werewolves, witches, immortals, and elves exist too, right?"

"Yes, sugar, and by exist, we mean live." Tristan looked straight at me, hoping to see the light click on.

"So, vampires are not the undead?" I looked at Nick, and he smiled.

"No, love, I am very much alive," he stated.

"How?" They could see the lifetime of fantasy trying to override the truth.

"Let me start from the beginning." Nick ran his hand through his hair and took in a long breath.

"Please do." I cast my eyes from one to the other, completely perplexed.

"You see," Nick began again. "We are all alive. I mean to say, living, breathing beings, just not from this world."

"You're from outer space?" This was really getting weird.

"No!" Tristan laughed as he looked at Nick. "You were right, Nick." He continued to chuckle.

"I was right about what, Tris?"

"You really do suck at this," Tristan said, shaking his head. Nick's eyes squinted at Tristan's remark.

"Well, if you can do better, please, the floor is all yours!" Nick huffed. Tristan nodded at Nick and turned back to me.

"All right, Olivia, try to keep up. I'm about to make a very long story short, okay?"

I just nodded as I continued to stare at him.

"Number one, we are very much alive. Two, we came from a different world, not outer space, a different dimension. Three, we're here because our world was destroyed by war. We are still at war. It has gone on for more than a millennium. That war is with what you refer to as werewolves. Four, in our world we are not vampires, shifters, and the like. Each race has a real name.

"Five, we still maintain a governing society, that is to say, we have our own set of laws and rules to live by. Now, baby, you try and process all that while Nick makes some more tea. Then we'll answer your questions." Tristan stopped, leaned back in his chair, and smiled.

"That certainly is a lot to think about," I said, making a low whistling sound. I sat back, let out a sigh, and began to attempt to process everything Tristan had said. Nikolas returned and handed me a fresh cup of tea. I took a sip and set the cup and saucer on the table beside me. Nick and Tristan sat quietly, waiting for me to speak.

"So..." I started. "It's obvious now the sci-fi story about worlds within worlds is true. I guess my first question would be, how did you get here?"

"Our scientists had discovered a portal between our worlds. It was used mainly to study this one and its inhabitants, but was ultimately the escape from our dying world," Nick began explaining.

"What was your world called?" I asked.

"Kardaun," Tristan answered.

"Go on," I prompted. "Tell me about Kardaun." My expression was frozen in wonder.

"Kardaun was a beautiful place, thriving with people, beautiful landscapes, and the colors were so vibrant! I can still see the dew glistening on the silver leaves of the Shayla trees. It looked like tiny diamonds in the morning sun." Nick looked as though he were there, his memories taking him far away. He caught himself and regained his composure. "Well, I'll tell you in great detail another time." He smiled.

"Kardaun was made up of six kingdoms, all governed separately by a king and queen. The kings and queens of Kardaun made up the judgment council; besides the rulers of each kingdom, we had one High King and Queen. The High King presided over the council and had the final say in decision making. He also presided over our world as a whole," Tristan continued.

"How many kingdoms did you say there were?" I wanted to know as much about Kardaun as they had time to tell me. The questions were starting to flood my mind faster than I could sort them out.

"Six," Tristan answered. "There were the kingdoms of Es'mar, Malvé, Dysier, Loxar, Chaldron, and Simin."

"You said you were not called vampires and shifters there, so what are you really?"

"I," Nick pointed to himself, "am a Larin." He looked to Tristan.

"And I am a Maldoran," Tristan continued. "Werewolves as you know them are Origs. Witches are known as Warins; elves, Avars; and immortals, Hulains." Tristan smiled as he could see me trying to commit these names to memory.

"How did you coexist without constantly attacking each other?" I was amazed that they were capable of cohabitation at all.

"The citizens of Kardaun were for the most part a very tolerant people. We had no prejudice against those different from our own kind, so we were a peaceful society, until Vladmar Scarsion, king of the Origs, planted the seeds of dissention and malcontent. Yet even he did not hate another for their race.

"Somehow his mind had become twisted, and he became convinced that he was superior to all. Some say he had developed an illness of the mind, others claimed he had been called by our Creator to rule Kardaun. Nevertheless, he was a ruthless person bent on overthrowing the High King. His only desire was power—absolute power," Tristan explained.

"I see. But I can't understand how the vampires could coexist without killing. Don't you crave blood?"

"Not in our world, love. You see, we were very much like you there. We aged; we were susceptible to illness, felt pain, all the things a human experiences in a lifetime. Our fangs were nothing more than defensive features should we fall into harm's way." Nick looked saddened as he spoke. I could tell he missed his home and would gladly give up the superstrength, agility, speed, hearing, sight, and most of all, the immortality to have his life back in Kardaun. It was apparent by the look on Tristan's face he felt the same.

"When we passed through the portal..." Tristan had picked up the conversation. "It changed us. We found that we stopped aging normally," he said.

"What do you mean normally?" It was my understanding that they were immortal.

"Well, we do age but very slowly. Recently we found that our aging process is like one year for every thousand here. Hence the so-called immortality, so I guess, in a way we are, since our hearts cannot die—at least not until we reach a certain age somewhere around one hundred, which means until that time, we will live. Since we won't reach that age bodily for at least another eighty thousand years, I guess we are as close to immortal as you can get." Tristan stopped speaking long enough to take a drink from his cup.

"I believe that's fair to say since you are bound to see this world repopulate a thousand times over," I concluded.

Tristan and Nick both chuckled. "Yes, love, I would have to agree." He seemed very pleased that I was truly paying attention.

"So, there is no way you can die in this world?" I asked.

"Oh yes, you see, our hearts cannot be extinguished by stabbing or shooting, hence the myths about wooden stakes and silver bullets. It cannot die. As long as a single tissue or the smallest organism lives, we will regenerate." Nick thought for a moment to put this into full perspective for me, but I spoke before he could continue.

"You mean if someone set fire to you, it wouldn't kill you?" This information fascinated me.

"As long as the fire wasn't hot enough to completely burn our hearts or destroy every living tissue, which most do not burn completely through, but it's not a theory I would want to test. But for the most part, if our heart is not destroyed, we will live. You see, love, unlike humans, whose hearts are merely an organ to sustain life, our hearts are a direct connection to our soul and literally carry the essence of our life," Nick continued his explanation very calmly.

"If that's the case, I don't see any way you could be killed." He smiled seeing that it was evident I would need more information.

"We can be killed, Olivia. If we are caught in a sleeping state, which by the way is only about two hours a day, or we are incapacitated, for instance, being stabbed or shot, which weaken us for a short time, we even lose consciousness. When that happens, someone can, during that time, remove our heart from our bodies and burn it. If the heart of a Kardaunian is burned to ash, the body will also turn to ash," he finished his explanation of Kardaunian death and waited for my response.

"Fascinating." I breathed. "In what other ways were you changed?" I felt privileged to be given this insight of what everyone else in this world considered mythical. Vampire movies held no fascination for me now!

"Passing through the portal affected each of us in a different way." Tristan had again picked up the conversation. "In Kardaun, I could shift into any animal I wished, as could all Maldorans. With the exception of small rodents, insects, and very large animals like elephants and giraffes. These forms were not feasible, much too small or too large to accommodate our bodies. It's the same with foul. We could only shift into larger predatory birds. When we passed through the portal into this world, we found that the only animal DNA in our system was that of the last animal we phased into before crossing through."

"Amazing..." I murmured under my breath. Tristan smiled.

"The Warins found their magic limited. A lot of their spells didn't work here, and many of the ingredients for their potions didn't exist in this world. The elves, or Avars, as we call them—and, sugar, I'm not talking about the little gnome-like creatures depicted as Santa's helpers. I'm referring to the ethereal creatures. They are a beautiful people, highly intelligent and creative. In Kardaun, they were scientists, engineers, and architects. They also have mystical healing powers and the ability to control nature, only in their immediate area. They are accomplished warriors, archers, and strategists. We were fortunate that none of the Avars sided with Lucas in the war. They are the one race that remained solely loyal to the king of Kardaun, not to mention our greatest allies in this war. The only problem is, they wish to remain neutral but will, if circumstances arise, lend a hand. The Avars did retain all their abilities and powers when they crossed through. Like the Avars, the Hulains were also affected little by the move to this world.

"Hulains were the most like humans; so there was no real physical change for them, again with the exception of immortality and being immune to illness or disease as the rest of us. They are the hardest from our world to detect or track and have served well as spies on both sides." Tristan stopped and stood up to excuse himself to get something else to drink. "Would you like something?" he asked Nick and me before he moved to leave the room.

"Yes, if you don't mind. Do you have any soda?" I requested.

"Yes, cola?" He grinned. I nodded. "Nick?" he waited.

"No, thank you, I'm fine." Nick turned back to me, waiting for my next question.

"This is all so fascinating," I commented. "What happened to the Origs and Larins when they crossed through?"

"The Origs," Nick started, "in our world could phase into the werewolf form at will, but here, they are only capable of changing at night. Vladmar was killed in battle, but his son, Lucas Scarsion, passed through into this world. He still believes, as he was raised and taught, that the throne of Kardaun rightfully belongs to the Origs and thus has continued the war we had hoped would end when our world was destroyed. Now as for the Larins, passing through the portal changed us more than anyone. We have always had a faster heart rate and thinner blood than the other races in Kardaun. The atmosphere in our world was much heavier and the gravity far denser than in this world. So, when we passed through the portal, our heart rate became even more rapid. It's far below a whisper and unable to be heard even with a stethoscope. That is where the tales of the undead come in. Our blood flow is so rapid we cannot keep the nutrients needed to survive flowing through our system. This causes a vitamin deficiency. We found ourselves needing or craving blood...human blood. It is thicker and rich with nutrients. Because of its thickness, it takes our body longer to process it, and we remain strong for a longer period of time." He looked at me, hopeful that I wouldn't be too appalled by what he had just told me.

"So, you do crave blood now. Is the craving constant?" I was beginning to feel nervous. I had been here four and a half hours and wasn't sure if I would remain safe.

"No, love, we can go a week without drinking," he stated.

"Have you...umm...satisfied your thirst lately?" I nervously asked. Nick smiled.

"Yes." He caught my expression. "Olivia, true Larins do not need to kill humans, at least not anymore. We have many resources now to obtain our vitamin." Nick smiled at me, noticing my slight embarrassment.

"Vitamin..." I knit my brow, wondering why he would refer to his drink of choice with that term.

"It sounds better in polite conversation to say, 'Please excuse me. I need to take my vitamin' than 'Hold that thought. I need a drink of blood.' Don't you think?" He laughed.

"I suppose it does," I answered, laughing with him. "Nick, I'm confused now." I told him, a little embarrassed that I may not have been following this fantastic story as closely as I thought.

"What about?" He was leaned back, very relaxed in his chair.

"Well, you said that Kardaunians were all immortal and couldn't die unless they reached a certain age, or their hearts were burned. Yet you just told me that without blood, you couldn't survive." I sat confused, staring at him.

"I'm sorry. I'll try to clarify for you. You see, any living being needs nourishment to live, the same with us. If the body is malnourished, it becomes weak. Well, without blood, my body would do the same. The weaker I become from the lack of nourishment, the more dehydrated my body would also become. Do you follow?" he patiently asked.

"Yes, I'm with you so far."

"Okay. If I were to completely stop taking in human blood, my body would not be able to sustain me but for a little over a week, since there are no nutrients to keep me strong, and as I start to dehydrate, so will my heart. Not only will my body become weaker, but my soul as well. Once my heart has withered, it could no longer function. It acts in the same way as a flame would." Nick was quick to notice the concern on my face.

"You needn't worry about that happening, love." He smiled tenderly. "There is an abundant supply in this world and in ways to obtain it."

At least he put that fear to rest, and I felt relieved. Tristan had reentered the room and handed me a glass.

"Have I missed much?" he asked, seating himself again in the chair between me and Nick.

"No, Nick was just explaining about his vitamin." I smiled.

"Oh, well, I hope he didn't make it too complicated," Tristan said as he leaned back to get comfortable.

"Of course not, Dr. Rilz. Complicated is your area of expertise," Nick joked.

"Good. I wouldn't want you trying to upstage me." Tristan laughed. Nick and I both joined him in the relaxed moment.

"What about the sunlight? You talked about dew on some kind of tree in the morning sun. I'm assuming you must have been able to go out in the daytime in your world." I just couldn't imagine Nick ever basking in the sun.

"I explained that our atmosphere was different, so too was the sun's rays. Just as earth has a protective layer, so did Kardaun, except there, that protective layer literally deflected all harmful rays, thus protecting the Larins, who, by the way, for the most part, are naturally pale skinned. This world, combined with lack of sun and a severe vitamin deficiency, only enhanced our pallid complexion." Nick turned up the corner of his mouth in a crooked little grin as he looked at Tristan. I assumed he and Tristan had some sort of inside joke about it.

"I think your skin is beautiful!" I admitted. I could see in Nick's eyes that he believed my compliment and accepted it graciously.

"Olivia, you have no idea how it affects me when you share your true feelings no matter how fleeting the comment." He leaned over and placed his cold hand against my warm skin. The pleasure just this one light touch brought left me trembling.

"Uh hum," Tristan interrupted. "Nick, the sunlight." He shrugged his shoulders and made a move-along gesture.

"Oh yes, because of your thin atmosphere and lack of protective layer, we Larins cannot withstand the day. Only ten minutes will burn our skin to the point that it would take days to heal, and thirty minutes could be fatal. Our scientists are working on a solution to this problem, so we hold out hope that we will someday walk in the sun." Nick leaned back in his chair. "There are many things you will learn in time." He drew in a long breath as if he had explained as much as he could about the Larins of Kardaun.

"Now I understand you both more, but as fascinating as all this is, it still doesn't explain me," I said. "Tristan..." I turned to look at him. He was so magnificent. I caught my breath when I met his steady gaze. I could feel the flames within him. I couldn't understand what he saw that would cause such desire. He seemed to be so absorbed in his thoughts he wasn't paying attention. "Tristan?" I repeated.

"Hmm...I'm sorry...what did you say?" he responded.

"Nothing yet," I said, feeling my face start to burn. "I was wondering...would you be offended if I asked to speak with Nick in private for a moment?" I tried to gauge his expression, but I saw nothing to indicate jealousy.

"Not at all, sugar. I'll go and make some sandwiches. Nick, you'll summon me when you're through?" Tristan paused to look at Nick.

"Of course, my friend, thank you." Tristan closed the doors behind him, and Nikolas turned again to face me from his seat. "Is there something wrong, love?" Nick seemed apprehensive, as if I may say something he would rather not hear.

"No, there is nothing wrong. I just needed to ask you something in private that would have made things a bit awkward if both of you were present." I started to feel nervous. I sat forward and cleared my throat in preparation for my next question. Nick sat patiently.

"Nick, in all the time we have been going out together, even on the last night I saw you..." Nick winced at the reminder of our last date. "I want to know why you have never touched me, with the exception of the one light kiss on the hand." I bit my lip, hoping his answer would not be one that would surely bring tears. If the thought of touching me repulsed him, I'm sure I would die.

Nick stood up, walked over to my chair, and knelt in front of me.

"Olivia, there are two reasons I have never held your hand, touched your face, or held you in my arms. The first reason is because you didn't know about me, and you would have known I was different." Nick's eyes were soft and shining as he explained his reasons for the distance he kept between us.

"I know now, Nick, I hoped you would consider allowing me..." I looked down, hoping I was not out of line by my simple request. I looked up to the soft shimmer of Nick's eyes. I couldn't help but think, as marvelous as he was in front of me now, how astounding he must have been in his own world.

SOULBOUND: DESTINY'S MOVE

He leaned forward toward me as I continued to look directly into his eyes. At that moment, I felt as if I had just experienced the most tender touch, one more intimate than anything ever experienced by a mortal. I just sat there still, wanting to hold on to the feeling he had just given me with nothing more than a look. I still ached to physically feel his touch on my skin. I could feel his longing as he remained poised in front of me. My body began to tremble as I started to burn with desire, excruciating desire! He leaned closer to me, and I could smell the scent of him, a scent that caused my mouth to water and my body to hunger for his lips to touch mine, just to have a taste of him. His cool breath brushed my lips as he leaned in closer to me. I caught my breath as his hand gently touched the side of my face. It was cold but gentle. I knew that I had never felt anything as sensual as this. The cold against the fiery heat of my skin felt as though it created a cool steam, like the melding together of fire and ice. I reached up and placed my hand on Nick's face and gently started to trace every line, every curve. Nick closed his eyes and shivered as my fingers lingered on his lips, those beautiful full lips I had ached for so long to touch.

He seemed to stop breathing as my hand ran tenderly down his neck to his chest. His muscles were like stone, and my breath caught. I continued back up to his shoulders, neck, and to rest again on the smooth, cold skin of his face.

Nick opened his eyes and pulled back, reaching out one last time to trace my cheek and neck, stopping to rest his hand on the throbbing pulse at the hollow of my throat.

"Olivia," he breathed, "I feel as if I have been brushed by the angels of Shalsmara!" He reluctantly stood up and moved back to his chair. We sat in silence as we both struggled to recover from the beautiful moment we had just shared.

"Ummm...so what is the other reason?" I managed to ask.

"That will require the presence of Tristan." Nick smiled, his voice suddenly sounded different toward me, softer and more reverent.

Tristan came through the doors carrying a tray of sandwiches. He placed them on the table beside my chair and handed me another soda.

"Tristan, it's time for us to let Olivia know why she's here." Nick informed him as he took his seat between us.

"Let's see, how to begin..." Tristan thought for a minute as I nibbled on one of the sandwiches from the tray.

"Tristan, before you begin, I need to ask you something." I hoped my asking this question would not upset the newly found closeness between Nick and me, but still I had to know Tristan's reason.

"What would you like to know?' Tristan answered as he leaned forward.

"Since we have been seeing each other, I want to know why you have never kissed me or put your arms around me. Why haven't you even held hands with me? With the exception of what happened today, it's as though you didn't have any romantic feelings toward me."

"What happened today?" Nick interrupted, looking at Tristan as he spoke.

"Nick, nothing happened that shouldn't on any normal date." I defended both my and Tristan's actions. Besides, I ruined it with my fainting spell."

Nick and Tristan stood simultaneously.

"Tristan, what did you do!" Nick's eyes were wide in horror.

"I am sorry, Nick. I almost let my desire override my reason. I stopped it. As painful as it was, I couldn't go on with it." Tristan looked ashamed as he spoke to Nikolas.

"Olivia, you said you fainted. How long were you out?" Nick asked.

"I'm not sure, a couple of hours maybe." I was starting to get scared. I wasn't sure what was about to happen.

"Tristan, do you realize what could have happened? Two hours! She was almost in a...a...coma!" Nick's eyes were even wider than before. He looked totally panic-stricken.

"Wait a minute, Nick! I have no idea what you're talking about, or what's got you so worked up. You have no right to condemn Tristan for doing the very same thing you did only four days ago!" I emphatically pointed out.

"Nick, you..." Tristan was unable to finish his sentence. He suddenly seemed to have trouble breathing. "My friend, I am so sorry. I didn't know. If I had known, I would have tried harder to control my emotions. Twice to be cut off from...in less than a week!" Tristan just sat down in the chair and cradled his head in his hand.

"I'm sorry, Tris. I should have told you what had happened Wednesday. This was just as much my fault. Forgive me, my friend."

"Tristan, Nikolas, listen to me" I demanded. "Whatever has upset you both need not be a concern now. You talk as if something catastrophic has happened to me. Both of you, look at me...now!" I raised my voice in fear.

They both slowly and quietly looked to where I was standing.

"I am unharmed. There is nothing wrong with me! Can you see that?" I stood with my hands stretched out in the air. "Now both of you listen to me. Whatever you were talking about is water under the bridge. Let's move on, okay?" I hoped I had gotten through to the both of them. They needed to realize there was ultimately no harm done.

"You're right, Olivia. I'm sorry for my outburst." Nick's apology was sincere.

"I'm sorry, baby, forgive me." Tristan looked so hurt. I wasn't quite sure what he was apologizing for.

"Tristan, sweetheart, you are forgiven, now please let's not allow this misunderstanding to get in the way of tonight's discussion."

Nick returned to his seat. He and Tristan looked at each other, conveying their silent apologies for their offense.

"You were about to explain why you both have kept your distance from me." I directed the conversation back to the subject at hand.

"You see baby," Tristan began. "We don't choose our mates in the same way as humans. They go through a process of trial and error. When they find someone, they feel they are compatible with, they try to live in a state of compromise to please their spouse. We, on the other hand, do not. We are drawn together instinctively by souls," Tristan explained.

"We know when our intended soul is born into this world. From that moment, we start gravitating toward it. Little by little, throughout the years, usually we are in the same vicinity as our mate before she reaches the age of twenty. In our world, that is the coming of age as humans refer to it. Until that time, we are not permitted by law to approach her," Nick informed me.

"What do you mean you are usually in the vicinity? Does it sometimes take longer?"

"Not under normal circumstances. If your soul was born in this world, it's easy to find it, but for some who came here through the portal, it isn't so simple," Tristan started explaining.

"I don't understand," I said.

"You see, there were many souls intended to bind when they entered this world and some that had not yet found their mates in Kardaun because of the war. When these women passed through the portal, the essence of their souls that which guides us to our mate got misplaced, so to speak. It's sort of like a signal being bounced from tower to tower; it's hard to get a lock on it," Tristan continued. "So there are some from our time still seeking their intended souls." There was a look in Tristan's eyes that told he knew someone with that problem, and it saddened him deeply.

"Then am I right in assuming this pull is experienced only by the males in your world?" I asked, trying to understand this process.

"Yes, love, you are right. Women do not have the burden of seeking us out. They never feel attracted to anyone physically or emotionally until their intended soul finds them." Nick watched me carefully as he spoke, hoping I would catch on to the meaning of this particular conversation.

"Remarkable," I exclaimed. "So that's why my attempts at dating failed. I was waiting for one of you!" I gasped.

Nick and Tristan looked at each other with one of those silent "Oh boy" looks. I immediately knew my assumption was wrong. My heart sank to my feet. If I was wrong, which apparently, I was, why was I here? I thought.

"Then one of you is not my intended soul?" I was stricken with total hopelessness.

"No, sugar," Tristan answered. "One of us is not your intended... both of us are! That's why you've been dating me during the day and Nick after dark."

"At first, this whole drawn by souls seemed pretty easy, now I'm confused. I'm sure this is pretty common for you, but—"

Nick interrupted. "No, love, this is not common!" he exclaimed.

"Sugar, believe me, explaining this is not going to be easy, by no means!" Tristan leaned forward, shaking his head.

"Well, easy or not, you're going to have to try!" My head was pounding; this is not going to end well. I just know it!

"To tell you the truth, Olivia, we're not sure how to explain this situation, only that it exists and our Creator has chosen it to be this way. We don't know what exactly to do about it right now, but at least you know why you're here," Tristan confessed their lack of understanding.

"Can you at least explain why you never kissed me?" I asked.

"That, love, we can explain." Nick smiled when he answered my question, glad to get back onto a subject he understood. "When we kiss our intended soul mate on the lips, it begins the soul binding, and it is irreversible. Since you knew nothing about us or what would happen, to allow that would be wrong."

"You see, to do something like that without your consent would make us no better than the man that attacked you," Tristan added.

"So, the binding of our souls without my consent or knowledge in your world is the equivalent of rape." I understood very well now why they never acted on their feelings.

"We have such an overpowering desire to bind with you, Olivia, that both of us almost committed that act against you, me on Wednesday night and Tristan yesterday morning." Both men dropped their heads in shame as I looked at them. "That, love, is what we have sought your forgiveness for."

"Well, now that I know what had both of you so upset, I can truthfully give you my forgiveness and know for what crime I am absolving." They both looked stunned.

"Now I don't understand," Nick stated. "How can you forgive so easily the terrible act we were about to commit?"

"Well, I understand now what you were doing, but at the time, even in my ignorance, Tristan, did I try to fight you off on the mountain?" I asked.

"No," he answered.

"Nick, down by the creek, did I try to stop you? Did I once move away?"

"No, love, you didn't," he responded to my questioning.

"I do understand that you wanted me to know who you really were and that you had to consider each other, but has it occurred to either of you at that moment I was a willing participant in this act?" I continued.

"No," came the flat answer in unison from both men.

"I did everything in my power to entice you both. By my own admission, I encouraged this act against me. In my world, that's called coercion, is it not Nick?"

"Well, yes, love...but—" I raised my hand to stop his sentence midstream.

"If there is anyone here that needs to ask forgiveness, it's me! I'm guilty of coercing you both to commit a crime. Since I was a willing and active participant, I believe you should be able to understand how I could forgive you so easily."

"Olivia, sweetheart, I don't think you understand the magnitude of what we were about to do!" Tristan protested.

"It doesn't matter, Tristan. I do not feel accosted or molested in any way. In my world, we have a saying that I think applies perfectly to this situation," I continued their defense. Nick had sat silently, his chin resting between his thumb and forefinger, listening intently to every word.

"What is this saying?" Nick asked. I looked at them and smiled.

"You can't rape the willing!" I sat back and waited for their reaction.

Nick's smile lit up the room. "Olivia, you are priceless! You'd make a very fine attorney." He laughed aloud.

"Simply amazing!" I heard Tristan say as I looked to see the gorgeous smile on his face too.

"I'm glad that we now have that behind us. I would like to know more about your world. Earlier you made a reference that I assume meant all Larins are not pale like you?" I decided a change of subject might relax the situation.

"No, every kingdom of Kardaun has people of many colors. Why do you ask?" Nick seemed confused by my question, as did Tristan.

"We, I mean humans, define our race by the color of our skin, and the country we come from defines our nationality."

Nick and Tristan both laughed. "Oh yeah, humans like to make things complicated," Tristan said, shaking his head.

"Complicated? I don't understand."

"Only humans would pay attention to something as trivial as skin color," Nick remarked as if he were thinking out loud. "In Kardaun, that means nothing to us. The kingdoms of Kardaun are just where we were born and raised. It's our abilities that define us as individuals, and each race has different abilities that work together in our world," Nick explained.

"I see. You gave me brief explanations of some of the abilities earlier. Larins have fangs, Maldorans shift, am I right so far?" I was sure I had this part down pat.

"Somewhat, there is a little more to us than that." Tristan picked up the conversation. "Larins are warriors by nature. They possess fangs and venom, a natural defense, along with the ability to levitate." I turned to Nick surprised.

"You can do that?"

"Yes, love, I can do that." He smiled.

"The venom is shared between Larins, Maldorans, and Origs. It has the ability to incapacitate or semiparalyze an enemy. Much like the way a cat bite affects a mouse." Tristan looked amused at Nick's cat-and-mouse comparison.

"I see, go on," I said.

"The Maldorans possess the ability to change their shape, as do the Origs. Origs, however, only phase into half man, half wolf. Maldorans phase into animals. Avars control nature, Warins control the mystics, and Hulains possess a variety of abilities ranging from the ability to move objects mentally to telepathy, with the exception of clairvoyance. No Kardaunian has ever possessed any precognitive abilities.

"So is it that each kingdom is populated by one race of people, like Es'mar is all Larin etc.?" I wanted to understand how their world worked, but I seemed to be losing track of who came from where.

"No, as I said, our race is determined by our abilities, not our kingdom." Nick was starting to look like someone trying to pound sand in a rat hole. I knew I was exhausting his explanations. I looked at Tristan; it was evident he could see my desperate attempt to arrange all the information into a cohesive thought.

"So, Tristan, the king of Malve' doesn't just rule over Maldorans?" I asked.

"No, sugar, there are just as many different races in Malve' as in all the kingdoms of Kardaun. Vladmar Scarsion was an Orig and ruler of Loxar. Naturally, the majority of the citizens of that kingdom sided with him in the war and remains loyal to Lucas. That's why there are Larins, Maldorans, Warins, etc., fighting with Lucas, along with a number of traitors that switched sides when we came here."

Now I understood their world much better and felt that I could continue our discussion with the ability to keep up. I smiled at both of them, and I could see the relief on their faces at the signal they had finally got through to me.

"I would like to know more about these kingdoms, especially your kings and queens." I was anxious to learn more about this fascinating world, but I knew this night did not hold enough time to hear it all.

We settled back as Tristan and Nikolas again began their rendition of life in Kardaun. They told the stories of each kingdom. I remained locked in my fascination of this beautiful world. Our discussion had continued on into the night. I had learned so much about their world, their lives, and their laws.

Around two thirty in the morning, there was a knock on the sitting room door. Nick and Tristan both stood up. They appeared anxious.

"Enter," Nick called. Two people entered the room, a man and woman.

Both bowed low and waited for Tristan as he walked over, hand outstretched, to greet them. The woman was absolutely stunning! She was so delicate and poised. Her hair was waist length and the color of chestnuts. Her face was so feminine and perfect. I couldn't help noticing her eyes. They reminded me of Savannah's brown doe eyes, only more of a brilliant amber color, and her skin, flawless, smooth, and golden.

Her escort was obviously vampire, pale skin, steel-blue eyes, and long brown hair pulled back. He was shorter than Nick by several inches, but very strong built.

I was staring rudely, but I couldn't help myself. I was surprised to see Tristan and Nikolas pay no more attention to this extraordinary woman than if she were an inanimate object. I stood up and walked over by Nick's side.

"Please, come in, my friends," Nick called to them as they crossed the room. "I hope all is well?" Nick's eyes moved back and forth between them, awaiting their response. A curt nod from both of them seemed to set him at ease.

He reached out his hand to the woman, who, instead of shaking it, kissed his fingers and placed her forehead to the back of his hand. The man repeated the odd greeting. Nick's eyes twinkled as he looked over at me. My expression was completely lost. Tristan just stood there beside me, smirking.

"I wish to present Ms. Olivia Ryan." Nick waved his hand toward me.

"Olivia, these are our dear friends Galen Marquis and Safrina Roux." He introduced them with such formality I was sure they were very important people in his world.

"It is our honor to meet you." Galen bowed low, speaking with a thick French accent, as did Safrina.

"Ms. Ryan." She spoke with a smooth, angelic voice.

"We have explained the danger you have been in for the past few years, but what we haven't told you is that Galen and Safrina have played an intricate part in our efforts to keep you safe," Tristan informed me.

"Then it is truly my honor to meet you both, that I may express my gratitude for your watchful eye." I smiled. Tristan and Nick seemed to beam with pride at the manner in which I addressed the couple before me.

I offered my hand to shake, and they also kissed my fingers and placed their forehead to the back of my hand, first Galen and then Safrina. *This must be some strange way of greeting people in their world...odd*, I thought. But when in Rome, they say. So, I stood silent and smiled.

After Safrina and Galen left, I turned to Nick. "You were telling me about your king."

"Oh yes." Nick smiled and gestured for me to take my seat before he continued. "Valmar and Daria Alberon were kind and just rulers. Their closest friends were King Jessom and Queen Lanai Xandier, rulers of Malve. In the last days of our world, they fought side by side at the battle of Daravey in the kingdom of Es'mar.

"Tristan and I had been instructed days before to gather as many of our people as we could to enter the portal into this world."

"We were privileged to share in this battle along with them," Tristan said.

"They were all four valiant." Nick's eyes lowered, as did Tristan's, most reverently.

"I don't understand, the queens fought in battle?" I couldn't grasp that many years ago women being allowed in harm's way. It had only been recently that women fought side by side in combat. "That long ago, weren't women considered too weak and thought of as needing protection?" I looked puzzled.

"Olivia, my dear." Tristan smiled. "We are not talking about your world, remember?"

"Oh, it's very hard to keep things straight sometimes." I blushed.

"In our world," Nick began to explain, "women did not have to fight for equal rights. "They were born equal. Daria and Lanai were accomplished warriors." Nick's eyes glistened with pride.

"The four of them, High King Valmar Alberon and his queen, Daria, along with King Jessom Xandier and Queen Lanai, took many of our enemies with them when they fell that day in battle."

I stood up and walked to the edge of the fireplace, looking into the fire, deep in thought. I tried to imagine the four just described to me. I admired them and their courage deeply.

"I'm sure you were much honored to have fought with them...and saddened by their death," I whispered.

"Yes, very honored," Nick responded.

"More sad than words can describe," Tristan added.

"What about your parents?" I directed my question to both of them. "I assume they too perished in the war." "Yes," they answered in unison.

"You told me you had changed your names several times throughout the years to protect your anonymity."

"Yes," they again chimed in unison.

"What were your names before you came here?" I needed to know them by their true given names.

Nikolas and Tristan both stood up. "I am Nixis Alberon." Nick bowed politely as he introduced his true self.

"My name is Traesdon Xandier," Tristan announced, also bowing politely. They both stood there, eyes fixed on me as I processed what they had just announced. As everything started coming together, I looked at them in astonishment.

"You are...they were your parents...you're princes!"

"No, love, we're not princes." Nick looked to Tristan.

"As you said yourself, baby, they were our parents." Tristan stopped for only a moment until I caught my breath.

"In our world, Nick is known as High King Nixis Alberon, and ruler of Kardaun," Tristan introduced Nikolas with pride.

"My dear friend Tristan is known as King Traesdon Xandier, ruler of Malve," Nick announced.

This was all my mind could withstand. I grabbed the mantel of the fireplace to steady my buckling legs and gasped for breath as I teetered and fell to the floor.

"Tristan, she's fainted!" Nick yelled.

"Calm down, Nick, she'll be fine in a minute!" Tristan swiftly picked Olivia up and placed her in the chair, propping her feet. In the blink of an eye, he had retrieved his medical bag from the kitchen counter and popped some smelling salts. I groaned as I started to rouse.

"Nick, get a glass of water," Tristan ordered. The words barely left Tristan's mouth when Nikolas returned.

"Are you all right, love?" Nick's voice was half concern, half fright.

"Uhmm," I mumbled.

"Here, sweetheart, take a sip of water." Tristan raised the glass to my lips. I took a sip and pushed his hand back.

"Thanks." I looked up at the two men and rose to a full sitting position. I was totally embarrassed.

"I'm sorry. I suppose I got a little overwhelmed."

"There is no need to apologize, love, after all, we have bombarded you with so much to take in," Nick comforted.

"That's for sure. You just seemed to be handling it so well we were taken by surprise when you fainted." Tristan looked as though he wished they had taken this talk in smaller increments.

"I'm okay," I said, waving them back to their seats. "At least everything makes sense now," I said.

"What do you mean?" Tristan looked at Nick with his eyebrows knit.

"It makes sense now why people are always bowing or giving low nods at the two of you when we were out together. I realize now those were all people from your world. I understand why I always felt like you both were so regal. It's because you are! I don't understand one thing though," I stated.

"What?" Nick was bent down in front of me, and Tristan was perched on the arm of the chair, stroking my hair.

"I understand why Galen and Safrina greeted you the way they did tonight, at least now I do. What I don't understand is why they gave me the exact same greeting." I looked at them with my eyebrow raised in curiosity.

"We've explained to you about being drawn to a soul," Tristan said.

"Yes," I answered.

"Well, you know the reason for both of us being here is that we're both drawn to you, right?" Nick continued.

"Yes." I patiently waited.

"Galen and Safrina know this too. Our entire world knows this, and who you are." Nick was still knelt before me, watching my expression carefully for any sign of another fainting episode.

"You were greeted as any queen would be by her subjects," Tristan added. "And by the way, you handled yourself like true royalty. We were quite proud." Tristan was smiling, as was Nikolas.

"But...I'm not a queen!" I still looked confused. "And thank you for the compliment by the way."

"You're right, love, you're not a queen, but once you choose whom you will bind with, either way you will be," Nick explained.

"Choose...I have to choose one of you." I couldn't believe this was happening, my moment of dread, the one thing that caused me more fear than death! "What if I refuse to choose one of you?" I said, hoping we could just continue as we were.

"Well, love. I'm afraid the council will do it for you when they convene again in a couple of months," Nick said. Something told me that was not their wish. I looked at Nick and then up to Tristan, my eyes almost glazed with fear at the thought of picking one of them.

"Making a choice between you is the only way?" I couldn't believe it. There had to be an alternative solution.

"Of course you could bind with both of us, but in your world, it is quite frowned upon to have two husbands. You yourself told me once that in your beliefs, you would be jeopardizing your soul to damnation if you were to do such a thing. Just so you understand, this situation is unique, even in our world." Nick let me know by the sound of his voice that he was just as clueless about what to do as I was.

"You mean two souls have never been drawn to one woman in the entire existence of Kardaun?' I questioned Nick.

"I told you this situation is unique, not that it has never happened before. It has, but only twice."

"What happened to them?" I hoped the solution of the past bindings may give me some insight as to what to do now.

"The first time it was two Orig men and a beautiful Orig woman. She, like you, was unable to choose. The council wrote into law, just in case this happened again, that the two men must engage in a duel of rights." Nick dropped his eyes as he spoke.

"What is this duel of rights?" It didn't have a good ring to it.

"The men were ordered to a battle to determine which would have the right to bind with her," Tristan said as he took over the conversation.

"So, the winner got the girl, right?" That didn't sound so bad, I thought.

"No, sugar, the one left alive got the girl." Tristan emphasized the word alive!

"This duel is to the death!" I was appalled.

"Yes, baby, I'm afraid so," Tristan answered.

"What happened?" I asked, feeling sickened and shocked that a civilization so advanced as Kardaun would still engage in something so archaic.

"The two men were quite equal in battle, and both ended up dying. The woman was so grieved by their death she took her own life."

"How tragic. I can relate to her though. I would feel the same if I lost you both to death!" I whimpered. "What of the second time?"

"This was two Maldoran men and a Maldoran woman. She decided to bind with both. The binding with her first mate went well, but she wasn't strong enough to withstand the second binding, and she didn't survive." Tristan looked at me, afraid on one hand of my attempting this feat and on the other, with conviction in his eyes that I was strong enough.

"What happened to the men? Wouldn't they have had only to wait, as you told me earlier, for her soul to be reborn? Seventy years isn't that bad. After all, you have waited on me for over five hundred years."

"We are talking, love, about the world of Kardaun. That would not be possible since immortality didn't exist then. So, the council ordered the duel of rights, only this time the one that died would be the only soul reborn in her time to bind with her. So, you see, Olivia, if you do not make a choice by the evening of the Winter Solstice, we will be ordered to the duel of rights, and one of us will die. The only thing is this time it will pit best friends against each other. To refuse the battle would mean death for both of us." Nick looked to his friend as he finished speaking.

"This is horrid!" I cried. "Nick, you're head of the council, aren't you? Tristan, you're a council member. Can't the two of you stop it?"

"No, love, because the law involves both of us. We would have no say in the matter." Nick again looked away with an anguished expression on his face.

"What happens if I do choose?" I fearfully asked.

"We have agreed that whomever you did not choose would go into exile, never to be in contact with you again, but remain alive," Tristan told me.

"For me it looks hopeless!" I said tearfully. "Why don't you do the same thing you did when you met me?" They both looked at me without understanding. "Flip a coin!" I said.

"You don't understand, because the choice is not ours to make, baby, it never has been," Tristan answered.

"This is so unfair!" I exclaimed. "Nick..." I looked at him through a haze of tears.

"Yes, love," he answered quietly.

"Why is our situation so unique?" I couldn't see any difference between us and the one's he spoke of in the past.

"Well, as I told you, the first time it was three Origs, then three Maldorans, but this is the first time three completely different races are involved, a Larin, a Maldoran, and a human, and this is the first time anyone has ever been drawn to a soul from outside our world."

"I see, this is very complicated. If I chose one of you, the one in exile, wouldn't he eventually find someone else?" I fervently hoped that there was some reconcilable outcome for this scenario. From the look on their faces, I could see the answer.

"No, baby," Tristan began. "You see, we cannot bind with anyone other than the soul created for us, therefore we are incapable of desire for anyone else. The, how do I put this..." he thought for a moment, "the carnal desire between a man and a woman does not exist within us until we meet our soul mates, and this mate is the only one we can produce children with, and then the males from our world can only produce two children, to continue his line, after that, we become sterile. It's sort of a built-in mechanism to Kardaunians, ensuring that our world would never be overpopulated." Tristan waited for my next response.

"Then there must be a huge number of Kardaunians in this world now, what with every woman that came through the portal and found her intended souls had children and they had children," I stated, knowing that there must be at least as many from Kardaun by now as there were humans in this world.

"I'm afraid that our population is far less than you think, love, and the numbers are getting smaller because of this insane war with the Origs. You see, when we passed through the portal for reasons, we have never been able to explain, all women, unbound or newly bound when they entered this world, found that they could not conceive. Only those that were expecting at the time of entry gave birth, but then they too were unable to conceive their second child. So, there are many Kardaunian couples that are barren. We believe that is why our intended souls are being born and reborn into different races, and as long as the souls are born into this world, they can conceive." Nick looked like, for this fact alone, he regretted ever bringing them to this world.

"Your people have suffered much to come here so that the world of Kardaun would not become extinct. Then to make matters worse, humans portrayed you throughout history as monsters, hunting you down, only diminishing your world more. How can you even tolerate humans after what they have done to you, to such a peaceful people?" I felt so horrible since I too was one of those humans who saw them as monsters.

"Olivia, this world belongs to the humans, and it is the goal of those that follow the crown of Kardaun to preserve the human race and help it to grow and evolve into a peaceful, productive world much like Kardaun was for thousands of years, before King Scarsion lost his mind. Tristan wanted me to see his people in their true light in hopes that any reservations I may have had would be dissolved. If only he knew how honored, I was to be brought into their world."

I smiled tenderly at him, hoping he would be able to see this in my eyes. "When did your people enter this world?" I directed my question to Nick.

"We passed through the portal in about AD 1200, earth time," he answered.

"How old were you then?" I continued my line of questions.

"Both of us were twenty-two in your years, why?" He stared, trying to understand my reason for asking.

I sat there mentally doing the math. "You're telling me that in your entire lives you have never been drawn or desired to have sex with any woman except me?" I was honored even at that thought, but totally shocked at the same time.

"Yes, love, as Tristan told you, we are incapable of those feelings until we meet the soul created for us," Nick reiterated.

"And you have never in one of my past births met me before now?" Nick looked at me curiously. "No, Lucas has always managed to kill you before you came of age. Why do you want to know this? I'm not following this trail of thought."

"If that's the case then, I'm sitting here in the presence of two eight-hundred-and-thirty-two-year-old virgins!" My eyes widened as I looked back and forth at them.

Nick looked up at the ceiling, and Tristan's face was scarlet. "Wow...in my world, to find someone at the age of twenty still untouched is rare!" I mumbled. Tristan and Nikolas both sat up straight with anxious expressions on their faces.

"Olivia are you saying that you—" Tristan started.

I caught onto his question and interrupted before he could finish. "No!" I blushed. "I'm one of those rarities. I've never, as you said, desired anyone that way, at least not until now," I admitted sheepishly.

Both of them seemed to release a relieved breath at the same time. Tristan moved from the arm of the chair to rest in eyes' view of me.

"Whichever you choose not to bind with will live alone. The pull of your soul on us is great. Olivia, and to not be near you is a torture we can't explain, but one we are willing to suffer for eternity, that Nick and I can both remain in this world. In order to try and put an end to this bloody war Lucas insists on continuing, we have to preserve the remnant of Kardaun from complete annihilation. Trust me, sweetheart, death would be far better than to be apart from you."

I could almost feel the agony caught in Tristan's chest as he explained this to me. I understood. Even if I did choose one of them, I would never feel whole, nor would I be able to live without sharing the same torture at the absence of the other. I wondered if they realized that.

"Nick, are the words and laws of your Creator written down in some kind of book, you know, like our Bible?" I asked.

"Yes, love, it's called the Ruhtt. Why?"

"Do you have a copy of it? I would like to read it. Maybe it would help me understand you both and your world better. I hope possibly that it will give me some insight on what to do," I explained.

"Certainly, love." Nick walked over to one of the long tables against the far wall and retrieved a small book from the drawer, just the right size to fit in a pocket. He walked back and handed it to me.

"Thank you," I said, slipping the book into my front pocket. "As for choosing..." I couldn't finish my thought.

"You know in your soul you will remain with one of us, that is absolute." Nick's voice trembled.

"But..." I looked at the two exquisite men in my life. "But I don't know if I can."

"I know it's going to be difficult, baby, but as we've told you, we cannot choose for you," Tristan said.

"I..." Tears filled my eyes. "I love you both—equally!" I confessed and started to cry.

"Olivia." Nick's cool hand pulled my face up gently. "We both love you too. More than words can tell."

"It's not the same as the love humans share; it far transcends any emotion you can imagine." Tristan's electric-blue eyes glistened with the purest love anyone had ever witnessed. I looked at Nick, his eyes mirrored the same.

"What am I going to do?" I began to sob uncontrollably. "I have to go. I have to go home! I need to think, sort this all out!" I stood up to start for the door and staggered as my head began to spin. I caught my balance on the back of the chair and took a deep breath. "Tristan, I would like for you to come and get me tomorrow. I don't think I could find this house again on my own. We'll discuss this more tomorrow, or rather later on today," I said, realizing it was only two hours till daybreak.

"Of course, I will, but I'm afraid you're in no condition to drive." Tristan had switched into doctor mode.

"Oh, wait. Nick, I came here with you. I don't have a car, and yes, Tristan, I'm fine now." My mind was overloaded. I needed to get out of here for a while. Nick looked at Tristan as he nodded. Nick reached into his pocket and handed me the keys to the Mercedes.

"Take my car, love. Olivia, if it's some time to yourself you need, you are welcome to the room upstairs. I promise you no one will disturb you." Nick pleaded, not wanting me to leave like this.

"I need to go home, Nick...please."

"I understand. But please take your time," he asked of me. His request was reasonable.

"I will." I walked toward the door and stopped before I opened it, looking back. Tristan and Nikolas were standing, silently watching; both looked frightened and worried. Both looked as though they were awaiting judgment, a bittersweet judgment left in my hands.

As the door closed behind Olivia, Tristan turned to Nikolas. "Nick, Galen and Safrina were here because there had been an attempt to breach the wall around the grounds."

"What? Why didn't you tell me, Tris!" Nick yelled.

"I didn't tell you because Galen said there was no need for concern. They had contained the situation." "Olivia. She's alone!" Nick's voice became panicked.

Suddenly they both straightened!

"We have to go—now!" Nick commanded.

SOULBOUND: DESTINY'S MOVE

They ran out into the night, hoping to reach Olivia's house before she did!

Abducted 17

I thought I would never make it home. The Mercedes was much more sensitive to touch than my Cavalier, and learning to drive a stick shift couldn't have hurt. As I pulled into my driveway, I noticed the porch light off. I was sure I had left it on, but then I was excited to see Nick, and it may have slipped my mind.

It was four thirty in the morning, and even with a full moon, it seemed almost black as pitch. The feel in the air made me uneasy. It was almost evil creepy.

I rushed into the house, anxious to shed some light around me. I quickly flipped the light switch by the door as I walked in, pushing it closed behind me in almost a singular motion. The second the light flooded the room, a horrified scream erupted from my very depths.

There in my father's chair sat a huge dark-haired man! It was like someone had glued me to the floor! I just stood there, my eyes wide in horror.

"Hello, my dear." The stranger's voice was deep and melodious, the type of voice that could sooth and hypnotize.

Gather you wits, Olivia! my brain instructed. "What are you doing here?" I managed to say before my throat closed up again.

"Is that any way to greet a guest?" he mocked. "I'm disappointed. I've heard so much about southern hospitality." He stood up to face me. The casual-dressed man's appearance matched the captivating voice. Besides the dark hair and well-groomed beard, his features were perfect, as if they had been chiseled from stone by a master artist. He stared at me for a moment. His gray eyes seemed to pierce straight through me.

I was glad he stood up. Even through my fear, I felt angry at his presumption to sit in my dad's chair uninvited. His massive body seemed to fill up the entire room! He took one step and was standing directly in front of me.

"So, you are the illusive Olivia. I'm so pleased to finally meet you," he crooned as he picked up my hand and politely kissed my fingers.

"Who are you?" I whispered.

"Oh, I'm sorry, forgive my rudeness. I am Lucas Scarsion." The very sound of his name sent another wave of terror through me. He just stood there, dripping with an evil eloquence. "I'm sure you've heard of me by now," he said calmly, smiling a beautiful, perfect white smile.

"What do you want?" I asked, even though I knew the answer.

"Hahaha, my dear little Olivia. Why, I want you of course." His eyes sparkled as he watched my expression. He seemed to relish in his power. In spite his pleasant mannerisms, his eyes gave away a cold, empty soul. "You are the key sweet, Olivia," he cooed.

"I don't understand. The key to what? Please, Lucas, I'm no threat to you!" I pleaded. My breath caught in my throat with every word.

"You are quite right. You hold no threat to me, but you are my answer. I have taken great pains to prepare for this night!" He flashed his sinister grin again.

I heard a loud commotion outside. "Galen!" I heard a woman scream, then the panic in her voice suddenly turned to agony as her scream seemed to echo for several seconds.

Safrina...A wave of nausea washed over me, and I began to tremble violently. The beautiful woman I had met tonight was gone, and the thought of her ruthless death angered me.

"What makes you think for one second that I would have any part in harming them?" I snapped. A thunderous evil laugh rang out. He was quite amused at my feeble defiance.

His eyes danced. "What makes you think you have a choice?" As we talked, I had begun easing back to the door. I turned the knob and rushed out, hoping to find an escape. I didn't even reach the front step when I saw a figure in the dark. I instinctively scanned the trees for any more creatures looming in the night.

"Hello, my darling," Lucas spoke from behind me. His greeting was gentle.

A flowing, musical voice responded, "Lucas, my love, is everything all right?" The porch light came on, revealing a beautiful slender woman with golden skin and shimmering sky-blue eyes. Her long platinum hair fell to her waist behind her.

"Indeed sweetheart," he said, wrapping his arm around her long slender waist. He placed his hand on her round face and kissed her tenderly. She looked up at him with such adoration, and he returned her gaze with the same emotion.

"Sweetheart, this is Olivia Ryan, Nixis and Traesdon's interest." He gestured to me as if he were introducing an old friend. "Olivia, this is Mariska, my mate."

This may be the only time anyone will ever see this soft gentle side of Lucas Scarsion, and I wasn't going to live to tell it! I thought. I started to move as Mariska reached out and took hold of my arm with a surprisingly strong grip for someone so petite.

"Don't be in such a rush, dear. We've just begun to get to know one another." She smiled sweetly as she tightened the already firm grip on my arm.

"Surely we haven't worn out our welcome so soon?" Lucas said in a mock hurt voice. He placed one hand on my face, gently tracing my jawline. His hand came to rest on the base of my neck, just at the top of my shoulder.

"Such a pretty little human," he commented. "If it weren't for Mariska disliking animals in the house, I'd consider taking in a pet." His bone-chilling laugh rang out again. "Be that as it may." He shrugged, and with a flick of his wrist, blackness consumed me.

"Hazon!" Lucas called as soon as Olivia's body fell limp. A woman dressed in a sweatshirt, jeans, and hiking boots stepped out from the trees. She made her way quickly to Olivia's porch.

"Put a sleeping spell on her. I don't want her rousing before we reach our destination," he ordered.

Mariska waited as Hazon bent down, whispering some words understood only by the witch. She breathed a soft, steady bluecolored breath into Olivia's face and stood up. "She's all yours, Your Majesty."

Then again, she bowed low to Mariska and started for the black Lexus that had just pulled into the drive.

Mariska scooped up Olivia's body as easily as if she were no more than a bag of flour. Hazon opened the front passenger door and got in while Mariska and Lucas took the back, placing Olivia between them.

"Where are we taking her, darling?" Mariska asked as she watched Lucas stroke Olivia's hair idly, like one would a sleeping cat.

"I want them to find her of course, just not too quickly. If I know Nixis, he will search the entire continent of Europe before he looks in his own backyard." He leaned his head back against the seat, smiling.

Nikolas and Tristan had taken the most direct path to Olivia's, straight over the mountain, but they knew. Olivia's front door stood open, only the faint glow of the dining room light shown in the house. Tristan rushed through the door, Nick behind him.

"You're too late, boys. They're gone!" came a soft but sinister female voice from the shadow of the hall. Tristan moved, but Nick had reached her first. He lifted the woman by the throat, holding her off the floor with one hand.

"Where, Mirabel? Where is she!" Nick demanded.

Mirabel's face lit up as she smiled evil and cold, no fear of the eminent death holding her.

"Lucas never said where he took her,"

Mirabel insisted. "He just ordered me to give you a message."

"Then spit it out!" Nick commanded.

"Tag, you're it!" And she disappeared in a waft of vapor. Nick stood silently staring at the hand raised where Mirabel hung in his grasp a second ago.

"What does that mean?" He turned to Tristan with his eyebrows knit.

"That's his way of saying it's his game now and we will play... by his rules!"

"Let's get back to the house, we have a lot to do," Nick said, passing Tristan with the speed of urgency he felt, leaving a cool wind blowing back against Tristan's long locks.

The second they entered the house, Nick headed for his study. "I'm going to make some arrangements. Call Taryn. Tell him to put everyone on alert in his area. Oh, and tell him to be here in one hour ready to fight. I'm sure we have a few lingering spies to deal with." Nick closed the study door behind him and dialed the phone.

"Nadya, we have a problem. Ready the guard, put them on standby, and be here in one hour."

Nadya could sense the anxiousness in his order. "Nick, what's happened?"

"I don't have time to explain on the phone. You have my orders. I'll see you in an hour."

He hung up and switched on the computer. He keyed in private flights on a secured site that he had procured access to a few years ago. Tristan knocked on the door, not waiting for Nick to invite him in.

"Taryn's on the way."

"Good, Nadya is too," he answered, scanning the list on the screen before him. "We know she's still alive. If all he wanted was to kill her, he wouldn't have bothered with the body," Nick reasoned. "There have been only three private jets leave in the past two hours. One flight plan for New England, one for upstate New York, and... ha!" He slapped the desk with the palm of his hand. "One left an hour ago for Europe!"

"You think he's taken her to his estate in Hungary?" Tristan asked.

"It seems only logical that he would secure her there. His estate is a fortress!" Nick was up and pacing.

"I don't know, Nick, something doesn't seem right," Tristan said warily. "It's too easy. Why would he go to the trouble of abducting her just to lead us straight to his doorstep?"

"Tris, we don't have a lot of time, and we have to start somewhere."

"I know what you mean, but I still feel like this whole thing is off." Tristan sat down on the leather sofa, wringing his hands.

"I don't even want to think about what he'll do to her!" Nick raked his hand through his hair. His eyes burning with fear.

"God, Nick, if he keeps her for any length of time..." Tristan's eyes were wide as the many tortures she could or would endure ran through his mind.

"This is not productive. Let's wait in the other room. Nadya and Taryn will be here soon."

They were standing by the fireplace, discussing plans and options, when Nadya entered into the sitting room. She bowed low at the door and moved into the room at Nick's motion.

Her waist-length blond hair was pulled back in a tight braid. She was dressed completely in the black attire of the Kardaunian guard. The dark eyeliner and thick mascara enhanced her pale, luminous skin and gave her black eyes the appearance of being larger, more menacing. The uniform fit like a glove, and a wide belt hung loosely around her hips, giving her slender athletic body the illusion of being taller than her five-nine height.

Nadya Ristov was not only the chief of the guard but also the best swordsman in Kardaun. She was certainly a daunting woman, her katanas strapped to her back and daggers sheathed on her wrists and legs. Her walk was graceful and fluid; there was no question Nadya was a vision of lethal beauty.

She walked up to stand in front of Nick. It was as if he were looking at a mirror image of himself in female form. She flashed a beautiful white smile as she reached out to hug Nikolas.

"What's the emergency, brother?" she asked, kissing Nick on the cheek.

"It's so good to see you. I just wish it were under better circumstances," Nick said as he released his sister from the embrace.

"Tristan, my friend, you're looking well." She smiled.

"Thank you, Nadya, so do you, as always." He returned the casual banter, trying to keep his emotions in check.

Taryn appeared at the door, bowed, and waited permission to enter. Nadya seemed taken aback by the striking man.

"Come in, brother!" Tristan called. Taryn walked toward them with such smooth, effortless movements, his brilliant aqua-colored eyes shining at the prospect of a good fight. He was as tall as Tristan at six five and every bit as muscular and broad shouldered.

He stood scarcely dressed in nothing more than black uniform pants and boots, bearing a single sword sheathed on his back. The leather strap cinched tightly against his smooth almond chest. The only difference between Tristan and his twin brother were the aqua eyes and Taryn's short cropped dark hair.

Taryn greeted Nikolas in the customary manner then reached for his brother's hand and a quick embrace.

"It seems we only see one another when there's a fight brewing." Taryn grinned as he stepped back.

"Yeah, it does seem that way, doesn't it?" Tristan smiled. "Taryn, have you met Nadya Ristov, Nick's sister?" Tristan gestured to Nadya, who was still involved in her conversation with Nick.

"No, Nadya, it is my pleasure. I wish the war had not kept us from meeting in Kardaun." Taryn reached his hand to her.

"Excuse me for a minute. I need to have a word with Nikolas. Take a moment to get acquainted."

Nadya reached her hand in response to Taryn's gesture and met his gaze. Taryn's breath caught the moment he looked into her eyes. His heart raced; finally, he had found his soul mate!

"I have been searching for you for eight hundred years!" he whispered to Nadya.

"And I have been waiting," she answered. "We will have time for this as soon as the task at hand is complete," she told him, turning back to business.

"Of course, I can't wait," he breathed. A quick smile flickered on her lips.

"Now that we are all here, brother, what has happened?"

"It's Lucas...he has taken Olivia."

"Forgive me, Nick, but who is Olivia?" It was clear by her expression that she had no clue.

"You don't know? The entire world of Kardaun knows about Olivia. How could you not?" Tristan looked shocked.

"My work keeps me isolated. Forensic pathologists aren't likely to hear any news from their clients," she informed him.

"Yes, but we would assume you would have heard when you were off duty." Nick entered the conversation just as astonished as Tristan.

"My dear Nikolas, I have very little contact with people, both human and immortal. So please forgive my ignorance. Judging from the urgency and your current state of mind, I feel I'm safe in assuming Olivia is your intended soul?"

"Yes, Nadya," Nick answered.

"As well as mine," Tristan added.

"What! This has only happened in our world twice in all of time!" she exclaimed.

"We know that Nadya," Nick said.

"Oh, I see. She hasn't chosen yet, has she?" Nadya suddenly felt her brother's agony.

"No, not yet" Nick answered, looking down as he spoke.

"I feel for you both, but I truly feel for her. I would not want to be in her shoes." She knew Olivia's decision had to be pure torture. "Well, bring me something to get her essence from, and it shouldn't be hard to track her."

"Nadya, there's more. Not only are a Larin and a Maldoran drawn to the same soul, but the woman that bears that soul is...human," Nick announced.

Nadya sat down, looking up at the two men in disbelief. Taryn knelt down beside her.

"Nadya, this is common knowledge to the rest of us. We have to find her and bring her back unharmed," he spoke softly, hoping she would see how important Olivia truly was to them and their world.

"You want me to track a human! They leave no more of a trail than a Hulain, and I've never attempted this feat before!"

"Nadya, not only are you the best swordsman in our world, you're also the most gifted tracker. I have every confidence you can do this," Tristan encouraged.

Nadya slowly stood up and looked at Nick. "Are you sure you want to bind with a human? What makes you think she's still alive? You could wait and hope your soul is reborn to a Kardaunian!"

"Nadya! How dare you question me! I don't care who you are! You will not speak to me in that tone! Do you understand!" Nick's voice was stern. His eyes burned with his disappointment in the princess.

Nadya dropped to one knee, head bowed.

"Forgive my impertinence, Your Highness. I had forgotten my place," she pleaded sincerely.

"Stand, Nadya." Nick looked into his sister's eyes. "Olivia is more incredible than words can define, and I love her deeply…we both do. Surely you are not as cold as you just portrayed yourself, sister. Have you become such a recluse that you've begun forming prejudice to other races?" Nick softened his tone, knowing she was in shock.

"No, brother, and what I said was contemptible. It's not my place to question the plan of our Creator," she spoke in a low, reverent tone. "Forgive me, Tristan, for my callousness," she said, turning to bow before him.

"You are forgiven, Nadya. Now let's get on with business. Time is not on our side."

"Taryn, you and Tristan take twenty of the guard and search the area, sweep a twenty-mile radius. Dispose of any spies you cross. Nadya, take five of your best trackers. See if you can pick up a trail," Nick instructed as he handed her Olivia's jacket. "I'll put the plane on standby and alert the members of the guard in Europe."

"Find her," Nick spoke to Nadya in a soft whisper. His eyes were pleading and desperate.

"I will, Nick. You have my promise," she spoke tenderly as she hugged him and disappeared from the room behind Taryn and Tristan.

Althea 18

I woke to find myself lying on a concrete floor in a damp, dimly lit room. I rose, maybe to quick. Everything began to spin, and my head was throbbing. I scanned the room, only to find I was locked inside a small metal cage. It was maybe five feet wide and six feet deep. There was a small open window with bars just at eye level. I tried to look out, but the only view was a huge stone wall, some shrubbery, and what appeared to be a large bowl-shaped birdbath. The outside air was colder for this time of day, so I was sure he had taken me out of the state. *Where am I?* I wondered. Will Nick and Tristan be able to find me before…I didn't even want to think about it.

I turned my attention back to the huge empty room. The only thing besides the cage and me was an old wooden worktable. There were no blankets or mats around me, only a five-gallon bucket in the corner of the cage. There was an old rag hanging on the handle. Big black letters were sprawled across the surface of it, spelling two words, Litter Box. Nick and Tristan had told me about Lucas's lack of respect for the human race.

"He thinks they're all animals," Nick had said. "Lucas doesn't believe humans have any true intelligence," Tristan had told me. Well, at least I knew for certain I wasn't dreaming again.

I knew there was no use in screaming for help, so I walked to the back of the cage and sank to the floor. There was something in my front pocket. I gently reached in and pulled out the small book Nick had given me, the Ruhtt, I think Nick called it. I opened it and adjusted my eyes. The print was small but still legible under the dim hanging light. I settled back against the stone wall and started to thumb through the book. I read mostly passages concerning the history and lineage of Kardaun, then I came across a passage that caught my eye. It was the story of the double binding Nick and Tristan told me of. I finished reading just before daybreak. Sitting there in the cold, damp quiet, thinking about what I had just read, it dawned on me.

She was unsure of her decision. The woman had to have been drawn more to one man than the other. She attempted a double binding for the wrong reason! In order to attempt this feat, there could be no reservations, no questions as to their Creator's motives for two souls. According to the Ruhtt, the woman was in total control of this situation. She had to enter into the bindings with the strongest conviction and absolute resolve that what she was doing was good and right. So completely opposite of the belief I was raised with. The second binding would make her an adulteress, thereby condemning her soul. By Kardaunian belief, should a double binding be successful, all three souls would be joined as one, making them stronger and wiser. A woman that attempts to bind with two souls had to have the desire to sustain the lives of both men and had to accept her mates unconditionally. Most importantly, her love for them had to be pure and equal!

I heard footsteps in the hall and slipped the Ruhtt back into my front pocket. The huge metal door opened to reveal the tall, thin woman I recognized from my dream. She carried a tray in her hands. I stood up and backed against the stone wall at the back of my cage.

"Who are you?" I asked in a cold monotone voice. She just glared at me as if I wasn't worthy of an answer and set the tray on the old wooden table.

"At the least, I should be able to address my watchdog by name!" I spat.

She whirled around quickly, her eyes narrowing. "You needn't address me at all!" Her voice was smooth and much more feminine than she appeared. "But since I am forbidden to bind your mouth shut, I am called Althea."

"Well then, Althea, perhaps you can tell me what day it is."

"Wednesday," she snapped.

"Can you tell me why I'm here? What does Lucas want with me?" I continued questioning.

"Perhaps I could tell you, but there is no reason why I should." She was definitely not going to make this easy.

"What are you doing down here?" I'm not sure why, but I felt as though I needed to draw her into a conversation.

"I've been instructed to feed you," she answered.

"By the way you're dressed, I'm guessing you belong to Lucas's army," I continued.

"I am the chief of King Scarsion's guard," she proudly announced.

"Oh, I'm sorry. Maybe you won't have to endure your punishment long," I snipped.

"What makes you think I'm being punished?"

I was gaining her interest. It was now evident she had never allowed herself to be engaged at any length in conversing with a human.

"Obviously you have done something that lost you favor in the king's eyes. Why else would you be placed on dungeon duty?" I paced impatiently as I tried to think of ways to extract information from her.

"I am here because of His Majesty's favor. I'm the only one he trusts," she defended.

"I see…and you believe that, huh? You really think he is that certain of your loyalty? After all, he is an Orig!" I baited.

She straightened to her feet from the edge of the table she was leaning on. "You referred to him in his Kardaunian name!" she said, surprised. "You are quite knowledgeable for a house pet!" She said this as if I should have realized my status.

"Why do you refer to me as a pet? I am a human being!" My voice had started to elevate with my agitation. Calm down, I reminded myself. Don't let her draw you away from your original plan. Get information.

"Human, animal...same difference," she stated flatly. "Humans are nothing more than animals, used either as pets or food, the same as a dog or cattle in the field." She seemed insistent on reminding me of her perception of my place in the world.

"Personally, to me humans are an infestation in the true Kardaunian world, which King Scarsion has assured, once he takes the high throne, will be exterminated!" She seemed pleased to announce.

I looked up at Althea, shocked at her words. So that's what he plans, to take over our world, destroy the human race, and restore his version of Kardaun under his rule. Had Althea thought about what would happen if the humans were exterminated as she put it? Well, if she hadn't, she's about to! I cleared my parched throat before continuing.

"Judging from your appearance, Althea, you're a Larin, aren't you?" I could again see I surprised her.

"Maybe if what you say is true, Larins are not part of Lucas's plans for the restoration of Kardaun," I said, standing in front of the bars with my arms folded in front of me.

My confidence was quickly thwarted when she crossed the room in a blur, rage emanating from her eyes. She grabbed the back of my head and slammed my face into the square edges of the bars.

"You impertinent little roach!" she rasped through clenched teeth. "How dare you speak like that!" This display of strength should have flagged me to keep my mouth shut, but instead only made me more defiant.

"Think about it, Althea. If Lucas destroys the entire human race, where will you get the blood you so desperately need for your survival?" I must have struck a nerve; she released her grip. I stood back, rubbing the side of my face, hoping she hadn't broken anything.

"I'm sure His Majesty doesn't intend to dispose of all humans." She sniffed.

"Exterminate, eradicate, whatever word he uses, means the same—no humans left!"

"I suggest you keep any further comments to yourself, or I may really lose my patience!" she snapped. I could see I was pushing my limits, but I didn't care. I was determined to get to her even if it did kill me.

"I've been instructed to feed you, conversing is not a requirement," she said, walking back to the tray on the table.

"Are you a citizen of Loxar?" I asked. I decided to ignore her warnings to keep quiet and tried to direct the conversation away from Lucas's plans.

"No, I'm from Es'mar. Why do you ask?" She looked curiously, wondering no doubt, if I were very brave or incredibly stupid.

"I just wondered why you sided with Lucas. If you had been from Loxar, I could have understood your loyalty. Have you always fought for the Orig king?" I continued, undaunted in my line of questions.

"What need have you to know?" Althea was beginning to show her irritation again. I needed to be wary about pressing her too hard. I had learned those results could be very painful.

"I'm sorry. I didn't mean to pry," I apologized with as much sincerity as I could muster. Althea played with the food on the tray. Her mind seemed to have wondered to another place, another time.

"I have pressing work to do, human. You seem to be able to solve mysteries, so here." She tossed some scraps onto the floor. "Solve the mystery of how to extract a drink from concrete!" She then turned the small tin cup of water up, pouring into a puddle at my feet. She laughed wickedly and walked out.

I quickly dropped to the floor. I had been here three days, and this was the first sign of food and water I had seen. I couldn't hold out for too much longer, I was sure. There before me were tiny droplets of moisture puddled in the uneven surface. I knew it wouldn't take long for the porous floor to completely absorb every drop. I leaned over and lapped as much of the moisture from the dirty concrete as possible. The rough surface scraped my tongue, and I could taste blood.

I picked up a small piece of bread and nibbled it gently then took another piece, pressing it tightly against the still moist spot where the water once stood. It probably wouldn't do any good, but it at least gave me a little hope.

The nights were cold, and the dark, damp room only enhanced the night air pouring through the open barred window. I spent my night pacing to keep my blood flowing.

Three more days passed before I saw Althea again. I would try not to make the mistake of angering her this time. I was lying on the floor next to the front bars, just content to let her drop the food and go. She wasn't going to leave things that easily. I saw the black boots, and in an instant, Althea grabbed me by the hair, jerking me up from the floor.

"Your food is here, roach, get up!" she demanded.

I rose to sit cross-legged, feeling weak and nauseous. After a few deep breaths, my stomach seemed to settle. I studied her for a few minutes, weighing my chances of survival if I dared to ask another question. *Olivia, keep your mouth shut!* I told myself. I never was good at taking my own advice, and I was sure I'd never have the reputation of being the "sharpest knife in the drawer."

"Althea, what made you turn against King Alberon?" I just couldn't help myself, and now that I started, I figured I'd either get an answer or wake up sometime tomorrow. There was just something about Althea that gave me the impression she wasn't the coldhearted monster she pretended to be.

"I was loyal to Alberon and fought with great conviction alongside my mate, Keve," she said.

"Keve didn't survive?" I asked.

"No, and it wasn't because he was a poor warrior. He was the second to Chief of the Guard Nadera. We were betrayed at the battle of Pria in Chaldron."

"What happened?" I asked her cautiously.

"I found Keve lying dead on the steps of the fountain...Queen Daria's dagger still piercing his heart!" The anger and grief glistened in her eyes with every word.

"Did you actually see Queen Daria take his life?" I asked.

"I didn't have to. Lazar told me he witnessed it and offered me the chance to avenge his death. In my anger, I took that chance and was made chief of Scarsion's guard." She turned from me, and my heart went out to her. To live with that kind of grief and anger for these many years must be equivalent to the fires of hell itself.

"Althea...Keve died fighting for his world, his king. I have no doubt he was a kind and just man." I felt bad for Althea, but I had to go on, to say what was on my mind regardless of the consequences.

"You must know his soul waits for you in Shalsmara."

"You don't need to tell me what I know!" she hissed at me.

"I'm just saying...you don't know for sure that Daria did this. You took the word of one of Scarsion's followers. Have you thought about the acts against others he has caused you to commit? You know these things are against the laws of the Ruhtt," I continued even though I could see her trembling in anger as I spoke. "If you continue this path, you will be damned to the veil of Ras, doomed to follow Keve unseen, within arm's reach, never to become one with him. Has that torture crossed your mind?" I was really pushing it now. I was surprised she had allowed me to go on this long. I decided to take advantage and continue, "Keve will only live in peace but forever remain in Shalsmara, never becoming one with the Creator, and you will be the only one to blame!" That was the final straw. Althea wheeled around, pink tears staining her face.

"Shut up! You are no one to tell me of my wrongs!" She grabbed my throat through the cage bars, pulling me forward.

"Althea, do you think Lucas will be pleased with you if you kill me?" I gasped. "Just please, listen to what is being said around you and think. You can change your fate, and I believe you want to." She released me, and I coughed and sputtered, rubbing my hand across my throat.

Althea started again to toss the food on the floor and dump the water but stopped. She looked at me as though she were trying to read my mind, to figure out why I would care. Leaning down slowly, she placed the water cup gently inside the bars and slipped the food through the slot in the door, then turned and left the room without a word. I drank the water in two large gulps and collapsed back to the floor.

I had become used to the constant pacing at night to keep warm but now had to push myself to keep going. My legs were becoming heavy and weak. I stopped to rest and saw a woman in the courtyard. She had built a fire in the huge concrete bowl and was walking around it in a circle, chanting something in an unfamiliar language. I watched as she continued, stopping intermittently to toss something into the blaze. It looked so warm, and I envied her that heat. I never got a good look at her face, but her hair was the color of copper, smooth and shining against the black cloak she wore. This odd ritual continued until almost daybreak. I watched as she made the circle around the flames one last time. A pink vapor started to rise from the fire, wafting out to each side. It drifted to the top of the wall and spread. As suddenly as it had appeared, it was gone.

The woman turned as if she heard something, and a tall, broad-shouldered man came up beside her. His hair was slightly gray on the sides, and his skin was a beautiful smooth mahogany color.

The stillness of the two as they stood talking reminded me of an oil painting of a time long past.

"Tell Lucas the binding spell is complete, and the veil is in place," the woman said.

"Excellent. Now all that's left is the waiting." The tall dark man sounded pleased. I was exhausted and unable to stand any longer. I slumped to the floor next to the wall and out of the direct path of the cold air.

My captivity had now lasted nine days. I'm sure I wouldn't have lasted this long if it hadn't been for Althea. She had changed so much since our first meeting. She still tried to convince me that Lucas only had the best interest of all Kardaunians at heart. Sometimes I wondered if she really believed her words of praise to the evil Orig king. Still, she was at least being nice, and I feared her less every day.

It was late that night; she paid me a visit. I had just dozed off for a minute when I felt the icy touch of her hand.

"Olivia," she whispered.

"What?" I jumped. "Althea, what are you doing here?" I dazedly asked.

"I took your advice and listened. I overheard Lucas talking to Mariska. You were right! He does plan to destroy us all and create a world of Origs under his rule!"

"I'm not surprised. It wasn't that hard to figure out," I said.

"You are exceptionally astute for a human. Had it not been for you, I would have gone on believing his lie," she admitted. "I owe you a great debt for opening my eyes."

"You don't owe me anything. I'm just glad you came to your senses," I told her. "Now why are you here?" I was positive she hadn't risked the wrath of Lucas by coming down here just to confess her ignorance.

"I had to tell you. Nikolas and Tristan are coming. I knew the news would ease your pain." Her voice was soft and compassionate. Looking into her eyes, I thought, another time, different circumstances, we could have easily been good friends.

"Althea, you have no idea." My heart was racing. "How long?" I anxiously asked.

"I don't know...a few more days maybe. My sources tell me they are planning their attack on Scarsion Manor, but they weren't privileged to the details," she replied. "Lucas is becoming suspicious. I know he senses the change in me since you came here." She turned quickly toward the door. "Quick! Lie down, someone's coming!"

I obeyed her command, and she vanished into thin air. The door opened slowly, and I saw the tall dark man from the courtyard step silently into the room. He never spoke, and I stayed perfectly still, pretending to be asleep. He scanned the room and stepped out, closing the door behind him.

"Who was that?" I asked Althea as she magically reappeared.

"Lazar, I have no doubt he was looking for me," she answered.

"How did you...where did you go?" I knew they had perfect night vision, and I couldn't see where she could have hidden.

"I hid out under there," she said, pointing to the underside of the huge wooden table and smiled. I started to ask how and recalled Tristan telling me about the Larins' ability to levitate.

"Quick thinking," I said with a smile in return.

"Olivia, I'm so sorry for the part I've taken in this war against the throne. I have much to atone for...if I live."

"If they're searching for you now, that means Lucas is trying to prove his suspicions. It won't be long till he knows about you," I warned.

"Don't worry. I can convince him of my allegiance for a few more days...at least until you're rescued," she assured me.

"You can't stay here! You have to leave now!" I urgently whispered.

"No, I can't just leave you here! Things will get very bad for you if I'm gone!" I could see in her eyes the desire to protect me and the desperate need to prove she could be trusted.

"Althea, listen to me. Your being here won't change one thing Lucas has planned! If he decides to kill me, you won't be able to stop him. You know when he figures this out, he'll kill you! You'll have your chance for atonement, but you can't put things right if you're dead! Now please go, get as far away from this place as you can!" I pleaded. Althea wasn't the bad guy, just another victim of Lucas's deception.

"I can see your reason." She contemplated for a minute then reached into a pouch on her belt.

"Here, take this. When Lucas realizes I'm gone, he'll question you, and I'm afraid you may not survive in your weakened state," she said, placing a tablet in my hand. "Take it at sunrise, and it will make you stronger, but the effects will only last until sunset," she explained.

"Don't worry, I won't tell him anything," I said with confidence.

"I have no doubt you are stronger than he realizes. I have to go." She reached through the bars and put her hand on my shoulder.

"Forgive me," she whispered and disappeared through the doorway.

Althea was gone, and I hoped that she would be able to evade Lucas.

Slowly I stood up on weak legs, my hands clutched into tight fists and my teeth clenched so hard it felt like my jaw was locked. The freezing air had left me numb. After a few laps around the confined space of the cage, my hands began to loosen. The tablet Althea gave me dropped to the floor. I reached down and picked it up. It will make you stronger, I recalled her words. I quickly put it into my mouth. It was sickeningly bitter and tasted like a wet dog smelled.

I noticed as soon as I swallowed my strength returning and my body temperature beginning to rise. "Thank you, Althea," I whispered under my breath.

Suddenly the door slammed open, and a pale young man entered the room. There was something unnatural about him, even for a Larin. I backed up against the wall, a knot tightening in my stomach as he stared at me. His fangs were showing. They weren't like Nick's or Althea's; they seemed permanent. It was the first time I felt truly frightened at first sight. His eyes were cold and empty, as if he were hollow inside. He opened the cage and grabbed me by the hair.

"Master wishes a word with you," he said, pulling me toward the door. "He told me to bring you unharmed, that you're not food. To bite you would mean death to me." He pulled my head back and breathed deeply against my throat.

"Mmmmm...it would almost be worth it!" he hissed. I didn't speak; something told me he wouldn't register anything I may have said. He then threw me over his shoulder like a sack of potatoes and whisked me upstairs, dropping me in the floor of what appeared to be a huge empty hall with two chairs on a platform, some odd-looking statues along the wall.

"What was that?" I thought aloud as I came to my feet. I heard a low chuckle and looked around to find Lucas peering down at me from the platform. I was again taken aback by the perfection of the man before me. I just couldn't understand how someone so beautiful could harbor so much evil.

"That, my dear, was a Luster," he stated. "They are quite handy to have around. They do exactly as they're told without question. The only inconvenience is they thirst constantly and they're easy to kill. The simple removal of their head, and they turn to ash. Lusters do pose time-consuming for the enemy though. They are incapable of strategy or reason and have no heart or soul, you see, since we have to kill them to create them. Take a good look, Olivia. They are what you humans encounter and have mostly encountered throughout history." Lucas smiled at the shock registering on my face.

"Yes, my dear, the undead as you call them do exist. Gavin there is literally a vampire. Well, enough chitchat. Let's get down to business, shall we?" His tone had hardened as he continued to stare down at me.

I realized I hadn't even attempted to speak the entire time I've been standing in this room. My skin began to tingle. This meeting was about to become very unpleasant.

"Althea is missing," Lucas stated. "I thought you might have some insight as to where she may have gone." He stepped down to stand in front of me.

I don't know what came over me. I felt angry and insulted that he would presume me to be so cowardly that I would be willing to rat her out! My answer came out dripping with bitter sarcasm.

"How would I know? It wasn't my day to watch her!" I snapped the words.

This enraged Lucas. He had me by the throat before I could blink.

"Do you know how close to death you are right now, little one?" he snarled. "I will have my question satisfied whether you are walking out of this room or carried!" He then gave me a sling as if I were a wet rag being tossed into the corner. I landed against the wall on the far side of the huge room.

Gavin "the Luster" looked down with a malicious grin. I could tell he was anticipating the chance his master might throw him a bone when he finished with me. Lucas grabbed my hair and yanked me from the floor. He glared at me for a second as he quickly thought of what to do with or to me next and instantly flung me back to the center of the room. He seemed to be standing there, waiting as my body came to a halt.

"Now, I'll ask again. Where is Althea?" he yelled.

"I don't know!" I screamed my response in defiance to his violent intimidation tactics. His hand struck the side of my face. I'm sure he withheld the force he may have used under other circumstances. It still felt like every bone in my face had shattered even though I was still intact. I wanted to cry, but my anger overrode the impulse as I wiped the blood from my nose with the back of my sleeve. Gavin started forward as Lucas turned toward him. He abruptly stopped and returned to the back of the room.

"The last place she was seen was downstairs. So, what did you say to turn her from me?" he asked through clenched teeth. Lucas was right in my face, his hot breath suffocating me. He was gripping tightly to the hair on the back of my head as he jerked me forward, and I could hear the roots loosening as he pulled. I had decided not to speak at all. It had always been clear that my life was of no value to Lucas, and if I was going to die by his hand, I was committed to keeping my word to Althea. I didn't know where she went, but I was afraid that something in our conversations may give him a clue. I was determined to die in silence. I'm not sure how long he kept me in that room, inflicting pain at every opportunity.

Blood was pouring from my mouth and nose. I knew that the only reason I was still conscious was because of the tablet Althea had given me.

"What did you say to her!" His impatience was growing with every word.

"I didn't tell her anything!" I screamed at him. "What could I have said? I'm only human, you know! I'm not that smart!" I hoped that playing on his ignorance of human intellect would save me from any further abuse. Finally, after what had seemed like hours of torture, he became still as my words registered with him. He released me and walked back to the platform.

"You're right. If you knew anything, you would have told it by now. I gave you more credit than you deserve. I need you alive, so Gavin will not be escorting you back to your chamber. Lazar, take her back," he ordered and walked out without another word.

Lazar was no less gentle as he returned me to the cage in the basement. I stood there relieved the torture was over, exhausted but pleased that he didn't get a word about Althea from me. The sun was starting to set, and the effects of the tablet began to wear off. The pain was far more intense than I realized as I collapsed under the tiny window.

Through The Veil 19

Finally, after ten days, Nadya and her trackers found Olivia at Scarsion's mountain retreat near the Canadian Border. The small group had settled in the woods just outside the boundaries of the estate, watching the fortress and those guarding it.

Nadya returned after a brief assessment of what to expect inside the gates.

"What are we up against?" Tristan asked as he moved to join Nick, Taryn, and Nadya knelt in a circle. The others had moved in behind them to hear.

"There are Larin, Maldoran, and Orig guards at the five key points of entry. Holden and Talia are at the main gates. They should be easy enough to dispose of. Rinehart and Yoa are at the northern entrance, Bail and Quillen at the south. The east is being guarded by Pyres and Gaines, and the west by Asdrew and Lochs," she informed them, drawing a quick layout of the main compound on the ground as she spoke. "Inside I could see at least a hundred Lusters just walking about aimlessly. Those are easy enough, but very time-consuming."

Tristan and Nikolas looked up and spoke in unison, "What about Olivia?" Their voices were filled with concern and their expression anxious.

"She's located here, at the side." Nadya pointed to the drawing on the ground. "There's only one barred window. It should be easy enough to get her out. From what you've told me, she's a tiny little thing anyway," she remarked nonchalantly.

Nadya's eyes were beaming with excitement. The mere thought of battle seemed to arouse her senses. Her eyes kept darting to her left at Taryn. The moonlight surrounding his beautiful face and perfect physique made him look extraordinarily amazing.

For the first time she was unsure if her heightened emotion was caused by the anticipation of the impending battle or the attraction to Taryn. She cleared her head and continued with the briefing.

"Here's what we do. Taryn and I will take out Holden and Talia at the main gate; same goes for Emeline and Darren at the north entrance," she instructed, pointing to them as she spoke. "Yarin and Nat will replace the guards on the south, Mitchell and Torrence on the east, and Edna and Jett will take the west entrance. Once all the points are procured, Taryn and I will open the main gates. Then...the fun begins. We'll keep the Lusters and the few Kardaunians that are about busy while you and Tristan rescue Olivia. Is everyone clear on this?" She scanned the group of soldiers around them as they all nodded their understanding and immediately dispersed to take their places.

"There's something wrong, Nick, it's too easy!" Tristan warned.

"There're no suspicious signs, Tris, maybe Lucas is just displaying his usual overconfidence," Nick replied. "Tris, take a squad to cover the back and then get into position by the front wall." Nick turned, pointed to a small squad of ten guards, and motioned them to follow Tristan.

Nadya turned toward Taryn. "I've never fought this closely with a Maldoran before. I'm looking forward to seeing you in action, Rilz. What's your cat, a lion or a tiger?" she asked, smiling sweetly but still unable to control the enthusiasm in her voice. Taryn just smiled at her and blushed slightly.

"It's nothing that regal...just a leopard," he said, slightly toeing the ground like a little schoolboy.

"A leopard...very nice. Will you be fighting in your animal form as well?" she asked, looking at Taryn admiringly.

He nodded slightly. "Only after I've lost my weapons. I'd look a little silly running across the battlefield as a large wild cat with a saber strapped to my back and a dagger at my hilt, don't you think?" he said with a low laugh.

Nadya giggled at the visual in her mind.

"Indeed, you would," she responded as she looked up at him, her eyes shimmering in the moonlight. Taryn caught his breath at the sight of her. It was clear to Nadya now that even in this dark corner of the wood, the attraction to her newfound soul mate was stronger than she had imagined and could prove to be a distraction to her usual concentration.

The group of warriors had begun readying themselves, drawing weapons, some phasing into their animal forms, but all awaiting Nadya's signal, ready to attack on command. Nadya and Taryn drew their swords, both gripping them tightly, eyes fixed ahead, breathing heavily. All at once, Taryn sighs and drops his blade.

"Nadya..." he said softly.

"What is it, Taryn?" she answered, straightening up to look at him.

Taryn stood there for a moment, speechless. She was so perfect, so beautiful he had forgotten what he was about to say. He impulsively stepped toward her and put his arms around her waist, pulling her close as he leaned over and kissed her tenderly on the cheek. She was surprised at first but quickly lowered her swords and wrapped both arms around him tightly. They were both perfectly aware of the situation and the eyes of everyone staring with gaping mouths, but they didn't let it spoil this moment—a moment they had waited eight hundred years for.

"Uhmmm...sorry to interrupt you two, but we have pressing business, and I'm sure Tris would agree if he were here, that we'd like to kill some Lusters and save our girlfriend!" Nick said with a hint of impatience in his lighthearted tone. He was glad to know his sister would no longer be alone in this world.

Nadya kissed Taryn gently on the forehead, both of them smiling as they pulled from their embrace. They retrieved their weapons and readied to take their positions.

"Stay alert!" Nick whispered to his sister, giving her a quick smile and a wink. This is what Nadya lived for. He could see the lust for battle in her eyes.

"You too, brother." She smiled. Her fangs already lowered in anticipation. Nikolas nodded and split off from Nadya and Taryn to take his place beside Tristan, already positioned at the front wall.

Taryn and Nadya secured the front gate with no problem. The north also was taken by Emeline and Darren quickly and quietly. Everything seemed to be going like clockwork as well with the south and west entrances, but the east gate was not yet secured. Mitchell and Torrence were struggling, so Richard and Gretta were sent to assist. Finally, after several minutes had passed, they received the allclear signal from Gretta.

Nadya and Taryn opened the front gates, and the charge began. Nadya had intended to levitate from the top of the wall, but a sudden wave of weakness came over her, and she fell hard onto the cold, dewy grass below.

"Nadya! Are you all right?" Taryn asked, quickly picking her up.

"Yeah, I just felt strange for a second. I'm fine...really." She wasn't accustomed to anyone showing concern for her well-being. The tender moment was fleeting as she turned on the approaching Luster, running her blade through his chest and taking his head in what seemed like one fluid motion. Black blood spewed onto both of them. Taryn touched her cheek as they both took off across the courtyard, fighting their way through the puppets.

Nick and Tristan were making way with a few of their own. Patches of the black sticky substance that ran through the veins of the Lusters had spattered onto them. Nick's beautiful blond hair looked as though he had dyed black streaks through it. The dark blood had spewed against his angelic face. Tristan was just as covered as they continued fighting. The clanking of metal on metal was deafening.

Nikolas went through one Luster after another, fangs bared, and his blade swinging meticulously, decapitating his enemy with precision. He looked to his left to see Tristan take down three in a matter of moments. He had so far only encountered two true Kardaunians, and their hearts lay in the fire still burning in the huge concrete bowl.

Nick could see the rage on Tristan's face and heard the growl as he suppressed the animal fighting to get out. His friend was so consumed with the Lusters in front of him he failed to notice an Orig had phased directly behind him. Nick immediately lunged, taking him down and paralyzing him with one bite to the jugular. Tristan whirled around to see Nick as he finished off the werewolf. He smiled and gave a quick salute to his friend.

Tristan stopped fighting when he heard Nick and Nadya cry out to him.

"Go get Olivia!"

"Taryn, come with me!" he called, and without hesitation, they turned and ran through the mass of fighting Lusters and their friends. The dark old blood of the mindless puppets had blackened the bright-green grass, giving it the resemblance of a tar pit.

They saw three of their comrades fallen by acid-coated arrows that were set aflame and shot from the rooftop. "Damn! Snipers!" Taryn hissed.

I heard the loud commotion coming from outside as I lay there on the cold, damp floor. The effects of Althea's tablet had worn off, and the full impact of my torture was excruciating. I wanted to look out and see what was happening, but I was too weak to move.

"Please, God, I prayed. Let that sound mean Nick and Tristan are here! I no sooner had thought it when I heard Tristan's voice call out to me.

"Olivia, can you hear me?" he yelled. I tried to answer, but all that came out was a low groan.

"Taryn, the window is too small to get through even in animal form!" Tristan cursed as he easily separated the bars from their concrete sill. He put his head inside as far as his shoulders would allow. His heart began to beat wildly in his chest when he saw Olivia lying there.

"Olivia, sweetheart, can you hear me?" he called again.

"Tris...yes..." I finally managed.

"Baby, take my hand!"

I reached up, but his fingers were still inches away. I tried to lift myself from the floor, but I didn't have the strength with nothing around me to grab on to.

"Taryn, I can't reach her, she's too weak to stand on her own!" he exclaimed, scanning the area for something long enough for her to grab hold of. There was nothing but a few brittle limbs on the surrounding bushes.

He suddenly turned with a half grin to look at Taryn. His brother seemed to read his mind.

"Now wait just a minute!" Taryn protested.

"It's all I can think of, and we don't have a lot of time!" Tristan explained. "Now phase and pull her up with your tail!" Tristan ordered.

"My tail...why can't you do it?" Taryn asked indignantly, finding the request a bit personal.

"First of all, your tail is longer than mine, and second..." Tristan continued, pointing to himself. "King, and it's not a request!" He stared, awaiting Taryn's compliance to his order.

Reluctantly, Taryn phased and backed his bottom up against the windowsill, vowing to himself that he would someday get even with Tristan for this.

"Olivia, grab on to the leopard's tail and pull yourself up!"

I reached up with trembling hands and grabbed hold of the wriggling furry rope. I must give a proper thank you to the man or woman at the other end of my lifeline, I thought. I barely reached my feet when I felt Tristan's warm hands whisk me through the window.

Taryn had phased back and dressed in a pair of pants he found in a pile of Luster ash while Tristan made a quick assessment of her injuries and gathered Olivia into his arms.

I wanted to speak, but my mouth and throat were too dry to form the words. I just looked at him through the hazy tears of relief as he talked to the man that had helped rescue me. I tried to see the face that had belonged to the leopard, but when I looked at him, all I could see was Tristan's face. When I relaxed my head against his shoulder, I looked up to see my beautiful electric-blue eyes staring down at me. I'm safe now, I thought. The warmth of his arms and chest was so comforting I allowed the peaceful darkness to overtake me.

"GO, TARYN, TELL NICK I have her!" Tristan said. Taryn was gone in a blur. Just as quickly as Taryn left, Nikolas was beside him.

"Is she going to be all right?" Nick asked.

"Yeah. She's dehydrated and badly bruised, but mostly just exhausted. She'll be fine when she gets some fluids," Tristan told him as he stood there cradling Olivia close to him. Nick ran his hand along her face, resting his fingers on each scrape and bruise.

"I did a quick examination when I pulled her from the window. Her back, shoulders, and legs are in worse condition. I can only imagine the pain Lucas inflicted to leave her in this shape." Tristan breathed the words as if he could feel her agony. His eyes burned with fury as he struggled with the silent rage growing within him. Nikolas understood how he felt even as he tried to maintain a calm exterior; inside he was boiling with a murderous lust for Lucas Scarsion's heart.

"Take her straight to the plane, Tris, take her home," Nick said as he stroked Olivia's hair back. "I'll fly back with Taryn and Nadya." He leaned over, kissed Olivia's forehead and returned to the fight with a raging vengeance. He signaled to Nadya that Olivia was safely off the grounds. Nadya acknowledged and called for her army to pull back. Nick held back, watching as Nadya and Taryn exited the main gate behind the remaining troops. He started forward to join them outside the gate, when two Origs and a Maldoran jumped him.

<hr />

NIKOLAS WAS DRAGGED through the front door and released into Lucas's throne room. The room was empty with the exception of a few rare pieces of art on the walls and statues placed in the corners of Orig kings before him. Against the far wall sat two large highbacked seats, Lucas and Mariska's throne placed in the center of what appeared to Nick as a huge stage befitting any actor.

Nick saw Hazon and Lazar standing on the platform before him. He started toward them, fangs bared, only to be knocked back to the ground. Lucas had entered the room and was now watching in amusement as Nick tried to find an opening in the invisible barrier surrounding him.

SOULBOUND: DESTINY'S MOVE

"Hazon, you contemptible witch! You will find death for this!" Nick promised.

Hazon stood on the stage beside Lazar and Lucas, laughing. She was a striking woman with copper locks and bright-blue eyes.

"I doubt very much it will be by your hand, Nikolas." She sneered.

Nick's eyes shifted to Lazar. "And you…traitor…will not be far behind!" He turned his attention to Lucas when he heard his thunderous laugh.

"Nixis…benetis otoglon," he addressed Nick as if they were old friends, using the ancient language of Kardaun, a language, though not forgotten, seldom used. Human languages have been encouraged for the past five hundred years. The Ruhtt had even been translated into the many human tongues to ensure an easier transition into this world.

"Ntoglon gohuen, Lucai! Kaspaeth gotunevnusmah!" Nikolas commanded.

"Very well, if this primitive language is your preference." Lucas sniffed indignantly.

"You have your chance now, face-to-face!" Nick stared at him, the hatred burning in his eyes.

"Nixis, you wound me," Lucas responded, clutching his chest mockingly. "I have no desire to battle with you tonight. Besides, you know all too well that would end as a chess game between two master players—in stalemate."

"Then why am I here?" Nick seethed.

Lucas gave a triumphant laugh. "Only to ensure that Traesdon returns with your little human first!"

"Enough with all the riddles. Stop chewing your bone, dog, and say what you mean!" Nick's eyes blazed with murderous desire.

"You passed through a binding veil tonight, both you and Traesdon, placed around us by Hazon," he said, gesturing toward her proudly.

Nick turned to Hazon with a contemptuous glare.

"She informed me of your little human's high morals, the fear she has of jeopardizing her soul. She has only seventy-two hours to bind with one of you…or both…which Hazon has assured she will not do by moral conscience, before one of you dies!"

"Nice plan, Lucas, but had you considered only one of us coming for her?" Nick wished now he had taken more heed to Tristan's warning.

"Indeed, Nixis, it is a clinging spell. Whichever, you or Traesdon would have need only to touch each other or your human to be infected by it. So you see, I win either way." He leaned his head back and laughed like Satan himself. Nick felt the pain of defeat in the pit of his stomach. There was no chance for him now.

Lucas was right. Tristan would bind with Olivia. Even though he knew death was eminent for him now, he found solace in knowing she would live.

"I am quite sure the little one will have bound with Traesdon before you can return. So, you are free to go, Nixis, and die in peace!" Lucas spat.

The Binding 20

I was relieved when Tristan carried me onto the plane. "Where's Nick?" I felt uneasy and frightened by his absence.

"Don't worry, baby, Nick is flying back with Nadya and Taryn." He was trying to ease my fear, but I could tell he was worried too. He continued examining me even though I kept insisting I would be fine. "Your bruises have already started turning. You must have a very strong blood flow," Tristan remarked.

"I've always been what my dad called a quick healer. I guess that's a good thing because I was a real klutz as a kid," I told him.

Abby brought some food and a pitcher of water. Tristan had insisted on pure liquids given my dehydrated state and lack of solid food. I wouldn't hear of it. I was completely ravenous, and Jell-O was not at the top of my list.

"Olivia, I know this is going to be hard, but...I need to know everything that happened to you."

"All right, where would you like me to start?"

"If you don't mind, from the time you pulled into your driveway."

I drew in a deep breath and began my recount of every moment from the time I arrived at my house. He sat patiently listening while the hatred for Lucas Scarsion burned in his eyes. I noticed as I spoke there were beads of sweat on Tristan's forehead. I had never seen him perspire before.

"Are you all right, Tristan?" I reached up to touch his face, but my hand was shaking so hard I could barely control it.

"I'm fine, sugar. Now, what about the copper-haired woman in the courtyard?" His eyes widened as I told him of her chant and the pink vapor coming from the flame.

"The last thing I heard her say was something about the binding spell being complete. She was talking to a man named Lazar." By the time I finished my story, I had begun to weaken again, and the cabin of the plane felt like it had turned into a sauna.

Tristan called Abby and instructed her to bring all the ice from the back. "Hurry, Abby, we have to stay cool until we land!"

"Yes, Sire." She bowed and rushed to the back of the plane, returning with two buckets filled. Tristan put some ice into his mouth and wrapped some in a towel, placing it on my stomach under my sweater, then did the same to himself.

"Olivia, you need to eat as much of the ice as you can," he said, placing another towel on my head and one around the back of his neck. I was thankful it was a short flight. I just wanted to get somewhere and lie down comfortably.

Tristan carried me to the limo already waiting when we landed.

"Markus, we don't have a lot of time. Get us home and hurry!" he ordered.

By the time he carried me into the house, I was barely able to hold my head up. I noticed Tristan's beautiful dark almond skin had started to pale, and the golden undertones had begun to fade. He laid me on the bed, and I noticed we were in the room at the end of the hall.

"What's happening to us, Tristan?" I whispered in a weak, shaky voice.

"Olivia, this is important, so please try to focus on what I'm about to ask, okay?" His voice sounded urgent and desperate.

"Okay," I whispered.

"The woman you saw outside was Hazon. She's one of the Warins that sided with Lucas. She placed a binding spell around the estate."

"What's a binding spell?" I managed the question through short gasping breaths.

"The spell affects anyone that has found their soul and not yet bound with them when they enter or exit through the veil."

"Like us," I said to let him know I was still coherent.

"Yes, baby, like us." He had started to tremble as he answered.

"What's going to happen?"

"Olivia, I need to know. Do you love me?"

"Of course, I love you, Tristan. Why?"

"I need your permission, sugar, and you have to tell me now!"

"My permission...for what?" Then it dawned on me what he was asking. "Tristan, I..."

"Olivia, I can't lose you," he barely whispered the words. I noticed how dramatically his appearance had changed. He was beginning to look ashen. Then I realized. The spell, he has to bind with his soul or die!

"Olivia, please, give me your answer!" he pleaded. "Do you love me?"

"Yes...forever" I breathed.

"That's all I needed to know!" His lips found mine, passionate and urgent. From the moment the beautiful kiss began, I felt my strength returning. The weakening fever suddenly became the electric sparks I always felt when Tristan touched me. The moment of my longing was so amazing it took my breath! I could never in my wildest dreams imagine this! I burned with every sweet brush of his hand, every kiss. His warm breath caressed my neck, my shoulders, and every time I began to relax, he would ignite another wave of passionate desire, sending the electric jolts coursing through every inch of my body. Oh, how I wanted this sweet agony to go on forever! I looked up into his eyes, his beautiful hair falling down, sheltering me. He placed his hand on my face, holding me in his steady gaze. Then I saw it again, the flame deep within him. I began moving toward it. God, how I ached for the fire to consume me! I stepped into the white-hot flame, and my body felt as if it disappeared! A low growl erupted from deep within Tristan the instant our souls touched.

NIKOLAS REACHED THE edge of the woods, a short mile from the confines of Scarsion Manor, where Taryn and Nadya waited anxiously. "Nick, what happened?" Nadya asked the instant he reached them.

"We were afraid he..." Taryn started.

"I assumed he planned to kill me tonight also, but Lucas had something far worse planned," Nick informed them. He could see the effects of the binding spell already beginning as he looked at his sister and her intended mate.

"We have to get to the plane. Is the car on standby?" Nick asked, his eyes urgently scanning back and forth at them.

"Of course, brother, it should be here any minute." Nadya smiled. No sooner had she spoken the words, a black Mustang pulled over at the edge of the road.

"What did you mean by Lucas had planned something worse?" Taryn asked, looking across the front passenger seat with concern for Nadya's odd lack of energy, yet directing his question to Nick.

"He wanted us to rescue Olivia. Are you all right, Nadya?" Nick too had noticed the change in his sister.

"I'm fine, now will you two quit staring at me!" She gave them an insistent wave of her hand.

"I'm afraid you're not fine, dear sister, none of us are. As I was saying, this was planned. We passed through a binding veil when we entered the estate grounds!"

"A binding veil!" Taryn exclaimed.

"Yes, and I was just detained to allow Tristan to get back with Olivia first." Nick's voice rang with the despairing sound of defeat.

Nadya reached across and placed her hand on Nick's arm.

"You don't know that she won't choose you," Nadya said.
"She will bind with Tristan tonight," Nick spoke with certainty.
"How can you be so sure?" Taryn asked.
"He won't wait, he can't! Tristan will not let Olivia die!" He was at least glad to know Tristan's love would keep her safe. They finished the ride to the airport in silence.

As soon as the plane was in the air, Taryn began treating Nick, Nadya, and himself the same as Tristan had Olivia—with plenty of ice packs. Suddenly, all three rose up in their seats. Nadya and Taryn instantly looked across the aisle toward Nikolas. A faint, bittersweet smile crossed Nick's lips.

"It is done, she has chosen," Nick said softly.

"Brother, there's still a chance."

"No, Nadya, we've explained the danger, and her morals and beliefs won't allow it. Tristan has taken his mate, and I'm truly happy for him. Now you have to prepare yourself," he said through labored breaths. "Prepare for what?" Nadya was finding it difficult to think.

Soul's Torment 21

"Prepare to take the throne, sister." He tried to smile but found it difficult. The loss of his love caused an ache so deep it overpowered the burning effects of the spell.

Nadya started to speak, but Nikolas raised his hand to silence her.

"Stay behind, send the crew away. Then come see me when your strength returns. I give you my congratulations for your new life together." I woke about three in the morning feeling warm and content. It was as if I was a jigsaw puzzle with a missing piece replaced one step closer to completion. I showered and dressed into some comfortable sweats I found in the center bedroom closet and went downstairs. I found Tristan in the sitting room, staring into the fire, lost in thought.

"Hey," I spoke into the silence as I moved to the chair across from him.

"How are you feeling?" he softly whispered and ran his hand along my cheek.

"I'm feeling great, well, better than great actually." I smiled timidly at him, and he smiled back.

"Tristan..."

"Yeah?"

"Who are Nadya and Taryn?" I asked.

"I forgot. We never got around to telling you about them. Nadya is the chief of the guard and Nick's twin sister. Taryn is a captain of the guard and my twin brother." Tristan was amused by the surprised look on my face.

"No wonder when I looked at the man beside you in the courtyard, all I could see was you! All this time, neither of you felt

I needed to know anything about your family?" It seemed odd that they would omit this very important detail of their lives.

Tristan laughed. "Sugar, we were so wrapped up in our preparation to announce the real us we never thought about family ties."

"I understand, you had more pressing things on your minds, so I forgive you," I said with a slight giggle. My tone and expression quickly became serious.

"Tristan, I understand the urgency for my answer tonight," I began.

"You do?" he responded with his eyebrow raised.

"If you didn't bind with your intended soul, you would have died."

Tristan stood up and stepped in front of the fire. "Oh, sugar, you didn't accept me just to keep me from dying!" He seemed positively stricken by the thought.

"No, Tristan. No!" I got up and stood in front of him. "I do love you, with all my heart and soul." I blushed.

He smiled and put his arm around me, drawing me close to him.

"There are no words nor will there ever be any that can express how I feel about you, Olivia. I'm glad you accepted me more out of love than fear, but it wasn't me I was concerned about." He smiled softly and kissed me with a feather's touch.

"What then made my decision so urgent?" I didn't understand. It was clear to me he was ill and growing weaker by the minute.

"I was concerned about you, sugar. The spell was affecting you much faster." He could see how confused I was and motioned for me to sit down. He knelt down in front of me.

"It's like this," he began. "Lucas, I'm sure, never thought his plan through. You were not in the forefront of his scheme. To him it was an easy way to dispose of us or at least one of us. He never thought about what would happen if you died first." He lowered his eyes and took a deep breath.

"What would have happened?" I asked.

"If you had died, then the spell would have no more effect on us, because our intended soul would no longer be part of this world. We would have been back to square one, seeking you out again in seventy years. So, you see, I needed to save you! I've waited too long to find you, and I couldn't bear to lose you now."

I reached forward, cupped his face in my hands, and kissed him gently. "Tristan..." My voice caught as I realized this wasn't over yet. "You saved me, and I know it voided the spell on you too, but what about Nick?" No sooner had his name passed my lips, he staggered into the foyer and collapsed.

"Nikolas!" I screamed and ran to kneel beside him. Tristan raised his head, and he opened his eyes.

"Tris..." He was weak and breathless.

"Don't try to talk, Nick, let me get you upstairs!"

"As you wish." He attempted a feeble smile and looked up at me. His eyes were so sad and full of pain. I could feel the blood drain from my face at the tormenting sight before me. Nick's weak, trembling hand touched my cheek; it was hot!

"I'm so glad you're safe," he whispered as Tristan picked him up and rushed to the room at the top of the stairs. I just sat there on the cold tile floor, tears streaming silently down my face. What have I done, my beautiful Nikolas? I started to sob violently.

Tristan picked me up in his arms and carried me back into the sitting room.

"Olivia, I'm going to try and make Nick more comfortable. Will you be all right here alone for just a little while?" He was as tortured by this as I was. I nodded my head, too hurt and too numb to speak.

"I'll try to hurry, baby, just sit tight, okay?" I nodded again, and he left the room.

TRISTAN HAD PACKED ice around Nick to help cool his burning skin. He held him up to drink, trying to get as much of the thick iced blood into Nick's system as he could stand.

"Thank you, my friend." Nick's voice was broken as he gasped for each breath. "I'm truly happy for you, Tris. Thank you for saving her."

"Nick, I knew you'd understand why I didn't...why I couldn't wait for you to return."

"It was all part of Lucas's plan. He detained me just long enough..." Nick's weakened state caused him to pause for rest.

"I know, Nick. I figured it all out on the plane home. Olivia told me about the binding spell. She didn't know how much time though."

"Seventy-two hours." The combination of ice packs and the large quantity of blood had given him more strength.

"I'll call Taryn. Maybe he can find a Warin that can reverse this," Tristan said.

"No, my friend, you know that a binding spell is irreversible. There's nothing you can do." Nick closed his eyes for just a moment to collect himself. "Tris, you have thirty-six hours to prepare Olivia for the inevitable. Then the pain will become unbearable. You must promise me..." He faded from consciousness but only for a second.

"Promise what, Nick?"

"Promise when that time comes you will ease my suffering." Nick knew he was asking much more than Tristan was prepared for. "Promise!" he pleaded.

"Nick..." Tristan started to protest, then looked into the agonizing gaze of his friend and sighed. "Yes, my friend. I'll honor your request," he answered, dropping his head in despair.

"Thank you. I have already told Nadya and Taryn to prepare to take the throne. They are bound by now," Nick told his friend.

"My brother and your sister?" Tristan smiled. "I'm glad for both of them."

"When Olivia is up to it, would you send her in to see me?" Nick asked.

"Yes, if you're comfortable enough, I need to get back to her."

"Of course, we'll talk again later." His voice trailed off again.

"I'll be back to check on you. By your leave, Your Majesty." Tristan bowed with great honor and reverence to his king.

TRISTAN FOUND OLIVIA sitting just as he left her, staring blankly into the fire.

"Baby, is there anything I can get you?"

"He's dying, isn't he?" I asked, turning my head slowly, still holding my blank expression. I didn't know what emotion to feel first, the sadness, the hopelessness, or the rage.

"Yes, sweetheart, I'm afraid so."

"This isn't right, Tristan! This shouldn't be happening! Look what I've done to you both and your world! Why didn't you let me die!" I screamed through my tears.

"Olivia! Don't talk like that!" Tristan's voice trembled. "Baby, please, listen to me. This is not your fault!" he said, kneeling down, wiping the tears from my eyes. "You didn't do this, Lucas did."

"You said yourself, if I had died first—" Tristan stopped me before I could finish.

"Neither of us would have ever allowed that to happen! I wish I could make you see how much you mean to us, Olivia." Tristan's words were from the heart, I know, but I was not as important as they are to me and to Kardaun.

"Tristan, how long does he have?"

"Till noon tomorrow," he answered solemnly. He knew that Nick would have longer, but he would end his friends' life early as he requested. He wanted to spare that knowledge to Olivia if he could. "Please stop blaming yourself. It's so painful to see you this way!"

"Don't you care?" I asked, looking at Tristan through a watery haze.

"Olivia, I can't believe you asked that! Of course I care; he's my best friend and has been since childhood!"

"I'm sorry, Tristan, that was totally uncalled for. Please forgive me!" I felt ashamed to doubt his feelings.

"It's all right, sweetheart. I know you're hurting right now." He wanted to console me, but I felt like I deserved to feel this pain.

"Baby, as soon as you feel up to it, Nick has asked to see you." Tristan's eyes let me know that he wasn't sure how long he would remain coherent. I knew if I wanted to talk to him, I needed to pull myself together and quick.

Another hour had passed while I sat staring into the fire. Tristan came back down from Nick's room.

"His strength is up enough to talk now," he informed me. "Are you prepared to see him yet?"

"Yes...I think so," I answered and walked to the staircase.

"Tristan...I'm scared."

"Shhh, baby, it'll be okay, trust me."

"I don't know what to say." The blur of tears was hampering my vision again.

"Say what's in your heart and everything will be fine," he whispered and gently kissed the top of my head.

I slowly climbed the stairs. When I reached Nick's door, I looked back to see Tristan still standing there. He gave me a quick reassuring nod, and I opened the door and entered the room, walking quietly to the edge of Nick's bed. The sight of him caused my legs to buckle. I felt the need to hold tightly to the bedpost.

He looked so frail. His skin was an unnatural gray color, and there were huge dark circles around his eyes. His once beautiful full lips were the color of light ash, parched and cracked. I shuddered, trying to hold back the agonizing sobs. My chest felt like it was caving in from the pressure of my restraint. Nick's eyes slowly opened, and a faint smile crossed his withered lips.

"Olivia, please come closer and sit here." He weakly patted the bed beside him. I moved to his side and sat down.

"Oh, Nick...I'm so sorry..." I couldn't finish. My voice seemed to shut down, and I couldn't hold back the tears.

"Hush, love, it's all right," he whispered. "I'm at peace with this." He feebly reached and took my hand. "But...I wish it had been me!" I cried.

"Don't even think that way, love. This is better, at least for me. You see, if you had died, I could never have been able to live in a world without you, and now that you've chosen, I know I couldn't bear to live not being near you."

The realization that either way I would never see Nick again hit me as if I'd been struck by lightning.

"Love, I had to see you. I needed to look into your beautiful green eyes one more time. You are truly the most breathtaking woman ever created!" He smiled. "I want you to know that I love you and will always love you, even in Shalsmara, for all eternity. I had to tell you before we said good-bye."

"Nick...I don't want to say good-bye!" I snubbed through my tears.

"We have to, love. Now please, you need to go, and for my sake and yours, don't return." A pink-stained tear rolled down from the corner of Nick's eye. He lifted my hand to his parched lips and kissed it tenderly.

I leaned down and placed my lips to his fevered forehead and whispered, "I love you, darling. I always will." I kissed his hand and reluctantly moved to the door.

I made it down the stairs on my trembling legs and collapsed on the floor. Tristan was there in an instant, carrying me back to the chair. He disappeared for what seemed like only seconds, returning with a cup of hot tea.

"Drink this, sweetheart, and catch your breath," he insisted.

"I need to be alone for a while," I told him. "I understand. I'll be upstairs," he said.

"No, I'm going up to the sunroom."

"Are you sure? I don't mind—"

I stopped Tristan midsentence. "It's quiet there. I need to think. I'll be fine, honey, really," I assured him.

"All right then, I'll check on you later and bring you something to eat."

"Thanks." I brushed his shoulder with my hand as I passed by him.

I had spent the entire day in the sunroom, desperately seeking an answer. To what, I wasn't sure. Why did this happen? Why would Nick be taken from me? How will Tristan cope with all this? How will he feel toward me when Nick is gone? What was right...what was wrong? My heart, mind, and soul were raging in battle, pulling at me in all directions. Tristan had been up to check on me several times. I watched the sun go down behind the mountain, and still I remained fixed in my chair.

Nadya and Taryn came by to see Nikolas.

"Nadya, I am so sorry." Tristan held out his arms, and Nadya accepted his embrace.

"It's hard to imagine I will never see him again in this world," she said, wiping a rose-colored tear from her eye. "Where is Olivia?" she asked.

"In the sunroom. She's been there since this morning," Tristan answered, releasing a wearied sigh.

"I need to speak with her."

"Nadya..." Tristan called. She slowly turned to acknowledge him.

"Be gentle with her. Remember, she is not to blame," Tristan cautioned.

"I know, brother," she said and gave him a reassuring smile.

Nadya walked into the sunroom as Olivia looked up through her swollen bloodshot eyes.

"We haven't officially met," Nadya began.

"You're Nick's sister," I interrupted. "I am so sorry. I feel like this is my fault and you have every right to hate me."

Nadya could see the anguish Olivia was suffering. She walked over and pulled her new sister-in-law from the chair, wrapping both arms around her.

"Olivia, I don't hate you, nor do I blame you. We are at war, my dear, and any one of us can become a casualty."

"Thank you for understanding even though you have every right—"

Nadya cut me off before I could finish my sentence. "Olivia, I want you to know that I do not desire the throne and would rather not have it forced upon me. I know the teaching and laws of the human world, so I can understand your dilemma. I need to know. Do you love my brother?" she asked.

"Yes, I do love him very much," I responded without hesitation.

"As much as you love Tristan?" If she was about to make a point, I wished that she would just do it.

"Yes," I answered flatly.

"Then will you do something for me?" she asked softly.

"If I can, what is it?"

"While you're searching your heart, remember that we are not talking about the human world. Their laws and rules don't apply to us." She leaned forward, kissed my forehead, and left me standing there in silence.

"She's right!" I whispered aloud. "All this time, I've been trying to sort this out through my perspective, not theirs!" I ran downstairs to find Tristan in the kitchen.

"I'm glad you finally decided to come down. I was just making you a sandwich." He smiled.

"Thanks, but I'm not hungry. I need to ask you something."

"Sure, what do you want to know?" He looked a little suspicious of my sudden change of mood.

"Promise me you'll answer truthfully, 'cause it's very important," I cautioned him.

"Baby, that's another little twist from my world. Once we're bound to our mate, we can't lie to them. If I tried, you'd know it." He grinned.

"Good, then I need to know…has there truly been no form of jealousy concerning me between you and Nikolas?"

"No, sugar, we told you before. We can't feel jealousy because your soul calls to us both. Sweetheart, try to understand that your soul is bound to mine for all eternity. Nothing can change that."

"Would things be exactly the same between us if I were bound to Nick too?" I continued.

"Yes, nothing would be different between us. Why, are you—" Tristan didn't get a chance to finish before I continued speaking.

"I'm just trying to see things from your perspective, that's all. So would your feelings for me change if I chose to remain bound only to you and Nick passed peacefully on to Shalsmara?"

"My sweet baby, no, my feelings would not change," he answered, running his hand through my hair and resting his palm on my cheek. "That would be your choice. Neither of us have ever had any control over that. Whatever you choose, we accept. Olivia, you are the center of our world and the keeper of our soul, so what you choose is totally accepted by us. I can't explain just how deep and unconditional our love is." His gaze was soft and loving.

"I think I understand that love much better now, since I have bound with you, Tristan," I explained.

"Olivia, a double binding is very dangerous. We told you how the last and only attempt turned out. I'm scared of losing you. If you were to attempt it and were the least bit conflicted or for the wrong reasons..." His voice trailed off.

"I'm well aware of all that," I said.

"Like I said, sugar, it's not my choice to make, but whatever you choose, I am behind you one hundred percent."

"That's good to know." I smiled as he leaned down and kissed me gently on the lips.

"I am still conflicted, Tristan. My moral upbringing in the human world is still there." I sighed. "I just needed to know for sure how you felt."

"Now you know, and I'm glad you understand how dangerous it would be. I'm hurting inside knowing I'm losing my dearest friend and will grieve for that loss for a very, very long time." Tristan's eyes looked glazed, as if the tears were about to start any second. I reached up and touched his cheek, allowing my tears to flow for the both of us.

"Baby, I know you don't want to hear this right now, but I have to go to the hospital. I have a patient being prepped for surgery." My heart thumped heavily in my chest. I didn't want to be alone.

"Couldn't someone else do the surgery?"

"No, baby, I have to go. Maybe you'd be more comfortable back in the sunroom." I guess he thought if I were up there, I wouldn't notice his absence. "You need to collect your thoughts and prepare yourself." He seemed to know how I was feeling, what I was feeling.

"I have to go now. Just remember, whatever you choose, I'm here for you." His look was so compassionate and understanding I didn't know how to respond. He leaned down and gave me a soft, lingering kiss before he turned to leave.

As soon as the silence set in, I panicked. All my doubts, fears, and grief seemed to flood my mind and heart at once. I rushed to the front door, giving no thought to the torrential downpour.

The combination of the crisp October air and the cold rain took my breath, but I didn't care. I dropped to my knees crying. I turned my face to the dark clouds above me, rain pelting violently against my face, and screamed through my tears.

"Tell me what to do! Am I no less evil if I let someone that I love die, than the man that caused this? Is my soul worth one ounce more than Nick's? Isn't it wrong and selfish to preserve my life and my soul above another?" Suddenly the tears stopped. It was as if all my questions had been answered. I knew what I needed to do, what I wanted to do.

Conviction 22

I stood up and walked back into the house. I had found the conviction I was searching for. I started up the stairs, discarding the articles of heavy, wet clothing as I went.

I opened the door to Nick's room and silently walked to the edge of the bed, pulling back the covers and discarding the ice packs as I slipped under the sheets beside him.

Nick's eyes gently fluttered open at the touch of my cold, wet body next to him.

"Olivia, what are you doing?" he weakly asked.

"Shhh...what I should've done hours ago," I whispered.

"I can't let you...it's too dangerous," he tried to warn.

"You told me yourself, love. It's not your choice, it's mine," I said, leaning over him.

"Tristan..." he murmured.

"He knows." I breathed as I tenderly pressed my lips to his. Almost immediately his dry, parched lips became soft and gentle. I could feel the touch of his hand as his arm came around my waist. It felt cool against my skin.

He became stronger with every gentle kiss, and his chest was again solid as stone and cool as ice. I gasped as his hand ran down the curve of my waist. I remembered how he used to make me feel with just a look and had imagined, but this! My god, he was extraordinary!

I lost track of the time I had been in this room, and I didn't care. The glorious scent of him was all around me, powerful and sensual. Nikolas gently placed his hand on the side of my face and looked down with his mesmerizing coal-black eyes. I again felt like I was floating, falling deeper into the black abyss staring back at me.

I gasped as I felt his very soul touch mine! Suddenly, everything disappeared into a blinding white light!

TRISTAN'S SURGERY HAD turned out to be a false alarm. Good news for the patient, but not for Aaron Yelton.

"Have you been taught how to read labs?" Tristan scolded the young man.

"Yes, Doctor, but—" His response was cut short.

"But you misread these numbers, so tell me, Yelton, how did you come to the conclusion that Mr. Layton needed emergency surgery?"

"Well, sir, after reading the labs and looking at the x-rays, along with the acute pain expressed by the patient, I concluded his gall bladder had ceased to function and become gangrenous. The x-rays were conclusive to my diagnosis."

"I see. Well, let's just take a look, shall we?" Tristan clipped the x-rays to the board and flipped on the light. "Mr. Yelton, show me the infected area." Tristan's suspicions were finally answered.

"Mr. Yelton, don't even bother," Tristan said, turning off the light. "Have a seat."

The young man sat down across from him and leaned back in the chair, an arrogant smile on his face.

"Aaron, just what made you think you could pull this off?"

"Doctor Rilz, I'm sure I don't know what you mean..." The young man attempted to look innocent.

"People's lives are at stake! The gall bladder you wanted to remove doesn't exist! Mr. Layton is in here for an impacted colon, and the acute pain was nothing more than a good bout of gas!" Tristan stared across the desk at the young man. "I need the one that took the classes in your name, the person that did all the work!

You are going to have some explaining to do when you find an attorney."

"This is absurd," Young Mr. Yelton began. "I certainly don't have to stay here and listen to this!" Aaron was exposed for the fraud he was, and his only concern was getting out of that office and disappearing.

He sat calmly as the young man made a quick beeline for the door, only to be met by the police. Tristan had left a note at the nurse's desk when he came in, alerting her to the problem. He watched as the impersonator was handcuffed and taken away.

Tristan took a long breath. "I need a cup of coffee," he mumbled to himself. As he closed the office door behind him, he spotted Taryn at the nurse's desk.

"What brings you here, brother?" Tristan smiled, and the poor nurse nearly fell out of her chair, no doubt wondering how to deal with the surprise at finding out there was two of these beautiful men in this world and still maintain a professional demeanor.

"Actually, I was looking for you," Taryn answered.

"Well, I'll buy you a cup of coffee." Tristan put his hand on Taryn's shoulder, guiding him to the break room.

"I went by the house. When I saw the jeep gone, I didn't bother to knock. I know Olivia is going through hell. I wish there was something we could do. I can't imagine Nick..." He lowered his eyes.

Tristan patted Taryn's shoulder and sighed. "I know it's hard to accept. What did you need to see me about?" he asked, glad to change the subject.

"I'm sure you know by now that Nadya was my intended soul and that we are bound now," Taryn started.

"Yeah, Nick told me. I'm so sorry I haven't given you a proper congratulation. I'm very happy for both of you." He smiled.

"Thanks, but I have need of some advice. Nadya...well, Nadya's not thinking clearly. She's planning to go after Lucas on her own, and she won't listen to reason," Taryn explained.

"I expected as much, after all, she's just like her brother. Tell her to hold off until...well, you know. She would never forgive herself if she missed his funeral. Give her your blessing and offer your help if she'll wait."

"Give her my blessing...Tristan, I've just found her! If she goes off hunting for revenge..." Taryn sounded even more distressed. He hadn't expected his brother to agree with his new mate.

"Taryn, I don't want her running off to commit suicide! I just want you to buy me some time to plan," Tristan clarified.

They stopped talking when Mercedes entered the room carrying a tray with cups and spoons to restock the coffee shelf.

All at once it felt like the air around them exploded! Tristan and Taryn caught their breath. Mercedes dropped the tray, and the clatter of spoons caused them to look.

"They should have killed her when they had the chance!" she muttered in an almost silent breath.

"Did you say something?" Tristan snipped with a huge grin on his face. She didn't respond. "What's the matter, Mercedes? Cat got your tongue?" he quipped as he let out a bellowing laugh. Taryn's loud guffaw joined with Tristan's as Mercedes bolted from the room.

"Congratulations, Tris. You have just gained a new brother!" Taryn was still beaming.

"I knew she'd do the right thing," Tristan said with pride. "I can't tell you how pleased I am. Nikolas lives. Our king has taken his mate!"

SOULBOUND: DESTINY'S MOVE

LUCAS AND MARISKA WERE enjoying some leisurely conversation and a glass of wine. The fire crackled in the fireplace as she sat nestled in his arms. He had been exceptionally gracious and cheerful since releasing Nikolas.

"Well, my dear, we should hear the sad news of the High King's death by noon tomorrow," he said, playing with a long strand of his mate's platinum hair.

"Will you be taking the throne soon?" she whispered.

"Not right away. I just have one small detail to take care of, a loose end so to speak."

"What loose end, darling?" Mariska asked, rising up from his shoulder.

"Nadya...she's the only heir, just a minor thing," he assured her as he gently kissed her cheek. "The tedious part will be the house cleaning, sweeping out the undesirables, so to speak." He laughed in a casual, relaxed manner.

"Victory at last!" He sighed, sipping from his glass and leaning back to relax.

"No!" Lucas screamed, jumping to his feet. Mariska sat silent and rigid on the sofa.

"This can't be!" he yelled. "Hazon!" Lucas ran into the hall and grabbed the first one of the house staff he found. "Where is she!" he demanded, holding the man by the collar.

"I...I...don't know, Sire. She...she...was by the kitchen door and after..." He stuttered.

"After, where did she go?" he screamed.

"She just...vanished, Sire, nothing left but a blue vapor!" the houseman choked.

Lucas threw the poor man, hurling him into the wall and leaving him in a crumpled heap on the floor. He ran out into the night, phasing into his hybrid form as he exited the front door. The tall silver half man, half wolf stood on the front stoop and howled through the brisk night air. A Maldoran guard and three Lusters lay dead in the courtyard.

Nothing would be safe tonight!

Awkward Beginnings 23

I woke to find Nikolas gone, and I was lying in the beautiful canopy bed in the center bedroom, dressed in a soft powder-blue nightgown. Nick entered the room carrying a tray. He placed it on the table by the bed and leaned in, kissing me gently. I shivered and smiled.

"Nick, I'm so glad to see you up and about so quickly." Just to see him smiling back at me made me even more certain of my decision to bind with him. I couldn't imagine never seeing his beautiful face again, and I didn't want to.

"I feel great, love, even better than I did before, but I guess that's to be expected," He grinned.

"What do you mean?" I asked.

"When we bind with our intended soul, it makes us stronger. Our senses are even heightened. Olivia, it was beyond wonderful!" His eyes were shimmering as he looked at me with the deepest love.

"I thought so, but after, everything went white. I can't remember a thing until now." I blushed, feeling that my fainting may have taken away from his experience.

"You were conscious for that?" He seemed stunned.

"Yeah, why? Didn't you expect me to be?"

"Well, love, when the High King takes his mate, it's usually a very extreme experience. It literally sends a shock wave throughout our world. It does with any king, just as we all knew the moment you bound with Tristan, but as I said before, the binding with the High King is much more intense. The woman usually loses consciousness before the final stage."

"So, are you saying that it wasn't everything it should have been?" I felt as if I had been a big disappointment.

"Oh, love, on the contrary, it was beyond extraordinary! The shock wave that passed through our world, I've been told, was beyond anything the people of Kardaun have ever experienced. The fact that you were still awake makes you even more remarkable, especially since you had bound with Tristan only twenty-four hours before! You really are the strongest soul in the entire existence of Kardaun!" The tone in Nick's voice was so reverent. I could see he was genuinely impressed. I was elated to hear this and to know that I was all Nikolas was hoping for. I reached up and placed my hand on his face, smiling.

"Why didn't you stay with me till I woke? What?" I asked when I saw the look on Nick's face.

"Olivia, my sweet love, that happened twenty-four hours ago!" Nick smiled proudly.

"You mean I've been out that long!"

"I told you our binding was extraordinarily intense," he reminded me with his beautiful proud smile still beaming.

"Well, I suppose that is never going to happen again, is it?"

"No, not exactly like that, but I promise you the future will not be disappointing." He kissed my hand and smiled his impish little grin. I turned a rosy pink.

"Oh, I almost forgot. I brought you something to eat." He placed the tray across my lap and braced the pillow behind me.

"I'll be downstairs if you need me. I'm sure you would like a little privacy to shower and dress. Tristan is very anxious to see you, love. I hope for his sake you won't be long." Nick stood up and kissed my forehead before he left the room.

Releasing a long blissful sigh, I began enjoying the delicious beef stew and roll Nick left for me.

As I searched through the massive closet for something to wear, I realized that every article was exactly my size. I picked out a nice sapphire-blue tunic and black leggings, then turned around and grabbed a pair of black satin slippers from the endless rack of shoes. The dressers were filled with a huge array of undergarments, stockings, and socks. I figured whoever had occupied this room no longer had need of these things, and they were all new, so I helped myself to those too.

I stepped into the massive bathroom and turned on the cascading shower. The steaming water was pure bliss. I seemed to have lost myself in this wonderful indulgence, when it occurred to me Nick and Tristan were waiting downstairs. The thought of being face-to-face with both of them now that I have bound with Nick made me feel jittery.

I turned off the shower and wrapped myself in a huge bath towel. I happened to glance into the mirror as I reached for a smaller towel to wrap my hair and noticed something unusual on my neck. My hand instinctively went up to touch the two tiny, raised marks. I turned my body slightly to examine them more closely and noticed two more on the top of my shoulder. They too were small but wider apart. My fingers ran gently across them. How odd, I thought.

All at once the bathroom door came crashing open! "Aaaagh!" I squealed "What the—"

"Olivia, are you all right!" Nick breathlessly asked.

"I was until you damn near gave me a heart attack!" I just stood there, looking at my two gorgeous newly bound mates, clutching my towel with white knuckles and looking like a half-drowned rat! "Lord, have mercy! I need to sit down. I'm shakin' like a dog passin' peach seeds!" I muttered, dropping the lid on the commode. Tristan couldn't contain the outburst of laughter.

"That's a new one," he said, still chuckling.

"What in heaven's name are you two doing?" I asked. "What possessed you to break down my bathroom door?" I just sat there, staring and dripping.

"We thought you were hurt!" Nick replied. "What on earth would give you that idea?"

"You touched your marks," Tristan answered.

"My marks? Oh, on my neck and shoulder...you put them there?" I questioned, staring at both of them.

"Yes, love, the one on your neck is mine, and your shoulder, Tristan's," Nick smiled as he realized the misunderstanding. "It's part of the binding, love, at least for Larins, Maldorans, and Origs. We place a small bite on our mate, and instead of releasing venom, we release a small amount of our blood, which causes the marks to rise permanently. Whenever you're in trouble or injured, you only have to place your hand on them for a few seconds, and it will summon us to wherever you are," Nikolas explained.

"Oh, um...how do you know for sure where I am?" I asked.

"It works like a GPS tracking system, sugar. No matter where you are, it draws us straight to you," Tristan said, smiling. It seemed as though Tristan suddenly became aware of the situation. He immediately turned scarlet and began to fidget.

"Oh...umm...I... ahh...I'll just be...I'll see you downstairs," he stammered and disappeared abruptly from the doorway.

Nick caught on to Tristan's embarrassment, and if vampires could blush, I'm sure he would have been a bright crimson.

"Yeah...ahh...sorry...I'm gonna...I think I better join Tris." Nick disappeared as quickly as Tristan had.

"Man, that was awkward!" I said out loud in the now-empty bathroom. I hurried and dressed, brushed out my hair, and tossed the bath towel on the floor to absorb the puddle of water. When I entered the kitchen carrying the tray Nick had brought to me, both of them shifted uncomfortably. Talk about your awkward silence!

"Thanks for the dinner," I spoke into the tensely thick air.

"You're welcome, love, is there anything else I can get you?" Nick asked, relieved that I didn't bring up the bathroom episode again.

"A glass of milk would be nice," I answered.

"Sure." Nick turned to the cabinet and retrieved a glass.

Tristan stood silent at the end of the counter. My eyes moved back and forth between them as I climbed up on the barstool and took a sip from the glass Nick handed me.

"So...is this..." I started.

"No!" they exclaimed in unison as if they could read my thoughts.

"Olivia, we are so sorry about what happened upstairs. Believe us when we say that will never happen again!" Tristan apologized, speaking for the both of them. It was plain that the entire incident was a misunderstanding.

"I'm sorry too," I said. "I should have realized immediately where the marks came from."

"We'll just call it a lack of communication and put it behind us, if that's all right." Nick smiled timidly as he spoke.

"Good idea, done." I smiled back.

"Sugar, we want your transition into your new life to be as easy and uncomplicated as possible." There were those words—easy, uncomplicated, the very description of the relationship I had hoped for. I was sure this situation was going to be far from either.

"This is not going to be...how would you explain it, Tris?" Nick looked to his friend, who, for the first time, stared blankly back at him. "Well, for the lack of a better description, some sort of ménage à trois, or weird triangle. We are bound together at a much higher level than humans can conceive. We are more of a circle, a circle that will continue to grow tighter with time. Do you see what I'm saying?" Nick asked as he illustrated his explanation on a piece of paper. He began with one large circle and continued smaller until it was no more than a dot. So closely knit that all space was gone.

"I understand what you're telling me. Our souls throughout the years will become so intertwined, so closely bound that it will be as if we were one entity, right?" I couldn't imagine being that connected to one person, let alone two.

"Right, love. You see, Tris and I cannot see any displays of affection like holding your hand or a kiss good-bye because that is normal behavior, so you don't have to be uncomfortable being yourself around us." He was so desperate to help me understand this way of life. I wasn't sure if he could see that he was getting through to me. I did understand. I was worried about facing the two of them together, but now that I'm here, it seems quite natural to be in the presence of them both.

"Are you saying that our physical desires will also change over time?" I was curious and hopeful that I wouldn't lose that beautiful difference in them.

"This is what you might call a honeymoon stage, sugar, but as time goes on, the physical need will diminish, but not like in the human world. The bond will be so close that just being in the presence of each other will bring total fulfillment and satisfaction." Tristan sighed as he finished speaking, hoping I had some sense of just how deep this love would become.

"Ohhh, I see, this bond will grow so strong it will be more of a celestial love than physical or earthly!" I was overwhelmed at the very thought.

"Exactly!" Nick exclaimed, looking relieved.

"That, believe it or not, is what every couple on this planet strives for and desires!" I told them. It sounded so wonderful, so perfect it was hard to imagine it would someday be real—at least while I was still alive. "So, the physical side..."

"We didn't say it would never happen, just that it wouldn't be necessary." Tris smiled impishly.

"I promise you that neither Tristan nor I will ever, and I mean ever, approach you in an intimate way as long as both of us are in the house or on the grounds. We will never again enter your room, your personal sanctuary, without your consent or invitation," Nick solemnly swore to me.

"Thank you for explaining these things to me. I feel a lot more relaxed now. The room I woke up in, I don't know who occupied it before me, and I hope they won't be put out, but...well, since all the nice clothes were my size, I sort of helped myself to some of them. I hope that's okay," I sheepishly asked.

Nick and Tristan laughed good-naturedly and leaned over to rest their arms on the counter.

"Baby, no one else has ever occupied that room but you." Tristan grinned.

"That room was designed especially for you and the clothes are all new, and they belong to you and you alone," Nick finished explaining.

"Oh, thank goodness! I was really concerned about invading someone else's space," I said. The rose color of my cheeks brought on another lighthearted chuckle from my two mates.

"Now that we have everything cleared up, Tristan and I have to go out for a couple of hours. I've called in more security around the house, so you should be fine until we return."

My stomach started to twitch. I wasn't sure if I was ready to be alone.

"Umm...I don't mean to pry, but where are you off to at this late hour?"

"Well, actually this is my daytime, remember?" Nick said with a slight grin. "We have to attend Nadya and Taryn's sealing ceremony."

"Sealing ceremony? I'm sorry. I don't understand."

"The night we passed through the binding veil, Nadya and Taryn did too, and they were intended souls, so tonight is their sealing."

"Oh, ohhh...I see. So, you two are not only brothers by soul, but brothers-in-law too. That is fantastic! You both must be so pleased. I know I am." I smiled then realized, if they're having this sealing ceremony, then...

"Does this mean we have to have one too?" I took a long breath. I had no idea there was so much to do. It seemed like this soul-binding ritual never ends.

"Yes, baby, your dress will be here tomorrow, and the ceremony will take place at nine tomorrow night." Tristan smirked.

"Great, thanks for the heads up, guys," I said peering up at the two smiling faces before me. "So why am I not invited to this special event? After all, they are family now, aren't they?"

"Of course they are, and they both love you dearly, but it's a sacred ceremony, and since we are not sealed yet, I'm afraid you're not permitted to attend. I'm sorry, love; it's just the way things are. I'll give them your congratulations if you'd like," Nick spoke kindly, feeling my disappointment.

"Yes, Nick, please do." I tried to smile, but I felt like an outsider for the first time since I learned of this world. "Nick, I thought that in Kardaun only souls of the same race like Larin and Larin, etc., were created for one another, I thought we were the only ones...different."

"I can only guess that our world had become so diminished by the time we were born that it was necessary for the Creator to design our souls in a different way, and apparently Taryn and Nadya are the first. They were never in a circumstance to meet in Kardaun even though Taryn knew his soul existed."

"Nadya and Taryn will be here tomorrow night. My sister has insisted on helping you get ready for the ceremony. We won't be long, love, I promise."

"I'll be fine. Both of you need to get going. I'll sit by the fire and curl up with a good book while you're gone." I flashed them one of my fake smiles that was no more convincing than it had ever been. I knew they both felt bad about leaving me, and I hated myself for making them feel guilty.

The flames in the fireplace swayed like a slow rhythmic dance, rising up and down, gently flickering from side to side. I watched the subtle dance, lost in time and space. My mind was recounting every detail that led to this day.

Everything had happened so quickly. From the moment I found out about their true identity, I hadn't really had time to catch my breath. This was the first time I was able to pause and reflect on the twists and turns that sent my life spiraling into a whirlwind of surprises and adventure.

I now have a healthy respect for karma, fate, and especially destiny! From one simple hello to events transpiring in a short eight months that have changed my views on everything I had known, events that have altered my life and my world, irrevocably and eternally.

Absolution 24

True to their word, Nick and Tristan were gone no longer than necessary to attend Nadya and Taryn's sealing.

Nick entered the kitchen to find me sipping a glass of wine and snacking on some cheese and crackers. He walked over and gave me a quick peck on the lips.

"How did it go?" I smiled.

"It was very nice."

"Did you give them my best wishes?"

"Yes, and I am to give you a heartfelt thank you. Nadya said to tell you she'd be here at six tomorrow evening." Nick was now studying my expression, and it made me uncomfortable. It was as if he could literally feel my apprehension.

"Nice snack," he commented.

"Help yourself." I slid the plate across the counter to him.

"Thanks." He took a cracker and a slice of cheese, still watching me.

"What's bothering you, love?"

"Nothing." That didn't wash! As soon as the lie left my mouth, Nick knew. "I'm sorry. I've been thinking too much again, is all."

"Thinking about what?"

"Things. Where's Tristan?" I asked, trying to change the subject.

"Putting the car in the garage. What things?" he persisted.

"I was just thinking, how my friends in town would react to the ceremony about to take place. In my world, they wouldn't see it for what it means or the reason for it. To them, it would be far less sacred and more of an abomination," I explained as I sat there, idly shredding a grocery receipt that had been left on the counter.

"Why are we having this ceremony anyway, Nick?" I really didn't see the point to it.

"Olivia, it's very important that our binding be sealed to the Creator Logsald."

"Why?"

"So that our souls may become one in Shalsmara and move on to become one with Him that created us."

"Nick, it's obvious that's not going to happen, no matter what kind of ritual you perform. You have to know I can't go there." Nick's eyes settled back on me as he realized I was talking about the damnation of my soul.

"You believe you're going to be cast in the veil of Ras?" He looked stunned.

"More like hell, which, for taking two husbands, I am going to split wide open!"

"Olivia, my sweet angel, you can't be serious!" Nick leaned over the counter and took my hand as he spoke. I looked up with tear-filled eyes. I could physically feel the pain in his touch and the anguish in his heart.

"If that's what you believe, I would rather you had let me die!" he whispered.

A solitary tear escaped onto my cheek as I reached across the counter between us and cradled his face in my hand. "Oh, Nick, I didn't mean it that way! I don't regret my decision, not for a second! My only regret is that you and Tristan will be without me in Shalsmara! It's you I'm thinking of, not myself!" I tried to clarify as the tears started to run.

Nikolas stepped around and took a seat on the stool next to me at the end of the counter. He gathered both of my hands into his, and the cool sensation was comforting.

"Olivia, when you made the decision to bind your soul with mine after you had already done so with Tristan, not only did that choice save my life, but it was a decision made out of love. This act, by what the human world teaches, put you in the position of jeopardizing your soul from entering into heaven. Is my interpretation of this biblical law, correct?" He awaited my answer, hoping he had not misunderstood what he had read.

"Yes, you're right," I answered.

"Doesn't this same book teach that humans are to love one another just as they would themselves?" I nodded, surprised at his knowledge of Christianity.

"Yes...but..."

"The teachings of my world are very similar. We are to respect all life and care for one another as we would ourselves. What you did, knowingly and willingly, at least in your belief, gave up your soul for us. That, love, was the most unselfish act a human can do! It was the ultimate self-sacrifice! You literally put the life and soul of another before your own. You did this for no other reason than the purest heart and truest kind of unconditional love!" He stopped to gauge my expression. I smiled at him.

"I know you're trying to justify my polygamist decision," I said, pulling his hands up with mine to kiss his fingers.

"That's what you need to understand, love! In my world, it's not polygamy! I'm going to try to explain it the best I can. I wish Tristan were here. He always seems to know how to do these things," he said, trying to smile through his frustration.

"Did I hear my name mentioned" Tristan grinned as he entered the kitchen.

"Yeah, Nick was just trying to explain why I'm not doomed for hell." I sniffed.

"I know, sugar. I was waiting in the sitting room. I didn't want to interrupt until Nick gave me the cue he needed my assistance." He chuckled.

"Look. I appreciate that you both care. You really don't have to console me. I'll eventually come to terms with any wrongs I've done concerning my faith," I said to them as Nick reached up and wiped a tear from my eye.

"Baby, do you feel one ounce of difference between Nick and me?" Tristan asked.

"No, absolutely none," I answered, surprised he would ask.

"If you had it to do again, would you?" he asked again a question I would answer without hesitation.

"Absolutely!" "Then no regrets?" "No!" I exclaimed.

"Well then, let's just get some insight into your world's history." He leaned down with elbows on the counter to look eye level at me. "In the biblical days, it wasn't uncommon for a man to have more than one wife, right?"

"Right," I acknowledged.

"It wasn't until the eighteen hundreds a law was passed by man, and only in what is referred to as 'civilized' parts of the world, that made it illegal to have more than one spouse. This law was initiated because humans mate by physical and hormonal attraction. They are also very possessive by nature. Humans feel like their mate or spouse belongs to them. They spend their lives trying to guard that possession. That's where jealousy comes into play. This kind of love cannot be sustained without conflict."

I just sat there silent, trying so very hard to grasp every word Tristan was saying. "Jealousy has destroyed a lot of lives," I commented.

"Yes, baby, it has. We, on the other hand, feel that we belong with our mates. We were created for one soul and them for us, so we don't feel as if we need to guard that relationship. Do you see what I'm saying?" Tristan was watching me, peering steadily into my eyes, searching for some glimmer of understanding.

"I think so." I grasped the thought, but the entire concept seemed to be escaping me.

"You see, in our world, adultery simply doesn't exist," Nick began. "We are joined at a level so far beyond human comprehension. We never desire anyone other than the soul created for us. So, there are no fights over mates, no jealousy toward another being, no divorce, no rape—at least not in the carnal sense—no question of our children's paternity. These things simply do not exist!"

"Nikolas, I know what you're saying, and it sounds wonderful! This is a unique situation in your world! Isn't that adulterous on my part?" I reasoned.

"No!" they protested in unison.

"You really don't feel any jealousy toward the time I spend alone with Tristan?"

"No, none whatsoever, because I am bound to your soul for eternity. I can never love anyone else, and I know you'll always love me," he explained.

"It's exactly the same with me," Tristan added. "Our Creator's plan is one thing we do not question. Sugar, your soul was designed and created as much for Nick as it was for me," Tristan continued his attempt to help me understand, but as always, I clung to the old human values.

"I just worry about how you both feel. I guess there's a fear in the back of my mind that eventually this will cause a problem between us." I couldn't get past what had been pounded into me since childhood about moral behavior.

Both men leaned back and took in a long-exasperated breath.

"Olivia, baby," Tristan started again. "This isn't a normal circumstance, but after the bindings took place, Nick and I became closer than just best friends. Through you, our souls are now bound as brothers—no, much deeper than any brotherly bond. You are now the center of our world and will always be." Tristan's voice was soft, and I could see in his eyes that nothing meant more to him than being part of my soul.

"There is no fear of Tristan taking you from me or of me taking you from him. If that fear does not exist, how can there be jealousy?" Nick asked. It was evident by the passion in his voice; he was not just saying these things to console my guilt.

"Olivia, during the time we spend alone, does Nick ever cross your mind?"

"No," I answered truthfully.

"When you're alone with Nick, do you ever think about me?"

"No." I blushed. Now that he brought it up, I realized that the alone he was speaking of didn't necessarily mean intimate alone, just alone. I never gave a thought to the one missing during those times, almost as if they didn't exist.

"There is no one else in this world when we're alone for me either. This is just as it should be with any monogamous couple. It's the same for Nick too." Tristan held such hope I would finally understand. I just looked at him, wondering how he could know that about Nick.

"Do you two talk about..."

"No!" they again exclaimed in unison. The shocked look on their faces was unexpected and priceless.

"We have no curiosity about that, sugar." Tristan grinned.

"All right, I get it—finally! If you're right, and I'm not saying I'm fully convinced yet. I'm human, so when I pass from this world, my soul goes to heaven. Whereas you two, being from Kardaun, go on to Shalsmara. So, you see, I still can't be with you for eternity." The tears fell like rain with this revelation.

Tristan held my hand as Nick cradled my head on his shoulder until I began to calm. He handed me a tissue and began to speak softly as my sobs subsided.

"Sugar, how do we know that your heaven and our Shalsmara are not the same place?" His eyes shimmered as he looked at me.

"He's right, love, and how do we know that your God and our Creator Logsald are not the same?" Nick added.

I rose up from Nick's tear-soaked shoulder, dabbing my eyes and nose with the tissue.

"I never thought of that!" My heart seemed to lighten in an instant. At least now I had hope.

"How did I get so lucky! You both are so amazing, and I love you!" I pulled both of their hands up and kissed them.

In light of last night's meltdown, Tristan decided I could use some fresh air. I came downstairs early as always to find two backpacks fully stocked at the edge of the bottom step.

"Let's get out of here for a while. The house is starting to close in on me," Tristan said as he greeted me at the bottom of the stairs. "Besides, there's nothing like a good Halloween hike!" He smiled that beautiful leg-weakening smile.

"You have no idea how good that sounds!" I grinned and stopped to examine my pack.

"Don't worry, everything's there." He nudged me playfully with his elbow.

"Did you remember my—"

"Camera? Yes, and a thermos of hot chocolate," he stated, feeling proud no doubt that he'd remembered even the smallest detail.

"Well then, what are we waiting for?" I said, picking up the gear. "Oh, wait a sec! I need to change my shoes!" I dropped the backpack and hurried back upstairs. When I returned, Tristan had already loaded everything in the jeep.

This trip seemed filled with endless conversation, and I paid no attention to where we were going. We stopped at the same trail we had hiked on our last date.

So much had happened. So much about me had changed in just a couple of weeks that it seemed like another lifetime since I had been here. I was so glad to be out, to feel my freedom again. I grabbed my gear and started up the trail, leaving Tristan behind.

"Wait up, sugar!" he called. "Are you after a fire or something?" he teased.

"I'm sorry, just a little anxious, I guess."

"I can see that, but if it's all right with you, I'd rather not rush this beautiful day." He smiled, and as always, my legs went numb.

"Okay, I'll slow down." I stepped aside and waved my hand in a long sweeping motion. "After you." My smile brightened as I watched him walk toward me. He leaned down and kissed me softly.

"Try to keep up." His laughter echoed as he disappeared just inside the tree line. I laughed and started off in a fast walk. Everything about this hike was easier and far less quiet than the last time. The air was crisp even though the sun was bright. I felt so invigorated, so alive!

We finally stopped at the huge rock overlooking the beautiful view of the mountains. The colors seemed exceptionally vibrant, especially the yellows.

We sat there drinking hot chocolate and enjoying the quiet beauty surrounding us. Tristan put his arm around my shoulder when a chill came over me as the breeze shifted. I leaned into his shoulder, resting my head against him.

"Thank you for bringing me here," I whispered.

"My pleasure. I've decided to give this place a name."

"Oh, have you already picked one?" I looked up at his soft, glistening blue eyes.

"Uh-huh," he mumbled and brushed my hair back. "I'm going to call it Angel's Peak."

"Why Angel's Peak?"

"Because...this is where I first touched an angel." His voice had become a soft whisper. As he leaned across me, I could hear the steady soft rolling sound of a cat's purr. I lay back onto the blanket, gazing up at him. The vivid October sky couldn't touch the blue of his eyes.

Angel's Peak was the perfect name, but he had the sentiment all wrong. I was the one in the presence of an angel, a gloriously beautiful and powerful angel.

The chill in the air disappeared. All I could feel was the longing and the sparks of electricity flowing through me. Nothing was left now but the fire within as I gave in to every pleasure of his perfection.

Dangerous Kinship 25

I walked into my room to prepare for the ceremony. I saw the garment bag hanging on my closet door, and it caused my heart to stutter. I had no clue what to expect, or even what I was supposed to do! What if I mess up, or do something really stupid? I thought. Will my ignorance cost them eternity?

My hands were shaking as I took hold of the zipper to reveal my ceremonial dress. As soon as I folded back the sides of the bag, I stopped breathing! This dress made the emerald-green gown I wore to the opera look like a secondhand rag! My dizzy spell reminded me to breathe. Before me hung a gorgeous white gown with a bodice of hand-woven silk. It was squared at the top to accommodate long flowing chiffon sleeves. Tapering down from an empire waist were layers upon layers of the soft, sheer material, leaving the bottom full and flowing. The entire gown looked as though it had been sprinkled with diamond dust! The light seemed to catch at every angle, glistening like tiny sun-touched drops of dew.

There was a light knock on my door. I slipped back to earth and called my permission to enter. The door opened gently, and Nadya stepped in.

"I see you've already examined your gown," she said as she walked toward me.

"It's the most beautiful dress I've ever seen!" I exclaimed.

"Well, we have a lot to do, so get your shower. I'll fill you in on the ceremony while I get you ready." She smiled and took my shoulders, gently ushering me to the bathroom door.

I emerged draped in a soft, plush robe to find Nadya had everything ready at the dressing table and my gown laid out on the bed.

"Have a seat." She grinned and gestured to the cushioned chair. "You don't know how much I appreciate your help."

"Think nothing of it. I'm glad to do it." She then began the task of trying to make me beautiful while she told me what to expect downstairs. Nadya was beautiful not only on the outside but in the heart as well, and I could sense a strong kinship forming between us.

When my makeover was complete, she turned me toward the mirror. I couldn't believe my eyes! I barely recognized my own reflection! Nadya beamed as my expression definitely had shown my approval.

"Nadya, my dear," I teased, "you have missed your calling."

"I wouldn't say that, but it's not bad for an amateur, if I do say so." She laughed.

I tried to laugh along with her, but a bout of nausea hit me as the nervous jitter in my stomach worsened. I swallowed hard and took a deep breath.

"Relax, Olivia, everything will go smoothly. I promise." Nadya seemed to sense the uncontrollable shaking in my stomach, and I was thankful for her calm voice.

"What was your gown like?" I asked.

"The sealing gowns are all alike. They're handmade by a Warin seamstress. It's the magic that makes them different," she explained. "The gown is designed to take on the essence of the woman wearing it."

"So, it never looks the same on anyone?" I was fascinated.

"Never. The color changes to blues, pinks, reds, yellows...every color imaginable with the exception of one."

"Oh...what color is that?" I questioned.

"Gold, it has never been that color. It's said that only a soul directly touched by the hand of the Creator can turn the dress gold." "I see. What color was your dress?" I smiled.

"Well, the woman wearing the dress can't see, but her mate and others can. Taryn told me it was vibrant lavender. He said, 'A color of gentle strength.'" She quoted and smiled.

"Oh, that must have been gorgeous! But then, I couldn't imagine anything not being beautiful on you."

Nadya lowered her eyes and accepted my compliment graciously. All the while she had been talking, I noticed an edginess about her. Something was beginning to feel unsettling.

I reached up and readjusted the collar on my robe as I picked up the lace undergarments.

"Would you excuse me while I put these on?" I nervously asked.

"Of course, dear," she absentmindedly responded. That's when I knew there was about to be a problem—a big problem! When Nadya opened her mouth to speak, I caught a glimpse of fang!

"Where is Taryn?" I tried to make it sound like idle conversation, hoping she didn't sense the panic rising inside me.

"He's waiting in the front foyer," she answered as she pretended to smooth out my dress. "The ceremony is being held in the back hall." I knew I had to somehow get to the door and call for Taryn.

"Oh, well then we better not keep everyone waiting," I said with the least amount of tremors as I could muster. "Would you mind getting the shoe box just inside the closet?" I knew it was a long shot, but it was all I could think of to put some distance between us.

"Of course," she spoke impatiently. As soon as Nadya stepped inside the closet, I bolted to the bedroom door. Just as I turned the doorknob, I heard a hissing sound behind me. I don't know where I found the speed, but I managed to jerk the door open.

"Taryn!" I screamed. He was at the top of the stairs in an instant. Nadya slammed the door on him and pushed me against the wall. Her hand was tight against my chest. For a moment I thought she would crush me!

"Nadya, get hold of yourself. Think about what you're doing!" I yelled. "Think of Nick and Tristan!" Her eyes were fixed on me, cold and hard as stone. I could hear the sound of Nick and Tristan's voice as they joined Taryn at the door.

"Nadya," Taryn called. "Let go of the door!" She quickly turned to the sound of his voice. I stood silent, not wanting to draw her attention back to me. The weight of her ice-cold hand was beginning to cut off my air, and I felt faint.

She turned back toward me and hissed as the door came crashing open, causing her to stumble backward. Taryn, Tristan, and Nikolas rushed into the room. Taryn and Tristan immediately grabbed on to Nadya, who was now oblivious to everything but me! She struggled to loosen their hold but failed.

Nick placed himself between us like a protective shield, wrapping his arms around me.

"Olivia, are you hurt?" he whispered in a panicked tone.

"No, I'm fine...really," I said, taking a long breath of relief. "Don't be angry with her. She's not herself." As I defended Nadya, a tear escaped onto my cheek.

"Shhh, love, I know." Nick breathed softly. "Take her to the kitchen and get her a very tall drink!" he ordered. "I'll be down in a minute." Taryn and Tristan whisked her from the room so fast it was almost like a blur!

"Are you sure you're not hurt, love?"

"Nick, relax. I'm okay!" I snapped. "Poor Nadya," I said, shaking my head as I sat down on the edge of the bed.

SOULBOUND: DESTINY'S MOVE

"Poor Nadya? Olivia, she almost killed you!" he said angrily. I knew his sharp words weren't meant toward me. I could hear the disappointment in his sister with every word.

"She didn't kill me! Can't you see? She was trying with every ounce of her power not to hurt me! She could have taken me long before Taryn was summoned! I know she feels awful right now," I told him, holding fast to my defense of her actions.

"You really care about her, don't you?" Nick seemed stunned by my forgiveness.

"Of course I do, Nick, she's like family to me and soon will be! Now go and see about her. Just give me a minute to catch my breath, and I'll be down," I ordered.

I walked into the kitchen. Nadya was sitting at the counter with her head cradled in her hands. She looked up when I entered the room. My heart ached for her when I saw the pink-stained tears streaming down her perfect porcelain-colored cheeks.

"Olivia...I'm so sorry..." She cried. "I feel terrible! I've ruined your ceremony! I...I..." Suddenly she began to sob uncontrollably.

"Is she all right now? I mean..." I stammered.

"Yeah, baby, she's fine," Tristan answered. I walked over to her and put my arms around her shoulders.

"Nadya, it's okay now. It's over, and you've ruined nothing," I calmly consoled her. I looked over to find all three men staring at me with disbelieving expressions.

"What are you three staring at? And close your mouths! There is no harm done! As far as I'm concerned, it's over, and I want it to stay that way! Do you three understand? Don't bring it up again, not to me or to Nadya!" I commanded. The only response I got was a slow nod from all three men.

"Now, you two need to get back upstairs and finish dressing, and you..." I pointed to Taryn, "back to your station!" I ordered. The obviously stupefied three left the room without a word. "Now that our audience is gone, I think it's time for you to get ready. I'll be waiting in my room. After all, you have the tedious task of getting me into that dress." I smiled and kissed Nadya's forehead. I started to turn, and she grabbed my hand. I wasn't expecting it, and a light gasp escaped from my throat.

"Thank you for what you've done for me tonight. I won't ever forget it. I owe you a great debt," she said as if my defending her were a matter of her own life or death.

"You don't need to thank me, Nadya, and you owe me nothing. I know you would never hurt me intentionally. I'll always be here if you need me."

"Why?" she asked, looking surprised and confused.

"Because, that's what sisters do." I winked and smiled as I turned to leave the room.

I went back upstairs and waited for Nadya to dress. She returned, looking exactly as I expected—a true vision of beauty. Her gown was a solid gray silk A-line with a high lace neck and sleeves. There was a row of tiny crystal sequins from her right shoulder to her left hip.

"You look gorgeous!" The words fell out with ease as I sat there looking stunned by her.

"You are too kind," she said with a wisp of a smile.

"Nadya, please sit down for a moment," I gently insisted.

She stopped fussing with me and sat down on the edge of the bed next to me in silence.

"I need to know what happened tonight. What brought this on?" I questioned softly.

"I'm sorry. It was my fault. I'm so accustomed to pushing myself to extreme limits, and this was no exception. It's been a hectic week. First, the battle at Scarsion Manor, then the binding veil. I was consumed by the fear of my brother's eminent death. Then there was my sealing ceremony and yours tonight. I kept telling myself I'll get something to drink tomorrow." She stopped long enough to take in a long breath as I listened without interruption. After a short pause, she began again. "I knew I was pushing it, but I was sure I could handle everything, and I'd get a drink when this was over. I hadn't thought about being alone with you for so long." She looked at me with pleading eyes, hoping I could understand. I did understand— more than she realized.

"Nadya, four days! You could have died!" I exclaimed.

"I was starting to weaken. That's why I couldn't put up a fight against Taryn and Tris," she admitted.

"Promise me you won't ever do that to yourself again! I was scared, not so much for me, but for you," I explained.

"Olivia, you are a remarkable woman and a true selfless soul. I hope my brother realizes how lucky he is." Her tone was soft and sincere.

"Lucky isn't exactly the word I would use to describe being bound to me for eternity." I snickered.

"Humph," she huffed and smiled. "Anyway, you were definitely born to rule. You handled those three like a true queen!"

"Ha," I laughed. "They were all just in shock! The look on their faces was priceless though." I giggled. Nadya too found humor in their behavior and giggled with me. At that moment, she seemed more human than vampire, but the visual in my mind would forever remind me that was not the case.

"We had better get you dressed," she said, rising to her feet. It was evident the tension had eased. Both of us were determined to go on with this evening as though nothing had happened. She handed me a pair of white satin slippers sprinkled with the same shimmering dust as the gown.

The Sealing 26

"Now stand up and let's get this on you." I tensed when she picked up the dress, and the nervous knot in my stomach returned. I stepped into the gown, and Nadya buttoned the back. She pulled me over to the full-length mirror.

"Oh, my heavens! That's not me!" I gasped, staring at the transformed reflection.

"Oh yes, my dear, it certainly is!" she gushed. Nadya had to be proud; after all, she had managed to turn the ugly duckling into a swan for one night, I thought.

"Well, what color is it?" I anxiously asked, turning to face her. She chuckled lightly.

"It doesn't change right away. It takes a few minutes to gather your essence. I promise it will turn by the time we enter the room with Nick and Tristan," she assured me.

As I walked to the top of the stairs, Taryn beamed a huge smile of approval. During all the commotion before, I hadn't noticed he was dressed in a well-tailored mourning suit. The wide ascot tie looked as though it was cutting off his oxygen, but otherwise he looked fabulous.

"You look stunning, Olivia! I am a little worried though," he teased.

"Why, is something wrong?" I nervously asked.

"No, you're perfect! I just wonder if they'll be able to speak after they see you."

"You, sir, are very gracious." I blushed.

We walked to the top step of the corridor, which luckily was wide enough for three people to walk side by side comfortably.

"Are you ready?" Taryn asked, holding up his right hand, and Nadya raised her left.

"Yes, I'm ready," I answered and took in a long deep breath to calm my shaking legs. I placed my hands on top of theirs, and we began our walk down into the back hall.

As we reached the bottom step into the corridor, I noticed Taryn's and Nadya's hands were trembling. Relax, I told myself. It's just your own shaky hands; they have nothing to be nervous about. Now concentrate!

The hall had been transformed into a beautiful ceremonial room. It was entirely lit by hundreds of candles in crystal votives. Vases of yellow and burgundy chrysanthemums lined the room. A long burgundy runner lay in the center leading to three satin-covered kneeling stools.

The Warin Gelcry stood behind a covered table, bearing three rings and three necklaces. Tristan and Nikolas were dressed exactly as Taryn. Both men were utterly breathtaking!

The Gelcry wore a gray robe with symbols lining the collar and down the front closure. He was a short portly man with gray hair, a round face, and wide hazel eyes.

I stepped onto the carpeted aisle with Taryn and Nadya still at my side. I swallowed hard, and my stomach began to flutter. I didn't know what to make of the expression on everyone's face. Never before had I seen Tristan or Nikolas look so stunned! The closer I came to them, I noticed the Gelcry's face had become flushed and the Ruhtt in his hands seemed to be shaking violently. Had I already done something terribly wrong? I worried.

Nadya and Taryn released me and took their places beside their brothers.

Stepping up between them, I noticed the dumbstruck expressions were still there. They slowly and reluctantly turned forward, and the Gelcry opened the Ruhtt and cleared his throat.

"I stand before you this night to seal the soul bound through Shalsmara to the Creator Logsald." We stood patiently as the nervous little man gathered his control before continuing. "Traesdon, have you bound with Olivia?"

"Yes, I have."

"Nixis, have you bound with Olivia?"

"Yes, I have."

"Traesdon, you may place your crest," the Gelcry instructed. Tristan took the delicate gold necklace bearing the Crest of Malve and gently placed it around my neck, hooking the clasp. It hung just at the base of my throat.

"Nixis, you may place your crest," the Gelcry said, turning to face him. Nikolas picked up the next golden chain with the Crest of Es'mar. As he latched the clasp, it lay directly below Tristan's pendant.

"Now," the Gelcry continued, "Traesdon, Nixis, together please place the Crest of Kardaun. Both men each took hold of the delicate necklace and gently slipped it over my head, leaving it to rest in perfect alignment with the other two. They turned to the Warin priest and bowed their heads.

"The kingdom's crests have been given and accepted." He then motioned for us to kneel. I pulled my dress forward, covering the small stool. As I knelt, the beautiful gown draped around me in a perfect circle, covering my feet.

The stubby-fingered man then picked up a delicate gold ring from the covered table. It had a sparkling clear diamond shaped in a semicircle. It was smooth and rounded on the sides and bottom, but the top of the stone was cut with a jagged edge.

"Traesdon, is this your ring?" he asked.

"Yes, it is," Tristan answered solemnly.

"Olivia, do you accept this ring to signify the eternal bond of your souls as one?"

"Yes, I do." My voice shook slightly as I answered the priest.

"Traesdon, place your ring on her left ring finger with the stone facing left." Tristan did as the Gelcry instructed then kissed my hand and forehead.

The Warin priest then picked up a second ring from the cloaked table. The stone was rounded smooth on each side but cut in the same jagged detail at both the top and bottom. The Gelcry himself placed this ring on my finger, with the stone facing up. He then looked at Nikolas as he held up the third ring. It was perfectly round on the top and sides yet again jagged on the bottom.

"Nixis, is this your ring?" Nick raised his eyes and answered.

"Yes, it is."

"Nixis, place the ring on her left ring finger, with the stone facing right." Nick slipped the ring on my finger and kissed my hand and forehead as Tristan had done. I looked down at the three rings on my hand. Beautiful and delicate yet odd as they lay offset on my finger.

"Traesdon, as you have given and Olivia has accepted, you may turn your stone."

Tristan gently turned his ring. I was amazed as it locked into place with the center stone.

"Nixis, as you have given and Olivia has accepted, you may turn your stone."

I watched as Nick turned the ring, locking it into place with the already joined stones, leaving a gorgeous circle-shaped diamond held together by three separate gold bands.

"Olivia." The still obviously nervous man held out his hand. I placed my left hand in his palm as he capped his left hand over mine, covering it completely. Tristan and Nick again bowed their heads. I was suddenly breathless! As the Gelcry began to speak the strange words, the rings began to glow under his hand with a bright golden light!

"Herat otherat. Luso otluso. Het rivigneth. Nitalrely dunnobot Evahen saeno thilg." When he spoke the last word, the golden beams of light shot out across the room as three separate beams flowed into the three of us. I stiffened straight from the intense heat radiating through my chest. In a second it was gone.

The poor nervous man seemed taken aback. I heard him catch his breath before he again started to speak.

"Traesdon Xandier, Nixis Alberon, and Olivia Ryan. Through Shalsmara to Evahen your binding is now eternally sealed to the Creator Logsald. Peace be unto you."

Tristan took my hand and kissed the ring that was no longer three separate bands and three separate stones but one solid, flawless ring, perfectly bound together for all eternity, never to be separated. Nikolas then followed kissing the ring.

"Olivia," the Gelcry started again. "From this day to eternity, you will be known as Her Royal Majesty, Olivia Xandier-Alberon! High Queen of Kardaun. You may rise and turn." I followed his instruction as Nick, Tristan, Nadya, Taryn, and the priest all knelt in front of me. Each of them kissing my fingers and placing my hand to their forehead before rising. Nadya and Taryn then hugged me as they uttered their congratulations.

"Excuse us while we prepare a toast for this exceptional occasion," Taryn said, and he and Nadya started across the room to a table set with glasses and champagne.

I glanced up at my two newly sealed mates. The love in their eyes was so overwhelming, so pure. I almost wilted to my knees. I breathed deeply and struggled to hold my legs steady.

"Nadya told me about the dress. What color was it?" I asked, daring to look up again.

"Olivia." Nick's eyes shined with admiration. "I have never literally had my breath taken from me until you walked into the room tonight. It was all I could do not to drop to my knees in your presence."

"I had no idea Angel's Peak would be so literal! You looked as though you were dropped straight from Shalsmara!" Tristan whispered.

"Thank you both." I blushed. "By the way, what was wrong with the Gelcry? He acted like he was scared to death." I saw the Warin glance over at me and realized this conversation was not private. I turned crimson and lowered my eyes.

Garan walked over and excused himself to attend another engagement. We expressed our appreciation for his services, and he bowed, walked to the edge of the corridor, and disappeared in a gray vapor. There were a lot of things I would need to get used to in this new world. I turned my attention back to the conversation.

"So did I do something wrong to upset Garan during the ceremony?" I asked.

"Olivia, Tristan and I are very honored and humbled that our Creator chose our souls for you." Nick touched my cheek, his midnight-black eyes staring down tenderly.

"We are very privileged to have found this favor in the eyes of Logsald," Tristan added with a quiet reverence.

"I don't know what all the fuss is about. I'm the one honored and privileged. I don't know what I've ever done to deserve either of you," I said, reaching up to lay the palms of my hands against their cheek. "Now...what color?" I was anxious to know if it was as pale as I expected it to be.

"Love, it was the most beautiful radiant gold I've ever seen! Poor Garan was so nervous to be in the presence of a soul directly touched by the hand of Logsald. I was afraid he wouldn't be able to perform the ceremony," Nick said as we slowly ambled toward the others.

"Gold! There must be some mistake! A flaw in the design or a word left out of the essence cantation! I'm sure it was meant to be a pale yellow or a peach color! Maybe it just doesn't work right on a human!" I was convinced the color was wrong.

"I'd like to propose a toast," Taryn said, handing us a glass. "To my brothers and new sister, peace and happiness to you as you begin this life."

We raised our glasses to him, and he took a sip of the champagne and set the glass back on the table. Nadya was just staring at him.

"What? I hope you weren't expecting some long philosophical speech! That just wouldn't be me." He sniffed. Taryn looked so innocent that it brought a smile to everyone, including Nadya.

The five of us ambled toward the front of the house. Now that the ceremony was over, I suddenly felt very tired. Nadya must have sensed it.

"Taryn and I need to get home. We are very happy for you." She leaned over to embrace Nick then Tristan. She then turned to me. "Olivia, just what do you see when you look into the mirror?" she asked softly.

"I see a plain, ordinary woman, not worthy of them," I answered honestly.

"Well, I'm sure time will prove otherwise. I'm anxious to see how the Creator's plan for you unfolds." She gave me a hug and walked out the door, pulling Taryn behind her as he waved good-bye.

Now that everyone was gone, I was taken by the awkward silence.

"Umm...can either of you tell me why I wasn't warned about the searing beams of light?" I asked.

"We couldn't warn you, sugar. It's never happened before," Tristan answered.

"This was an extraordinary ceremony, but then, everything about our situation is extraordinary." Nick smiled. "It was intense though, wasn't it?"

"Yeah, it definitely was," I agreed. "If you two don't mind, I'd like to change and maybe get a little rest. This day has been exhausting!"

"No, sugar, of course we don't mind. I'd like to put on something more comfortable myself." Tristan had already removed the tie.

"We'll talk tomorrow, love, go on and rest," Nick said and kissed my cheek. Tristan did the same, and I bid my goodnights before starting up the stairs to my room.

After changing and putting everything in its place, I sat crosslegged on the bed and picked up the picture of my parents from the nightstand. I wiped a tear from my eye as I traced my finger around the image of their smiling faces.

"You may not have approved of the choice I've made, but I know in my heart you would have understood. I so wish you could have been here. I miss you," I whispered. I dried my eyes, set the picture back by my bed, and slipped my feet under the covers. I looked at the perfect ring on my finger. *I hope they didn't take the golden gown serious*, I thought. "I don't think I could handle the stress of trying to live up to some kind of celestial expectations," I mumbled aloud, sighed, and turned out the lamp.

My mind was still busy as I lay back on my pillow. I usually have dreams when my life is about to be threatened. I wonder why I never dreamed of Nadya's attack. Was it just too spontaneous? I thought. Or could it be that I was never in danger of dying at all?

Bittersweet Good-Byes 27

The next two weeks went by quickly. Nick was often taking me out somewhere at night while Tristan and I spent our days enjoying nature. With the exception of a few hours of rest, we spent our remaining time in the sitting room, just talking and laughing. They had so many stories to tell about their lives since coming to this world.

Everything was so relaxed; it was as if we had always been together. They had gone to such great lengths to make sure my transition into their world was as effortless and comfortable as possible.

It was the middle of November, and even though the air had cooled considerably, I still enjoyed sitting on the patio. This morning was no exception. I was sitting at a small table in the garden area, sipping on a hot cup of spiced tea. Most of the leaves had disappeared, and everything was taking on that dismal gray appearance. It was then that it occurred to me that I had been so caught up in my new world that I had been neglecting my old one and the friends that surely by now would be wondering about me. I let my thoughts trail off to another time, to memories forever frozen in time, bittersweet thoughts of a thousand yesterdays gone by. I was so absorbed in my walk down memory lane that I didn't even hear the rustling of the leaves across the ground.

"Hey is everything okay?" The soft, smooth voice startled me. I looked over to see Tristan leaned casually against a pine tree by the walkway. His long black hair was pulled back. He was dressed in a denim jacket, blue tee, and jeans.

He looked positively radiant. It never seemed to fail; I had to catch my breath before I could speak.

"Hey, I didn't hear you walk up. What brings you out here this morning?" I smiled and sipped my tea.

"You, we got a little concerned. You've been out here a long time." He shuffled some dried leaves with his toe as he spoke.

"Oh, I'm sorry. I guess I was lost in thought and didn't realize," I said apologetically.

"Is there something wrong, baby?" I still loved it when he called me that. Just the way he says it sends the tiny jolts buzzing through me.

"No, I was just thinking about my friends in town and the house. I do need to check on things at my place, and I should stop in to see my friends for a short visit at least.

"That's all?" he asked. "Nothing else?"

"Well, maybe a little more than that, I guess. I'm not so sure I'm ready to let go just yet," I confessed. I looked down, hoping he wouldn't take my longing for past things the wrong way.

"I understand," he said.

"You do...really?" I sat my cup down and motioned him over to sit with me.

"Yeah, really." He smiled as he took the seat across from me and picked up my hand. "I used to go back to the very spot where I first arrived in your world every month. I would just sit there remembering. I suppose I was hoping the portal would open so I could have just one more glimpse...you know."

"Yes, I do," I spoke quietly as we sat there looking into each other's eyes. No words were needed to convey the deep and agonizing sadness that would forever remain a part of us.

"I think that you should go into town this afternoon and have some barbeque for lunch." Tristan flashed a tentative smile at me. I bit my lower lip as I looked down at our joined hands and smiled.

"You know, I believe I will!" I rose from my seat, and Tristan followed suit.

"If you want to go by your house, I'll meet you there." His tone let me know that going there alone was not an option, so I didn't argue.

"How does three o'clock sound?"

"Sounds like a plan. I guess we should go inside and fill Nick in on the day's agenda." He put his arm across my shoulder as we slowly walked to the door.

Nick was in his study working on the computer. "I'll be finished in just a minute," he said without looking up from his task. Nick was dressed in his "hang around the house" clothes, as he liked to call them. Even in the casual faded jeans and green tee shirt, he was still mouthwatering to look at. Tristan and I sat on the sofa, chatting idly as we waited. I heard a quick tap, tap, tap, and then Nick walked over and sat down in the wing-backed chair across from us. I glanced down as he leaned back, stretching his feet out in front of him. He wasn't wearing shoes! I had never seen him so relaxed! Tristan leaned forward, resting his elbows on his knees as he clasped his hands together.

"Olivia has decided to go into town today and visit with her friends and then stop by to check out her house," he announced to Nick, who in turn remained silent as if he knew Tristan had more to say.

"I think she knows that we're not too keen on her going out alone, and especially back to her place," Tristan said. Nick sat there looking at me as if he were trying to think of a good reason for me to abandon the entire plan.

"I don't know why the two of you can't relax a little. Lucas isn't going to try the same thing twice! He didn't strike me as stupid! It's broad daylight, and it's very unlikely they would try anything now."

"Even though you're probably right, I'd feel better knowing you weren't alone," Nick said.

"She won't be, at least not at the house. I told her I would meet her there this afternoon. I'm not comfortable with the idea either." Tristan glanced over just long enough to catch the irritated expression on my face.

"You too have got to stop treating me like a child! I'm a grown woman for Pete's sake! I don't plan on taking any chances, and I'm certainly not going to put myself in any position to be harmed by strangers. I have full knowledge of the danger that awaits me and the risk I'm taking by leaving this house alone."

"I'm sorry, love, you're absolutely right. You have the right to go wherever you please and certainly don't need our permission. I would, however, appreciate it if you would at least let us know where you're going." Nick seemed quite calm as he addressed me and my frustrated attitude. "I still agree with Tris, that he should be with you at the house. It is, after all, a secluded place, and I'd rather we didn't take any chances."

"Fine. I can handle that at least."

"Good, then go see your friends and have fun." Nick smiled.

"I do have a little problem though," I continued.

"Oh, what kind of problem?" Nick raised an inquisitive brow.

"What do I tell them about my absence and how do I explain this?" I said, holding up my hand and pointing to the ring on my finger. "They're going to ask where I've been and what I've been up to the past month. I can't just casually say, 'Oh, I've been hanging out with a shifter and a vampire! I would have stopped in sooner, but I was kidnapped by a werewolf, beaten within an inch of my life, and held in a dungeon for ten days! Oh, don't worry, obviously I was rescued, but there was this magic veil conjured up by this witch named Hazon, and I ended up being bound and sealed to two mates, who, by the way, are the same said shifter and vampire!' I'm sure they'll take that story with a grain of salt or have me committed!" I ranted.

Both men sat quietly until my nervous tirade was over. No one said a word as I sat there wide-eyed, staring straight at Nick. The corners of his mouth began to twitch, and suddenly he burst out in shrieks of uncontrollable laughter! As beautiful as the sound was, I remained annoyed. Tristan only encouraged the raucous by joining him!

"I don't think this is one bit funny!" I scolded" How am I supposed to explain my absence and who or whom am I supposed to tell them I'm married to?" I asked, still very annoyed that they found humor in my dilemma.

"Love, I'm sorry. It's very simple. Tell them you slipped away to Vegas or something and married me," he said, trying to catch his breath and regain his composure.

"So just lie." I glared. My agitation with them was still evident.

"Well...yeah. You may not have gone to Vegas, but..." Nick shrugged his shoulders, still holding the amused smirk on his face. Tristan snickered, and I immediately shot him one of my "don't you dare say a word" looks.

"Oh, I see what you mean. A lie in this situation is much more believable than the truth."

"Exactly, sugar," Tristan squeaked as another round of laughter escaped. I crossed my arms and peered at Tristan with one eyebrow raised and a menacing scowl on my face. He immediately straightened in his seat and fought desperately to control himself.

"What about Tristan? Everyone knew I was dating both of you. What do I say happened with him?" I continued, trying to cover every question I thought they might ask.

"Well, tell them if they ask about Tris that he transferred to some hospital down south. Then tell them I'm taking you on an extended trip to Europe before we move to my apartment in New York. That ought to satisfy their curiosity."

"What about my house?"

"Um..." Nick hesitated a moment. "Tell your friends I found a nice older couple to rent it." He then leaned back in the chair, comfortable that his explanation was satisfactory.

"It all sounds good to me. The only thing that worries me is my ability to sound believable. Darla has always been able to tell when I'm not telling the whole story, so to speak." I stood up and started unconsciously pacing. I just stopped still. The room seemed to get quiet—eerie quiet. The fire crackling in the background sounded like firecrackers being tossed about. A sick feeling began to burn in the pit of my stomach as the true reason for my trip to town started to sink in.

"I won't ever see them again, will I?" I choked on the words as I tried to force back the tears. Nick's expression became somber, and the lighthearted mood changed in an instant.

"My dear sweet love," he cooed. He stood up and put his arms around me in a gentle, consoling manner as Tristan stood tenderly stroking my hair. I could tell by the look in their eyes they felt the anguish of loss as deeply as I.

"Of course you'll see them again, I promise," Nick assured me. "We'll stop by occasionally with the excuse that I came down on business." He was now standing back, holding both of my hands in his.

I felt like a huge weight had been lifted from me! My life in the human world wasn't about to disappear! I hadn't lost myself in the chaotic insanity of the past month!

"You have no idea how you've just made me feel!" I sighed. "I suddenly feel like every worry in the world has been taken from me and my life is perfect." I beamed at the two loving souls before me.

"I need to go up and change," I said. I was about to leave the study when it occurred to me that my Cavalier wasn't running. I had given my parents' car to Grace Butler. It seemed the least I could do to show my gratitude for all she had done for me.

SOULBOUND: DESTINY'S MOVE

"I can't go to town." I felt let down, and my disappointment couldn't help but show.

"Why, baby?" Tristan asked, looking confused.

"I don't have a car! I can't drive one of your vehicles." I pointed out to Tristan. "The Hummer's way too big and awkward, and the Mercedes...let's just say I'm not that coordinated!" I squinched my nose with the comment, and both Nick and Tristan chuckled as if I had done something memorable.

"I knew that you would eventually want to wonder off alone, so..." Tristan had done something without my knowledge; his look was that of the cat that ate the canary, and I wasn't sure whether to be excited or worried. "I bought a car and had it delivered while you and Nick were out a few nights ago. I hope you don't mind. I picked something that I felt would get you home if the weather turned bad. If you don't like it, we'll take it back and you can pick something else," he explained.

"What did you get?" I asked, hoping it wasn't anything too ostentatious or hard to maneuver, like anything with a stick shift!

"It's a small Subaru. They're good in the snow," he stated.

"Tris!" I squealed. "That's perfect!" In my excitement, I flung my arms around him and kissed him. I realized Nick was still standing there, and I dared to look over at him, afraid my reaction to Tristan's gift may have offended him. I couldn't have been more mistaken. He stood there beaming, genuinely pleased by my joy.

"Tris, you'll show her where the keys are kept in the garage?"

"No problem," he acknowledged. "Don't you think you better get ready?" Tristan laughed as he reminded me, I wanted to change.

"Oh yeah...um...I won't be long," I stammered. I started to leave the room but instead turned around and ran over to kiss them both on the cheek before I left.

When Olivia left the room to change, Nick had the opportunity to speak to Tristan.

"Tris, I know she needs her freedom to come and go, but I can't help but be apprehensive about it. Regardless of what she may think, Lucas isn't going to give up on her so easily," he said as he walked slowly back to his desk.

"She won't even know I'm there," Tristan answered his silent request. Nick nodded, and Tristan left to wait in the foyer for Olivia.

After going through about twenty garments, I decided on a black ribbed turtleneck and faded low-rise jeans. I slid a wide black and-silver belt through the loops on my jeans and slipped on pair of black ankle boots.

I never was one for jewelry, but I did find a nice silver chain and some silver loop earrings I liked. My hairbrush was on the bathroom counter, so I walked in and picked it up, stepping back from the mirror to examine my look. I hadn't really paid attention to how much my hair had grown since I stopped cutting it. It was already to the center of my back and seemed twice as thick.

"Good grief!" I mumbled aloud, running my fingers through the thick locks. I was in too much of a hurry to deal with pinning it up, so I just ran the brush through and left it hanging.

Now where did I put my driver's license? I rummaged around through the dresser drawer. I couldn't seem to remember. I just stood in the center of the room with my hands on my hips, scanning every surface.

"The nightstand!" I thought aloud, snapping my fingers. I pulled the drawer open, and sure enough, I picked up my license along with the twenty-dollar bill I had clipped to it weeks ago. I slipped them into my hip pocket as I closed the door behind me.

I came bounding down the stairs with a preoccupied mind and my eyes set on my feet. I slammed into Tristan's chest. He caught me before I became an addled heap on the floor. It felt sort of like running headfirst into a brick wall!

"Sorry." I smiled. Tristan didn't answer, instead he just stood there gawking at me with an unfamiliar expression.

"Is something wrong?" I asked, looking down to examine myself. His silence made me feel as if I may have dressed too hastily. "This doesn't look right. Maybe I should go back up and find something else to wear," I said, now feeling very self-conscious.

"No," he quickly responded. "You look amazing!" His gorgeous electric-blue eyes scanned me from the top of my head to the tips of my toes. His reaction to me was so unexpected I wasn't sure how to respond. My mouth seemed to dry up, and I could feel goose bumps beginning to rise on my arms.

"What...are you looking at?" I asked.

"You," he answered.

"What about me?" I looked back down, trying to see what the big deal was all about.

"I'm not used to seeing you like that," he said, still staring at me with glazed eyes.

"Like what?" I stood; arms outstretched.

"Like...like that!" he answered, gesturing outward with both hands. A wisp of a smile crossed my lips as I looked up. *So, this is what turns Tristan on—simple and rustic. This outfit is definitely going to the front of my closet!* I thought. "Thank you for the compliment, now show me to the keys," I teased, gently nudging him toward the door.

I just couldn't get over my fascination with their ability to conceal things in plain open sight. I can't count how many times I had walked right by the garage and never once had a hint of its existence. I was again amazed when Tris walked over to a tree trunk and pressed the switch to open the door. The side of the mountain slid gently to the left rather than having a door open upward like a normal garage. I just shook my head.

"How did you manage to camouflage the entrance without disturbing the natural growth around it?" I asked. "I've never seen an engineering feat like this in my life!"

"Ha-ha! And you won't unless the engineers and architects are Avarian." Tris laughed.

"Huh," I muttered in my preoccupation with the shifting forest.

"The elves, sugar."

"Oh...ohhh, man, I don't know what I was thinking. Of course, the Avars are extraordinary builders," I said, still marveling at their work. When Tristan motioned for me to come into the garage, I noticed my new car parked just inside the entrance. "Oh my, I love it!" I breathed, walking up to examine my gift more closely.

"The keys to all the vehicles are kept in here," he said, pointing to a small box hanging on the far wall. "I'll get them for you; just remember to hang them back here when you get home," he said as he walked across the room.

"Okay." I couldn't see what was so important about replacing the keys to that particular spot, but if that was their wish. If there was anything I was sure of, it was that Nick or Tris never did anything without purpose. I opened the door to the Subaru and was elated to find it was an automatic! Tris was walking back toward me, keys in hand, when I squealed in delight.

"Oh my gosh, Tris!" Tennessee doesn't require a front tag, so he had something special made for the empty space. It was a tag that bore a full moon over a dark forest with a blue-eyed panther, face peering out from the trees. "This is perfect!" I exclaimed. The car definitely showed Tristan's good taste and his preference for blue.

"Here's your key," Tristan teased, dangling the key ring high above his head.

"Okay, Tris, hand it over!" I ordered. After a few minutes of playful scuffling, he dropped his hand.

"All right, here you go," he said. "Have fun and be careful." His words seemed to stop me cold. I hadn't heard the phrase "be careful" since my mom passed away. Tris knew he had said or done something to pull me from my recent playful mood. I just swallowed hard and tried to pass the heart-wrenching words with a soft smile.

"I will...promise," I said as I climbed into the driver's seat. I waved and started to back out of the garage. I knew that both of them would be worried; after all, it was the first time since they rescued me that I had been out from under their watchful eye.

I started down the winding road, excited to partake in some girl talk. I rehearsed my story over and over in my head. Damn! I thought. Why do I have to be such a terrible liar?

I had picked the perfect time to stop by the restaurant. The lunch rush was over, and there were only a couple of cars in Rooter's parking lot. I pulled into a space near the front door and walked in. The aroma of barbeque sauce and french fries filled the room. The familiar scent was comforting and helped me relax. I glanced around to find only three people working the front and the last two customers at the register.

Darla and Kandi hadn't noticed me yet, and I didn't know the tall, lanky brunette at the counter. As I stepped around the corner, Darla looked up and shrieked, "Olivia!" She ran over and flung her arms around my neck. "I'm so glad to see you! I was getting worried," she rambled. "I wanted to call in a missing person report, but Kandi talked me out of it!"

"Well, I'm glad she did." I laughed. Kandi walked over to greet me with a wide smile.

"Hey, girl, it's good to see you," she said, gently giving me a hug. "Come on over and sit down." She motioned toward a booth as she started walking. She seemed nervous and unsure of what to say. Maybe she's just had a hard day, I told myself.

"You want something to drink or a sandwich?" Darla asked. I ordered a barbeque sandwich and a cola. Kandi sent the new girl to the kitchen with the order.

"That's Tracy. She was hired when you quit," Kandi answered before I had the chance to ask.

"So where are Danny and Michelle?" I asked. It seemed odd not to see at least one of them here.

"Girl, hold on to your socks. You're about to get a shock." Kandi snickered. "When you left, Dan was a wreck. Michelle stepped in to 'console' him, and after a whirlwind romance, they up and got married last week. Dan took her to the Bahamas for their honeymoon." She laughed as she looked at my gaping mouth and wide eyes.

"You're kidding!"

"Nope, serious as a heart attack!" Kandi retorted.

"Well, I'll be...I'm happy for them. They'll make a great couple." I smiled.

"So, what have you—oh my god! Let me see that ring. Is that a..." Darla couldn't seem to finish a full sentence as she pulled my hand across the table.

"Yes, it is." I grinned.

"Who...I mean, which one?" she stammered.

"Nick."

"I knew it!" Darla said as the palm of her hand smacked the table. "Deep down I knew he was the one! I just have a sense about these things, ya know." Her head was bobbing up and down with every word.

"Well, damn, Darla. Why didn't you tell her six months ago? You could've saved her a lot of trouble!" Kandi seemed a little sarcastic, but Darla didn't seem to notice.

"Cuz it wasn't any of my business," she stated flatly and stuck her tongue out at Kandi.

"Now, ladies," I said, hoping there wasn't about to be ill words. Kandi smiled and shook Darla's shoulder playfully. "Don't worry, she knows I'm kidding."

Tracy had returned with my food and muddled through a quick introduction. She informed Kandi that she needed to leave early because her little boy was sick. Kandi told her to clock out. She excused herself and walked away. Kandi and Darla then turned their attention back to me.

"Okay, Liv, start from the beginning and tell us everything!" Darla leaned forward, crossing her arms on the table as she spoke. I took a bite of my sandwich and began the story Nick came up with.

The time went by quickly as we talked and reminisced. I looked at the clock above the register. I needed to say my good-byes. I didn't want to keep Tristan waiting at the house.

"I really need to get going. I've got a lot of packing to do," I fibbed.

"Awe...I wish you could stay longer." Darla whined.

"I know...me too. I promise to stop in when Nick comes down here on business," I assured her. Kandi had been fidgeting for quite some time. She never did seem to relax back into her old self.

"Um...you won't see me on your next visit. Today is my last day here," she informed me.

"What? You're leaving!" I exclaimed.

"Yeah, I got another job offer in Miami. You know how it is, better pay and more to do." She grinned. We had walked to the front door as Kandi announced her plans.

I hugged Darla and promised again to visit before she went back to work. I stood there, silently looking at Kandi. I don't know what had happened to change her and wished I had time to find out.

"I'm going to miss you." I couldn't hide the tears I was fighting to hold back.

I'll miss you too. Don't let it get you down, it's a small world. I'm sure we'll cross paths again," she said with confidence.

"I hope so," I whispered as I hugged her. She pulled back and smiled.

"I know we will, trust me!" She winked, and I saw a glimmer of the old mischief in her eye. Tristan was waiting at the house as promised.

"Did you enjoy your visit?" he asked as I got out of the car.

"Yeah, it was great," was all I said. There was a hint of sadness in my voice. Tristan picked up on it but opted not to ask.

I walked through the front door, and a rush of emotions flooded through me. Most of the personal things were gone. Nick and Tristan had moved those things to my new home. The pictures were gone from the walls, and the huge shelf in the corner was void of the vast movie collection.

"I'll wait here for you," Tristan said and took a seat on the couch.

"Thanks. I won't be long," I whispered.

I walked into the kitchen. So many memories lingered in this room. I guess there was a farewell in my trip to town. This good-bye hurt deep, and I wiped away a tear. I wiggled the kitchen chair with the loose leg, remembering the numerous attempts my dad made to fix it. He never did get it right.

The dishes were still placed neatly in the cupboard, just like Mom would have placed them. My eye caught a cup in the back of the shelf. I reached in and lifted it out. Anna was written across the front. Mom's coffee mug. I visualized her at the table sipping from the cup while Dad ate his breakfast.

I tucked it into my arm and walked into the hall. I stopped at the long row of marks on the wall. Dad would stand me up here and measure how much I'd grown every year. Stand up straight,

Olivia. Now if you don't stand still, you're going to start shrinking. I smiled at the memory.

I moved on through the house and rummaged through a few things on the back porch. I picked up my dad's fishing pole. This should bring some luck at the lake, I thought. I went back through the house to find Tristan hadn't moved since we came in.

"I'm ready to go now," I said, wiping another tear way. He rose and silently followed me out. I put my things in the backseat and turned back to the house.

I stood there with one foot in the car and one on the ground, committing every detail to memory. Finally, I placed my fingers to my lips and blew a kiss toward the house and hurried to back out of the drive, making every effort not to look back.

After another one of Nick's fabulous meals, I spent the rest of the evening alone, sitting in the sunroom.

I sorted through every detail of my life. I suppose, in a way I had passed through a kind of portal of my own, from my world into theirs. It's the sixteenth of November. Tomorrow will make one month since I first learned of Kardaun.

At first, I felt sort of like Alice falling down the rabbit hole, landing in a fantasmic place that made little sense. My trip to town had proven my perception of fantasy and reality was very different. Oddly, I felt like my return to this place was more like the reality of Alice waking up under the tree.

It's a curious thing, this destiny and just how quickly things can change. I had gone in four short weeks from Olivia Ryan, insignificant misplaced human, to Olivia Xandier-Alberon, ruler of kingdoms.

Invasion Of Es' Mar 28

My night was restless. I suppose my mind was overstimulated with the thoughts of people and places in the past. I couldn't get Kandi out of my mind. I kept thinking of how much she seemed to have changed and the sense that something about me was instrumental in the cause.

I dreamed of Mike Zita, McKenzie Roberts, Kandi, and strangely the sweet older lady in the hospital, Emeline. I concluded she was in my dream because of Nick's remark of an older couple renting my house. She was the first image that came to mind. It wasn't that my dream was bad, just odd. I saw Kandi and her beautiful big brown eyes; for some reason, I seemed fixed on them. She winked, and suddenly they were the huge brown cat eyes of a puma. It winked again and ran into the woods. Then I saw a bird, large and graceful, floating above the trees. All at once I was talking to Emeline. As for Mike and McKenzie, they were there one second and then nothing, but blue vapor remained.

I sat up on the edge of my bed, tossing my hair back, mulling over the strange images. Hmph, I'm losing my mind! I thought. My life is getting so jumbled up I can't even have a coherent dream!

I took a hot shower and decided to put on a pair of sweats and tee shirt since I had plans to stay in today. I slipped on a pair of big fuzzy house shoes and pulled my hair back in a ponytail.

I clunked down the stairs in the awkward shoes and went to the kitchen. A plate of fruit and some tea was all that sounded appealing.

At first, I thought Nick and Tristan were gone. The house was quiet as a church. Then I heard the muffled sound of their voices coming from the sitting room. I only caught pieces of their words.

They were talking about some pass closing. I picked up my plate, tediously balanced my cup on a saucer, and started for the other room to join them. The sound of my slippers scuffing across the floor seemed exceptionally loud and annoying.

Both of them stopped talking when I entered the room. I continued over to the chair by the fire, set my cup down, slipped off the atrocious shoes I had decided never to wear again, and positioned myself cross-legged in the seat.

"What pass is closing?" I asked as if I had been included in the conversation from the beginning.

"Pass...how did you hear that?" Tristan asked in surprise.

"I don't know. Sound always travels better in the fall and winter. It must have something to do with the air being thinner," I said, popping a grape into my mouth. "Besides, this place is so quiet. Every little sound seems to reverberate off the walls." I grinned. "So, what were you two plotting?" I asked as I took a sip from my cup.

"Actually, we were plotting the invasion of Es'mar," Tristan answered, showing a hint of mischief with his sidling grin.

"Huh..." I stared with knit brows. "Es'mar?"

"Yes, love, how would you like to take a trip?" Nick asked, his eyes gleaming.

"Okay, you two can start making sense anytime now." They both laughed as they reveled in my clueless expression.

"How would you like to go to Switzerland?" Nick announced the question rather than asked.

"Switzerland—are you serious!"

"Of course I'm serious!" Nick laughed.

"I've never been any farther than Florida," I exclaimed. "When are we going?"

"The end of the week," Tristan answered.

"I'll see to your passport," Nick stated.

"You won't need to; I already have one...in my maiden name of course. Will that be a problem?" I asked.

"No, your driver's license is still Olivia Ryan. We'll need to change that to Riggs though, when we return." Nick smiled.

I glanced at Tristan. He seemed perfectly at ease with my use of Nick's pseudonym in the human world.

"So where in Switzerland are we going?" My excitement was evident in my tone of voice.

"Come with me. It'll be easier to show you," Nick said, taking my hand in his.

We entered the media room, and I went straight to my usual seat directly in front of the screen. The three of us had spent several late nights in there watching old movies. I relaxed into the soft chair beside Tristan as Nick turned on the DVD player and seated a small disk, then walked back and sat down.

The screen lit up to reveal still shots of a beautiful city. He pushed the Pause button before the picture could fade away to the next.

"Okay, this is the city of Bern, where we'll land," Nick began. "There will be a Hummer waiting," he continued, releasing the Pause button. "We'll travel south down through the St. Gotthard Tunnel," he continued as the pictures of the Swiss countryside faded in and out. I sat quietly, taking in every detail.

"Hope you're not claustrophobic. The tunnel is over ten miles long," Tristan teased. I just rolled my eyes and huffed.

"It really is that far through the tunnel. As far as I'm concerned, the best part of the ride." Nick grinned.

"Where to next?"

"Well, from there down the St. Gotthard pass between the Tocino and Rhine Rivers, into the Canton of Tocino in the Southern Alps."

"Is that the road?" I asked, pointing to the squiggly lines on the screen.

"Yeah, oh, so you get car sick," Tristan started again.

"Humph, no, I just wonder how someone could maneuver so many hairpin turns. It looks like a can of worms." Nikolas laughed at the comparison to my favorite pastime.

"Actually, the road can be treacherous, at least to humans. The pass is closed in the winter. We'll turn off the main road here," he said, casting his shadow onto the screen.

"Then it's only a few miles to Kardaun Valley. It is completely anonymous to the outside world." The screen then went black. "Don't you have any pictures of the valley, or Es'mar Estate?" I asked.

"That, sugar, we're saving as a surprise."

"That is so not fair!" I felt like a starving animal left one bite short of a full meal. "I can't wai—" I stopped dead. Tristan and Nikolas never go anywhere without a reason. There was more to this European "vacation" than they were saying. I just knew, whatever it was, I wasn't going to like it.

"Why are we going to Switzerland?" I asked, standing up to face them.

"We always go this time of year. Besides, it's been our home for over six hundred years."

I got a sick twinge in the pit of my stomach with Tristan's evasive answer. "Okay, but what is the reason for going every year?" I knew it when they both shuffled in the seats and their expressions resembled two boys caught with their hand in the cookie jar.

"Well, love...um..." Nick started as if he wished I wouldn't have caught on until we were already there.

"Come on, Nikolas, spit it out!" I exclaimed as I stood before them, arms folded, patting my foot.

SOULBOUND: DESTINY'S MOVE

"Well, Tris and I host the Yule Ball every year, and we like to be there to see to the final preparations," Nick finally admitted.

"Yule Ball!" I certainly did not like the sound of that.

"Yes," Nick meekly answered.

"What is this Yule Ball? I assume it's some formal affair?" I said curtly.

"Uh...very formal." Tristan stepped in, apparently trying to rescue Nick from the wrath that he assumed was about to come down on him.

"Every year we invite a few of the citizens of Kardaun to celebrate the Winter Solstice," Tristan explained.

"Few huh...just how many is a few?"

"There isn't near as many attending as, say, a couple of hundred years ago." My eyes lowered on Tristan as I took on a hard, steady glare.

"The ball used to entertain over a thousand guests, but as Tris said, through the years, the number has lessened considerably. For that, we can blame Lucas and his insanity."

"How m-a-n-y?"

"This year, the guest list included seven hundred, but sadly we've lost fifty of our kinsmen."

"Six hundred and fifty people!" I felt faint.

"Relax, Liv, it'll be fun, you'll see!" Tristan always seemed to find a way to distract me from matters at hand.

I jerked my head around to look at him, surprised at what he just said. "What did you just call me?" A crooked smile crossed my lips as I exhaled in relief.

"I'm sorry, I meant Olivia." Tristan's eyes gave away his uncertainty as to whether he should have apologized or let it stand.

"No. I was beginning to worry either of you would ever get comfortable enough to call me that!"

"You prefer the short version of your name?" Nick asked.

"It's not that I dislike my name, it's fine occasionally, but everyone I've ever known, my parents, friends, teachers, all felt comfortable enough to use that familiarity. Well, with the exception of the two people that means the most in the world to me." I smiled and blushed. "I'm closer to you than anyone on earth, and I've been patiently waiting for one or both of you to say it...comfortably. The use of my full name coming from you seems so impersonal."

"We've refrained from it because we thought you'd feel disrespected by us," Nick explained.

"Well, I'm glad we have an understanding now, Olivia sometimes, Liv most of the time." I laughed. "Now back to the Yule Ball and the six hundred. It's obvious to me that my attendance is not left to choice," I said, watching Nick and Tristan's head move simultaneously from side to side. "I suppose I'm going to have to take it like a woman." I grinned.

"No, love, like a queen," Nick said. There went that twinge again.

"What if I do something stupid and embarrass you both?" I needed to express my fear and hoped they would understand how uncomfortable this made me.

"Don't worry, Liv, you'll do fine." Even with Nick's reassurance, I wasn't convinced. At this moment, I didn't feel quite like the fish out of water, but more like the fish being tossed into the piranha tank!

"Sugar, you're worrying over nothing. All the guests are anxious to meet you. After all, they are curious about their new High Queen." Tris meant well, but his words only heightened my anxiety.

"Uhgg..." I growled. "All the more reason to worry about screwing up!" The knot in my stomach felt like a cannon ball. I knew there was no way around it, so I had better just resign myself to this fate and hope it passed quickly.

"I don't know about you two, but I'm starved!" Tristan announced.

"I'll see what I can do to remedy that," Nick responded.

"I'll give you a hand," I offered.

"Great, then I'll put these things away and meet you two in the kitchen." Tristan ambled toward the shelf to replace the movies Nick had taken out to find the slideshow.

Nick got the makings for a salad out of the refrigerator, and I pulled the cutting board from under the counter and seated myself on the barstool.

I started slicing the carrots; my mind was busy with the thoughts of Switzerland. I had to reveal my greatest concern to Nick.

"Umm...Nick?" I began.

"Yeah."

"I know what my being bound to both you and Tristan makes me in my world. I'm sure you're aware that what I'm called isn't very kind."

"I know, love, and I'm sorry for that."

"Will I be looked at the same way by the people of your world too?"

"Of course not, Liv. In my world, you're the strongest soul ever born in the existence of Kardaun. You're worthy of the highest praise. You, love, are held in the hearts of the people with great admiration and reverence." As Nick spoke, I could see this admiration in his eyes.

"I'm nothing special to deserve anyone's admiration. I'm sure there's someone much more worthy of their praise," I told him.

"Well, you're not looking through our eyes." He smiled and continued cutting the vegetables.

"I'm just glad I'm part of your world now. If the humans knew about me, they may consider taking up a custom of the past." I sniffed.

"What custom?" he absently asked.

"Well, in the old days, I would be labeled a harlot and would've been stoned for my actions." Nikolas looked totally appalled by what I had just said.

"I told you before, my friends would never understand. They wouldn't be able to see the reason for my choice. To them it would just be immoral and vulgar." I was looking down now, idly rolling the carrot back and forth.

Nick stopped working and stared across the counter. I could see that he wished with all his heart he could make the pain of my rejection disappear. It wasn't hard to see that a part of him would, without remorse, kill any human that showed the slightest hint of contempt for me.

"I'm sorry, love, that you have been so far removed from the human world, because they can't see how wonderful you are." He reached across the counter, tenderly touching my cheek.

"Don't feel pity for me, sweetheart. I'm where my heart tells me to be." I smiled and kissed his hand before he pulled back. "Besides, in spite the flaws in the human race, there are a lot of good people," I defended.

"I know, love, if we didn't think they were worthy—" he dropped his sentence when Tristan entered the room.

He walked straight to the fridge and removed a plate of chicken.

"He's being truthful with you, baby." Tristan smiled and proceeded to take down a piece of chicken in two bites.

"Privacy, Tristan." I grinned.

"Yeah, what about it?" He winked.

"Have you ever heard of it, honey?" I teased.

"Yes, sugar, and personally, I think it's highly overrated." He laughed.

Nick chuckled at our playful banter.

"We can't help that our hearing is so sensitive. Eavesdropping is really unintentional, you know," Nick intervened.

"I know, I'm just teasing. Besides, there is nothing I would say to one of you that I couldn't share with the other." I smiled.

"All jokes aside, baby. You are the most admired soul in the world of Kardaun. If we were actually back in our world, there is only one that would be held in higher regard than you."

"Why only in Kardaun?" I looked curiously at Tristan.

"Well, some believe the time of the Fire Queen has passed, since our world was destroyed."

"The Fire Queen." They had my full attention now, and I was very curious to know the story behind this woman.

"There's a prophecy in our world," Nick said.

"Tell me about it, please." I knew he would take the time to humor my request as I looked at him, my eyes glassed with anticipation. I kept my eyes on Nikolas as I reached to the plate on the counter, taking hold of a chicken leg just as Tristan did. Surprisingly, he didn't let go until I scowled at him! He smiled sheepishly and released it. I leaned forward, resting my arms on the counter as I nibbled the cold snack.

"Let's see..." Nick studied, recalling the words of the prophetic writing. "It is said," he began, "a queen will be born, blessed and good. She will be of the House of Hulain and once removed from the house of Kardaun. It's told she will be a mighty warrior in the time of the fallen," I interrupted the tale.

"What is the time of the fallen?"

"Well, love, as with any mysterious prophecy, we're not sure when that particular passage refers to. We believe that time had not yet come before Kardaun was destroyed. We also believe that destruction was caused by our own hand before its time," Nick said.

"So, you believed in an end-of-time prophecy too?" I was surprised at this similarity to my world.

"Of course, sugar, nothing lasts forever," Tristan spoke up.

"I'm sorry for interrupting, Nick, please go on." I propped my chin into my palms and leaned forward on the counter expectantly.

"As I told you a few minutes ago, she will be a mighty warrior in the time of the fallen. The queen will be cloaked in the veil of tomorrow and carry the blood of kings like a sword of fire!"

"Oh, this queen sounds glorious!" I exclaimed. Nick and Tristan, I was sure, could see my admiration for this age-old tale and the woman depicted.

"Her children," Tristan had picked up where Nick stopped, "are also heroes in the prophecy."

"She had children?" I looked surprised as if this warrior should have been void of maternal instinct.

"Yes, she did bear children in the story." Tristan grinned.

"What is prophesied about them?"

"It's said," Tristan continued, "her children will be just and strong. They will hold tight the crests of three kingdoms and will be the key to the destruction of an evil shadow on the land. They will draw upon them all the blood of Kardaun and reign peace to the kingdoms as one forever." Tristan and Nikolas had worked their way around to stand on either side of me as they gave their rendition of the story told throughout their history.

"What a wonderful tale of hope and peace! So, back in your world, they hold this story as truth?" I asked, looking up from side to side.

"Oh yeah, it's even in the Ruhtt." Nick said.

"I'll have to look it up. I didn't get a chance to read it all while I was in Scarsion's dungeon." I shivered when I recalled the dark, damp prison. Nick and Tristan simultaneously placed a comforting hand on my shoulders, and my very soul shuddered. Something had changed, but I couldn't put my finger on it. I pushed past the strange sensation and continued my questions.

"So, does anyone still believe that this prophecy will come to pass?" I asked, craning my neck to look up to where they stood. They leaned down on each side of me, elbows resting on the counter.

"Yes, many as a matter of fact." Nick grinned.

"Some I've heard are circulating rumors that you are the Fire Queen," Tristan added.

"What! Are you serious?" I laughed.

"We're very serious, love." Nick's smirk gave me to know he didn't agree with them and neither did Tristan; just the same, they seemed to enjoy the reaction.

"Well, I hope it doesn't take long for them to realize that their hope for the future is far misplaced in me!" I exclaimed. "It's pretty obvious from the kidnapping I'm not some mighty warrior! I'm certain that I'm not cloaked in some veil and absolutely positive I don't carry any blood of kings!" I scoffed. "I'm not even from Kardaun, I'm human."

"Nevertheless, that's what some believe, and you're just going to have to live with it." Tristan chuckled. "Well, baby, I have to go to the hospital, it's my last day before we leave." He smiled and kissed me good-bye. "I'll see you tonight."

"All right, call me later," I yelled as he started out into the hall.

"I will, and you don't need to shout," he called back, and I heard his laughter echo as the front door closed behind him.

Nick had taken a metal goblet from the cupboard and poured himself a drink from its matching pitcher in the fridge. I used to cringe inside when I would see him sipping the thick red substance, but now it was beginning to feel normal to me. He stood there, casually drinking, totally unaffected by Tristan's display of affection.

"I guess I need to get some things ready for the trip. Would you mind giving me a hand? I had never been on a real vacation, and I was unsure what to take."

"Sure, I'd be glad to," Nick answered and turned to rinse his cup. He took a drink of water followed by some apple slices to cleanse his mouth. "After you." He gestured. We walked to my room, and he followed me straight to the spare room they referred to as a closet.

"You really don't need to pack anything, unless it's something you really want to take. Everything you'll need is in your room at Es'mar."

"I have a room at Es'mar?"

"Of course you do. It's always been there, just waiting for the day you'd finally come," he spoke in a low whisper.

"Is the closet as big as this one?" I asked.

"No."

"Thank goodness!"

"It's bigger." He laughed.

"Ohhh," I moaned. "Nick, there is really no need for that much excess. I don't even need all this! When we return after the first of the year, maybe we could thin this out a little and donate some to the homeless shelter," I suggested.

"You truly are an exceptional soul!" His voice sounded softer as he nuzzled my neck, and his arm came around from behind me. The closeness of him caused my heart to speed up, and I knew he heard it. The slightest touch from him always caused me to tremble. He slowly turned me to face him, still holding my body close. I looked up into those mesmerizing black eyes, barely breathing as he brushed his free hand down along my cheek and neck. I could smell the sweet scent of him and became almost limp in his arms. His eyes held the same steady gaze as that first night alone in the sitting room. I again felt the intimate sensation he had caused before. My god, how does he do that? I thought. I eagerly awaited the tender touch of his lips to mine as my arms came up around him.

He lifted me from my feet, carrying me to the huge bed. The beautiful, gentle kisses continued as the glorious intoxicating scent, my scent, enveloped me completely. I reached to his waist, discarding the cumbersome sweater. The feel of his cool stone-hard chest against mine seemed to push the trembling deep within me. His lips came down on mine with more force as the world outside disappeared.

A Visit to Kardaun 29

As we began our descent into Bern, Tristan had taken me to the back of the plane and told me to have a seat beside the window. He closed the panel between us and Nick, then reached across to slide open the shade. The sun was shining brightly over the beautiful city, and I smiled.

"Tris, why don't you have the same tinted windows on the plane as we do at the house and in the cars?"

"To tell you the truth, sugar, we never thought of it. Nick usually keeps the shades down when he travels by day. Now that you'll be making longer flights, I think we should get this updated."

The plane had safely found its way to good ol' terra firma, and I was relaxed. I had managed to get used to flying, but that didn't stop the jitters I seemed to keep as long as we were in the air. I assumed, since the sun was still high, we would be waiting onboard for dusk before we disembarked. So, I sat back and picked up the book I'd been reading.

"Don't you plan to get off the plane?" Nick asked.

"Of course, but since it's still daytime, I thought we'd be waiting here till the sun sets," I answered.

"We've got a long ride ahead of us," Tristan piped in.

"But...how..." I said, pointing to Nick.

"Love, there are times, like this, that I have no choice but to pass through the sunlight. Once I'm in the Hummer, I'll be quite safe," he explained.

"Okay, but what about getting to the vehicle, Nikolas?" I bobbed my head sarcastically as I answered.

"I'll use these and move very fast!" His comeback was playful as he held up a pair of sunglasses and a long-hooded cloak that resembled the one worn by the third spirit to haunt Ebenezer Scrooge. "The Hummer will be close to the plane on the tarmac." He winked.

"Oh, well I guess you've done this before, so I'll just shut up now." I smiled, a little embarrassed at my mother-hen attitude.

"You and Tristan go on ahead and I'll be right behind you." He had opened the cloak as he spoke.

We were barely seated when the door opened, and Nick jumped in beside us. He dropped the huge hood and began to unbutton the robe, when I noticed the burn on his hand.

"Nick, your hand!" I pulled his arm over to examine the damage.

"Don't worry, love, it's nothing. That happens sometimes. It'll be healed before we reach Es'mar." He didn't seem concerned, so I supposed I shouldn't be either.

"Rohan, we're ready to go," Tristan said to the driver.

He was a nice-looking young man with dark hair and brown eyes. "Yes, Sire," he acknowledged respectfully.

"Don't we have to go through customs?" I asked.

"Yes, but with Nick's condition, we'll drive into that building there, and someone from customs will meet us," Tris said, pointing to the large bay doors in front of us.

"Hmmm...don't they get suspicious about his 'condition'?" I questioned.

"No, we told you, sugar, we have people working in almost every occupation on this planet." His eyes danced as he watched my expression. "Customs doesn't take long. It's not like we're foreigners," he teased.

"You're not?"

"No, baby, we're citizens of Switzerland and the United States."

"Well, how convenient for you. I suppose as a 'foreigner' I'll be searched and asked a blue million questions!" Neither of them was aware of just how truly foreign I felt going into this Yule celebration.

"We could stop and let you go through the usual way if that's an experience you feel a need for," Nick said, breaking his long moment of silence. I turned my head slowly toward him. He remained seated in his relaxed position, elbow on the arm rest, head tilted to one side, and his chin resting casually between his thumb and forefinger.

"They certainly won't recognize her as Kardaun's High Queen," Tristan added.

"Nope...humph...then we'd have to come back tonight and kill them for their disrespect," Nick nonchalantly commented. I caught on to their bluff quickly.

"All right, you two, have had enough fun at my expense!" I scolded. They broke into snickers and guffaws the moment I chastised them. "Both of you," I said, "that's enough now, behave yourselves!" "Yes, dear," they chimed in unison.

"Ughhh! You two are impossible!" I huffed, all the while smiling to myself. It was obvious just being here had lifted their spirits. This may prove to be fun after all, I thought and settled back to enjoy the ride.

The trip was tedious but beautiful. The farther down into the Southern Alps we went, the higher the mountain peaks. I was completely enthralled with my surroundings.

Finally, we turned off the main road onto a rough, narrow trail leading back into the dense forest. It came to a dead end at the base of two enormous mountains. I sat there staring ahead at the stone wall before us.

"Now where do we go?" I asked, feeling a little put out at the thought of a longer delay in reaching our destination.

"Straight ahead," Nick answered calmly.

Rohan spoke into a headset only a few words that sounded like Italian. To my surprise, the stone barrier started to shift. The rocks seemed to effortlessly glide apart, revealing a cleft in the mountains. I immediately thought of the garage back home. As we drove through the now-obvious gate into the small dark tunnel, the wall slid shut behind us.

The Hummer emerged high up on a ridge and came to a stop. It was true dusk now. The sun was barely visible behind the mountain peaks of the horizon. Still just enough light to take my breath away.

"Oh my god." Before me was the most beautiful, pristine valley covered in a new blanket of snow. It stretched as far as the eye could see. In the distance, I saw the edge of what appeared to be a lake. The entire valley was surrounded by five mountain peaks that seemed to reach to the sky. They reminded me of long pointed fingers that literally grasped the clouds to hold this peaceful place away from the world. Along the base of the mountains were lush green forests that encircled every inch of this tranquil paradise. Tristan touched my arm and pointed to my left. I looked to where he motioned and saw a huge three-story gray stone manor set on what appeared to be several acres and seven smaller buildings to the east of the main house.

"This is beyond words!" I breathed in awe.

Nick gently leaned over and whispered softly in my ear, "Welcome home, Olivia."

We started down the winding road as the sun faded slowly out of sight, transforming the purple sky to a dark-ink-colored canvas dotted with tiny diamonds.

The driveway to the front of the manor was lit up like midday. We pulled up in front of an extraordinarily large set of concrete steps, and I realized just how much I had underestimated the size of this place. It wasn't an ordinary manor—it was a palace!

No sooner had the vehicle stopped moving that a tall, lanky young man reached for the door handle. My mouth suddenly seemed to lose every drop of moisture, and my nerves were dancing wildly. Nikolas exited the vehicle and held out his hand to me. I hesitated for a moment, then took a deep breath and stepped out. I immediately felt a strong kinship to a goldfish. I could see people peering out virtually every window. Talk about your awkward self-consciousness.

"Nick, ummm...I'm beginning to feel like this wasn't such a good idea," I whispered.

"Nonsense, Liv, you're going to love it here." He smiled confidently. "Pay no mind to the onlookers. That's just the house staff anxious to get a glimpse of their new queen."

More like a look at the plain mortal, undeserving of the station, I thought. I stood there for the longest time, just staring up at the huge heavy wooden doors laden with hand-forged iron latches and hinges. Just being at this entrance left me feeling, if it were possible, even more small and insignificant.

"Well, sugar, don't you think we should go inside and get settled?" Tristan asked with an amused smirk. "Or do you plan to spend the entire month on the front stoop?" He chuckled. I looked up and smiled faintly at him.

"I was just admiring the craftsmanship," I said with conviction. I so hoped they couldn't see the nervous twitch in my legs.

"Come on, baby. Let's admire it from the other side of the door." Tristan winked to relieve the anxiety he could obviously feel.

I nodded and smiled as he ushered me through the portal that would transport me entirely into their world.

The first thing I noticed was the design in the center of the floor. The crest of Kardaun was inlayed in black tiles against the beautiful gray Italian marble. The dark crimson walls were filled with gorgeous and rare paintings. I made out the signature on the two hanging on the wall nearest to me. One was a Monet, the other Renoir. These works of art, I was sure, had never been or ever would be known by the human world. It made me wonder who sculpted the breathtaking statues that adorned the corners of this room. There were four corridors leading from this room, and in front of me was an enormous marble staircase at least eight-foot wide. I counted four steps to the landing where two more stairways led to the second story, one to my left and one to the right. I walked up the steps with Nick and Tristan to find three more steps in the back that led through a door to yet another corridor.

"My stars in heaven!" I exclaimed. "I've never seen anything like this place!"

"If you're impressed with the entrance hall, you're going to love the rest of the house!" Nick loved the pure innocence of Olivia's childlike wonder.

"House, this isn't just a house!"

"Well, you can call it whatever you like, love, but to me and Tris, it's just a house."

"Come on, Liv, I'll show you to your room while Nick checks in with the staff." Tristan took my hand and pulled me gently behind him as he started up the staircase to my right. My room was on the third floor. Tristan opened the door and guided me into the space designed for me. My hands immediately flew to my mouth. My room in Tailors Mountain paled in comparison. I felt like I was again wandering through a dream. I sauntered around the room, admiring the detail and care they had taken to the décor. The bed was made of hand-carved mahogany with huge, squared posts holding the canopy rails. It was adorned with antique lace and gold bedding.

The windows were dressed in gold satin drapes and antique white sheers covered the French doors that opened to a large balcony.

My private bath was half the size of my room back home, and the closet was my room back home. The marble floor was graced with Persian rugs patterned in swirls of gold and crimson. Set comfortably around a large mahogany fireplace was a soft cushioned sofa and chair; the accent tables matched the dark wood décor with crystal centerpieces. From the seats, it was easy to enjoy the view from the balcony windows.

"So whatdya think?" Tristan anxiously asked, breaking the stone silence.

"Oh, Tris, this is magnificent!" I breathed.

"I'm glad you like it," he said, releasing a huge sigh of relief. "We weren't sure what your taste would be, so if there's anything you'd like to change—"

"I wouldn't change a thing! This room is like a dream. It's absolutely perfect!"

Tristan brushed his fingers gently through my hair and whispered softly,

"It is now." I had no response, but he knew exactly how he had made me feel. I walked over to the window, working desperately to discreetly gain control of my breathing. I turned back to face Tristan, only to find my efforts futile. My breath literally left me. The golden undertone beneath his smooth almond complexion appeared to be glowing. Our eyes were locked. My heart quivered in my chest, and I ached from my very soul to be closer to him, so close we would be one entity.

"Uhmmm...I...ah...I guess I better see how things are going downstairs. I'm sure you want to freshen up. Umm...I'll send one of the staff with your dinner," he stammered.

"Uhhh...yeah...I would like to relax tonight," I awkwardly answered.

"I'll come back in the morning and show you around," he said, avoiding any further eye contact.

"Okay. I'll see you in the morning then." I blushed. Tristan wheeled around and disappeared through the door. I fell onto the sofa, fighting to gain composure. *They did say, never when they are both in the house...even if the house was as big as two counties!* I thought.

Rest did not come easy. The short time I slept was rocked with anxiety. I worried about interacting with the house staff and what they expected of me. The thought of meeting the guests when they began to arrive panicked me beyond any fear I had ever known. The moment the purple haze of dawn started to show in the sky, I began readying myself for the day. The early start afforded me the time for a nice hot bubble bath. The task of getting dressed was much more of a chore than I would have liked it to be, but I finally found something comfortable to wear. I was waiting patiently by the fire when Tristan tapped lightly on my door.

"Come in," I called. Tristan entered the room positively radiant!

"Good morning, beautiful!" he complimented as he walked up and gave me a big kiss.

"Good morning!" His cheerful demeanor was contagious. "Are you ready to take a stroll around the house?"

"I am. Lead the way," I said, motioning him to the door.

"Oh, after you. In this case, it is definitely beauty before age!"

He was so joyful and comforting I just wanted to wrap myself up in him and stay right here. We stepped out to the hall, and he took my hand and started forward.

"My room is just next door, and Nick's is at the end of the hall," he said, pointing in front of us. "This room," he said, opening the double doors, "is our commons room."

The large room was decorated with beautiful antique furniture that appeared to be seventeenth century. The woodwork on the tables and fireplace mantel all hand carved. It was like stepping back into a time when elegance and craftsmanship meant something.

"This is such a peaceful room. These antiques must have cost a small fortune," I commented as I brushed my fingers along the edge of the mantel.

"Actually, sugar, it wasn't that expensive when we bought it new." He chuckled. "It's just been well preserved."

"Oh, right." I felt embarrassed. I should have thought. Of course, everything in this place was brought in during its time.

"Come on, there's a lot more house to see." He reached out and again took my hand.

"The second floor," he said as we began our descent to the next level, "is mostly recreational. This is the gym and rec room."

"Why would you need a full-sized gymnasium?"

"Well, for one, we like a good game of basketball now and then, and in the summer, the young ones are sent here for training," he explained.

"I see. I keep forgetting about those just coming of age."

"It's not only the young adults, the children from the age of five up as well."

I was sure that the training groups were sparse. I felt sad for them, the people of their world, that so few could have children. The thought depressed me, so I decided not to question any more.

"What's down there?" I asked, pointing to a long corridor with a row of doors.

"That's the staff quarters," he answered.

We turned the corner and stood atop another wide marble staircase that led down to an enormous room void of furniture, with the exception of a platform at the far end of the room. There were three high-backed chairs raised in the center and four chairs on each side just slightly lower.

"This, sugar, is the ballroom." His voice echoed through the open space.

"What are those chairs for?" I pointed.

"That is where the kings and queens of Kardaun will be seated during the ball. The center chair belongs to you, and Nick's to the right, mine to the left." He grinned as he felt the tension rise from within me. "Don't worry, baby, everyone is going to love you."

I swallowed hard and turned my attention to the gorgeous view of the mountains and lake visible through the row of huge heavily tinted windows. Long flowing blue and silver valances draped down along the sides, just dusting the marble floor that, too, had the Kardaun crest in the center. Statues, beautifully sculpted, were spaced precisely along the walls, and a massive crystal chandelier hung from the center of the ceiling.

Nikolas was on the far side of the room, giving instructions to one of the staff as we approached him.

"So, what do you think?" Nick grinned, waving his arm to encompass the room.

"About what?" I asked as Nick bent down and kissed me lightly. "Oh, the house. So far, what I've seen is remarkable!" I answered.

"No, I mean the decorations," Nick said again, sweeping his hand around the room.

I hadn't noticed the wreaths decorated with silver and blue ornaments or the eighteen-foot Christmas tree in the corner being lavishly adorned with silver, blue, and crystal bulbs. I noticed too the perfectly placed silver bows lining the branches.

"I didn't think you celebrated Christmas."

"We don't, love, usually we just celebrate the Winter Solstice, but you do." Nick smiled. "The entire house is being decorated in your honor. Several of the guests have accepted our invitation to stay after the ball for a Christmas Eve banquet."

"You didn't have to go to all this trouble for me!" I was glad though; the festive decorations made me feel more comfortable with the celebration.

"It was no trouble. Everyone was happy to do it. It seems the tree trimming is everyone's favorite." He beamed.

"What's behind the French doors?" I asked.

"Oh, that's the dining room where the Yule banquet will be served." Nick placed a hand against the small of my back as he walked me to the doors. It too was decorated with the sapphire blue and silver colors. Each white linen table held crystal hurricane lamps placed in the center of ornate wreaths. Another long row of tinted windows draped the same as the ballroom, and yet another chandelier hung from the ceiling. My stomach knotted again as I realized how many people would be seated at these tables.

"We better move along if you want to see the rest of the house." Tristan seemed a little hurried. I wondered what could possibly have him pressed for time. "Nick, have you had breakfast yet?" Tris shuffled as he spoke.

"No, come to think of it. I've been so busy I hadn't given a thought to eating."

"Why don't you join us?" I figured Tris wouldn't mind the invitation since I was sure he was about to ask.

"That sounds good. You go ahead. I'll meet you in the main dining hall in just a few minutes." He smiled, kissed my cheek, and walked back to the young man he was talking to when we came in.

The main dining area was much like the banquet room with its linen tables and large tinted windows.

"You know, this reminds me of the restaurant Nick, and I went to on our first trip to New York City," I remarked.

"It does resemble it a great deal, now that you mention it. There's a private dining area over there, if it makes you more comfortable," he said, pointing to the doors on the back left-hand side of the room.

"No, this is fine. It's not like there's a crowd." With the exception of two young women on the house staff, we were the only people in the room.

Along the far wall was a table set in buffet style with every breakfast food imaginable. Some of which I was familiar with and some not quite so sure of.

"Why is there so much food for just the three of us?" I knew things were extravagant here, but that seemed like such a waste.

"Actually, we have several guests that have already arrived. This late in the morning, many of them have most likely already been here and gone. I'm sure there will be others later."

"How come I haven't seen anyone yet?" The house was enormous, but still I expected to see more people about.

"Some of the guests stay in the guestrooms on the west wing, others in the houses you saw when we came in."

I filled a plate with bacon, eggs, toast, and a small bowl of fruit. I hadn't realized until now how famished I was. I wasn't able to eat last night. Nerves can do that to a person. My last full meal, I guessed, was dinner the evening we left the States. I took my seat at the table with Tristan and was about to ask what might be keeping Nick when he walked through the door.

Breakfast was very relaxed. Tristan and Nick both dressed in tee shirts and jeans at least made me feel as though I hadn't underdressed this morning.

"Tristan, do you mind if we skip the rest of the tour?" I could tell by the way he fidgeted as he talked to Nick that he had something pressing to do.

"Are you sure? There's a lot more to see, you know."

"Well, I'd like to do a little exploring, if it's okay." I smiled and took another bite of my toast.

"You do have the main rooms down, and I have a little something to do this morning. This afternoon though, I've got some plans for us." Somehow, I wasn't sure I liked the sound of that. I felt sort of like I did the morning he leaned over the counter at Rooter's and said,

"How do you feel about horses?"

"You're welcome to hang out with me until then," Nick offered.

"Thanks, but I don't want to be a bother or get in the way." They could sense just how awkward and misplaced I felt.

"You, love, are not now, nor will you ever be, a bother." Nick smiled.

"Just the same; I'll find something to occupy myself for the next few hours. What exactly do you have planned today, Tris?"

"Do you ski?" He flashed that mischievous grin at me. I knew it! It was the horses all over again!

"Ski? I've never even seen a real pair, let alone had them strapped to my feet!" They both laughed at the fearful expression on my face with the simple mention of the sport.

"Don't worry, Liv. I'm not going to let anything happen to you. We'll start on the beginner slope." He winked.

"I just told you, Tris. I don't know how!" I hoped my protest would change his mind.

"Well, sugar, you're not going to learn any younger," he teased.

"Right," I huffed. "Is there something in that massive closet for me to wear?"

"No, but I had a ski suit sent up to your room." Tristan's smug expression was a giveaway this outing was definitely going to take place.

I found my way back to my room with Nick's assistance, unaware that this would be the first of many trips outside of the valley. I was about to prepare for the ski trip when Tristan called out through the door.

"Olivia, may I come in?"

"Sure, Tris," I answered. He opened the door, smiling as always. This place seemed to intensify everything beautiful about him, and Nick for that matter.

"Tell me you've come to cancel the trip this afternoon." I grinned hopefully.

"No, Liv, you can't come to Switzerland and not enjoy the fabulous slopes. That would be like a sin or something!" His eyes danced. God, he was beautiful!

"Oh, I almost forgot; you better pack an overnight bag. We won't be back until tomorrow." That sly, mischievous look was still in his eye.

"You mean we're staying at the lodge?" I could learn to love this sport. As a matter of fact, I felt a strong fondness for the slopes already.

"Not exactly at the lodge, we own a private cabin on the resort grounds."

"Oh, sounds great! You didn't come here to talk about the trip though, did you? Obviously, there's something you're just bustin' to tell me."

"Not tell you, sugar, show you. That's why I was so anxious this morning. I wanted to get everything ready."

"Oh, well I can tell by your beaming expression I'm not going to regret it," I said.

"You're gonna love it, promise. Come on, Nick's waiting for us." We went down the front staircase and headed for the west wing corridor, a part of the house I planned to explore tomorrow.

"This is our special media room of sorts," Tristan said as he ushered me into the room. I looked around curiously. There were no chairs or movie screens. No televisions or shelves of movies. Nick was standing in the center of the room on a circular platform. He had a metal device strapped to his wrist.

"Uhmmm...where is everything? Are the screens hidden in the floor or behind some wall panels?" I asked.

"No, love, this room is for viewing our home movies. We are about to give you a firsthand look into our world." His eyes were dancing wildly. He seemed as anxious as Tristan. This was obviously something they looked forward to very much.

"Literally," Tris added with a smirk. "Brace yourself, sugar."

Nick pressed a couple of buttons on the wristband, and the room darkened. Almost immediately we were surrounded by buildings. They were so real! Tall, majestic structures trimmed with silver and gold etchings around the doors and windows.

Above us a cloudless lavender sky; it was like one of those extraordinary movies from the futuristic imagination of a genius writer!

"What is this!" I gasped in awestruck fascination.

"This is the city of Es'mar." As Nick answered me, the scene changed. We were standing now in a large room. There were four people gathered at the far end engrossed in conversation. I knew right away who they were. I looked quickly at Nick and back to the group.

Nikolas had definitely taken mostly after his father. Valmar was a strong-built man with black eyes and sun-kissed blond hair. Daria was a very elegant woman with hair the color of golden honey and chocolate-brown eyes. Both were very regal, but you could see the signs of a warrior in Daria's movements.

The couple standing beside them was obviously Tristan's parents. I studied Tris for a minute, trying to assess which parent he had taken most after in appearance. Jessom was a mountainous man. He had long brown hair and perfectly smooth light skin that resembled the color of fresh cream. He and Tristan had the same electric-blue eyes. Lanai on the other hand was without a doubt the most beautiful woman I had ever set eyes on!

She was tall and slender, her every movement graceful and poised. Her ink-black hair fell sleek and straight all the way to her hips. Her eyes were the color of copper, and her skin, flawless. Tristan's face was shaped like hers, and he definitely had her smile and soft supple lips. Even though her skin was the color of polished ebony, the golden hue of the Maldorans glistened around her. She was absolutely magnificent! I looked up at Tristan and placed my hand softly against his face.

"You favor your mother."

He straightened and smiled with pride.

"This is so amazing! Holograms are just a dream in my world!"

"It's coming, sugar, I guarantee it." I was privileged to the major cities of the kingdom, all designed differently. It was like traveling to a different world from kingdom to kingdom.

"Now this is the last of the visions we've saved."

The beautiful cities disappeared, and we were standing on a hill overlooking a meadow filled with tall aqua-colored grass. There was an unusual tree with huge silver leaves just below us.

"What kind of tree is that?" I pointed.

"That's the Shayla tree I mentioned the night you learned about us," Nick answered.

"I see what you meant. It's so beautiful!" All at once I heard the laughter of two boys as they came into view. They were riding some sort of cycle that skimmed across the tips of the grass. It was easy to tell, even with their blinding speed, that I was looking at Nick and Tris. The cycles came to a stop just in front of us.

"How old were you guys?" I was smiling as I watched them play.

"Eleven." Tris laughed. "We spent a lot of time in the Calvas Field as boys."

"You were both so adorable! That's not surprising though." I could see my comment embarrassed them, and I thought that was priceless.

"This is so wonderful. I could stay here all the time." "I know, love. We feel the same way; but we try to stay away. It's far too easy to get caught up in the past." Nick sounded overly melancholic, and Tristan never spoke.

The visions of Kardaun and the lovely boys disappeared. The room was back to normal. My visit to their world had ended.

"You know, after seeing you as children, it makes me wonder," I started.

"Wonder what, love?"

"It makes me wonder what your kids would look like." "You!" they exclaimed in unison.

My mouth went dry. I slowly looked back and forth between them. It hadn't even occurred to me—they expected children! My heart was suddenly pounding in my ears. I couldn't even think about this!

"Umm...I need to get ready for the slopes. Ahh..." The awkward situation seemed to amuse them. "Thank you for showing me the beautiful world of Kardaun. I...I'm just gonna go..." There was no way to regain my composure, and I just wanted to get out of there to catch my breath.

Nick and Tristan watched as Olivia sprinted across the entrance hall toward the stairs.

"Hmm...I don't think she's ready for that," Tristan commented.

"Nope, at least not for a long while," Nick responded.

Transitions 30

The next couple of weeks they kept me busy. I got used to being airlifted out by helicopter. Tristan had taken me skiing again and on a sightseeing tour of Switzerland. Nick introduced me to the nightlife in Milan. The short trips almost always lasted at least a couple of days. I loved the cabin at the resort, and the apartment in Milan was very cozy.

During the times I was actually at Es'mar, I had met a few of the guests and become acquainted with some of the house staff. I walked into the commons room this afternoon to find Nick propped up on the sofa. He was dressed in a tee shirt and a pair of faded jeans with a hole in the knee. He had on a headset, tapping a bare foot against the couch arm.

"Hey," he said, pulling the headphones down around his neck.

"What were you so wrapped up in?" I asked, leaning down to listen. My eyes lit up when I heard the music. "I didn't know you liked alternative music! I love this group!" I exclaimed. Nick smiled broadly; apparently, he had learned something new about me too.

"They are performing tonight in Milan. I have tickets if you want to go."

"You have to ask! I'd love to see them. I tried once to get tickets last year when they were playing in Charlotte, but the concert was sold out," I told him.

"We'll leave just after dark. That will give us time for a nice dinner before we go to the show."

"Great!" I squealed. "I'll go and get ready then."

I was ready for my night out a little early. I stood by the window watching the sun fade slowly behind the mountain. My mind wondered back to Nick and how wonderful he looked in the ballroom. I had only seen him in the light of day then and inside the car when we arrived. I couldn't think of anything but how striking he was even though the heavy tinted windows obscured the light. I would love to see him in the natural light, any natural light. I pulled myself from the daydream when Nick knocked on the door.

Tristan was in the entrance hall when we came down the stairs. He was going toward the west-wing corridor.

"Where are you two headed tonight?" he asked.

"Nick is taking me to Milan to see Sinez."

"Signs? That's an odd pastime, sugar, but if that's what you like, there's a real big one in the square."

"Not s-i-g-n-s, silly, the band S-i-n-e-z." I laughed. "I take it you don't listen to alternative?"

"Nah, that's really not my cup of tea." He chuckled.

"Well, I was about to ask if you wanted to join us," I said.

"Thanks, but that music seems to start at the base of my skull and works its way to the bottom of my spine. You two go and have fun. I have some business to take care of anyway." "Oh." Nick's eyebrow rose inquisitively.

"Yeah, it seems I need to have a talk with one of the staff." He looked straight into Nick's eyes as he spoke.

"Do you need me to stay?" He knew the answer before he had even asked. Nick knew full well Tristan was very adept at handling these particular problems. "All right then, the concert is going to run late, so we'll probably stay at the apartment in Milan till tomorrow night."

"Okay, I guess I'll see you two tomorrow then, enjoy," he said as he kissed my cheek and whispered, "I'll call you tomorrow." Nick said nothing, only smiled.

Tristan stood on the front stoop and watched until the helicopter was out of sight before heading back to the west corridor and the lower level. He worried more for Olivia's safety here than in the States. Being this close to Romania and Hungary was an even greater temptation for Lucas. Hopefully the interrogation of Scarsion's spy would shed some light on any upcoming interruptions Lucas may be planning. For this reason, he was glad Olivia would be away should there be any trouble brewing tonight.

Mariska Scarsion stood in front of the fireplace, holding back tears as she stared in disbelief at her mate.

"Mariska, my dear, you need to relax. You trust my judgment, don't you?" Lucas spoke softly, yet there was a strain in his voice. Patience was never a trait of the Scarsion men.

"Of course, Lucas...but..." Mariska's voice trembled, partly from her disappointment and partly from the fear of bringing down the anger Lucas was famous for. In the entire world of Kardaun, she was the only woman to fear the one she was designed for. There was something missing in the soul of Lucas Scarsion, something that would forever leave her incomplete. "It's just that..."

"Just that what?"

She heard the annoyance in his tone but couldn't stop herself from continuing, "It's customary for the man to ask permission of his mate before—"

Lucas cut her off midsentence. "I am the King of Loxar, and my decision is all that matters! I need no one's permission!" he yelled. Mariska flinched back as he took a step toward her. "My sweet darling, I apologize for my outburst, but I assure you that you are more than ready for what lies ahead. You will make a wonderful mother."

She stood gazing into his eyes, fear gripping her with every breath. She looked for the compassion or remorse for his presumption, but there was nothing. His soul was cold and blank. The tears fell from her eyes as her hand went to her abdomen and the child growing within her.

We had been here almost a month, and even though I was much more at ease, I still stumbled across new rooms. It was the day before the dreaded Yule Ball, and my nerves were a bit on edge. I decided to take yet another stroll about the huge house.

I heard the sweetest music coming from a room just off the main hall. I don't know why I hadn't noticed the entrance...maybe because the door was slightly obscured in the far corner behind one of the enormous statues that lined the wall. I found Tristan seated at a beautiful grand piano. The huge open windows were a perfect backdrop. The soft snowflakes drifted gently down behind him as if they were part of the slow melody. The picture was so serene. Tristan seemed to be so absorbed, so far away in another place or time that he was oblivious to everything around him. As the keys faded to silence, I spoke, "I didn't know you could play."

"You—" Tris began.

"I know. You never asked, right?" I smiled.

"Yeah." He laughed softly and moved over for me to sit beside him.

"What were you playing?"

"It's a song from Kardaun called 'Hesrat Uthoc.'" he answered, continuing to play softly.

"It's beautiful." I watched his fingers move with such precision and ease. It surprised me since his strong-built hands had no resemblance to that of a pianist. There were many personal things about my two mates I was sure I would learn in time. "Does Nick play too?" I asked.

"Yeah, we both play several instruments. His preference is the guitar or saxophone. As for me, I like the guitar and drums, but this...this calms. It's true what they say, you know."

"About what?" I asked.

"Music does soothe the savage beast." He bit his lower lip and looked down at the keys. I quickly averted my eyes. The possibility of Tristan's "inner self" being a force to reckon with had never occurred to me. Suddenly I could feel his struggle within myself.

"Things weren't always so easy for us," he began. "When we first came here, it was a very tumultuous time. We didn't have the resources we do now, and entering this world took a lot of adjusting." The soothing music continued to play as Tristan looked over at me. His eyes held an unexplainable sadness.

"You don't have to talk about it," I said.

"No, it's okay. I want to tell you. Our people haven't always been so...compassionate toward humans. We crossed through, and for reasons we can't explain, there was a terrible rage inside of us. At least those of us that were less human. We were consumed with a... bloodlust...for the lack of a better word."

"So, you..." I just couldn't imagine either of them as murderous monsters!

"Yes, we killed humans, without regard." He lowered his eyes again, and I could feel the shame he held in his confession. "We couldn't control the emotion in us. It was like when you do something in anger and then have a painful regret after."

I put my hand consolingly on his shoulder as he continued.

"How is it that you killed? After all, you have the choice of shifting." I understood this rage within Nick but not him.

"It's not that simple, sugar, I wish it were. You see, I crave raw meat and, just as much as Nick...blood. Maldorans cannot go for more than four days without phasing. We have to, for our sanity and life's sake, release the animal within." He watched as my expression changed from sympathy to shock!

"I had no idea...I understand now why there are times when Nick's pitcher empties so fast." My words seemed to run together, but then it's a wonder I could speak at all.

"Well anyway, as to the turmoil upon our arrival, Nick and I were in separate parts of the world then," he said, gently reaching up to brush my hair back. "It was especially hard for the Larins. If they refused to kill, it was suicide, and just one bite to leave the victim alive. Well, it would sustain them for a short time, but it was like starving to death and not being able to die."

"How awful that must have been!" My heart ached. Now I understood that look. It wasn't sadness but a deep soul-wrenching remorse! I didn't want him to feel pressured to talk about it, so I tried to change the subject.

"Why isn't there a piano at the house?" I asked. "There is," he answered.

"Where? I haven't seen it."

"There are parts of the house you haven't seen yet," he told me with a tongue-in-cheek grin.

"There can't be. There isn't anywhere else to go except...down! Oh, I never even thought of a lower level! Why hasn't either of you taken me down there?"

"We just didn't feel you were ready yet. There are some areas that are quite pleasant and some, well, you may not approve of," he said, wishing he had left well enough alone. I studied about what could be so unpleasant, then my mind flashed to Scarsion's dungeon, and I gave Tristan a knowing stare.

"We are at war, sugar, and some things are just a necessary evil," he tried to explain. "It's not that we hate the followers of Lucas. They are in their own way as much victimized as the rest of us."

"The whole situation is sad for both sides. Why isn't the piano in one of the foyers?" I just wanted to change the subject and get the vision of dungeons and the like out of my head.

"It used to be in the entrance near the stairs. Nick had it moved after..." He didn't finish the sentence; it was as if he felt he had said too much.

"After what?" Now he had my curiosity in full swing.

"It's kind of a long story," he said hesitantly. I don't think I could have dropped it now if I wanted to.

"I've got time. It's not like I have any pressing engagements, you know." I smiled. Tristan smiled and gave a little sigh.

"All right then, I guess the beginning would be the best place to start. When we arrived here, the portal didn't just drop us all in one place. We were scattered throughout Europe, Asia, and Africa.

"I was in Asia, Nick ended up in England, Nadya in Russia, and Taryn in Africa. Lucas actually started in Romania. It took a little over seventy-five years just to get our bearings, you might say. Had it not been for Nikolas, we may have remained in the same mind-set as Lucas regarding humans."

"How did Nick manage to get order back to your world? Wasn't he just as enraged as you?"

"He was, but this emotional turbulence didn't affect the Avars and Hulains. Nick came across a Hulain woman in London. Her name was Delry, and they quickly became friends. She helped him gain control and taught him what she had learned about the human world," he explained. "Nick set out to let our people know that he had survived. He taught all that he could find how to deal with their new life. Those in return, being loyal to the throne of Kardaun, began seeking others, and it kind of came about through a relay system.

"The kings and queens of each nation of Kardaun came to London seeking Nikolas, and the council was reformed."

"So, a new order for Kardaun was established here in this world?" I asked as I tried to keep up.

"Yes, and new laws were written in the year twelve seventyeight. That's when we found out that Lucas wasn't willing to give up the war his father began. He refused to attend the council meetings and announced that the rule of Kardaun lay in the wrong hands."

"It sounds like Lucas has always been as demented as his father was," I surmised. Tristan nodded in agreement.

"We have always felt that the illness of Vladmar was a genetic trait inherited by his son. He started then, placing spies to watch Nick's movements." Tristan paused for a moment, obviously contemplating how to proceed. I sat silent and patiently waited for him to continue. So far the story of their beginning had me completely captivated.

"He is the reason for the vampire and werewolf stories," he stated matter-of-factly.

"I figured that would have stemmed from the disregard of humans all of you had." I didn't understand how Lucas could have been the sole beginning of the bloodbath caused by vampires and werewolves in the Middle Ages.

"We may have killed humans in the beginning, but not in a way that made it obvious. Never did we seek innocent or extremely young humans. Instead, we tried to seek out only the bad element of your society or the very old and sick, not that this practice made the act of killing any less reprehensible." He lowered his eyes in shame. "You see, Lazar had sworn his allegiance to Lucas and by accident discovered how to create what we call Lusters." Gavin's unnatural face flashed in my mind for just a brief second.

"By accident? I thought that was something all Larins and Origs could do instinctively."

"No, sugar, we had no knowledge of this phenomenon until Lazar meant to kill a human wandering the countryside of Romania one night. Something interrupted his meal, and he failed to drain the mortal. Rather than let it go to waste, he injected his blood into the victim in hopes of preserving his food source for later. When he returned, he found the human waiting. He dropped to one knee and called Lazar master. Well, you can imagine the sense of power that gave him. And the creation of the undead went on from there."

"The first Luster wouldn't have been a count, would he?"

Tristan smiled and began the gentle music again. "You're exceptionally quick, sugar."

"But I thought Lusters did only as they were told."

"They do and he did, but they were free to hunt as they pleased with no restrictions. They instinctively used the Larin abilities for predatory purposes. That's why more women than men were killed by vampires. Lucas learned he too could create a facsimile of himself, and the human stories of werewolves began. Nikolas viewed the practice as a vulgar abomination against the Kardaunian people, and hence he and the council banned the practice among those loyal to the crown. There is a very stiff punishment for the creation of a Luster for the purpose of slavery."

"But didn't both you and Nick inject some of your blood into me in order to raise the marks?" I unconsciously reached up to touch my neck as I asked the question. Tristan quickly caught my hand.

"You better not touch your mark. You may just scare poor Nick to death!" He chuckled. "Figuratively speaking that is."

"Oh, sorry, but isn't that the same thing? Shouldn't I be a Luster too?"

"No, it's a very different thing. You see, the mortal must be at least half drained, and the amount of blood combined with a touch of the venom is a far more considerable amount."

"I see, well, I'm curious. Both Larins and Origs can create Lusters, but what about Maldorans?"

"Actually, Lucas did try that experiment, and as far as we know, it never worked out. The human did phase, but it seems they lacked the ability to phase back into their natural form and exhibited no human traits; since that would not benefit Lucas's cause, the attempt was abandoned." He paused at that moment as if he were trying to gather up all the memories of regret and remorse, he had scattered onto the table to put away again in the locked file from which they came.

"How did Es'mar Estate come about?" I asked, trying to lighten the conversation. Little did I know I was opening an all-new barrage of unpleasant emotions.

"Well, that's another story." Tristan smiled and turned back to the piano keys.

"Are you pressed to be somewhere?" I asked.

"No," he answered.

"Well then, walk with me while you tell me about this wonderful place." I smiled, holding my hand to him as I stood.

He rose from his seat and ambled slowly beside me. "Let's see, uhmmm...although I had met with him and the other rulers in London, and as good as it was to see my friend again, I had returned to China. It was about fifteen years after the reformation of Kardaun that Nick and I sensed our soul had been born in this world. I began migrating slowly again toward Europe. Nick remained for a time in London. Just a year before your soul reached twenty, we found ourselves in Scotland in around twelve ninety-seven." He paused again but only for a moment. "Scotland was engaged in war as Robert the Bruce had joined with William Wallace against the oppressive rule of King Edward I. We had both joined Wallace and Bruce in the battle against England. That's how we reunited, so to speak." His story held me in an almost hypnotic fascination.

"Why would you fight in a war with humans, when you were in the middle of your own bloody battle?" I asked, astonished that the human's war would interest them at all.

"We figured it was as good a way as any to start helping the inhabitants of this world. You should know we'd always take the side of the oppressed." He grinned. "Besides, we were in no danger of being killed. It was also an easy way at the time for Nick and me to get nourishment."

"I'm probably going to regret this, but how so?" I asked with a puzzled expression.

"By walking the battlefield at night, feeding on the recently deceased and dying. For those barely hanging on to life, it was more for mercy than sustenance." He stopped speaking when he saw the color drain from my face. "Are you okay, Liv?" he asked, placing his arm around me for support. The vision of them...ughhh! My stomach churned, and the bile started to rise in my throat. I swallowed hard and steadied myself.

"I'm fine. I just wasn't expecting to envision the scene in such vivid detail." I half smiled.

"I told you, sugar, life was very different back then." I could tell by Tristan's expression that he was contemplating ending the rendition of life in the Middle Ages.

"So, you actually met Robert the Bruce and Wallace?" I'd hoped my question would alleviate his worry as to my ability to handle the facts.

"Yes, you'd be surprised at how many of those in your history we were privileged, and not so privileged, to meet." He gave me a little smirk. "Where was I? Oh yeah, we didn't realize that we were seeking the same soul until six months before your twentieth year. Lucas's trackers found you first. As soon as your life expired, we felt it and put two and two together. That's when we vowed to stay together until we found you and one of us had bound with you. That was the closest we would ever get until now."

"How is that?" I wondered how Lucas could always find me first.

"His trackers had your soul's essence from the first encounter, and we never got close enough for that, so it made it much easier for them to find you." I could see in Tristan's eyes the feeling of failure he carried, allowing my soul to be destroyed so many times.

"I'm glad you never gave up." I lifted his hand and kissed it tenderly.

"Sugar, we could never do that!" he exclaimed. "We had found that in this world, everything was based on wealth. The more money you had, the easier it was to make yourself invisible. So, we worked on building a wealth for the next fifty years that would ensure our ability to maintain our anonymity," he explained. "We lost you again in thirteen sixty-five in Prussia, an area you refer to as Germany. By then, we had amassed a fair-sized fortune."

"How did you manage to gain this financial freedom in such a primitive time?"

"It really wasn't that hard." He chuckled. "Remember, sugar, we did come from a very advanced civilization. We were easily able to figure out the trade system, and early on we discovered the value of historical artifacts, not to mention a few tiny innovations that made little impact on your world but very lucrative for the times." His smile was bright and gleaming.

"Well, judging from what I've seen and see before me now, I assume you've continued building that wealth?" I was curious. I knew they were very well-off, but I wondered just how well. If they could do that in a short fifty years, what have they managed in eight hundred!

"Yes, it is the means to our secrecy and has provided a comfortable life. It has also been helpful to many of your world's charitable organizations. Cumulatively, the world of Kardaun is very self-sufficient. We don't actually need the jobs we hold in the human world. They're only a means of interaction and supporting the needs of our people. Just as in our old world, there is no poverty among us," he proudly announced.

"Wow, I wish you would share that secret with my world."

"Someday, when we don't have to spend so much time and effort on just surviving, we may just do that." We had wondered aimlessly into a huge room with yet another enormous fireplace and soft overstuffed furniture. There were rows and rows of books. It wasn't a library, yet it didn't seem like the sitting room at home.

"What room is this?" I looked around. It was decorated in an earthy sort of way. The windows were undressed, and the view was breathtaking.

"Oh, this is my private study," Tristan answered nonchalantly.

"Nice," I commented.

"Thanks, now where was I?" He gathered his thoughts again as we sat down by the fire.

"Uhmmm...Germany, I think," I answered.

"Oh yeah. Along about fourteen twenty-five, Nick and I were being drawn west again. As we passed through Switzerland, we sort of stumbled onto this valley by accident. It was perfect for what we had in mind. We wanted a place where the people from Kardaun could gather without drawing attention to ourselves. Nick sent for Tabius, the Avarian king that ruled Chaldron. He too agreed that the valley was perfect. Tabius called in his finest architects and builders. It took thirty years to build. Es'mar was finished in fourteen fifty-five. But," he sighed and rubbed his hands together, "it's remained a work in progress, always being updated to fit the time."

"Well, it's absolutely magnificent! How do you keep it so well hidden? Can't the planes and helicopters see it from the air?"

"No, you forget again. This is not made of the human world. I sent for a group of Warins that cast a concealment spell around the valley. Human eyes are very susceptible to illusion. From the air, the valley appears treacherous because of the peaks and constant cloud cover. Since they can't see through it, they don't try to land here," he explained.

I glanced out the window at the sky. "I don't see a thick cover over us."

"Hmmm...we wondered about that. It makes sense though. You are the only human to ever be actually inside the valley. Now we know it truly works only on the outside world." He laughed. "I don't know about you, but I'm getting hungry."

"Yeah." I giggled. "I could use a little something."

Tris took my hand again, and we started down the long corridor toward the dining room.

"You never did explain Delry and the piano," I said.

"Oh yeah. Well, I told you Nick had formed a very close friendship with her. She came to visit us often at the house in Tennessee. She was very fond of music and loved to hear Nick play. He's an exceptional pianist. Anyway, about three months before we found you, Delry had gone to Romania to work with a small group of Kardaunians that had been isolated in the mountains. They were attacked by Scarsion's guard, and Delry was taken captive. She was very strong willed but..." Tristan paused as he revisited the obviously painful memory, "her death was very slow and painful."

"I don't understand. I thought you didn't feel pain as we do."

"We don't, at least not outwardly like humans, but pain of the heart can be excruciating," he told me. "There are many ways to inflict that pain, and Lucas has perfected them all."

"I'm sorry." I couldn't think of anything to console his loss. It was obvious that Tristan had also cared a lot for this remarkable woman.

"Nick took it very hard. She was like a sister to him. He moved the piano downstairs. It was nothing but a painful reminder of her gruesome death. He hasn't touched the keys since."

I felt the sorrow in his soul, not only for the life of Delry but for the anguish of his closest friend. I decided to abandon the questioning. We continued our leisurely stroll toward the dining room. The conversation had turned to idle chitchat.

I stopped at the end of yet another corridor and listened.

"What is it, sugar?" Tris asked.

"I thought I heard...there it is again!"

"What?" He seemed perplexed. "I don't hear anything unusual."

"It sounds like children laughing." I figured it must've been the acoustics in this place playing tricks with my hearing.

"Oh that, it is." He laughed softly.

I was stunned by his answer. "You mean there really are children in the house?" I don't know why I assumed all the guests arriving were childless.

"Uh-huh, the nursery is down there on the left." He pointed.

"Can we go in?" I asked.

"Sure, the kids will be thrilled to meet you." He smiled. Tristan opened the double doors, revealing a very large room partitioned into several sections.

"The actual nursery is to your left. This to your right is the teen lounge," he began explaining. There were only two teenagers seated on the sofa. Both were wearing headphones, each engrossed in movies playing on laptops. We passed by them unnoticed. Through the first section at the front of the room were three children ranging from the ages of six to about nine, I guessed.

The area had plenty of room with tables, art supplies, and ageappropriate games and toys.

"The youngest girl is Nolema. She is Hulain, and her parents hail from Simin." Tristan pointed to a tiny girl with a large quantity of play dough scattered on a table. "The boy there is Tavan; his parents are from Dysier. He's a Warin, and this one..." he smiled as the young girl walked over and bowed, "is Meara. She is nine, and her parents are Origs from the Kingdom of Es'mar."

"Your Highness." She bowed low as she addressed me and then Tristan. The tiny girl was beautiful. She had big brown eyes and long strawberry-blond hair that lay in curls to the center of her back.

"It's nice to meet you, Meara." I smiled. The rosy-cheeked girl looked up with a beaming expression.

"Each section of the room is set up for a specific age group. This one is for children six to eleven. The teen lounge for twelve to sixteen," he continued. "Run along and play, Meara. We'll see you again before we go," Tristan spoke softly to the bright-eyed child. "Here is the toddler section for two- to five-year-olds," he said as he bent down beside a girl with auburn hair, sea-green eyes, and a very pale complexion. She looked up from her doll and smiled. She was absolutely precious!

"This is Kylea, she's two. Her parents are Larins from the kingdom of Es'mar. This young man," Tris said, picking the child up into his arms, "is Crispin. He's four, and his parents, as if you couldn't tell, are Maldoran, and they come from the kingdom of Malve." He tickled the toddler, and the most exquisite laugh echoed through the room. Crispin had gorgeous charcoal-gray eyes. The golden undertone against his pale skin and dark-brown hair gave him a rustic appearance. Tristan gently sat the boy back down beside his toys, and we started for the infant section of the nursery. One of the nursery assistants came through the doorway in front of us and caught her breath as she dropped instantly to one knee. I would never get used to this.

"Your Highness, King Xandier, my apologies. I just came in..." she stammered nervously.

"Rise, Zira, we didn't mean to startle you. Queen Olivia wanted to meet the children. We apologize for not announcing our visit." He smiled kindly at the nervous woman, and she shifted anxiously.

SOULBOUND: DESTINY'S MOVE

"No, Sire, you are welcome to visit as long as you wish. I didn't mean—"

"Relax, dear, no offense was taken. I'm pleased to meet you. Zira, was it?" I smiled and held my hand out, which she quickly acknowledged by kissing my fingers and placing my hand to her forehead.

"The pleasure is all mine, Your Highness," she answered.

I wish they could address me in some other way. I just didn't fit the title, I thought. "Please go about your duties as if we weren't here. We'll try not to interrupt your routine." I tried to be gracious, but it seemed to me every time I opened my mouth to speak, all that came out was southern country.

"Thank you, my lady, by your leave." She caught my eyes and seemed to relax as she gave a quick smile and swished quickly around us to tend to the children. We received the same surprised response from the nanny, Shaloen.

"Please stand, we didn't mean to interrupt," I apologized. She was a petite woman, obviously Larin, with long corn-silk hair and deep sapphire eyes.

"Oh no, my lady. I am sorry for not greeting you when you came in. I was busy with the baby," she explained. I looked around at the walls lined with cribs and rocking chairs, all empty except one. "Sadly, there is only one baby," Tristan said, answering my silent observation. "She is three months old and is the daughter of the Warin rulers of Dysier. Her name is Shadow, our only little princess." "May I?" I looked to Shaloen for permission.

"Of course, my lady." Her sapphire eyes glistened as she stepped back from the baby. I leaned over the crib, gently lifting the babe from her resting place.

"She's so tiny!" I remarked. As soon as I looked down at the cherub-faced infant, my heart melted. I loved everything about this delicate little person. The softness of her skin and the sweet smell of lotion and baby powder filled me with a most unusual sense of calm. I whispered and nuzzled the child as it wriggled and cooed in my arms. I remembered how scared I was three weeks ago when Nick and Tristan commented about their children, but now looking at this innocent babe, I ached to hold my own. Tristan stepped up to my side, and I glanced up to find him smiling as he watched me. His expression was soft and warm. What a wonderful father he would be. I pushed back the errant thought.

Little Shadow lay still in my arms, and I kissed her tiny fingers and placed the sleeping angel back in her crib.

"Thank you." I nodded to Shaloen.

"You're very welcome, please visit with us again," she said and curtsied to me.

"I appreciate the invitation," I answered, knowing I wouldn't be able to stay away now if I tried. Tristan took my hand, and I reluctantly followed as he too thanked the kind nanny.

We were met by the two teenagers as we started for the door. After the usual greeting, Tristan introduced them.

"I'd like you to meet Quila. She is sixteen and Larin from Simin. This young man is Chaldon. His parents are the Avarian rulers of Chaldron and our only prince."

"Not to be rude, but your name and the name of your parents' kingdom are almost identical." I felt embarrassed after voicing my thoughts. The young man didn't seem at all

"I know. My mother thought it would be nice to honor the 'old' world, so..." His smirk was meant good-naturedly. It was plain he was accustomed to royalty, being a prince himself. He didn't use titles in his conversation. My impression of this young man was definitely a good one. I had not met any Avars until now, and it was easy to see what Tristan meant by ethereal. He didn't look at all elfish. He wasn't extremely tall but very strong in appearance.

His features more resembled someone of Asian descent. He carried himself with confidence, and I was sure of his parents' pride.

"Why are you here, Chaldon?" Tristan asked.

"I just thought I'd hang around and keep Quila company," he answered and smiled at his friend.

"That's very considerate." Tristan patted the young man on the back. "I'll see you tomorrow night."

"I'm looking forward to it." Chaldon bowed.

Once outside the doors, it was as if Tristan read my mind.

"Chaldon is seventeen. This is his first time attending the ball."

"Oh, that's right. Kardaunians come into their special abilities at that age. So, they're not permitted at the ball until then?" I asked. It seemed unfair to me, especially for Quila.

"Don't worry, sugar. They're going to have a party all their own. The children are not left out of the Yule celebration."

"I'm glad to hear that!" I was about to protest the exclusion of children until that moment. "So, I noticed the circle in the floor of the teen lounge. Do they get to view the 'old' world as Chaldon put it?"

"Actually, it's a video game of sorts. It works like the visions, as it too is holographic but more interactive. The players become part of the game. It's not dangerous, but very intense. I'm sure Quila or Chaldon would be happy to show you how it works when you go back tomorrow."

"What makes you think I'm going back?" I asked.

"I could see it in your eyes, sugar. Just like the rest of us, you're hooked." He chuckled and nudged me playfully.

"Humph." I sniffed and then laughed. "You're right. Tris?" My tone turned serious as I came to a halt just outside the dining room. "How is it that out of six hundred people, there are only seven children under the age of seventeen?"

"You already know that many of the couples from our world are barren, and many of those that were able to give birth were either killed or their children lost their lives before they came of age. Lucas Scarsion's evil holds no compassion. So, like we said, our world is losing more than gaining," he answered solemnly.

"That wretched evil man. I hate him!" The tears filled my eyes, tears of anger that went far deeper than any words could express.

"I know, baby." Tristan pulled me close to him. "We keep a special eye on little Shadow because of this." I pulled back and looked up at him, horrified.

"Are you saying Lucas wants to kill that sweet innocent little girl?" I just couldn't imagine that kind of evil.

"Not Lucas, but Hazon," Tris answered.

"Why?" I gasped. "That tiny infant couldn't do anything to her!" "It's not what she could do but who she is," he stated.

"I don't understand."

"You see, Hazon, like Lucas, kept Barnabus from binding with his soul mate until just this year. He found Lathra before she did. Now he has an heir to his throne."

"I'm confused, Tristan. What does the throne of Dysier have to do with Hazon?"

"Well, sugar, it's like the humans say, you can't pick your family. If not for Shadow, she would be in line for the crown if Barnabus and Lathra die, which is another endeavor Hazon has been unsuccessful at."

"You mean Hazon is related to Barnabus?" I knew it was a dumb question, but I was so thrown by this news.

"Yep, she's his sister."

"It must be awful for him, knowing what his sister has become, knowing the evil deeds she has committed!" I felt very sad for the man I had yet to meet.

"Hazon would take the lives of her own family?" I asked, my voice dripping with disdain.

"She's been so brainwashed by Lucas that she no longer feels a kinship or family bond with them. It breaks Barnabus's heart knowing if he meets her, it would mean kill or be killed."

"How sad, and that poor child has to grow up with that cloud hanging over her," I thought aloud.

"Don't worry, Liv. Barnabus and Lathra have a protection spell on her. They'll keep her safe as we all will. The spell is hard to hold when they have to be away from her, like in this instance. We all keep a watchful eye during those times." He seemed confident enough as someone as small as Shadow, and more so on an adult. "Besides, protection spells, as I said, are very hard to maintain the child's safety," so I relaxed.

The Yule Ball 31

"Why don't you have the Warins put a protection spell on me, then you and Nick could relax?" I asked. It seemed like a logical solution to me.

don't think you'd like to have someone on your heels twenty-four seven to keep the spell in place." He laughed.

The day that had fueled my anxiety for weeks was finally here. The house was completely filled with people now, and the very foundation of the manor seemed to be vibrating with the anticipation of tonight's festivities. Nick had stopped to ask me down for breakfast, and I politely declined. I didn't even want to think about food, let alone try to eat! Bless him, he was very understanding and had a tray sent up.

I had been pacing the length of my room for what seemed like hours and was sure by now there was a perfect path worn into the Persian rug. I wish Nadya was here. My dear sister-in-law would know how to calm my nerves. I stopped midlap when I heard someone knock.

"Come in." Just the sight of Nadya brought some relief. "I was just thinking about you!" I exclaimed, practically running to hug her.

"You were on my mind as well." She laughed. "Nick told me how nervous you were, and I couldn't just leave you up here. Your imagination can sometimes get the better of you." Nadya pulled back and smiled sweetly. The smile only lasted a second when she got a good look at me. "Olivia, you really don't look well. I know I'm pale, but you look completely drained!" She immediately took my hands and led me to the sofa. "Here, Liv, have something to drink, and for goodness' sake, breathe! You poor dear. You look scared to death!" Her observation wasn't even close.

"Terrified, and that's putting it mildly!" My voice was raised slightly, caused by the overwhelming tension.

"Hahaha! Olivia, you're making way too much of this. The hardest part of the evening is the introduction. After that, it's all fun."

"That's easy for you to say. After all, you aren't out of your element, and you won't have six hundred pairs of eyes searching out your every flaw!" I was nigh onto tears at this point, and I wasn't sure how long I could hold the breakdown back.

"That's what you think? That everyone at the ball will be scrutinizing your every move? My dear, we are not the kind of people that look for the worst in others. We simply don't have that mindset. They're just very excited to see you in person!" She put her arm across me in an attempt to comfort my fear, and I could sense a true empathy for my feelings. "Nick and Tristan have explained the ceremonial walk, right?"

"Of course." My mind pulled up the vision of everyone staring up at me, and I felt like I was about to hyperventilate.

"I promise, Liv, before the first hour passes, you'll be wondering why you stressed to begin with." She smiled and patted my shoulder. "It's almost time to get ready, so I need to go." She acted as though I might try to run if she left me alone. "You'll be all right when I leave, right?"

"Don't worry, Nadya. I'll be okay. I just don't know how to begin getting ready for this nightmare."

"That's a worry I can take away right now. You have an entire entourage coming to help you."

"Thanks, that makes me feel sooo much better." I forced a half smile, hoping to lighten the uncalled-for sarcasm.

SOULBOUND: DESTINY'S MOVE

"I'll see you in a couple of hours." Nadya started out then peeked around the door and called out to me, "Breathe."

The minute the door closed behind her, I took her advice. I pulled in a deep breath and released it slowly. "You have to do this, Olivia, so get a grip!" I said aloud to myself. Another long sigh escaped as I walked to the window. The sky was gray, and the clouds hung low around the mountain peaks. I could see the fog rolling in across the lake. It looked as bleak as I felt. I jumped as the sound of another knock on my door pulled me from the dismal trance.

"Come in," I called again. The door opened, and a petite woman who appeared to be my age. What was I thinking? Almost everyone from Kardaun appeared to be my age.

"You Highness." She bowed as she spoke. I was never comfortable with that title, or Your Majesty for that matter, and now I was even more unnerved by it.

"Please, there's no need to be so formal." I suddenly realized I didn't know how to address her.

"I am Sylviana, your—" I cut the poor girl off.

"Please, Sylviana, address me in a manner that is a little less... royal." The poor dear seemed taken aback by the request. She quickly rallied her senses and began again.

"I'm here to do your hair and makeup, my lady." She had a very sweet voice and fragile features. I was taken by her femininity. Her long brown locks were pulled back in a loose bun that was held in place with a makeup brush. Her bright-blue eyes shined in awe, obviously honored to have been chosen for this daunting task.

"Well, I guess we'd better get started." I smiled and walked to the dressing table. I reached under the back collar of my robe and pulled the thick mass from under and let it fall behind me.

Sylviana gasped. "Your hair is beautiful!"

"Thank you, but I doubt you'd feel that way if you had to brush it every morning." I laughed. The young woman giggled, and the ice was broken. She went to work brushing and tugging. Her hands, though delicate and small, worked through my hair, nimble and precise.

When Sylviana stopped to get some pins, I looked into the mirror. She had managed to twist my thick hair into a perfect braid that lay just below my shoulder blades. "I swear," I mumbled to myself as though the young woman couldn't hear me, "this mountain air must be very agreeable." It seemed as though my hair had grown another two inches since I've been here.

She began twisting the braid until it was formed in a perfect bun set just below the crown of my head and began accentuating it with diamond-tipped pins.

"Now, let's get your makeup on." She took extra care around my eyes, using only soft subtle blues for color. To my cheeks she applied a soft rose blush, and for my parched lips, a light rose lipstick and gloss. Sylviana examined me for a minute and decided there was nothing more she could do, so she turned me to face the mirror.

I was astounded at the reflection. I looked like the same me, only softer, more fragile than I really was. "Sylviana, you are amazing!" I exclaimed.

The petite young woman beamed with pride. She excused herself and was met at the door by a young man, at least I presumed him to be young. His hair was white as snow, and his face, that of a boy in his teens.

"Good evening, Your Majesty. I am Rueben," he announced. "I have your dress for tonight's gala. I hope it is to your liking." He smiled, and his deep ocean-blue eyes sparkled like diamonds. I stared at the garment bag hanging on the small portable rack he had pushed through my door moments ago. My stomach began to churn, and I didn't dare speak until the nausea subsided! Master Rueben was quick to sense my tension.

"If I may speak freely, Your Highness," the young man started. I had decided young was the more appropriate description. I only nodded my permission.

"You are very beautiful, and you truly have nothing to fear. Trust in His Majesties." I smiled sweetly as he put "His Majesty" in the plural. He was right. I had two of the most exquisite escorts, and I would without a doubt come in a far third to their powerful presence.

"Thank you for your reassurance, Rueben. Now, may I see the dress?" I smiled softly.

"Of course." He removed the cover gently and waited for my approval.

"Oh my..." I gasped, walking over to examine the gown more closely. The sleeveless dress was designed to fit snug from the bodice to knee and from there belled out naturally. The color was a perfect sapphire blue that looked as though it had been generously kissed with silver stardust! A small slit in the bottom revealed a delicate panel of silver pleats designed to gently peek out with each step.

"It's magnificent!" I exclaimed.

"May I get you anything else?" he asked.

"No, thank you." I smiled, and he bowed and left me gawking at the beautiful gown. Two more women entered my room just moments behind Rueben, one, a timid red-haired girl, the other, an older heavy-set woman. After a respectful curtsy, the older of the two made the introductions.

"This is Cheri," she said, gesturing to the quiet girl with the soft smile. "The poor thing doesn't speak since Scarsion cut her tongue out in Kardaun. It's a shame, is what it is." I was speechless to respond to the gruff-talking woman. I was at a loss for how to address this situation. Should I offer my sympathy, or remain silent? I looked at the young woman as she stood head bowed, unable to interrupt the older woman. I decided to do her the favor.

"I see, and you are?" I glared at her for being so crass.

"I'm sorry, my name is Gretta, and I meant no disrespect to Cheri, she knows that. I was just saying it's a shame that we come to a world where we can live virtually forever, all injuries heal, except those inflicted before…" She stopped short of her sentence as if she had some painful memory that she was about to resurrect. "Me and Cheri here come to put on the finishing touches, you might say." Gretta flashed a warm smile. I had misjudged the woman, and I felt bad. Gretta was only trying to help me understand Cheri's silence, in her own way.

Although her appearance was gruff by Kardaunian standards, she had a very amicable personality. I liked her confidence and the fact that she left out words like Your Highness. I looked at Cheri, still standing there with her head slightly lowered. What a cruel hand fate had dealt her, to have suffered such unimaginable torture, only to be brought here to spend an eternity in silence. I was in awe of the tiny breath of the woman and humbled by her strength.

"We'd best get started, that is unless you plan to enter the ballroom in your personables." Gretta chuckled.

I dropped the robe and stepped into the snug-fitting gown. Cheri began securing the back, and Gretta brought out the shoes. A faint smile crossed my lips as I remembered the Cinderella comment I made to Nick. God, that seemed like a lifetime ago! It was a special sentiment that he remembered. They resembled Cinderella's glass slippers except for the sparkling silver heels and the light dust of silver on the toe. I hoped this wasn't a sign the dream would come to an end at midnight. I felt panicked for a brief second.

"Have a seat while Cheri sets your earrings," Gretta said. I obeyed without hesitation. As much as I liked her, I couldn't help the feeling of being instructed by a well-seasoned drill sergeant.

Cheri began setting the diamond-and-silver studs. In the meantime, Gretta brought out another box.

"You are going to love this!" She grinned. "This bracelet was designed especially for you." She opened the box and placed it on the table in front of me.

I literally lost my breath! The wrist cuff was latched with a delicate silver chain that would adjust to fit my wrist. A row of white diamonds formed one upward and one downward arch. Filling the gap between the two was...the crest of Kardaun.

The prominent K in the center was designed in black diamonds; the sparkling white diamonds formed each intricate letter of the kingdoms entwined with the centerpiece. It was absolutely gorgeous! I had no idea how many carats I was about to clasp to my wrist, and the way I was shaking now, I was positive I didn't want to know.

Gretta cinched the chain to a snug fit. "Too tight?" she asked.

"No, it's perfect, thank you, Gretta."

"Well, stand up, lass, and let's have a look," she ordered. I hadn't noticed the Irish accent until that moment. Gretta's large hands clasped together.

"My word, give us a turn now," she said, waving her hand in a circle. I held out my arms and did as she asked. Cheri was beaming as she stood there with her hands locked against her chest.

"Glory be to Shalsmara! I'm looking at an angel!" she proclaimed.

Her eyes were shining as she continued smiling proudly. I blushed.

"Gretta, you are very kind," I said.

"Kind!" she bellowed. "My dear lass, I've been called many things, but kind has not been among them, honest to a fault though!" She laughed. "Come, see for yourself." She took my hand

and pulled me in front of the full-length mirror. Gretta was indeed a lovely woman—a lovely, motherly woman.

"Oh, my goodness!" I was in shock at the transformation. I looked like a fairy-tale princess! Maybe everything was going to end at midnight after all. The sickening twinge hit me again. Cheri bowed low and left Gretta alone with me.

"Well, child, I have to go. Enjoy the celebration." She leaned over and hugged me gently. "Don't want to muss the hair." She smiled. "There is a special glow about you, lass. You're bound for great things," she said, giving me a wink as she quickly exited the room.

Nikolas and Tristan only knocked once and entered Olivia's room before she answered.

I was looking out the window when I heard my two mates enter the room and turned slowly to greet them. The minute I made the full turn and smiled, they stopped dead in their tracks and stared at me. Instantly I became self-conscious. My heart fluttered as I waited for them to speak. I wasn't sure I would be able to respond to anything they might say. The sight before me had me entranced. Both men wore a black tuxedo that was accentuated with a vest and tie, Tristan's, sapphire blue, and Nick's, silver. Somehow, I just knew they were not bowtie men. As I began walking slowly toward them, I continued my gaze. I noticed the silver-and-diamond cuff links—Nick's bearing the crest of Es'mar, and Tristan's, the crest of Malve. I had compared myself to Cinderella once; now I felt no comparison. This had surpassed that fantasy—two Prince Charmings! It just couldn't be better!

Tristan's sleek black hair was pulled back into a tight ponytail that lay flat against his back. His eyes—no, their eyes—seemed intensified, and I could barely breathe! I was certain now no one would be watching me. I flinched slightly when Nick spoke. I was so captivated I seemed to have drifted from reality.

"Olivia, you look stunning!" He seemed to barely breathe the words.

"Sugar, you are beautiful beyond words!" Tris uttered in almost the same breathless tone as Nick. I couldn't speak; my heart was pounding too hard to form words.

"Uhmmm...I think we should go; we do have guests waiting," Tristan urged. Suddenly I was as anxious to get out of this room as they were.

We walked down the back stairway to wait on the last step as we were to be announced one at a time for the ceremonial walk.

"Take a deep breath, love, you're going to be fine," Nick said and lifted my hand to his lips. I noticed a ring on his right finger that bore the Kardaun crest. The insignia from their world was definitely of great importance to the people. Tristan, I noticed, was wearing an identical match to Nick's ring.

"Ready, baby, it's about to begin," Tris whispered as he kissed my hand as well.

"I'm as ready as I'll ever be. Let's get this show on the road." I plastered a smile to my face that I prayed looked authentic and confident.

A whistle sounded above the crowd. It was very high pitched like the ones used on ships, then the thump, thump, thump of a staff hitting the marble floor.

"Announcing...the ruler of Malve and second to the crown of Kardaun. His Majesty, Traesdon Xandier!"

Tristan stepped out and stopped on the first step of the wide marble staircase. The short balding man again blew the whistle and thumped his staff to the floor.

"Announcing...the ruler of Es'mar and High King of Kardaun. His Royal Highness...Nixis Alberon!"

Nick left my side to take his place on the top step with Tristan, and I caught one last breath to steady my shaking legs. Thump, thump, thump.

"Introducing the queen of Malve, Es'mar, and High Queen of Kardaun...Her Royal Highness, Queen Olivia Xandier Alberon!"

I stepped down to stand between my mates, the smile still holding. My nerves started to edge a little more when I heard the involuntary gasps from some of the guests. I expected no less than their disappointment; after all, no matter how much effort they put into it, I still looked human and plain in comparison to the beauty of these people. Nonetheless, disappointed or not, this was as good as they were going to get.

I took the arm of my mates, and as we began our descent, the crowd erupted in a thundering applause. The guests had parted, leaving the center of the room open as we made our way to the council seats. Everyone looked so beautiful! The women were elegant and poised, the men flawless and debonair. Ohhh, I just wanted to disappear!

I managed to regain my focus as I glanced occasionally from side to side, nodding politely as Nick and Tristan had instructed. I noticed a young Larin woman in front of us. She was slightly heavier set than most of the women. Her hair was short and black; it fell in layers against her delicate round face. As we drew closer, I was captivated by her beautiful sea-foam eyes. She was wearing a sapphire-blue gown that set off the shoulder with a puff sleeve. I couldn't quite put my finger on it, but there was something about the woman that made her stand out from the rest of the crowd. As soon as we stood even with her and she bowed her head to curtsy in respect, Nikolas stopped and smiled.

"Delcie." She was the only guest he acknowledged verbally.

"Your Highness," she responded, looking up. Her name was uncommon and lovely just as she was.

Finally, after what seemed like an eternity of humiliation, we made it to the end of the uncomfortable walk. The other six council members were already seated and rose to greet us as we stepped onto the platform. The first couple I met was Kalem and Vada Marpayz, the rulers of the kingdom of Simin. He was a tall slender man with onyx-black hair and eyes the color of dark caramel. He sported a wellgroomed beard and mustache. His Queen, Vada, was a lovely darkskinned woman. She would easily pass for Polynesian in my world.

Kalem seemed a bit hesitant when I reached my hand. It was as if his mind was somewhere else. So, I thought it best that I speak first.

"It is an honor to meet you, King Marpayz," I said. The sound of my voice seemed to bring him around. "My apologies, Your Highness. It's just that..." "Just what?" I gently inquired.

"Well...it's just that you remind of someone I once knew." He seemed slightly embarrassed for his blatant stare.

"Oh, friend, I hope." I gave him my most gracious smile.

"Indeed, my lady, like a brother." He smiled back, looking far more at ease, and resumed the customary greeting. Vada was softspoken and content to show her respect and leave it at that. We moved on to the king and queen of Dysier, Barnabus and Lathra Winden. Lathra was an amazing woman with sky-blue eyes and thick strawberry-blond locks that lay in rows of curls to the top of her hips. It was pulled neatly back and held on the sides with diamond combs.

Barnabus was a medium-built man. His shoulder-length hair was light brown with natural smooth copper highlights. He was very charming. His eyes were a dark violet and a little unsettling. I held my hand to him as I spoke.

"It is my pleasure to meet you both. I was privileged to see your daughter in the nursery. She is an angel and, if I may say, takes equally of both of you."

"Thank you, Your Highness," he responded. It was obvious they were very proud parents.

The last council members I met were Tabius and Rochelle Sullivar, the rulers of Chaldron. Tabius spoke with a smooth, soothing voice, and it was obvious Chaldon was his father's son! Rochelle was a petite woman with long dark-brown hair. Her thick French accent took a moment to adjust to. She had a very outgoing personality, and I believed, had we met under less formal circumstances, she would have been content to engage me in a lengthy conversation. This was someone I could definitely become close friends with.

I glanced at the two empty chairs as Tristan and Nick turned to take our seats.

"That's the council seats of Loxar," Tris whispered. Nothing more was needed. Maybe someday, I hoped, they would be occupied again. We took our seats, but Nikolas only remained for a few moments to give the guests time to gather. He then stood and raised his hand; a hush fell over the crowd.

"Good evening and welcome to our annual Yule Celebration," he began. "We are honored that everyone could be here tonight. Before we begin the festivities, as you know, several of our kinsmen are not among us. I would like to request that we take a moment of reflection in honor of those that have given their lives this past year for the sake of Kardaun." The room fell into a deafening silence, not a mumble, not even a breath. Nick spoke into the silence.

"Thank you, my friends." He stepped over beside me, looked down, and winked. I could literally see the royal air dissipate. "Now, if Olivia will do me the honor." He smiled and held his hand to me. I took it and rose from my seat.

"High King Nixis Alberon had suddenly disappeared, and Nikolas Riggs had taken his place. I have but one more thing to say...let's get this party started!"

The throng of guests roared with applause. Nick led me to the center of the room, and the musicians began with a slow waltz.

The lights dimmed, and the faint glow of the tall Christmas tree in the corner twinkled lightly.

"Everyone is watching." I couldn't help but tremble as I kept my eyes fixed on the crowd.

"Just look at me, love, and everything will be fine." Nick smiled and placed his arm around my waist. I looked into his glistening black eyes as we moved and turned to the music. The crowd disappeared, and it was just the two of us. Nick's movements were so smooth and light that it felt more like I was floating than dancing.

Tristan stepped up to cut in, and he took over without missing a beat. He was every bit the partner Nick was. The rest of the council entered the dance floor, and other couples began mingling in.

"It wasn't the nightmare you expected, was it?" Tristan smiled that beautiful, brilliant smile that always turned my legs to Jell-O, and I stumbled a bit. I wondered if he knew how that affected me.

"No, I suppose not."

"Nick and I want to introduce you to some very special guests. Are you ready for some serious mingling?" he asked, continuing the leg-weakening smile. The look in his electric-blue eyes was so intense, so sensual the tingling sparks ignited within me.

"I guess I am, but you have to stop doing that!" "Doing what?" The mischief gleaned in his expression.

"You know what." I laughed softly.

"Come on. Nick's waiting."

We stopped dancing, and he gently took my arm. As we made our way to the opposite end of the room, I caught a glimpse of the dark-haired woman Nick addressed as Delcie.

"Tris, why was Delcie the only person Nick had actually spoken to when we entered the ballroom tonight?" I asked, watching the woman as she enjoyed her dance and what appeared to be lighthearted conversation. Her smile was positively radiant.

"He has a great deal of respect for her, and, in a way, I guess feels indebted to her. When we were in Kardaun, Delcie had just bound with her mate Ludac Krspa. They were so newly bound that the sealing ceremony had not yet taken place. Lazar had headed yet another invasion on the city of Calmera, the place you saw in the visions of Kardaun. She, like most couples, fought by her mate's side. During the battle, she saw Queen Daria in jeopardy and had to make a quick decision between holding her ground with Ludac or splitting off from him to help Nick's mother."

"I'm guessing she chose the latter," I said.

"Yeah, and she did indeed save Queen Daria's life, but Ludac was lost in the battle."

"That's terrible, so what happens to them in Shalsmara since they were never sealed?" I felt so anguished for her and for the sacrifice she made on Daria's behalf.

"They will be together but will never become one with each other or the Creator since they were never sealed," Tris explained. Now I understood why she stood out to me. It was because I sensed Nick's feelings toward her.

"That is so sad," I concluded as we approached Nick.

"You, my love, are a vision on the dance floor!" Nick said as he kissed my cheek. I looked up at him and suddenly felt very warm. I simply had to stop making eye contact with them!

"We want you to meet some of our special guests," Nick reiterated Tristan's words.

"I wasn't told I'd have to mingle," I muttered as we walked.

"Oh, trust me, sugar, you won't wanna miss this." I looked up at Tristan with my famous "deer in the headlights" look, and he laughed out loud.

Even though the ballroom was filled with over six hundred people, there was plenty of space for walking. The three of us approached an older couple, both white haired. The gentleman had deep-set blue eyes and white bushy eyebrows. His mustache matched his hair and hung thick across his lip. The woman turned to greet us, and I nearly stumbled into her.

"Emeline!" I exclaimed.

"Olivia, I'd like you to meet Emalia and Dorhan Dagius."

"It's wonderful to see you again, Your Highness," Emeline said with the same twinkle in her eyes I remembered from my stay in the hospital. It was obvious to me now, by her golden hue, she and Dorhan were Maldoran.

"They use the human names Emeline and Darren Davies in your world," Nick continued. "They're the couple that has taken up residence in your house."

"Emeline was brought into the hospital to make sure Mercedes didn't try anything while you were there," Tristan added.

"Mercedes? The tall blond nurse?" I asked.

"Yes, my dear," Emeline answered. "A nasty little Hulain spy for Scarsion."

"Oh my...I should thank you for keeping an eye on things," I muttered.

"It was my pleasure. I enjoyed watching her squirm." The saucy little woman laughed. "I told you not to mistake the white hair and dimples for sweet." She grinned and squinched her button nose.

"I thought so then and am positive now, Emeline. There was no mistake." I chuckled lightly.

"Ahh, you are a gracious queen. It has been our honor," Dorhan said.

"Dorhan is the historian for our world," Tristan informed me.

"That's wonderful. I would love to talk more with you. I'm anxious to learn as much about Kardaun as I can." I sounded a little exuberant, and Dorhan smiled politely.

"At your convenience, my lady. I look forward to it."

"If you will excuse us, we have other guests to greet." Nick smiled politely, and they nodded.

I felt good knowing the sweet elderly couple wouldn't be passing of old age anytime soon and they could enjoy a long full life together. I smiled to myself. I couldn't think of anyone more perfect to occupy the loving home my parents had built. As we made our way across the room, we were greeted, it seemed like every few seconds, by those wishing to express their gratitude for the invitation.

My eyes wandered to the dance floor where Chaldon was dancing with his mother Rochelle. How sweet, I thought. They moved out from under the lights, and I blinked quickly.

"What is it?" Nick asked.

"I think the lights are affecting my eyes," I told him.

Tristan looked in the direction of my stare and snickered. "Nope, your vision is fine—they're green," he said flatly, and I slowly looked up at him and turned my head to one side.

"Ookay..."

"It has something to do with their ability to control the elements." He grinned, finding my expression amusing.

"All Avarians have a green undertone, love. It can't be seen in the daytime or under bright light," Nick explained.

So, they do have an Elvin quality after all, I thought.

"If you think that's weird, you should see them in the dark of night. Now that's creepy!" Nick teased, waving his fingers under my chin.

"Now that's weird." I giggled.

"What is?" Nick asked.

"A vampire using the word creepy." I burst into laughter, and it didn't take long for the two of them to join me. After enjoying the revelry, I sobered myself enough to reprimand Nick's teasing.

"Now, Nikolas, stop it. If you ask me, I think they're beautiful!"

"I'm only kidding, Liv. They're a very beautiful people." He smiled, and we started moving forward again. We finally stopped at the far end of the ballroom.

"Where are the guests you wanted me to meet?" I looked around and saw no one approaching us. Tristan caught a tentative breath as he tousled a crystal bulb hanging from the Christmas tree.

"Ah...Liv, before we introduce you to them, we'd like to give you a...an explanation," Tristan said, still clicking his fingers against the delicate ornament that I was sure would hit the ground any moment.

"All right...go on." I was puzzled as to why they needed to explain the next guest, but if I'd learned anything these past months, it was to trust them. They always had good reason for their actions.

"You know that our laws wouldn't allow us to approach you until you turned twenty?" Nick began the explanation.

"Yeah."

"So, when we found you at the high school in your third year—"

"My junior year."

"Yes, well, we couldn't exactly be close to you, and we had to keep you safe from Lucas." For some reason, Nick was dragging this out, and I couldn't understand what made them so nervous.

"For heaven's sake, Nick, just tell me! It's not like I'm going to be any more shocked than the night I learned about you and Tris! Give me a little credit here!"

"You definitely have a point. In order to keep you safe, we called in some actors from our world to position themselves close to you in your day-to-day life." Nick looked worried as he waited for my reaction. I studied this strategy for a minute.

"That makes sense. It didn't arouse my suspicion and alleviated your worry, so what's the big deal?" I shrugged.

"That's just it, there is no big deal, at least not to us, but we were kinda worried you might get upset about being 'spied on,' sorta," Tris concluded.

"There was a time I might've thrown a hillbilly fit but not after meeting Scarsion. I'm really glad you were watching over me."

"I'm so glad you feel that way. You have no idea how relieved that makes us feel. Now let's go meet our guests. They're waiting in the banquet room." Nick gestured to the French doors and ushered me forward again with a gentle hand to the small of my back.

To our right, standing in the dim lights by the decorated tree in this room, were three people. Two had blond hair, and the third was a mountainous man with short dark hair, olive skin, and a booming voice. As we approached the group, the two blondes turned to greet me, and I nearly fainted at the sight of them.

"McKenzie Robbins...Mike Zita?" I just couldn't believe it! Mckenzie curtsied and introduced the strong dark-haired giant as her mate, Luther. The appearance of her fragile petite frame next to Luther didn't seem at all the couple I would have imagined. Then I glanced at Tristan and then Nick. I really didn't have room to judge. I smiled as Mike and Luther bowed.

"Forgive me for being so shocked. I always thought you and Mike..." I suddenly felt awkward and turned a rosy pink.

"That's what everyone was supposed to think." Mike chuckled. "Kenz is pretty good at the shy teenager, don't you think?" he continued, smiling, and his blue eyes danced.

"So that night at the lake, you two weren't..." I stammered.

"Heaven's no!" Mckenzie answered.

"King Alberon summoned us to assist you and make sure you weren't seriously injured," Mike said.

Now I was thoroughly humiliated knowing they were aware of my lie all along. "I'm glad you were there, and I do appreciate everything you had to endure for my sake. High school is a part of the human world all its own."

"You can say that again!" McKenzie laughed. "I've never seen a group of such irrational and rebellious people in my entire two hundred years!" She was certainly not the shy girl she had portrayed every day for two years. She was indeed a very confident and outspoken woman. As easy as the conversation seemed to flow, I could sense a difference in their posture and attitude toward me.

That feeling didn't set well with me.

"How did you get to me so quickly?" I asked.

"We, that is McKenzie and I, are Warins. I'm from Dysier, and Kenz hails from Simin."

"Remember the Gelcry, love," Nick whispered.

"The Gelcry. Ohhh, I see." As pleased as I was to see them, I wished at that moment we were not having this conversation. It seemed the more I opened my mouth to speak, the more ignorant I sounded!

"There was someone else we wanted you to meet," Tristan filled the awkward moment. "I wonder where..." He turned and smiled. "There she is!"

I turned around and couldn't believe my eyes! "Kandi!" I squealed. In my excitement to see my dear friend from Rooter's, I flung my arms around her neck, but my excitement was short lived. The moment I embraced her, I felt her entire body go rigid. I slowly pulled back, and even though she looked flustered by her own reaction, there was a dull ache in my chest. I suddenly felt like one of those fancy-dressed dolls in the glass boxes with a sign plastered across the front "Do not touch!" I wasn't Olivia anymore. I was "Her Royal Highness!"

"I'm sorry. I was just so pleased to see you," I apologized.

"No...you don't need to..." It was obvious she still didn't know how to respond. I turned my attention to Rohan, plainly her mate.

"It's nice to see you again, Rohan. I didn't get a chance to thank you for picking us up at the airport."

"It was my pleasure, Your Highness," he respectfully answered with a polite bow.

"Kandi, I should have known the last time I saw you..." I began. She seemed confused by my words. "Well, judging from your beautiful golden tone, I feel safe in guessing you're Maldoran?" I said to clarify myself.

"Yes, you guess right. Rohan and I are from the kingdom of Malve." There was that horrible silence again.

"Your Highness," Kandi started. "I've been waiting for a chance to tell you how sorry I am." She shuffled nervously as if what she was about to say warranted some sort of punishment.

"What could you possibly need to apologize for?" I looked up at Nick, who did nothing more than shrug, looking as clueless as I was.

"I was given two tasks, and if I hadn't left before you that night, that human boy wouldn't—"

Tristan cut her off midsentence. "Wait a minute, Kandira. Nick and I gave you the 'all clear' to go, so that episode falls solely on us," Tris told her.

"It was no one's fault," I interrupted. "None of you could have known what was on that deviants mind!" I wasn't going to allow this conversation to continue. "What other task were you given?"

"I was supposed to press you to make a choice between His Majesties, and I failed miserably." She half grinned.

I slowly turned my head from Nick to Tristan; my eyes narrowed. Tristan averted his eyes, and Nick ran his fingers through his hair and attempted a smile.

"Well, Kandi. I'm glad you failed at that job." I smiled, withholding the laugh pushing up in my throat. Judging from her broadening grin, she too was as pleased as I was. "As wonderful as it is to see you, there's a party going on, and I...well, we..." I said, gesturing to Nick and Tris, "need to get back." I wanted to spare her any further discomfort. "I would like to talk to you tomorrow if it's all right. Would you meet me in Tristan's study at one o'clock?" I hadn't even thought of asking Tristan. "You don't mind, do you? I didn't think you'd be using it." I smiled up into his beautiful blue eyes.

"Of course not, Liv. What's mine is yours." He grinned.

"Thank you, sweetheart." I turned back to Kandi. "So, tomorrow then?" I looked expectantly at my friend.

"Certainly, Your Highness," she politely answered. This just wasn't right! Kandi was my friend, and I promised myself come hell or high water tomorrow she would know it! I didn't think I could mentally stand one more Your Highness or Your Majesty. I wanted to scream out "My name is Olivia!" Instead, I took her hand and wished them a gracious good night.

I knew these exceptional people held tightly to the royal heirs of their world, and in so many ways, it gave them comfort, gave them somewhere to belong and a way to honor all that was left of Kardaun. It wasn't my intent to disrespect there custom or way of life. I wished they could see that I wasn't what they deserved!

They never questioned the Creator I knew, yet I couldn't escape the notion burning inside me that something had gone terribly wrong in my creation. No matter how hard I tried or how patient the good people of Kardaun were, I was an outsider, taught in a different culture, and raised in a fierce and volatile world! Somehow, I had to find a balance between their world and mine, if for nothing else than my own sanity. "Liv, penny" Tris tugged at my hand.

"Huh...what were you saying, Tris?"

"I said penny...for your thoughts," he repeated softly.

"Oh, trust me, sweetheart, it wasn't worth that much." I smiled. He knew something was bothering me. He could feel it flowing through me, but thankfully he chose not to press. I pulled in a deep breath, pasted the smile back on my face, and forced myself to move on. I greeted several more guests, but the behavior of my friends remained prevalent in my thoughts. The words and conversations taking place seemed to waft around me like echoes in a barrel.

I couldn't have been more relieved when the banquet was announced. I managed some casual conversation throughout the magnificent meal, and somehow, somewhere between the main course and dessert, I found my focus again.

"It sounds like the tempo has picked up in the ballroom." I guessed the DJ had taken over while the members of the orchestra had dinner. I had to give them credit; the eclectic genre held something for everyone.

"So, Tris, are you going to ask me to dance?"

"Sugar, I would like nothing more, but I have this one promised to another fair maid." He chuckled.

"Oh, well then, you better not keep her waiting." I smiled. He kissed my forehead and bowed politely. "Nick, what about you?" I asked, stopping near the center of the dance floor.

"It's not that I wouldn't love to have you in my arms, but..." Nick gave me that impish look, a dead giveaway something was about to take place, something I wouldn't be thrilled about. "You see, our guests haven't been able to enjoy the custom of the 'Draw' since, well, forever."

"Custom of the 'Draw'?" I took a long breath and released the sigh.

"Uhmmm...yeah, all the male guests, aside from Tristan and myself of course, draw for the privilege of dancing with the High Queen, and since there's never been one until now...well..." He was so enjoying this.

"Ughhh! Nick, why didn't you tell me?" I moaned.

"I am telling you, love. Do you see those gentlemen? They have won the honor."

I looked to my left and noticed a line forming, a long line. "Oh, good grief!" I complained. "What am I supposed to do now?"

"Hahaha! Liv, don't look so tense. Just turn toward them, curtsy politely, and have fun." He continued his mischievous smirk.

"I have to dance with every single one?" I asked, noticing two more enter the line.

"I'm afraid so, love. You wouldn't want to disappoint anyone, would you?" He smiled sweetly as he put his hand under my chin, causing me to look directly into his mesmerizing black eyes.

"I suppose not," I answered weakly.

He then kissed my cheek, bowed, and left me standing solitary in the middle of the floor. I turned to the line, pulled up the ol' Yule smile, and curtsied. It didn't take long to realize that immortality was not a prerequisite to rhythm or dancing skills. The modern dance was easier. I could keep a safe distance between myself and my partner, but the slow dances...

In the next hour, I had been stepped on, stomped, pushed, pulled, flung, slung, whirled, and twirled until I felt like a loose thread unraveling with every step! Nick must have been watching the torturous ordeal. When the last man literally lifted me off the floor, he must have taken pity and decided to cut in.

"Oh, thank God." I breathed in relief. "I thought it was never going to end!"

"Hahaha! You held up beautifully, love! I'm very proud of you." He beamed.

Ohhh, why did I have to look up into his eyes? I wonder if he knew how desperately I wanted him. "Uhmmm, Nick?"

"Yes..."

"As wonderful as this has been, would it be considered rude if I called it a night?"

"Of course not. I have to admit, we're surprised you're still standing." He laughed. "Any other human would have collapsed by now."

"Ha, ha, very funny," I teased. "Then you won't mind if I go upstairs?"

"I'll get Tristan to walk with you," he said.

"Thank you for this lovely evening," I cooed softly.

"It was my pleasure, love. Good night," he whispered and kissed me gently on the lips.

"Goodnight, darling."

As Olivia started toward the staircase to meet Tristan, a redhaired man dressed in casual clothing was whispering something to Nikolas.

"Well, what did you think of the party?" Tris asked, taking my hand.

"It's after midnight and nothing has turned into a pumpkin, so it was perfect." I chuckled. The minute we turned the corner to the second-level stairs, he whisked me up into his arms and carried me to the door of my room.

"I've wanted to get you close to me all evening." He smiled. Ohhh, there were those eyes again.

"Thanks for the lift." I tried to make light of the obviously tense situation being this close to him caused. He sat me tenderly on the floor and placed his arms around me.

"I don't know how we ever celebrated anything before you," he whispered. "Go and rest, baby. I'll see you in the morning." He kissed me softly and whispered, "I love you."

"I love you too, good night." I pushed the door closed with a dreamy sigh and made my way to the dressing table. As I unwound the long braid, I saw the tea tray by the fireplace. I smiled to myself. Nick never forgets a thing. Slipping out of the dress and into my robe, I started for the shower.

The herbal tea smelled sweet as the warm steam filled the air. I settled back on the soft cushions to replay the night and unwind before going to bed.

"Tris, there's some trouble," Nick said, catching him at the bottom of the stairs.

"What's up?" Tris asked.

"Lucas, what else? He's sent his goons out to attack the village up the road. If we hurry, we might get there first. You get Nadya, Taryn, Barnabus, and Lathra. I'll get Mike. Have the women change quickly and meet me on Loxar Ridge."

"Will that be all the help we need?" Tris asked.

"Yeah. Apparently, he's only out to create some new Lusters. He sent one Orig and two Larins. Nadya, Taryn, and Mike can handle them along with any new Lusters they may have created should they get there first."

"You need Barnabus and Lathra to clean up the mess, so to speak. What are we doing then?" It was such a small raid he didn't see the need for Nick and himself.

"It's too close to home, and I don't like the feel of it. Besides, we're doing the mercy run. You and I will seek out the injured. You patch up those that have a chance, and I'll end the suffering of those who don't." Nick hated this duty. The poor humans didn't deserve this—no one did.

They reached the edge of the woods by the village only minutes too late. The despicable traitors had already unleashed their evil. Two buildings were ablaze, and Nick counted three dead in the street. People were trampling the bodies as they ran for their lives, screaming in horror. Four new Lusters, one Orig, and two Larins were seeking out their friends and neighbors to quench their insatiable thirst.

"Nadya, Taryn, Mike, end this quickly!" Nick ordered. They were gone in a breath, fervently engaging in the fight. "Barnabus, I'd like for you and Lathra to wait here. I'll summon you when it's over. You'll have your hands full."

"If you should need some extra help," Barnabus said, putting his hand on Nick's shoulder.

"Thank you, my friend, I'll be sure to call on you," he responded. "Tris, let's go." They started with the edge of town just inside the tree line.

"Over here!" Tristan called out. A man and his wife lay in a thicket. Tristan only took a second over the man and began working on the woman. She was pregnant and had been clawed about the face and chest by the Orig, most likely his first victim once he phased into the werewolf form.

Nick knelt down by the man and looked to Tristan. There was no need for words as Tris shook his head from side to side and continued to bandage the crying woman. From the look of the huge hole in the poor man's stomach, Nick could tell but still wanted that confirmation. He hated these human raids. The smell of mortal blood was everywhere, and the sweet scent filled his nostrils, pulling at him. He loathed the awakening of the secret rage that dwelt inside of him, the monstrous demon that they, the less human of Kardaun, still struggle to tame.

"My wife!" the man cried out.

"Your wife is fine, she's safe now," Nick consoled him as he lowered his fangs, the blood from the wound causing him to salivate.

"Please, mister, the pain...stop the pain!" he screamed.

Nikolas honored the man's request and bit down on his throat, pulling the warm, thick fluid from his veins, ending the dying man's agony.

They repeated this same scenario several more times, amazed at how much damage the invaders had done in such a short time. Nadya, Taryn, and Mike had made quick enough work of the new Lusters and the three immortals sent by Lucas. They had begun looking for the injured as well. Barnabus and Lathra had already begun altering the humans' memories.

"Brother!" Nadya called to Nick.

"What is it?" he answered.

"We managed to get all but one, a new Luster. He got away and ran into the woods. Do you want me to see if I can find him?"

"No, he's probably in Romania by now," Nick said. "Just keep looking for those that need help." He looked drained and despaired.

"Hey, are you all right?" Tris asked. He had never seen a look quite like that in his friend's eyes before.

"This is what's wrong. This is their world, and it's just another reminder of why we should never have come here!" he yelled and walked away. Tristan understood very well Nick's feelings. These poor humans were defenseless against those from the world of Kardaun.

Nikolas heard a noise inside of an old barn. He slipped quietly through the half-open door and scanned the area, stopping beside one of the stalls. The dim lantern behind him illuminated his blond hair and across his shoulders.

A tiny little girl with sun-kissed braids stepped out in front of him. She stood there looking up with big round blue eyes and a tearstained face, clutching a hand-sewn doll tightly to her chest. He just stood silently looking down at the beautiful child that struck him barely above the knee.

"Granny's been praying," the toddler said. "Are you an angel?" she cooed. A tear formed in the corner of his eye. Never before had he felt more compassion for a human than at that moment. This tiny innocent soul had rendered Nixis Alberon, High King of Kardaun, speechless.

Decimation Of Innocence 32

My sleep was restless despite the wonderful "Cinderella Ball" I had just experienced. My foreboding dreams had again returned. This time, the Luster Gavin was in the forefront of my nightmare. I kept seeing his menacing fangs and the sheer bloodlust in his eyes. There were screams and growls all around me. The deafening sound of metal scraping metal and Mike Zita's face!

I rose not with the dreamy visions of the Yule Ball but instead with a searing sense of fear! I dressed quickly and hurried down the marble staircase in search of Nick or Tristan. There was a young woman from the house staff working in the entrance hall. She bowed low as I approached her.

"Please, stand up," I requested. "What's your name?" "Eileaha, Your Majesty," she answered softly.

"Eileaha, that's a very pretty name." I smiled. "Would you be so kind as to address me as ma'am or something a little less regal? Your Majesty is a bit much for me to take in this early in the morning." I chuckled softly, hoping to put her at ease.

"Of course, Your—I mean, ma'am." She blushed.

"Eileaha, I've only been there once, and I still have trouble finding my way around. Would you mind pointing me in the direction of Nick's study?"

"Yes, ma'am, King Alberon's study is down that corridor and to the left," she answered.

"Thank you very much." I started to walk away, and she bowed again. I sighed and smiled. "Your respect for the crown is admirable, my dear, but it won't be necessary to bow every time you see me. A simple nod will suffice."

She seemed surprised at my request for lesser acknowledgment, but that's exactly what I thought I deserved.

"Yes, my lady, as you wish."

"Thank you," I said softly, then turned in a rush toward the corridor she had pointed to, hoping to find Nikolas in his private space.

I raised my hand to knock and heard Tristan and another man whose voice I didn't recognize. I hesitated for only a second and decided that my news was important enough to interrupt whatever conversation was taking place.

"Enter," I heard Nick call.

I walked into the room and saw Tabius Sullivar, the Avarian king of Chaldron, and Kalem Marpayz, the Hulain that ruled over Simin. They were standing in the back of the room with Nick and Tristan, obviously engrossed in a serious discussion.

I suddenly felt very intrusive and wished I had waited until later to address my concerns with Nick.

"Olivia." Nick beamed as he walked to meet me at the door. "You look exceptionally beautiful this morning."

The second he kissed me, I felt something different about him. He gave me a quick we'll-talk-later look as he took my hand. I glanced down to examine my attire. I had dressed in such a rush I wasn't really sure of what I threw on. I was satisfied that I was at least matching. I had a pair of soft calf-length leather boots, a creamcolored knit dress with a wide brown belt loosely fitted around my hips, and a matching chocolate-brown sleeveless shrug that fell flush with my hem. I reached up and tugged the suddenly tightening turtleneck and mustered a nervous thank you. All four men were dressed similar in button-up shirts and slacks. I followed Nick to the now silent group.

"Olivia, you remember Tabius and Kalem," Nick said.

"Of course, it's so nice to see you both again." I smiled sweetly and offered my hand. They greeted me in the usual way.

"It is our pleasure, Your Highness," Tabius said with his flawlessly smooth voice.

"Please pardon my intrusion, gentlemen. I wasn't aware Nikolas and Tristan were entertaining guests this morning."

"There's no need to apologize, my lady. Your presence is very welcome," Kalem said with a polite bow.

"Nevertheless, gentlemen, my business with Nikolas can wait. With your permission, I'll excuse myself and leave you to your discussion. It has been a pleasure, and I hope to see you both again before you return home." I smiled again as both men bowed graciously.

Nick and Tristan exchanged a quick glance. It was so weird. Since the sealing ceremony, they seemed to be able to pick up on even the slightest change in my emotions. Nick took my arm and walked back to the door with me.

"What's wrong, Liv?" He seemed concerned as if he knew I came bearing ominous news. It was like they could read me as clearly as a printed page in a book.

"Can you step into the hall with me?"

"Certainly," Nick said, opening the door for me.

Once outside the doors, I began revisiting my dream. His pleasant demeanor changed instantly. He seemed to become distant, and there was an unfamiliar look in his eyes. I wondered if he was hearing a word I was saying.

"Nick, hey, are you listening?" I asked, nudging him.

"Yes, love, I heard every word." He smiled faintly.

"Something's going to happen! I need to warn Mike! Is he still here?" I started to turn, anxious to find my friend, when Nick's hand caught my arm.

"There's no need to trouble yourself, Liv. I'll be seeing him in a little while. I promise to relay your concern and explain your dream." Nick's voice had an almost monotone-like sound. I just stood there peering at his stone expression, searching for hint of a familiar emotion.

"Liv, why don't you wait for me in the dining room?" He had obviously made a conscious attempt to soften his voice, but I could still sense something different. Something was deeply troubling my loving mate, and I was convinced my dream had little to do with it.

As much as I wanted to know what it was, I chose to humor him.

"Okay, I'll see you in a bit then?"

"I promise not to be long." He looked at me softly. "Liv..."

"Yes, Nick..."

"I love you." I caught my breath! Even though I knew his feelings from the beginning, it just wasn't like him to just say those words!

"I love you too," I quietly responded, and he smiled. I leaned up to his ear and whispered, "Which way is the dining room?"

He chuckled and kissed my forehead. "Eileaha," he called to the young woman I had met in the front hall. "Please escort Queen Olivia to the dining area," he commanded.

"Yes, my lord." She bowed.

I felt embarrassed. After all, I'd been here almost a month, but the house was so massive I just couldn't keep my bearings.

Nick watched Olivia turn the corner with Eileaha before reentering the study. No sooner had the door closed behind him, Tristan spoke up.

"What has Olivia so frightened?"

"She had another dream," he answered and turned to Tabius. "You recall my telling about Olivia?"

"Yes, the queen is prone to precognitive dreams. Is there a problem?"

"I'm really not sure."

"What do you mean you're not sure?" Tristan was confused by Nick's response to Tabius. "Her dreams definitely spell trouble, and you usually welcome the foresight."

"This time I'm not so sure it is foresight, Tris."

"You lost me." Tristan took a seat in one of the high-backed chairs by the fire, looking very disconcerted. Nick began reciting Olivia's dream. When Nick finished regaling the nightmare, Tristan stood up and looked to Nikolas with a confused expression. "This is just too weird!"

"I know. Tabius, what do you make of it?" Nick asked his friend. Tabius began to pace slightly as he contemplated the scenario.

"Normally, I would take measures to prepare for trouble. If it hadn't been for our confrontation last night," Nick said, trying to make sense of things.

"You're positive she was unaware of last night."

"Positive," Tristan answered. "I escorted Olivia to her room myself."

"She described it so well—me, Tristan, Nadya, and Mike! I don't understand."

"I suppose it's possible the double binding could have caused some sort of psychic connection. That would certainly explain her dream." Tabius was intrigued by the depth in which the three souls had melded in such a short time.

"Let's just see if there are any more dreams like this before we get concerned." Tristan couldn't help feeling a little wary of his own advice. It was possible, after all, that their dismissal of Olivia's warning may prove to be a grave mistake. He planned to keep his guard up just in case.

"I agree, Your Highness. It is possible you may be reading too much into this. It may be nothing more than a coincidence," Kalem added. "If there is nothing further to discuss, I have promised my lovely mate a trip to the slopes today."

"Of course, Kalem, enjoy your outing, and give my best to Vada." Nick realized he had detained Tabius and Kalem most of the morning.

"Then by your leave." Kalem bowed respectfully to Nikolas and exited the room. Tabius also excused himself and followed behind Kalem.

Tristan made no effort to leave. Instead, he remained silent, studying Nick as if he could somehow look straight into his soul and surmise what had changed in his friend.

"Okay, Nick, now that we're alone, do you wanna tell me what's really wrong?"

"Tristan, take me to the nursery." Nick caught him off guard with his surprising request.

"The nursery?"

Nick just stared at Tris for a moment. "Is there something wrong with your hearing?"

"Maybe...okay, Nick, follow me." Tristan walked in silence until they stopped just outside the nursery door.

"Nikolas, what brought this on? As far back as I can recall, even to Kardaun, not once have you visited a nursery or even spoken to a child for that matter. We all understood you had obligations, but then you never expressed an interest either. Now, out of the blue, you want to visit the only room in Es'mar Estate that you've never seen.

Why? What's changed? Don't tell me it's curiosity. I can sense the difference, my soul-bound brother!"

It was true; their souls were bound through Olivia, and it would only be right that Tristan knew what took place last night.

"All right, Tris, have a seat," Nick said and sat down on the bench by the door. He regaled the incident with such heartfelt emotion that it touched Tristan. He stared at his friend and brother with watery glazed eyes.

"Now you know why I'm acting this way." Nick sat with his head down and hands folded. This emotion was foreign to him, and he needed to make peace with it.

Tristan pulled in a short breath and wiped his eyes.

"It's something, isn't it? The power the young possess? It's miraculous how one look into the trusting eyes of innocence can bring even the mightiest of men to their knees."

"I would never have known if it hadn't been for the human child," Nick quietly spoke.

"Well then, brother, let's meet the most powerful citizens of Kardaun, shall we?" The moment Tristan opened the doors, Chaldon and Quila halted their game and dropped to one in knee in total shock! Tris waved them to stand up.

"I remember that game. We used to play it a lot when we were young," Nick recalled.

Chaldon and Quila looked at each other as if they had just heard some fairy tale. Their minds just couldn't process High King Alberon or King Xandier as ever being children or playing games!

"Hahaha! You were pretty good at it as I recall. Maybe we can come back later and challenge Quila and Chaldon to a game. How would you like that?" Tristan asked the teenagers.

"It would be an honor!" Quila replied, wide-eyed in disbelief.

"Come on, Nick, let me introduce you to a younger group."

Nick was completely taken with the younger children, and he was quick to find his comfort zone. They were so refreshing. The young ones didn't distinguish royalty; they didn't expect any particular behavior. To them he was Nick, someone new to talk to, tell their stories, and share their art with. He was amazed at the fact they kept getting smaller as they went along.

"This is the infant area." Tristan was totally enjoying this.

Nick approached the children with an almost childlike wonder of his own. "Shaloen, His Majesty has come to meet the baby." Tristan smiled.

"We are honored, Your Highness," she muttered nervously.

Nick walked up to the crib and peered down at the infant. "My word, it's so tiny!"

"They do start out that way brother. Why don't you pick her up?"

"Pick it up! I'll break it!" Nick exclaimed.

"*It* is she, and her name is Shadow. They don't break that easily. Immortal children's bones are just as strong as ours, although until they come of age, they do have many human traits," Tris told him.

"What kind of human traits?" Nick asked, not taking his eyes off the infant.

"Well, they don't get sick like human kids. They are susceptible to cuts and bruises, but the older they get, the quicker they heal. They also need naps and feel some pain like aches from fatigue or muscles, and they get tired. They feel heat and cold, and by the time they are twenty-one, they come into their full immortality," Tris explained to Nick in the short, condensed version.

"They are very complex beings then." Nick seemed awed by all this.

"Very. Now you need to see what they feel like," Nick tried to protest, but Tristan wasn't having it. He scooped little Shadow up from the crib and turned to face his friend. "Now hold out your arms and make sure you cradle her head for support."

Nikolas stood very still as he held the babe in his arms. Tristan guided him back to the rocking chair and took a seat beside of him.

"How do you do that?" Nick asked.

"Do what?"

"Handle these tiny beings with such ease."

"Hahaha! Do you have any idea how many of these tiny beings, as you say, both mortal and immortal, I've brought into the world? It gets easier with practice."

"I had no idea, Tris. I certainly have a greater respect for your profession now." The baby wriggled and cooed contently. Nick seemed surprised when Shadow stretched her hand, and it came to rest on his face. He reached up and took her tiny hand in his, examining it very carefully. "You are so amazing," he whispered.

Nikolas was so totally captivated by this tiny wonder he had lost track of time. "Nick, I hate to rush, but poor Olivia has been waiting in the dining room for an hour."

"Oh, I told her I wouldn't be long. We better get going. Uhmmm, are you going to take..."

"No, you can put her down." Nick stood up and gently placed the baby back into the crib and followed Tristan into the hallway. Tristan didn't say anything as they walked on to the dining room but couldn't help smiling as he noticed Nick look back toward the nursery and then look at his own hands.

"It's amazing, huh, how something so tiny turns into...well, us."

Olivia was sitting at the table, patiently waiting. "I thought you two forgot about me." Nick sat down without a word or response at all to Olivia's comment. "What's wrong with him?"

"Pay no attention. Nick just made his first visit to the nursery." All at once the entire room became dead silent, and all eyes were turned their way.

"I had no..." Nick stopped speaking and looked around the room. Just as suddenly, the sound of forks scraping plates and low mumbles began again.

"I had no idea how amazing children were!"

"You see, sugar, Nick had never experienced children before."

"You mean at all, ever?" I was totally stunned. "How could someone live over eight hundred years and never..." It was beyond comprehension.

"I never seemed to be in the right place. They are so extraordinary."

"Oh, my dear sweet Nick, don't think you're alone in these feelings. They affect us all that way." I ran my fingers along his cheek and smiled at him.

"Well, I have some things I need to do, so I'm gonna grab a bagel and run. I'll catch up with you later, sugar."

"Okay, Tris, have fun or whatever." I laughed. As soon as Tris was gone, I directed my attention back to Nick. I was still unnerved by my dream and needed to know about Mike.

"I don't mean to dust aside your new experience, but did you see Mike?"

"No, I haven't talked to him yet. I thought we might have something to eat first."

His calm reaction to my dream was unusual. It seemed as though he wasn't taking me as serious here as he did back in the States.

"I don't get it! Back in Tennessee, the very mention of one of my dreams set you on your heels! Why is it you seem so complacent about them now?" He may not see a threat, but I was sure of it!

"Liv, I do take you very seriously. I've learned that there is usually a week at the least before any event happens. So, I feel confident Mike will be safe until after breakfast." He smiled.

I just sat there staring at him. He was being cavalier about it, but why? I thought.

"Okay, love, if it'll make you feel better, I'll summon him right now." He barely finished his sentence when Mike entered the room and headed straight for us.

"You summoned, Your Highness?" Mike asked, bowing low.

"Yes, Mike. I'd like to speak with you in private. Would you meet me back at my study in an hour?" Nick's polite request wouldn't be denied. He had a way with the people of Kardaun, always polite and friendly. Orders always seemed left to the discretion of the recipient.

"Of course, Sire," he answered then turned to me. "Good morning, Your Majesty." He bowed low again as he spoke.

"Good morning, Mike." I sighed. This was all I could take. "Look, I understand my station in this world, but I don't feel like you need to be so formal with me. After all, you were my classmate and friend long before I became your queen." I just couldn't allow this royalty thing to alienate me from everyone I knew prior to this life, even if they weren't human. "Please try to address me as a friend, formalities excluded." I smiled.

"As you wi—uhmmm...I mean, I'll try...Olivia." My name rolled off his tongue as if he would be struck dead the second, he said it! I couldn't help but giggle as I watched poor Mike's eyes dart apprehensively between me and Nick. For a split second, I saw the gleam in Mike's eye, the one that always gave away his love of danger and that familiar smirk. Nick leaned back in his chair, a wide smile on his face.

"Mike, if Olivia considers you a personal friend, so do I. Please do as she requested." Mike started to bow but was stopped as Nick reached out and shook his hand. The gesture eased the tension I had obviously caused.

"I hope we get a chance to talk before you go," I said.

"We will. You can count on it, Liv." He smiled with gleaming eyes and turned to leave.

"Feel better now?" Nick asked.

"Yes, now you can explain something to me."

"What, love?"

"You said only a Hulain had mental abilities, so how is it you can think of someone, and they appear?"

"Oh, well, that is the only mental ability I have, as do all the kings and queens of the council, and only because we have royal blood."

"I see, with the exception of me." No matter how comfortable I became, there would always be something to remind me I was different. Nick picked up very quickly on my feelings.

"Liv, you belong here as much as I do, as any of us." He took my hand as he spoke. It was obvious he believed those words with his whole heart. "So, what are you planning today?" He changed the subject.

"Well, Kandi is coming to see me, but I think she's as nervous about it as Mike was."

"Be patient, love, after all, she probably feels embarrassed, given some of the comments she made about her kings." He snickered.

"You heard all that?" Nick just tilted his head.

"Of course you did, but that was her job." I began to defend her, when I realized my words, her job. "Oh goodness, Nick. Mike, Kandi, and McKenzie—they're all actors! Was I wrong in assuming we were really friends?" I felt embarrassed that I may be pushing something on them that compelled them to continue their act.

"No, they had all become very close to you! They were afraid of how you'd react when you found out," he explained.

"I'm glad to know that was real. I hope I can ease Kandi's mind when we meet today."

"I'm sure you'll have her gossiping in no time," he teased. "You have the day to yourself, but Tris and I have plans at dusk."

"I assume these plans include me, so what are we doing?"

"Of course you're included, I'm not going to say anything more except dress warm." He stood up and kissed me lightly. "I'll see you tonight."

SOULBOUND: DESTINY'S MOVE

I wiled away the bigger part of the day relaxing in conversation with Kandi. I felt as though our old friendship had rekindled before she left to meet Rohan. The reminiscing was more emotional than I thought it would be. There was an unusual emptiness in the air when I left Kandi in the hall and started aimlessly down the corridor. It was almost as if I had dreamed my life before this, and it saddened me to feel so distanced from even myself. How was I ever going to find a way to truly reconnect? Hmm...funny before this amazing journey I was loved, involved in life and still separated, different, and alone. Now, I'm loved, involved in a completely new life, and still separate, still different, and still...alone. Maybe if I could find a way to join the old me with the new, I might actually find some fulfillment or at least a comfort in my own skin. I just shook my head silently, trying to shake the empty feeling. I found myself standing outside the nursery door. I had subconsciously guided myself there. Maybe it was a good place to find some solace and a temporary cure for my melancholy.

I was greeted with smiles and enthusiasm. I so enjoyed playing with the children. Quila and Chaldon were happy to show me how the Kardaunians' "video game" worked. They introduced me to their favorite, Balmira's Quest. Quila explained that the holographic images or my opponent couldn't actually harm me physically, so I could relax. She could evidently sense my hesitance.

"You lose points each time the light from the blades passes through your body and gain points when you strike the image 'opponent.' It's really quite simple, but it takes a lot of concentration and strategy. The images learn from your movement, so they can calculate your weakness and your strengths," she explained.

"We use this game as part of our battle training," Chaldon added. The three of us stepped onto the platform, and immediately we were surrounded by a different world. We seemed to be standing at the edge of a city much like the ones I saw in the visions of Kardaun. I was totally fascinated, but my amazement was cut short when three warriors came out of nowhere, swords drawn! They were so right; this was the most intense game I had ever played, and though the youngsters made no teasing remarks or criticized, I could admit I was horrible at it. I noticed during the game how easily they dropped the formality of my status and viewed me as just Olivia, another teammate. I felt so relaxed. They asked me a million questions about my world. They seemed to hang on my every word, and I became aware that I wasn't the only one learning something today.

I thanked them for allowing me to play and moved on to the smaller kids. I was so caught up in the activities I hadn't noticed the time until Shaloen, or Shay, as she used in the human world, announced baby Shadow's four o'clock feeding to her assistant.

I made it to the front hall just in time to greet Nick and Tristan. I had dressed as Nick requested: sweater, jeans, boots, and winter coat. It hadn't seemed that cold out when I walked with Kandi this afternoon, but then the temperature was sure to drop as the night falls.

"So where are we going?" I asked.

"We're taking you on a sleigh ride to show you some of the sights of Kardaun Valley," Tristan answered.

"Are you sure those jeans will be warm enough?" Nick asked. "We don't want you catching cold."

I was more concerned with having a heat stroke! Nick was sure being overprotective. That trip to the nursery today must've had a profound effect on him, I thought.

"Nick, you don't need to fuss. I'm fine, and I promise not to get sick," I joked.

"Don't worry, we have plenty of blankets," Tris reminded him.

"All right, all right." He waved his hand in understanding. "Are you ready then?"

"Yeah, but it's only dusk. It won't be sunset for another hour." I looked puzzled at Nick.

"I can go out during this time of day. Well, actually an hour before sunrise and an hour before sunset. The rays aren't strong enough to do us Larins any harm then. It's the only daylight I can enjoy."

"Well then, let's not waste another minute!" I was ecstatic to find out I could enjoy some things in the light with Nick. Even if it was only two hours a day!

A fabulous two-seated sleigh was waiting out front. It was wide enough to accommodate six people easily, three to a seat adorned with bells and lanterns and hitched to a gorgeous team of sleek black Belgian horses.

"Ohhh, they're beautiful!" I exclaimed, running my hand along the horse's neck.

"I knew you'd appreciate them." Tristan smiled proudly. "We better get going before we lose the light." Tristan helped me up to the seat and gathered the reins, and the sleigh started off toward the open field. It seemed like only a few minutes before Tristan reined the horses to a stop. Nick stepped down from the sleigh and reached up to help me down. The three of us stood at the edge of the lake. It was obviously closer to the house than it originally appeared from atop the ridge. The view was spectacular!

"When we found this valley, Nick and I decided to pay homage to our families and kingdoms. So, we named everything around us after them," Tris began to explain. "This is Lake Lanai."

I looked out across the lake at the reflection of pink clouds dancing and shimmering across the top of the gentle rippling water.

"This is so serene. No wonder you love it here," I said.

"Over there," Nick said, pointing to the mountain on the other side of the lake. When I looked to where he was pointing, I saw something moving along the rocks and unconsciously sauntered down the embankment a few feet from Nick to get a better look.

"What is that? It's not really a mountain sheep, but not a goat either," I said, pointing toward the curious-looking animal.

"That's an Ibex. They're indigenous to this area. Sometimes they can be a bit of a nuisance," Tristan answered. I could tell he wasn't very fond of the creature but respected it just the same.

"I'm sorry, I got distracted, Nick. What were you about to show me?" I turned back toward him and froze. Everything disappeared but his dark silhouette etched against the purple sky, now adorned with a silver moon. The reflection off the water danced along his pale skin. He was sooo beautiful! I reveled at the sight of him in this glorious violet hour, no longer day yet a breath from night! Slowly I made my way toward him, hypnotized by the wonder of him in the light. I remained oblivious to everything as I stood before him, breathless. His eyes glistened in the dim light, and I felt as though I were falling again. This time, to touch the soul of this perfect being would not be close enough. Suddenly I remembered Tristan was standing there, yet he made no attempt, no sound to distract me. I broke my gaze and turned abruptly toward the lake. I felt embarrassed and awkward.

Nick cleared his throat as he too was obviously struggling to regain his composure.

"It's easy to get distracted out here. The beauty is overwhelming," Tristan said in a calm, low tone. I immediately felt the heat in my cheeks.

"As I was saying, over there is Loxar Ridge, and just beyond it is Dysier meadow. We'll take you there when we come back in the spring. By then, the fohn will have arrived and melted most of the snow."

"The fohn...what's that?"

"It's a warm breeze that blows up from the south the same time every year. It ushers in the spring thaw," Tristan answered. "We better get moving, there's a lot more to see." He smiled and took my arm as I climbed back into the sleigh. Tristan gave the reins a tap, and we started moving again. I heard the sound of rushing water.

"There in front of us is the Malve River. We'll follow it upstream for a ways." Tris turned the team, and we began a climb along the tree line. I could feel Nick's eyes on me as he sat in silence. My heart sped up just a notch, and I caught his smile from the corner of my eye.

The incline was much steeper than it appeared, but the horses seemed to manage the trek with ease. Tristan reined them to a halt, and Nick got out, offering his hand again. I still hadn't managed to find the courage to look him in the eye. We stood at the edge of a huge precipice overlooking the river.

"This is Valmar Canyon," Nick announced. He seemed to relish in this particular view.

"This is absolutely magnificent!" The canyon was breathtaking!

"Up there." Tristan pointed to a high peak with an enormous waterfall cascading down the side of the mountain. The roar of the water sounded like thunder! "That is Jessom's Peak and Daria Falls."

"Ohhh..." I breathed. "There are no words to describe this! You couldn't have found a more glorious monument to your parents!" I just stood there, breathlessly taking it all in. Tristan reached over and brushed a loose strand of hair from my face, and I shivered at his touch.

"As much as I'd love to stay here all night," Nick said. I looked over at him, holding a steady gaze as the last of the light faded. Tristan lit the lanterns that I was very aware were only for my benefit.

Still, it gave a sort of Currier and Ives ambiance to the scene. "We'll cut down through Chaldron Forest and take Simin Trail back to the house." Nick smiled.

I am way too easy to read, I thought as I settled back into my seat and sighed.

"Are you cold, love?" Nick asked, pulling a blanket from the back of his seat.

I was sure the temperature had dropped considerably because I wasn't roasting like I expected, but I wasn't really chilled either.

"No, I'm fine, but I will take some of that hot chocolate you've been guarding over there," I teased.

"Make that two, Nick, if you don't mind."

"Coming right up." The casual banter and playfulness started to flow along with the warm liquid. Nothing could be more perfect, and I was so content.

Without warning, Tristan pulled the horses to an abrupt stop just inside a clearing. Nick had whisked me to the ground in a flash. I turned around, disoriented by the sudden displacement. The horses reared and bolted into the woods, leaving us on foot.

"What is it? What's happening!" I shouted.

"We have company, sugar," Tristan said, pulling me behind him.

"Olivia, get back and stay behind us!" Nick ordered.

I slowly backed up against a mammoth-sized pine. My heart was pounding, and my breath quickened. I scanned the trees all around. The moonlight and clear skies gave off a glow against the snow. At least I felt more in control being able to see. I could make out shadows moving slowly through the trees. Tristan had begun easing out away from Nick; he was poised for a fight. I looked back to Nikolas just in time to see him pull a sword from the inside panel of his coat. I gasped when he pushed off from the ground, levitated about six feet, and hovered!

It was one thing to hear about, yet entirely another to see it! I swallowed hard; my eyes fixed on him. The realization of his immortality had now gone from a mental vision to reality! I was more thrown by this exhibition than I expected. Suddenly he stopped being my Nick. This blond angel is a true vampire—cold and deadly!

I felt a tingling sensation run down my spine as I turned toward the low growl on my left. The black panther was crouched low.

The kitten-like face I had witnessed that first night was nowhere to be found. The face I saw now was contorted. His mouth was drawn back over a row of long razor-sharp teeth, and his eyes were narrowed. Every muscle in the panther's body was tensed. This was not my gentle, loving Tristan! This animal was wild, unpredictable, and lethal! I wasn't sure what scared me more, the shadows or the ones I loved!

"Lucas is growing weary of this game, Nixis," came the familiar voice of Lazar from the shadows.

"Then why won't he face me, Lazar? Tell him to meet me, and we'll end this once and for all!" Nick hissed.

"Oh, he will, old friend, when the time is right and if your luck holds tonight." Lazar sneered as he stepped into the clearing.

"You had just as well call out the rest of your band of traitors and let's get on with it!" Nick's voice had changed to a rough, menacing tone. There was an edge to his words, as if he were impatient. I started to shake as I felt the emotions racing through my mates. It wasn't impatience; it was a thirst—a pure, all-consuming bloodlust!

A tall Amazon of a woman emerged to stand beside Lazar. The moonlight was too dim for me to make out any of her features. She reached into the waistband of the black Kardaunian uniform, pulled out a small red orb, and tossed it into the center of the small clearing. As soon as it touched the ground, a fire erupted.

She continued to stand silently at Lazar's side. In the new light, I could see deep-set blue eyes and sallow cheeks. She wasn't as young as most of the immortals I had met, but very strong in stature. Her hair was dark with the exception of the very front along her face; there it was snow white! My guess, Lucas's new witch, Hazon's replacement.

Just as more of Scarsion's soldiers began to emerge, a small army seemed to appear from behind me. First, Kandi and Rohan, then Emeline and Darren, Nadya, Taryn, Kalem and Vada, Tabius, Rochelle, Barnabus, Lathra, several others I didn't recognize, and finally in a blue vapor appeared Mckenzie, Luther, and last, Mike!

"Hahaha!" Lazar laughed. "This will be a sweet victory. Lucas will be so pleased. The rulers of all five kingdoms at once—no loose ends. Shalsmara smiles on us." With a turn of Lazar's head, the fight was on!

The sound of battle whirled around me. I tried to cover my ears to squelch the sound of metal scraping metal and the screams, the sickening screams of the dying! The flames of the fire blazed up a bloody red with every heart thrown into the tormenting heat. It seemed to flicker outward like long greedy fingers reaching to fill a gluttonous appetite.

My stomach wrenched so violently I dropped to my knees, yet I couldn't turn my eyes from the carnage taking place before me. I swallowed hard, holding my hand over my mouth as I witnessed Nikolas lunge at the throat of a phased Orig, sinking his bloody fangs deep into its throat. The werewolf fell limp and helpless to the ground. They were ugly creatures that stood upright like a man. Their fur was scraggly and coarse. The face of the Orig was hideous, with its bulging eyes, wide mouth, and teeth sharp as needles, dripping with drool. It made a sort of sucking sound like breathing through water, and suddenly there was the body of a beautiful young woman lying there. In seconds Nikolas ripped the heart from her chest and tossed it to the hungry flame. The Orig vanished into a pile of ash. The noise of metal blades clashing started to dissipate as Maldorans began phasing to their animal forms.

Kandi changed into a sleek muscular puma just as Rohan became an extraordinarily large polar bear; both disappeared into the throng. I looked up toward a screeching sound to see the shadow of a hawk circling just above where Tristan stood. Emeline immediately phased, becoming a stealth falcon, and took flight in what seemed like one fluid motion. The birds began to whirl in the air as they engaged in their death dance.

Taryn, now in leopard form, was fighting at Nadya's side. They moved and turned with such precision it almost seemed choreographed. I realized each woman remained close to her mate as they fought, each just as connected as Nadya and Taryn, fighting as if they were one warrior, twice as strong and twice as deadly. There I stood, the mortal queen, clutching desperately to a tree, frightened, weak, and vulnerable. I was unable to aid Tristan or Nikolas, unable to defend even one of my protectors. This was wrong. I wasn't worth dying for! I jumped at the sound of yet another agonizing scream.

Vada was quick with her Hulain attribute as I saw a dagger hurled by another immortal frozen in midair just inches from Kalem's heart! Emeline's mate, Darren, was the only one apart from his mate. The beautiful gray wolf was in a desperate fight with two Maldoran hyenas. They were growling and gnashing, and I feared for my new friend. Suddenly the flames rose again as Emeline swooped over the fire, dropping something from her talons. In the next instant, she was on one of the hyenas.

Barnabus and Lathra were engaged in true Warin fashion, hurling the blue orbs and casting shielding spells with fury. I was fervently trying to keep track of my family and friends, the salty tears streaming, stinging my eyes and hampering my vision.

I was so focused on the action in front of me I hadn't noticed the protective wall of bodies before me had been breached!

"Gavin!" I screamed. The Luster from Scarsion manor was suddenly standing directly in front of me! His eyes looked like smoldering red embers, staring a burning hole straight through me. I knew death stood before me, but I couldn't find the fear. All I could feel was rage. I screamed the first thing that came to mind. "Why?"

The Luster stopped cold. His head tilted slightly to the side, confused and surprised by the simple question.

I scanned the chaos behind him. Everyone was absorbed in the fight and oblivious to Gavin. My only defense was to keep talking in hopes of buying myself a little more time. "Why would Lucas plan an attack when he knew he'd be outnumbered?" I knew the soulless creature didn't understand, but questions seemed to keep him at bay.

He stood silent for another moment before he spoke. "Master expected everyone to be gone since your celebration was over," he answered. "Why are so many remaining?" Now it was my turn to be surprised. His ability to form a question of his own had caught me off guard. Could it be? I thought.

"Gavin, you were human, don't you remember this time of year? Think. I know you can remember!" I desperately pleaded. He stared intently. I could almost physically see the struggle to recall his human life.

"December..." he muttered, and then an expression of recognition. "Christmas!" he exclaimed.

"Yes, Gavin. They stayed on to honor me by joining us for a Christmas Eve banquet." I couldn't believe no one had noticed him yet. I could see that he was tiring of the chitchat, and my lifespan was dwindling by the second!

"I see...well, it appears the guest of honor will be joining me for dinner instead!" Gavin threw his head back and laughed at his own witty response. A second later, his eyes narrowed, and his demeanor hardened. There was the bloodlust in my dream!

The last thing I saw was his fangs before I closed my eyes. "No!" I screamed and flung my hands out to push him away. I felt his stone-cold body for a brief second, and he was gone! I opened my eyes to find Gavin sprawled on the ground a good six feet from me. He raised his head, staring at me as though he were in shock! Before he could get to his feet, Nadya's sword came down, and the Luster Gavin was no more. I wish I had seen who pulled him from me. I owed them a debt for saving me a horrible and painful death.

Nadya had turned around to assist Taryn against two Lusters; she didn't see the Maldoran phase behind her. Before the bear could strike, an arrow came out of nowhere, piercing the beast straight through the heart. The woman screamed and fell to the ground, slowly turning ashen. Nadya instinctively wheeled to the sound and witnessed the slow, agonizing death of her attacker.

She bent down and retrieved the black arrow from the ash and quickly scanned the trees. Taryn nudged her with his nose, and she held the arrow out. "It seems there is a traitor among the traitors. No honor among..." Taryn's eyes narrowed in a nonmenacing way. "You're right, my dear, too cliché." She grinned and rejoined the fight.

Just then, I heard a panther's scream and jerked my head toward the sound. A lioness had clawed his side, and blood was pouring from the wound. An Orig had joined her, and they were bearing down on him.

"Oh God...Tristan...they're going to kill him!" I whispered to myself. I wanted to scream, but all I could do was watch. Rochelle

Sullivar stepped out, and I saw her hand move toward the fire, and the flames reached out, grabbing hold around their bodies. The two fell to the ground, returning to their natural form. McKenzie and Luther removed their hearts in less than a second, and I breathed a sigh of relief. I heard a bone-chilling screech. Oh, dear God, that sound came from Nikolas! It was so terrifying the hair on my neck stood up.

Lazar and the witch were about to engage him when Tabius merely lifted his hands and the wind began to swirl around them like a fierce tornado! Nick was so concentrated on the two still pushing toward him he didn't notice the huge black werewolf behind him! I tried to call out to warn him, but I was so petrified no sound could escape.

Just as the Orig raised its paw, Mike Zita jumped between them and took the hit. As he fell to the ground, his sword split the beast open. Kalem yanked the heart from the Orig, but not before it had done the same to Mike!

"No...Mike...No!" I screamed as I watched his body turn to ash. I slumped to my knees, sobbing bitterly. I heard the sound of the enemy retreating. All the sounds seemed hollow and slurred, as if everything was moving in slow motion.

I looked up, wiping away the burning tears. Maldorans and Origs were now phasing back to their human form, gathering in a circle around the fire, heads bowed in reverent silence. No victory celebration, no handshakes or pats on the back in recognition of a job well done, just mourning for all their kinsman, friend and foe. The peaceful snow-covered clearing was tarnished gray with ash and strewn with puddles of black and red blood. This was no longer a place of solitude; it had been transformed into a tomb that will forever bear the stench of death. Nick and Tristan were at my side instantly.

"Olivia, are you hurt?" Nick anxiously asked as he and Tristan knelt beside me. I looked up at him through tear-filled eyes. I couldn't speak for the bile rising in my throat. In the release of my panic, I just leaned forward and vomited.

Tristan gathered me in his arms and kissed my forehead. "Come on, baby, let's get you back to the house." He carried me all the way to my room as Nick walked beside us in silence.

Locked Away 33

They had left me to clean up and calm down. I wasn't sure I would ever be calm again after tonight. I was standing at the window, staring out into the night, when they returned to check on me. I heard them come in and sit in the chairs behind me, but I continued staring out the window.

"Olivia, what are you thinking?" Nick asked with a soft, uncertain tone.

"This just doesn't seem real, but it was real! What were the blue orbs being hurled about?" I asked.

"Uhmm...plasma orbs. Warins—"

I didn't give Tristan time to go into an explanation. "Plasma orbs, incantations, vampires, werewolves, people transforming, manipulating the elements—it was like watching some fantastic sci-fi movie!"

"Where do you think the ideas for these movies come from, sugar?"

Every occupation on the planet, I recalled Tristan's words at the airport. "But this wasn't a movie or some story. This was real and people—good people—died! Lives were decimated right before my eyes! Mike...I warned you, but you didn't listen!" Not a word was uttered as I continued to stare out the window at nothing. "Never again," I calmly stated, "never again will the good people of Kardaun fight and die for a helpless queen...for me...a useless mortal!" My words were bitter with self-contempt.

Nick started to protest her last comment but decided to remain silent. There would be another time more appropriate to argue her self-loathing. I turned slowly to face my two mates, my expression stolid.

"I want to go home." My voice was calm and monotone.

"Certainly, love, when do you want to leave?"

"Now. Before this dreadful night ends."

"The plane is always ready, so we'll be in the air in two hours. I'll inform the staff and guests." Nick bowed his head, as if acknowledging the command of a higher authority than himself.

"Thank you, Nick. Tristan, I know you have the same ability as Nick, being king of Malve, so as you leave, would you summon Nadya for me? I need to talk to her."

"Done," Tristan said as he too bowed his head in reverent compliance.

Nadya was at the door as Tristan and Nikolas exited the room. I called for her to enter, and Tris closed the door behind her.

Once in the hallway, Nick turned to face Tristan. "I can sense a great turmoil in her soul."

"I know, but I can't read it. It's frightening!" Tristan exclaimed, rubbing his palms together.

Nick raked his fingers through his hair. "Damn Lucas. Damn Lazar! I would give anything to have spared her the horror she experienced tonight!"

"I know, but it was bound to happen sooner or later." Tristan rested his hand on Nick's shoulder and sighed.

Nadya walked over and had a seat across from Olivia. "Liv, I am so sorry for what you had to go through tonight. It must've been horrifying, not knowing what to expect."

"That's what I wanted to talk to you about. I know it's going to take some time before I come to terms with what I've witnessed, but..." I took in another deep breath, trying so hard to vanquish the memory.

"But what, Olivia?" She remained patiently waiting.

"But I just can't allow this to happen again. I need you to train me, teach me how to fight!" I stared into the astonished eyes of my sister-in-law, waiting for her answer.

"Olivia, you don't know what you're asking! It's not as if you would have any more of a chance against those from our world if you were an accomplished swordsman!" She tried to reason with me.

"I can't just sit idly by and watch everyone around me die!"

"Olivia, the training is very intense. You wouldn't survive."

"You don't know that for sure. If you won't train me by request, then you will train me by your queen's command." I hated doing that to her. "Leave this between us."

"As you wish, Your Highness." She stood and bowed respectfully.

I was thankful to be home. Nick took my jacket when we came through the door, and I walked down the steps to the comfort of the sitting room. There was a fire already burning. He had obviously had someone come in and ready the house for our return. I slipped off my shoes and leaned back in the soft chair.

"Can I get you something to eat?" Tris asked in a low voice. It was almost as if he were afraid of waking someone or something.

"No, thank you. I would like a cup of herbal tea, if it's not too much trouble."

"Not at all, sugar." He hurried out to fulfill my request as I sat there staring into the flames, the sights and sounds of the past night echoing in my mind. I could see the face of the Luster Gavin as clearly as if he were standing in front of me at this very moment.

There was more to these Lusters than the Kardaunians were aware of. It wouldn't do any good to say anything. I was sure they would pass it off as my imagination. I would have to have proof to back up my theory. I thought of my friend Mike. Why wouldn't they listen to me? If they had, maybe Mike would still be alive, I thought. Then I realized it wouldn't have changed a thing. Mike lived for danger, and nothing could have kept him away.

In the days following that horrible night, Nick and Tris were very patient. I kept mostly to myself, spending time in the sunroom or my bedroom.

Two weeks had passed, and I had barely talked to either of my mates. I wondered if the lighthearted kinship I shared with them would ever return. Everything was so wonderful before. There is truth in the saying "Ignorance is bliss." If I could just turn back time...I was happy in my naïveté. Now, that innocence was gone, and it left me feeling as if I had been savagely defiled.

"Liv," I was startled at Nick's voice. I was lost in my self-inflicted depression. That's what it was. I knew it deep down. I just didn't seem to have the strength to overcome it.

"Liv," he repeated. "Can I talk to you?"

"Of course, Nick, what's on your mind?" As if I didn't know.

"We're very worried about you."

"You needn't be. I'm fine," I lied, knowing he could tell, knowing they could feel my emotions.

"It's not healthy, love, to let this go on."

"Tell me, Nick, how do I forget? Is there a witch out there somewhere that can take it all away?" I instantly regretted my sarcasm. He didn't deserve to be insulted. None of this was the fault of either of them, and I was a horrid, despicable person for trying to take my anger and pain out on them.

Nick stood silently, contemplating his options. He could easily summon Barnabus or Lathra to alter her memory—a solution that would be far more compassionate than allowing her suffering—but he knew it would only happen again, and as hard as it was, she needed this memory to prepare her, to give her strength.

SOULBOUND: DESTINY'S MOVE

"Olivia, I wish I could have spared you, but it was an inevitable experience. What's done is done, please try and put this behind you," he pleaded.

"Nick, I want to...I just don't know how." As I watched him stare helplessly back at me, I could feel the anguish in his soul. Tears started to well up in the corners of my eyes. I hated myself for causing him one ounce of pain.

He knelt down in front of me, wrapping his arms tightly around my shoulders. As he pulled me into the embrace, the tears began to fall. I don't know how long he held me there as I wept. The release of pain was overwhelming. This was what I needed all along. The one thing I didn't allow myself: grief.

It was the tenth of February; things seemed to be more relaxed now. The playful camaraderie was slowly returning. I had finally managed to get Nick to take me downstairs. Just as Tristan said, the baby grand was sitting in the middle of a large room filled with musical instruments. There were shelves upon shelves of sheet music and an enormous stereo system. I saw a mixing board and rows of disks, some blank, some recorded. The unpleasant side of this level wasn't at all like I expected.

The containment rooms were designed for the comfort of any detainees from Scarsion's army. I could live with that. Tristan had told me once they didn't hate the people that followed Lucas. They were just as much victims as the rest of us.

We walked back into the music room, and I sat down on the piano stool.

"Do you play?" Nick asked.

"No, I'd love to learn though. Would you play something form me?"

Nick suddenly became uncomfortable, and his expression turned somber. "You should get Tristan to play. He's much better than I am. I'd be happy to play you a tune on the saxophone." He half smiled.

Baby steps, Olivia, I told myself. I decided to humor his request. "I'd like that." I walked over to the chaise lounge and relaxed. Nikolas began playing a soft, smooth melody, every note perfect. My eyes gently closed as I let the sweet sound envelop me. The music faded, and as I opened my eyes, Nick was sitting beside me, eyes glistening.

"That was wonderful." My hand rose to caress his face. I would never get past the feeling of being in the presence of an angel when I looked at him.

"That was nothing, love. There has never been a song written that could define you," he whispered and leaned in to kiss me. It was so soft and lingering. He drew in a long breath and pulled back.

"We'd better get back upstairs."

"Yeah, we should go." Upstairs we found Tristan in the kitchen.

"Dinner's ready," he announced with a bright smile.

"Where?" Nick looked to the table.

"Right here," he answered, pointing to the pizza box on the counter.

"It was my night to cook, right?" I just shook my head and pulled a slice from the container.

"Nick, about the piano lessons, would you teach me?" I watched him carefully for his reaction. The uncomfortable look crossed his face again for a split second.

"I told you, love, Tristan is better at it, and he has more patience." He flashed a quick crooked grin at me. I was determined to help him get past the grief of his friend and vowed to myself, somehow, I would get him to play again.

"All right then, Tris, are you up to the challenge?" I said, biting down on the pizza slice.

"Challenge is what I live for." He laughed. "We'll start your lessons whenever you want."

"Great, tomorrow suits me. Oh, and earplugs might come in handy." I giggled.

Nick's cell phone rang out, and I nearly jumped out of my skin! They usually kept their phones on vibrate, so I wasn't accustomed to the sound anymore.

"Yes," he never answered with a customary hello. Tristan and I sat quietly as Nick listened to the caller. I could feel his emotions change. The anxiousness was building inside him, something was terribly wrong! Tristan sensed it too.

"What's wrong?" I blurted as soon as he ended the call.

He flashed a quick glance at Tristan and then turned to me. "Nothing you need to be concerned about." He smiled confidently and brushed my hair back. "I don't mean to be rude Liv, but I do need to speak with Tristan in private."

"Oh, no, you don't. I know something has happened, and I'm not going anywhere!" I folded my arms and remained stubbornly seated.

"We just want to protect you, sugar." Tristan was standing across from me with pleading eyes, hoping I would let it go, but I wasn't budging.

"I can see you're determined, so if you must know, Lucas has decided to bring the battle here. That was Nadya on the phone."

"What did she say?" My heart was beating wildly! No matter how gently he tried to put it, the news was not going to be good!

"There's been two attacks right here in Tailors Mountain. I don't have the complete details. She wants Tristan to meet her just outside the south end of town." He looked to Tristan and nodded.

"I'll be back as soon as I can." Tristan's jaw was clenched, and I could tell he was expecting a fight.

"Be careful, Tris, and try to get the names of the victims. I grew up here, and there's a good chance it's someone I know." He just gave me a quick nod and a kiss on the cheek before he hurried out the front door.

"Nick...I'm scared."

"Don't worry, love, you're safe here." He pulled me close to him in an attempt to comfort and reassure me. I didn't see anywhere as safe after the invasion of Kardaun Valley.

"We don't have the details, so let's not borrow trouble. Now go in and have a seat by the fire, and I'll bring something to drink. We'll have a go at a game of cribbage while we wait." He was such a remarkable man, so confident and strong. I followed his advice and got the cribbage board from the edge of the bookshelf.

The game was so quiet I could hear every tick of the clock on the mantel. My concentration was completely lost.

"Liv, relax, Tristan will be back soon. He always comes back." He winked playfully. His beautiful, perfect smile didn't hide the worry though.

Time crept by. Every second felt like a minute, and every minute an hour.

"What's taking so long!" I tossed the cards onto the board and threw myself back in the chair.

"Come over here, love." I walked over and knelt down beside him, resting my head against his leg. He began to stroke my hair.

"I understand how you feel. I've never been good at waiting either."

"Funny, you certainly could have fooled me. How do you do it?"

"Haha! I guess I've just got a few years practice on you." He wanted me to trust that this was going to turn out well.

"I guess you're right though. Tristan is very capable of taking care of himself."

"That's my girl," he cooed softly. He sounded very fatherly. I bet he would be a wonderful parent. I jumped at my own thought. I can't be thinking this, especially now! He pulled me onto his lap and cradled me in his arms.

"Tristan's coming."

"Are you sure?" I asked.

"He'll be here in a few minutes. I told you, didn't I?" He smiled.

"Yes, you did." I was elated to know he was unharmed. I jumped to my feet and started for the door, anxious to know what he found out.

"Tristan! I'm glad you're okay. I was worried!" I exclaimed, grabbing him around the waist the minute he came through the door. "Hmmm...maybe I'll take a few more midnight strolls!" "Stop it," I teased, tapping against his massive chest.

"What's the problem, Tris?" Nick called from his seat by the fire.

Tristan took my hand and led me back into the sitting room. "There were two attacks—three people, two killed, one injured. Nadya caught the essence trail of a Maldoran and an Orig. They split off on the south side from two Lusters." He paused to take a drink from my cup.

"Orig or Larin?"

"Larin."

"Did you find out who they were?" I asked.

"Yes, Nadya tried to get to the Lusters, but she was too late. It was a woman by the name of Rebecca Sorenson." I gasped when he named the victim.

"You knew her?" Nick questioned.

"Yes, she was my history teacher in high school," I answered. "Who were the other two?" I sensed Tristan's hesitation. "Tris, who were the other two?" I repeated.

"A man named Chad McCoy and his wife—"

"Darla...oh god...is she..."

"No, she's injured, but she's going to make it." "Who is Darla?" Nick asked.

"You were never introduced. She's the short red-haired girl at Rooters," Tris explained.

"Chad...he's..." I stammered.

"I'm afraid so, baby, I'm sorry."

"Poor Darla and those beautiful little kids. She has three. It's going to be so hard for her. I need to go to the hospital!" "No!" both men protested at once.

"Why? I can't just leave her lying there. I have to do what I can to help. She's my friend!"

"Don't you see, Liv, that's what Lucas wants! He's targeting people you know!" Nick reasoned. "He's trying to draw you out in the open!"

"I don't get it! First, he wants me dead, then he sets it up, so I'll have to bind with you, and now he's trying harder than ever to take me out! Why?"

"He underestimated you the first time. He was sure Nick would be dead by now, and that was his mistake. Now he's trying to rectify it."

I was confused, but I didn't have time for long explanations. I had to help Darla!

"Olivia, please try to understand. Darla is going to be fine. I'll see to her recovery myself, but we just can't risk taking you out where you'll be in a vulnerable position. Lucas could care less if the humans know about us. He only has one objective: kill Nikolas and take the crown."

"I know what Lucas's plans are. I had my suspicions about his real goal, and Althea confirmed it."

"Althea?" Nick seemed surprised that I had spoken with her.

"Yes, we sort of became friends, and I talked her into leaving." Now they were standing there with their mouths hung open. "You mean Althea is no longer with Scarsion?" Nick suddenly seemed more interested in her than the immediate danger.

"That's what I just said, and before she left, she gave me a tablet to take, which I'm sure gave me the strength that saved my life! I owe her—"

"Hold on a sec. Just what plan did Althea discover that would turn her against Lucas? She is, or was, not only loyal to a fault and chief of his guard, but the deadliest warrior in his army. You made friends with her and turned her allegiance in only ten days?" Tristan acted as though I'd performed some kind of miraculous feat!

"Don't act so shocked. She is a very intelligent woman. She does have the capability to listen to reason and come to conclusions of her own, you know," I defended. "As for Lucas's plan, I can positively tell you it doesn't include anyone that is not of Orig descent." Nick's eyes widened in horror!

"My god, he is insane! For nearly a millennium, we've gone on the assumption he just wanted the crown, when in reality, he wants the world!"

"This changes our entire strategy," Tristan mumbled.

"Indeed, it does, my friend."

"What about Darla?" My question brought them back to the immediate problem.

"Sugar, if it'll make you feel better, call her, but you simply cannot leave this house until we get the situation under control!" Tristan wasn't asking; he wasn't giving me an option. He was giving me a direct order!

"For how long?"

"As long as it takes." Tristan's expression was stern. I almost believed he would lock me in our own basement dungeon if I refused.

"Fine!" I yelled and headed for the stairs.

"Where are you going?" Nick called to me.

"To exercise my right!" I snapped.

"What?"

"I'm going to do what every prisoner does—make my phone call!" I stormed out of the room and up the stairs, slamming the bedroom door behind me. I was angry that I had been imprisoned in my own home, hurt that everyone in my life was dropping like flies, and their injuries and deaths were all because of me! Most of all, frustrated that there wasn't a damn thing I could do to stop it!

The Seduction 34

Five days had gone by since my "grounding," and my temper had settled. I understood the danger now and was resigned to waiting this thing out.

"Liv," Nick called to me from the door of his study as I passed by. I had decided to change my routine and went for an early swim.

"Yeah?"

"Would you come in here a minute?"

"Sure, is something wrong?" I asked, entering the study. Nick was listening to his music without headphones and walked over to lower the volume as I sat down in the high-backed chair.

"Just got a call from my office in New York, and as much as I hate to, I have to go up there for a couple of days. I can't help but be apprehensive about leaving." He did seem to be a bit nervous. I could tell there was something more to this sudden trip than he was saying. Maybe he was afraid I'd ask, and he knew he couldn't lie.

"Don't worry, darling, I'll be fine. Tristan is here, and you've doubled the guard around the house. I promise to be good," I teased. "I won't try to sneak away or anything like that."

"I promise to make it as quick as possible. I should be back by Monday night." He smiled.

"That's just two days. What could possibly go wrong?" I shrugged my shoulders and smiled. It was pretty clear from the look on his face he was thinking—plenty.

"I hate to be away from you," he whispered, wrapping his arms around my waist. He gave no thought to the water dripping onto the rug at my feet.

"I know. I hate it too. When do you have to leave?"

"Actually, the car will be here in a few minutes." His eyes held the disappointment for the separation.

"I'll call you often," I said.

"Promise," he whispered. I nodded and kissed him tenderly.

The limo pulled up outside, and Nick grabbed his briefcase. "See you Monday," he called on his way out. I sighed and started up the steps to the kitchen for some toast and coffee. I wonder where Tristan is. The house was so quiet and empty feeling. I poured the coffee and put the toast and jam on a tray. I decided to eat in my room.

I took a long, relaxing shower and sorted through the jungle of clothing for something to wear and made a call to Darla. She wanted me to believe that she had everything under control, but her voice gave away the truth. She was a wreck. I wished I could be there with her right now. I knew how difficult it was to lose someone you loved.

The time seemed to get away from me, and I had spent two hours on the phone.

It was odd that I hadn't heard Tristan thumping around somewhere in the house. I opened the door and called out to him, "Tristan...Tris..." No answer. I felt a tiny bit frightened by his absence, but common sense told me he couldn't be too far away. I settled back into a chair and picked up my book. I thought I would just read a couple of chapters before I got dressed. It wasn't like I had anything important to do anyway.

That didn't turn out the way I'd planned. It was late afternoon, and I had finished the book. I dressed and went downstairs. Tristan was still nowhere to be found. I was beginning to get concerned, when the front door swung open, and Tris walked in carrying a huge pile of boxes and bags.

"Where have you been all day?" I asked, relieved to see his smiling face.

"Well, I initially set out to just go pick up a few items to make my specialty dinner, and it occurred to me that you must be getting bored by now, so..." He began stacking things on the counter. "I went out of town and bought you this." He sat a new laptop in front of me. "And these." There was a wide assortment of video games. "And a set of good headphones, oh, and an iPod so you can download some new music, and these CDs to listen to." He stood there watching me in hopes that he had chosen the right bands.

"My stars, Tris, you didn't have to go to all this trouble!" I said, thumbing through the stack of games. "Oh, I love this game! Where did you ever find it?"

"It wasn't easy. After I heard you mention it at Es'mar, I knew for certain that was at least one that you would like. I had to go to three stores to find it. The clerk said it was a very popular item." He had begun putting away the groceries as he talked.

"So, what is your specialty dinner?" Tristan's cooking was good, but he was nowhere near the chef Nikolas was.

"Spaghetti, complete with meatballs." His expression was utterly priceless! "So, where's Nick?"

"Oh, he got a call this morning and had to jet off to New York. He said he would be back by Monday evening," I told him, thinking nothing of it. Nick had made several trips on short notice.

"You mean you've been here alone all day?" I could literally see the blood drain from Tristan's face.

"Relax, Tris, obviously everything is fine."

"Nick should have called me. I would have come straight home."

"I suppose he assumed you were on the grounds somewhere. I'm sure it wasn't deliberate," I said in Nick's defense. Tris took a long breath as he stood there rubbing his palms together. I could always tell by that simple unconscious action when he was upset.

"It's over. You're here, and all is well."

"I know, but I'll make sure we communicate better in the future."

"I'm going to take this stuff up to my room." I began piling my arms full and realized I would have to make two trips to get it all. Tristan noticed as well.

"I'll finish putting the groceries away and bring the computer up to you, okay?" He smiled.

"Thanks, and thank you for everything." I smiled sweetly and started to my room.

After putting a few of the items away, I went to my dressing table to brush my hair and pull it back. While rummaging through the drawer for my brush, I came across a small vial. A mischievous smile crossed my lips. I had picked this up from the health store before we left for Switzerland. I had aimed to try a little experiment on Tristan when we were alone. *Well, this is as good a time as any,* I told myself. I opened the vial labeled "Catnip Oil" and shook a tiny bit onto my fingers and brushed it gently through the tips of my hair.

I met Tristan in the hall, carrying the computer box. "Oh, thanks, Tris, I'll put this in here, and we can go work on that lovely dinner you were making." When I stepped back out and closed my door, I noticed his expression had changed just a little.

"Are you sure you want dinner right now?" he asked lazily as he leaned in, nuzzling my neck. "I'm not really hungry," he purred. The light nuzzles were becoming more forceful, and I kept stepping backward.

"Tris, are you okay?" I asked, taking yet another step to hold my balance.

"I'm perfect, sugar, and you are so beautiful...so ir..." he began the word and stopped to kiss me, "resistible," he finished saying. His kisses were soft at first and grew more intense by the minute. I had finally run out of hall and was standing against the wall by Tristan's bedroom. My heart was beating wildly in my chest, and the fire he always created when he touched me felt white hot!

He reached over and opened the door. I stepped into his room, still walking backward until my legs touched the edge of the bed. Tristan stood with one hand on the top edge of the door and looked at me with glazed eyes. "Sugar, you have no idea what you've done." He growled as the door slammed shut.

My eyes fluttered open. Tristan was sleeping quietly beside me, his arm draped across me. I stirred, and he pulled me closer as he awoke. I smiled at how beautiful he looked lying beside me. His electric-blue eyes were clear and vibrant again.

"Good morning." I smiled.

"Mmmmm...so this is what it's like to wake up in heaven," he cooed.

"As much as I would love to stay right here all day, I do need to get up."

"Why?" he whispered, kissing my neck softly.

I shuddered and sighed. "Nature calls." I wouldn't say nature wasn't exactly calling; it was shrieking. Reluctantly he let me go, and I dashed to the bathroom. I came out wrapped in a bath towel. Tristan was still lying on the bed, resting on his elbow. My lord, he was magnificent! I started forward, and something crunched under my foot. I looked down at the remnants of what used to be the clock from atop his dresser. Slowly I scanned the room. It was totally destroyed! My mind raced, trying to remember just what took place last night! It was like I had developed some sort of amnesia. Bits and pieces flashed through my head in a blur—a wonderful, glorious blur.

"Tris, is that claw marks on the headboard?" I pointed as I spoke.

He stood up and tucked the sheet around his waist. "Uhhh... yeah...I..." he stammered.

"I didn't know you could do that!"

"Do what?"

"Partial phase."

"I didn't either, but apparently," he said, kicking away a piece of the splintered footboard. He was standing in front of me now; the closeness again ignited my flames.

"Olivia, last night was so extraordinary." It must have been, at least from what I could recall. "I love you so desperately," he whispered.

"I love you, Tristan." I could barely speak as my breaths were so shallow. I sighed heavily and wrestled for control.

"I can smell a hint of it on you," he said.

"That's why I'm going to take a shower. Another night like last and you'll have a downstairs bedroom," I tried to tease, all the while I ached to start all over again.

"All right," he said with reluctance. "I'll grab a quick shower and make you a fabulous breakfast."

"I'll meet you downstairs then." I kissed him and went to my room. As much as I enjoyed my time with Tris, I couldn't shake this empty feeling. I dressed and flipped open my cell.

"Nick," I said when I heard his voice. "I miss you. Is everything okay?" Now I knew what was wrong; my emptiness was the absence of him. It was getting harder to be away from either of them, even for a day. They too seemed to feel this need to stay near me.

"I am so relieved to hear your voice. I have been on edge since I left the house," he said.

"You know I'm safe here. Why would you even worry?"

"I don't mean it like that. I can't relax unless you're near me. I won't be gone as long as I planned, love. I'll be home tonight." I felt such a relief, and the butterflies fluttered in my stomach with the anticipation of his return.

SOULBOUND: DESTINY'S MOVE

"Great. I'll be counting the seconds," I said. "I'll see you tonight. I love you."

"I love you too, more than you know," he whispered. I closed the phone and sat there for a minute, just reflecting on the change in me and in them.

Our souls seemed to be growing closer. I could actually feel Nick's emotions from this distance.

End Of A Winter Dream 35

I had been confined to the house for fifteen days straight. I desperately needed some fresh air.

The attacks on Tailors Mountain had been coming in a constant succession. Nadya and the guardsman had thankfully thwarted their plans and saved the lives of many of my human friends, yet Lucas remained relentless in the attempts.

Nikolas had turned our peaceful home into some sort of headquarters. People had been coming and going in an endless procession. I wondered if they were even close to a resolution that would end the bombardment of evil that had been unleashed on my hometown.

Tristan had all but tripled the guards around our already secluded and well-hidden property, making it virtually impenetrable. It was beginning to feel like I was doomed to a life of imprisonment. I don't know how much longer I could stand the confinement.

Somehow Tristan had convinced the Avarian king to meet with them. Tabius and Rochelle Sullivar were in the study now. Under normal circumstances, I would have been included in these meetings. Since I had so much yet to learn about the world of Kardaun, we agreed that I would remain in the background a little while longer.

The days were filled with meetings and planning strategies. The new knowledge of Lucas's plans had literally escalated the war. The nights were set aside for me and a rigorous study program as Nick and Tristan tried to get me up to speed with their world.

Kardaun was a world old as time itself. I wondered if I would be able to learn the Kardaunian history and laws in my short lifetime (being human certainly didn't allow for time).

I was feeling stifled and restless as I ambled back to the rear hall. Tabius and Rochelle were just leaving Nick's study. I approached them with a smile, holding my hand out for the customary greeting.

"Tabius, Rochelle, surely you're not leaving so soon?"

"I'm afraid so, Your Majesty," Rochelle answered in her eloquent flowing voice.

"We have some urgent business to attend," Tabius informed with a polite nod. His perfect angelic smile gave the illusion all was right with the world.

"I do hope you will return for a visit when things have settled." My invitation was graciously accepted as they bowed low and retreated to the front entrance.

I stood at the door of the media room. *I just have to get some fresh air, or I'm going to go crazy!* I thought. I turned around, opened the small closet by the stairs, and took out a jacket.

As I climbed the steps to the sunroom, I had convinced myself a small stroll in the garden wouldn't do any harm. I could be back easily before Nick and Tristan realized my absence.

I turned on the outside lights and watched the gentle snowflakes drift to the ground. February always seemed to carry the heaviest winter snows. It was dusk but still bright enough to see the walkways without the artificial lights, but I figured there was no harm in a little caution. At least the guards would know someone was outside the confines of the house.

I stepped out of the door and breathed in the crisp, cold air and felt an overwhelming sense of relief. Slowly I began ambling along the snow-covered path, just embracing the beauty I had always taken for granted.

The delicate white cover surrounded every limb, lying gently like a blanket protecting the world around from the bitter harshness of the winter's cold.

So absorbed in my thoughts, paying no attention to where I was going, I found that I had wandered into the woods and strayed far from the quiet garden. I must be near the back of the property, I thought. I could see the bars of the tall wrought iron fence that surrounded every inch of the estate.

The dim light of dusk was beginning to fade. I'd better get back, I warned myself. Nick and Tristan would be furious if they found out how far I'd wandered from the house.

I had started back down at a quicker pace and then froze in my tracks. A hooded figure stepped into my path. I could tell immediately it was a woman.

"Abby," I called. No answer. The silence triggered a sense of alarm. My mind was slowly beginning to register the danger, and my breath quickened.

"Abby isn't coming." The woman's voice had a familiar ring to it.

"What are you doing here?" I demanded, trying to sound brave even though everything in me was screaming run!

The woman took a few steps and dropped the hood. Now I recognized the face that accompanied the familiar voice!

"Mercedes!" I gasped. "What do you want? How did you get in here?"

"Abby was too confident," she said. "A Hulain didn't seem like much of a threat to her. She was wrong!"

A tear came to my eye at the vision of Abby turning to dust. She was a Larin and loyal to Kardaun. I would miss her deeply.

"Mercedes, you know what will happen when they catch you here!" I threatened. "They'll be looking for me now!" I lied and, true to myself, not convincingly.

"Hahaha!" she laughed. "It won't do them any good. I said Lucas should have killed you when he had the chance!"

"Why? What does it matter about me? I'm no threat to Lucas!" I knew her intention now, and my panic was fast rising.

"You don't know?" She seemed surprised at my ignorance.

"No. Tell me why my life or death is so important!" I had hoped to keep her talking until Nick and Tristan discovered I was gone and prayed they would have time to find me before she fulfilled her mission.

"He allowed you to bind with them!" She spat with disgust. "You are the source of their combined strength! When you're gone, they'll be weaker, easier to overcome! I will be favored by him after this. My standing in King Scarsion's guard will be exalted!"

I stood silent as the demented woman continued to ramble. "If he only knew how easy it would be, you wouldn't have lived this long!" she gloated.

"Mercedes, if you do this, you won't live to tell Lucas!" I threatened again.

"You pitiful little mortal! No one knows I'm here. It'll be hours before they find you! You'll be dead, and I'll be a hero!" She smiled a proud evil smile. "The good thing about humans, they die quickly!"

I caught my breath as I saw the flash of her blade being unsheathed. She lingered with it, prolonging the moment to relish in her victory.

Suddenly, I remembered what Nick said about his and Tristan's mark. I slowly raised my hand and touched the tiny scar on my neck. I ran my hand down under the collar to the raised mark on my shoulder. Just as I touched it, I felt a piercing sting in my chest. I was too late! Mercedes had thrust the sword deep into my heart!

I felt the warm blood ooze behind the blade as she pulled it from my body, and I collapsed to the ground.

Tristan and Nikolas appeared, and a smile crossed my lips for the gift of one last glance. I felt no pain, no fear, no regret. Strangely, the last lines of a poem written by my mother would be my final thought: The sands of the hourglass have been washed clean. And so, the night falls on a winter dream. Then...oblivion.

TRISTAN PHASED THE moment he saw Mercedes. His razor-sharp claws came down across her back before she realized what was happening. Nikolas grabbed her as Tristan took on his human form and rushed to Olivia's side.

Nick felt the soft flesh open up as he sank his fangs deep into Mercedes's throat. Immortal blood has no sustenance for Larins, but he found a deep satisfaction as the warm liquid pulled from her veins. He finished Mercedes quickly and set fire to her heart. Turning around, he saw Tristan crouched over Olivia's body. The cold air against Tristan's heated skin pulled up a vapor around him like warm breath. Nick joined him as he knelt beside their soul mate lying still and pale.

"Tristan..." Nick's eyes were searching, not wanting to hear what Tristan had to say.

"She's gone, Nick. We're too late," he said in a sorrowful whisper. Nikolas leaned back and screamed a mournful, bloodcurdling screech for a second time over Olivia's still body, then reached down and gently scooped her into his arms.

As he walked back to the house carrying his limp, lifeless mate, a tear fell from his eye onto her pale cheek. The drop gingerly rolled down to rest in a rose-pink puddle against the mark on her throat.

Tristan followed silently into the house and returned to Olivia's room dressed as Nikolas lay her on the white linen bed.

"Tristan, check again," Nick ordered.

"Nick..."

"Just do it!" he shouted in desperation.

Tristan checked her pulse and listened in vain for a heartbeat. He stood up straight and looked at his watch. As tears streamed down his face, he announced to Nick, "February twenty-fifth, time of death 6:32 p.m." Then he dropped to his knees and wept unashamed. Nikolas too dropped to the floor, the rose-colored tears flowing like the blood of his soul.

Each raised her lifeless fingers and kissed them, placing them against their forehead, then kissing her cold lips, first Tristan, then Nikolas.

Nikolas called their private mortician to send his assistant to prepare Olivia's body for the funeral. Raven stepped from the queen's chamber and offered her condolence before each of them took their turn for a private farewell.

Tristan entered the room first. Olivia was dressed in the white sealing gown. The three necklaces lay against her chest, and her thick black locks softly surrounded her face and shoulders, and her arms lay still at her sides.

He stood there trembling. Her pale skin reminded him of perfect bisque. She looked like a beautiful porcelain doll waiting to be placed on a shelf. He fell to his knees, wiping the tears from his eyes.

"Olivia, my beautiful baby. Never in my life have I questioned the will of my Creator. This leaves me wondering why he would allow me to touch such a magnificent soul. Why he would give me life, only to take it away! You, sugar, were not just my life, but my very existence. Now, I'm nothing. I promise your death will not be in vain. Then, I'll be with you again in Shalsmara. I promise, baby. You won't have to wait long. I love you." Tristan leaned down and kissed Olivia's cool lips one last time.

He walked into the hall head down. Nick placed a consoling hand on his shoulder. "Wait for me at the front door, my friend."

SOULBOUND: DESTINY'S MOVE

Tristan again brushed the tears from his eyes, nodded silently, and walked away.

Nikolas stood quietly for what seemed like the longest time, just looking down at her, then knelt by her side.

"My dearest love, even in death you are the most beautiful woman ever created. My soul goes with you, love. I don't understand nor can I accept a life without you. It's like being given a taste of heaven's ambrosia and told to be content. That could never be. I will always hunger for that which has been taken from me. Death will be sweet, knowing the most beautiful angel in Shalsmara waits for me." Nikolas kissed her softly, and as he rose, a tear fell to the eyelet cover unnoticed. He bowed and backed to the door. There at the tips of her ring finger, the tear had formed a tiny, pink-stained heart with a hole in the center.

Nikolas slowly walked down the stairs, his every step labored and heavy. The ache in his heart made him weak, and for the first time, he faltered on trembling legs.

Tristan watched from the front door. He stood silent, clutching his chest. This pain of the heart was the one thing their immortal bodies could not spare them. The one pain that was unbearable, and Tristan wanted to rip it from his own chest!

Nick stepped up beside Tristan and opened the door. The cold night air rushed in. Two withered leaves salvaged by a cornerstone of the entrance swirled in and spiraled to the floor, settling at their feet. They stared down as if they were peering straight at a reflection of their soul.

The two bereaved men stepped out into the darkness and disappeared into the night, leaving the front door wide open and the house unguarded. They had gone to ready the platform and funeral pyre where Her Royal Highness, Olivia Xandier Alberon, would be cremated.

Nick walked along, head down, and thought of the guests that would be arriving. He called Nadya, and he winced as she released a grief-stricken shriek at the news. She had become as close to Olivia as any sister. Once Nadya calmed down, she agreed to inform their guests of the tragedy.

They had begun their journey for celebration; instead, they would mourn. Their sweet Olivia had turned twenty-one on the day of her funeral.

"I can't imagine one day without her, let alone seventy years," Tristan thought aloud.

"Lucas will never allow it again," Nick said.

"I know. Seventy years will never come," Tristan acknowledged. As they approached the house, Nick realized they had left the door ajar.

"Tris, we forgot to lock the house!"

"It doesn't matter. They can't hurt her anymore." Tristan's voice was void of emotion. His jaw clenched in another attempt to hold back the tears.

If only they hadn't been so consumed with their grief, if they had been more attuned to the signs, maybe they would have been more prepared for what awaited them through the sitting room doors.

As they stepped across the threshold, both men froze.

"No!" Tristan breathed. Nikolas caught a sharp breath.

"Oh my god!"

About The Author

The quiet solitude of southern Appalachia has been the home of Amanda Albery since birth. It is in this rich cultural environment that she has chosen to raise her two sons. She considers one of her greatest loves to be the everyday blessings of inspiration and joy brought about by big brown eyes full of wonder, freckled noses, and hearty laughs.

Amanda grew up helping her parents on a small farm. Animals have always been a part of her life. She has two cats, Percy and Phineas Poe, two dogs, Willamina and Navia, all of them very much a part of the family. She enjoys many activities associated with her country lifestyle such as canning, crocheting, and cooking to name a few. Amanda's passion has always been sharing her love of literature and the gift of imagination.